GW00789569

The Val Sagas

Volume Two

Hel

Dr. Gregory Pepper

Copyright 2010
All rights reserved — Gregory Pepper

No part of this book may be reproduced or transmitted in any form or by
any means, graphic, electronic, or mechanical, including photocopying,
recording, taping, or by any information storage retrieval system, without
the permission, in writing, from the publisher.

ISBN: 978-1-4461-9145-3

Cover art by Chris Beatrice ©2010
Typography and page composition by J. K. Eckert & Co, Inc.
Published and printed by Lulu.com

To my wife, Bina, and my children, Nicholas, James,

Xia, and Karishma Pepper

Contents

Note: Chapter titles shown in italics are based on original Norse sagas.

Acknowledgments

I would like to start this second installment of *The Valkyrie Sagas* by thanking all those readers who so kindly bought *Mimir's Well*. If you are reading this introduction, then you have probably already read the first novel and have generously decided to continue with my tale. For that I thank you warmly. I hope *Hel* will exceed your expectations.

I would like to begin my acknowledgements by reiterating my thanks to the unknown bards of old. These talented storytellers first created the wonderful Norse sagas around which my story has been woven. I would also like to thank the scholars and academics who over the centuries have put so much effort into writing down and translating this powerful, elegant prose. Without their efforts I would never have been introduced to these intriguing tales from a time now faded into antiquity.

Along with a foundation of good storytelling, knowledge is the bedrock of writing, be it fiction or nonfiction. To this end, I would like to take this opportunity to thank three great institutions whose contributions have been incalculable. *New Scientist*, which I read avidly every week and which fuels my imagination, Google, and *Wikipedia*. These latter, fabulous, free resources prise the 'search' out of research. Nowadays, anyone is just a few clicks away from being an armchair expert in any subject he chooses, no matter how obscure. Tasks that used to take days or weeks to accomplish can now be completed in a matter of minutes. In my opinion, these two extraordinary research tools are among the finest achievements of the twenty-first century so far.

Who knows what other wonders lie ahead?

If knowledge is the bedrock of writing, then daydreaming has to be its cornerstone. Countless hours of boring journeys to work; long, leisurely bubble baths; and that grey, twilight zone somewhere between sleep and wakefulness make fertile hunting grounds for a restless mind. It is these times that I would like to thank for joining the random dots of my creativity.

Friends and family have borne the brunt of my artistic angst and I would like to thank all those who have put up with my ceaseless ramblings about Valkyries. I have been a bore for some time and I am grateful for your continuing patience and understanding.

It can be tough eating, sleeping, and obsessing your dreams.

Enough of this. Tick-tock—*Hel* is growing impatient and demands your company…

I do hope you enjoy your read!

1

Hel's Hole

"Aargh!"

This wasn't at all unusual.

"Aaargh!"

Oh, dear—there went a bowl of cabbage hurtling across the room.

"AAAARGH!"

It looked as though a plate of onions was about to follow suit.

Sadly, and within an embarrassingly short time of Cole's departure from Hel's reception room, business—and tantrums—had returned to normal.

Loki hated to see his daughter throwing hissy fits, but by now he'd got used to them. They were a regular occurrence, something that happened each time he visited Niflheim, which was about once every three to four months.

Hel had a dreadful temper, and these outbreaks were nasty while they lasted. Food was thrown around, plates would get broken, and glasses would be smashed against the room's beautiful panelled walls. The outbursts were scary, but when they were done Loki's daughter would eventually calm down and life would get back to normal. It was a bit like like throwing a switch.

A few moments before, when Cole was in the room, Hel had been all sweetness and light, hugging and kissing him and whooping for joy now that she'd got a weapon to destroy Odin. Unfortunately, with Cole gone—*hey-ho*—normal service had been resumed.

Loki sighed deeply and shook his head. In the early days he had tried to comfort her, giving her cuddles or stroking her forehead, but this never really helped. Nowadays, he just shrank quietly into the shadows and let her get on with the hysterics, blasting the fomenting rage out of her system.

In a way, he understood and shared her frustration, but her scenes were still demeaning and not befitting the queen of Niflheim, the supreme ruler of the damned. Sometimes he wished she would behave more like Frigg or Freyja. They had such a wonderful sense of decorum, smiling and gritting their teeth in the face of adversity. But he guessed that Hel wouldn't be his daughter if she were well-behaved and, besides, neither of those goddesses had suffered banishment for all eternity to a stinking, rotting, lawless realm.

No, Loki's daughter was hot-blooded and temperamental just as he was, and he wouldn't change that for all the gold in Valhalla. Her fury and capacity for violence was truly terrifying and was the reason she had been so spectacularly successful in this ghoulish, ghastly, nightmare of a realm.

Interestingly, Loki mused, he found her outbursts were predictable, always commencing when they were about to sit down to eat. Their meal had just been laid on the dark oak table before him and it looked wonderfully appetising. Venison, pheasant, rabbit, and mutton broth, served with all manner of vegetables and delicious roast potatoes. These latter were items not found in Asgard and something he always looked forward to when visiting. They were a culinary treat from Midgard, and he kept his fingers crossed that tonight they wouldn't end up on the floor next to the red cabbage and onions which were already lying mournfully there.

Dodging a well-aimed goblet that clattered noisily against the panelled wall behind him, Loki crept over to the small window and looked outside.

"Yes, dear…Quite so, dear…If you say so, my dear…" Loki absently muttered soothing, meaningless platitudes as he let his mind wander out to the world that lay beyond the hot, leaded glass window.

Love it or hate it, there was macabre beauty to Niflheim, or 'Hel,' as his daughter preferred her kingdom to be called these days. Niflheim was a stunning and unusual world, one situated in the same universe as Asgard and permanently connected to that realm by a wormhole. This acted like a giant umbilical cord, one which spewed a continuous cascade of water and corpses onto its gloomy surface. This flow was a one-way trip, strictly Asgard to Niflheim only. Other than Loki, nobody ever went back.

The world was a Mars-sized planet and had a captured orbit (the same side of the sphere always facing the sun) as it circled tightly around its dying brown dwarf star. From the window, Loki could see this huge, fading remnant of a star sitting in the same position in the sky day after day after day. Or he would have done, if there were days in Niflheim.

Because the sun's darkened orb never moved in the sky, time was frozen. Perpetual day never followed perpetual night, unless you happened to travel from the twilit side's murky gloom to the darkness of the frigid, icy wilderness on the other. In Niflheim, time passed without measure.

Being an ancient star, the surface of Niflheim's sun was very different to those of the younger incandescent fireballs that bathed Asgard and Midgard with their brilliance and splendour. Looking like some gigantic, blackened sunspot, the sun's surface was only occasionally pockmarked by outbursts of fiery, orange explosions—the last burning remnants of its once-mighty store of hydrogen fuel.

It was a sad display, pitiful almost, watching the dying star's nuclear swansong that provided so little warmth to the orbs that circled forlornly around it.

By rights Niflheim should have been a cold, burnt-out husk of a planet—a barren rock circling its sun like some useless lump of spent charcoal, devoid of life, atmosphere, and vegetation. Instead, looking out through the misty gloom Loki could see the realm's surface rippling and heaving. The side of the planet facing the sun was alive, seething with a living carpet of black poppies, rotting flesh, foul insects, and giant maggots.

This vision reminded Loki of a carnivorous pitcher plant, whose 'guests' arrived in the realm by falling through the wormhole and landing on its decaying, maggot-infested surface. This putrid, liquefying mess quickly became their toxic, syrupy grave, a tomb where worms and hideous bugs feasted on their flesh. Just like the *Hotel California,* the damned could check in any time they pleased, but they could never leave.

Into this macabre arena of death had stepped Hel's horrific genius. Her grotesque and brilliant mind had turned the realm's unique habitat into a business, one that was thriving through deals struck with worlds both in their universe and beyond.

Her pitch was simple. Re-branding the planet as a one-of-a-kind opportunity, she sold the realm's facilities to deities as a vast, rotting, waste disposal site, one that welcomed their unwanted dead and disposed of them permanently and in accordance with their wishes.

No soul was ever refused. The good, those who died from old age or natural causes, would spend their eternities entombed peacefully in the frozen, lifeless night of the planet—'Old Niflheim,' as Hel sarcastically called it. The bad, the evil dead, would be revived by the magical, regenerative power of the poppies and then forced to suffer eternal damnation on the cursed, living, twilit side of the planet—her side, the side called Hel.

For these services, Loki's daughter was rewarded handsomely by gods eager to 'off' their former subjects. Over the endless years since her arrival, Hel had amassed a vast fortune, huge vaults of treasure that dwarfed those of Valhalla, Asgard, Jotunheim, and even Midgard all rolled together. Hel had become fabulously wealthy, but therein lay a terrible paradox.

Like some sailor marooned at sea, what was the use of having all these riches if she could never spend it? Hel had more gold, toys, trinkets, and jewels than any king or queen could ever want for, but it was all completely worthless. She could never leave Niflheim, so her infinite riches rotted beside her.

Loki was briefly stirred from his daydreams by a large earthquake that shook the room and caverns around them. Through the window he could see a plume of molten lava erupt from a rent in the planet's surface. Sizzling and bubbling violently, this rapidly turned into an incandescent flow that meandered like a slick of glowing treacle through the rotting landscape.

Eruptions weren't unusual. Two other planets circled the sun, their eccentric orbits tugging at Niflheim and whipping its rocky core into a molten frenzy. Hidden fingers of gravity tore at the planet's sunlit side, causing earthquakes, lava flows, and the venting of toxic gases in a continuous, never-ending cycle of hostility. These natural phenomena, so feared on other, more tranquil worlds, were in fact the planet's salvation. Their destructive forces kept the surface hot and provided warmth and a noxious atmosphere in which the plants and bugs could thrive.

This trauma completed the realm's horrific cycle of life. Violent upheavals and the rotting flesh provided warmth and nutrients for the plants and bugs to thrive on, with the poppies thanking the generosity of the dying by releasing a pungent odour that kept the decaying flesh alive and wholesome.

This made death on the planet's surface a terrifying ordeal. Those damned for all eternity faced the prospect of being pegged out and eaten alive, each cell of their bodies living and feeling until the very last. This was the true, hideous horror of Hel—a realm where evil suffered a remorseless, agonising death.

"AARGH!" Another penetrating scream erupted from Hel's mouth and the thud of crashing onions startled Loki back into the room.

"No, please! Not the roast potatoes!" Loki entreated as his eyes pleaded with his daughter's. Hel had hoisted them high above her head and was threatening to hurl them at him.

"You haven't listened to a word I've been saying, have you?" she challenged angrily, eyes smouldering with rage. "Why won't you help me, Daddy? WHY? Every time you visit you keep saying the same old things—'Trust me Hel. Be patient Hel. Just a little while longer Hel.'—and look what happens: absolutely nothing."

Loki cringed as she spoke. He hated it when she mimicked his voice. She could do this to perfection, sounding exactly the same as he did. It was a unique talent and one he found particularly irksome.

"But darling, you love it here really, don't you? I mean, you enjoy your work and the presents you receive? And what about Cole? Isn't it fabulous having the starter of Ragnarok here in your realm with you?"

"Yes, of course, I do enjoy my work and he is wonderful but…Oh, Daddy, I'm so sick of the place—the constant stench, the heat, the disgusting food—"

This was it: the moment Loki had hoped wouldn't arrive today.

Slowly, Hel waved her arm across the wonderful feast before them. Its effect was both instant and stomach-churning. The wonderful joints of venison, lamb, and beef all turned into an ugly, grey, gelatinous goop before his eyes.

This was the truth, the harshness of her reality. Every dish before them was an illusion, a desperate attempt to make the only food available look appealing. There were no deer, no cattle, no sheep in Hel. There weren't even any potatoes, roasted or otherwise. The only source of nourishment was skimmed and boiled from the rotting mess of flesh, insects, and plants outside.

Hel was right. It was disgusting. Suddenly, Loki had lost his appetite. "And my presents?" Loki tried tentatively once more.

"Yes, they're always lovely. Cole will make a fine addition, but Daddy, they just get so boring. I can't stand it here anymore. I want to feel the warmth of a living sun, to chat with normal people again, and to smell fresh, clean air once more. I'm sick of being here, sick of being stuck in my, in, in…" she faltered, momentarily lost for words.

"…in my, in my—in Hel's hole!" she finally blurted loudly.

Collapsing into a chair, Hel's head slumped forward into her hands. She had lost count of the number of years she'd been trapped down here in this timeless, miserable tomb, but it was too long, far too long. She had done her punishment and it was time to return to Asgard. It was time to take her rightful place alongside the other gods and goddesses. It was time to be a Valkyrie again. *How dare Odin treat her so badly, binding her to this stinking realm with such devilish, dark enchantments?*

Loki walked over and stood behind her, stroking her luxuriant hair and massaging her slumped shoulders in a desperate attempt to ease his child's agony. Usually this would be all he could do, gestures of comfort for a lonely, grieving daughter. However, on this occasion, things were very different. He'd been saving his best present for last.

"Darling, what if I told you that I'd brought you not one, but two fabulous presents?"

Hel looked up, eyes wide with expectation but devoid of hope. *How could another 'Cole' help her return to Asgard?* There could be only one starter of Ragnarok and by the looks of things, he didn't seem all that special.

"Would you like me to give you a clue?" Loki offered. "Would you like to know why your dad is the mostest bestest dad in the whole, wide universe?"

Hel nodded her head enthusiastically. Perhaps her father wouldn't disappoint her for once with extravagant—but empty—words.

Grinning mischievously, Loki pulled an object from his bulging trouser pocket. He began to bounce this from his hand, to the crook of his elbow, and back again. The object was an apple.

Gazing intently, Hel quickly realised that this was no ordinary apple. Its skin shimmered a beautiful golden colour in the flickering candlelight. Hel's eyes widened dramatically. *Surely not?* That was impossible!

"I believe you already know the name of my second, even more exciting surprise?" Loki teased playfully before tossing the apple into Hel's eager hands.

Grabbing the fruit anxiously, Hel examined it intently. Rolling the apple slowly between her fingers, she scrutinised every millimetre of the succulent skin. Finally, satisfied that it really was what she thought it was, she took a deep bite. It tasted delicious.

"Mmmm. Oh, Daddy, thank you—thank you so much. I LOVE YOU!"

Leaping dramatically from her chair, Hel threw her arms around her father and squeezed him tightly once more, kissing him passionately on both cheeks. She knew what this meant and finally she could dare to hope. *With Idun hostage, how could Odin refuse her return to Asgard?*

The evil god was doomed.

"I thought you'd be pleased," Loki beamed, understating the obvious. He chuckled quietly as she held him in her arms. "Now you must promise me you'll look after her?" he continued anxiously when at last Hel released her grip. Loki knew his daughter only too well. Never take anything for granted.

"Oh, absolutely. Of course I will. You can trust me completely," Hel nodded enthusiastically, keeping her fingers crossed tightly behind her back.

"And do you have your trunk ready for his lordship?"

"Yes, of course, Daddy. It's right here as always," Hel replied obediently, pointing to a large trunk lying in one corner of the room.

Strolling leisurely over to the container, Loki lifted its lid and checked that she wasn't fibbing. Like he said—NEVER take anything for granted.

The trunk was full, just as Odin commanded it should be when Loki returned to Asgard. This was Odin's prize, the price he demanded for Loki's continued visits to his lonely, beleaguered daughter.

"So my dearest little angel, when would you like me to return to Asgard and start negotiations?" Loki jested.

"Now, you idiot—NOW!" Hel screamed, her voice wild with jubilation.

Loki laughed. As if his daughter could possibly have said anything else.

2

The Suitcase

It was a late afternoon in early March and Marcus was almost home. The sun had already begun to set on what had been a glorious day. Marcus loved this time of year, the time when the first hints of spring lay tantalisingly all around.

The day had been cold and cloudless, with the dawn heralded by a heavy frost that had cleared slowly throughout the morning. Now as he trudged home through the park he could see the first flowers of spring, snowdrops lying in small clusters around the roots of leafless trees. The earliest daffodils were also in bud, and tightly-closed crocuses struggled to raise their heads above the dormant blades of grass. His warm breath left a thick trail behind him as he walked; the tip of his nose tingling in the chill of the evening air.

It was a wonderful time, a time when the joy of spring promised to banish the misery of winter.

Arriving at his apartment block, Marcus decided to take the lift to their fifth floor flat. He was feeling lazy that evening, even though he hadn't had a particularly strenuous day. As the aging lift slowly shuddered and groaned its way skyward, Marcus reflected on the conversation he had had with Woods just moments before leaving his office.

Approximately a week had passed since their interview with Dr. Nyran, and every day Marcus phoned Woods to check on progress. Each day the conversation started with a tingle of excitement—and ended in disappointment. There was no news. No one from the Valkyrie cult had appeared to collect Herja's knife.

Marcus knew he shouldn't expect too much, but he was just so excited and impatient. He was desperate to find out more about the mysterious women who turned up and then disappeared, leaving a trail of death behind them.

Despite their failure to reappear, it hadn't all been inactivity and boredom. Woods had already undertaken some tests on the dagger and had made some startling discoveries.

X-ray analysis of the weapon had revealed a sophisticated and complicated structure. The handle of the knife appeared to be hollow and contained some sort of battery and electronics. No further details had been gleaned because Woods didn't want to damage the knife, at least not before the cult came looking for it. He had, however, managed to take some small scrapings of the metal for spectroscopy and this had shown a bizarre chemical structure. The knife was definitely made from an alloy of metals, but in a composition that had his boffins baffled. They desperately wanted a larger sample to work with, but Woods resisted their pleading for the same reason. It really was essential the knife remained intact.

With an overly enthusiastic bump, the lift finally arrived at the fifth floor. Marcus waited patiently for the doors to open. They took their time as usual, groaning and shuddering in protest.

"Hi, honey!" Marcus called out his customary greeting when he eventually battled his way through the front door. *He really must get that lock changed.*

Anna was in, but she hadn't replied, probably because the television was blaring loudly in the sitting room—she turned it up way too high.

"I'm starving—just going to make a sandwich and grab a beer. Would you like one, too?" he enquired. Still no answer. She was probably asleep, or couldn't hear him over the noise.

"What's this?"

Marcus had finally noticed the large, bright suitcase that practically filled their small entrance hall. It looked new and expensive, well-made, with a smart pink and brown floral pattern. These types of bags were all the rage these days, their lurid colours helping you identify your luggage quickly in the airport carousel when travelling. With a smile, Marcus wondered what would happen when everybody owned one of these. He guessed his battered old leather bag would be back in fashion by then.

"I didn't know you were going away?" he continued from the kitchen, voice heavily muffled as he licked butter from a knife he'd used. This was a disgusting habit and one for which Anna would have given him a good bollocking if she'd caught him doing it. He hastily cut a generous slice of cheese and dumped it crudely with some tomato chunks onto a slab of brown bread. His snack was complete.

PHSST! This had to be the most satisfying sound in the world: the sound of a top leaving a bottle of beer. Marcus could almost taste his 'Bud,' but decided to show some strength of character by waiting until he reached the sitting room before enjoying his first refreshing gulp of paradise.

"Would you like a beer?" he called out plaintively. This was her last chance—but Anna still didn't reply.

Balancing his sandwich on a plate in one hand and with his beer in the other, he carefully negotiated the suitcase in the hall. *Where could she be going?*

Perhaps Liz'beth was ill again? Anna's mum had turned eighty in January and was plagued by ill health. Anaemia, angina, leg ulcers, and arthritis…the list went on and on with new ailments being added annually. 'Liz'beth' (as they affectionately called her) could write a book on medicine if she wanted to, poor thing. Still, she was a tough old bird—and Anna had inherited her genes. No doubt she would get over whatever it was that was ailing her this time.

He gingerly pushed the sitting room door open with his foot. "Hi, hon—"

The words died instantly in his mouth, sandwich and beer falling in slow motion from forgotten hands to the carpet below. He didn't hear them hit the floor nor did he remember dropping them. His shock was too great.

The woman sitting on his sofa and watching TV wasn't Anna. The smile that came from her lips as she rose to greet him wasn't Anna's familiar and homely smile. The bright red hair and beautiful, ice blue eyes told their own story.

The Valkyrie Brynhildr, Officer Jessica O'Brien, was back—and it looked as though she was going to stay.

3

Odin Expects

Kat found herself shivering as she waited with the other warriors at the base of Odin's citadel. Her shivers were as much to do with nerves and excitement as they were to do with the unexpectedly cold start to the day. It was early September, and after a blazing summer the sudden transition to autumn chills was going to take some getting used to.

The forty-eight hours since Kat had won the tournament had been something of a whirlwind. In fact, her head still felt as though it was spinning now.

Dr. Katarina Neal was no more, having been replaced by the Valkyrie Sangrid—or, 'Sangrid the Terrible' as Silk had already unkindly dubbed her. Kat didn't blame Silk for this. When she, too, learned of her name's terrible legacy, she understood Silk's reasons. All she could do now was to prove her wrong, with actions speaking louder than words. Kat wouldn't walk the same evil path as the Black Valkyrie had done before her. She simply couldn't accept that this had to be her fate, to become so cruel and treacherous, her destiny as prophesied by Mimir.

No. This wouldn't happen.

The unwelcome shock about her future hadn't been the only unpleasant surprise in the process of becoming a Valkyrie warrior. Bathing in Mimir's well had also been traumatic. Experiencing your body exploding into trillions of photons of light before hurtling through a black hole and back was certainly no picnic.

13

Kat would dearly have liked to blame this incandescent journey for the hangover she was feeling, but unfortunately an overindulgence in mead, ale, and wine at yet another celebratory feast the previous night had been the culprit. She had got pretty wasted again, but fortunately not so hammered as to repeat the mistakes of the night before. Using Jess as an excuse, she had managed to wriggle out of an awkward encounter with Hod.

It wasn't that she didn't care for him—she did, desperately. It just wasn't fair to inflame his passion further, at least not until she'd got her feelings straightened out in her head. He wanted love—but was friendship all she desired?

Hod was a good man, a kind man, and a god hopelessly devoted to her, even more so now since her drunken tryst. He needed her, and her culpability about his blindness bound her, too, with invisible chains.

Friendship, guilt, need, and flattery were all strong emotions, but did love lie hiding behind any of these? She didn't know. *Was it right to play with his heart while feeling so unsure?*

Kat couldn't shatter his pride again so, choosing the cowardly option, she had decided to dodge his verbal bullets and field excuses until she could be certain. For both their sakes, she had to sort her feelings out.

"Should we knock?" Zara asked, plucking up the courage to suggest this course of action. There was obvious anxiety in her voice. The jet black door before them looked imposing and none of the girls could ever remember being called to such a meeting with Odin before. It was all terribly mysterious and completely hush-hush.

Large meetings were usually held in Gladsheim; with Oden only holding private audiences in his lofty citadel. Indeed, it was this irregularity and the whispered need for secrecy which heightened the nervousness of the warriors today. Only they had been invited, and not the maids, their protégées, which suggested something very important was going to be said. Even Odin's wolves Geri and Freki looked concerned as they paced irritably around the base of the tower, eyeing the warriors suspiciously as they did so. It was most unusual for them both to be awake at the same time.

"I—" Ruby was about to answer Zara's question when the door before them opened silently.

Odin was ready.

"My dear warriors," Odin began when they had finally assembled in the chamber at the top of his spire. The room was beginning to feel claustrophobic with the nine of them, Odin, and Freyja assembled in the small, circular space.

"Thank you for coming to see me so early this morning. I'm afraid there are many things we need to talk about and much that mustn't stray beyond these walls. I need your help and ideas in tackling the serious problems that are engulfing Asgard."

Odin paused and looked slowly around his chamber. He wanted to gauge the attention of his Valkyries and they didn't disappoint. You could have heard a pin drop.

"I will start with the easy problems. Gunnr, I need you to stay close to Balder without making this too obvious. His dreams are getting worse and I fear for his life."

Silk nodded her agreement, relieved that at last her concerns were being taken seriously. Balder's dream spoke of death and she prayed it wasn't his own. It was common knowledge that Odin's second son was invulnerable to any weapon of Asgard, but his dream suggested a different fate. Balder was her one true love and she feared for his life. Now that Odin had given her authority, she would stick to her man like glue. If anybody or anything tried to harm Balder, they would have to get through her first, and that wouldn't be easy. Gunnr was a ferocious Valkyrie.

"Brynhildr?"

"Yes, my lord," Jess looked up in surprise. She hadn't expected to be mentioned in any of the problems today.

"Herja has left her Valkyrie knife in Midgard and I understand you know one of the people who may be holding it."

Jess looked blankly. She knew about Herja's dagger but not where it was.

"Detective Marcus Finch?" Odin volunteered.

A warm smile crept across Jess's face. *Oh, goody!* Marcus was handsome, clever, and on her last trip to Midgard she had sensed he was a future hero. The attraction was instant; he was her hero and one destined to join Odin's Einherjar, the army of heroes massing in Valhalla. A mission to collect him would be most welcome.

"I need you to go to Midgard as soon as possible and keep an eye on him. He may lead you to Herja's knife."

"Oh gosh, well, I suppose if I have to…," The warriors laughed loudly at Jess's show of mock reluctance. It was a nice moment of light relief in what looked to be a tense and depressing meeting.

"I guess you'll be wanting this," Odin continued, feeling under his throne for a large yellow book which he then passed over to Jess. Eagerly she began flicking though the pages looking for the letter 'P.'

"Now, Prudr, I need you to stay close. You all know that Cole is missing?" The warriors nodded and murmured. "Well, I think he will come back and I'm guessing sooner rather than later. If he does materialize, then I want you to capture him and this time do sort him out straight away, okay?"

Prudr nodded grimly. She had been looking forward to many weeks of fighting with Cole, breaking his spirit, but his kidnapping had changed things. Keeping him intact and strong made him an irresistible target for their enemies. If Cole were destined to be the starter of Ragnarok, then the sooner she took his manhood—and the aggression that went with it—the better.

"Herja and Sangrid?" Odin hunted each of them out in turn with his eye.

Jameela and Kat looked up, with Kat by far the more surprised.

"I need you to go back to Midgard to recover your knife," Odin focused his gaze briefly on Jameela before turning his attention to Kat. "And Sangrid, I would like you to accompany Herja as you are more familiar with this part of the world than she is."

Kat could hardly believe her good fortune. She had been a warrior for only forty-eight hours and was already being offered a mission home. The brilliant smile that lit up her face could probably be seen from Heimdall's watchtower, and it certainly didn't pass unnoticed by Odin.

"Sangrid, do take this mission seriously. It's not a joyride. It could be very dangerous and you are only to assist Herja in finding her way around. Please, I don't want any more accidents. The people holding her knife are both clever and dangerous."

Kat nodded; she understood what he was saying and tried her best to look calm and solemn. She felt like dancing and jumping around the citadel screaming 'Hallelujah' at the top of her voice, but she knew she mustn't—at least not just yet.

"Now we come to the serious troubles." Odin paused, and he gathered by the shockwave that rippled around the room that his warriors hadn't been expecting further bad news.

"I learned from Heimdall last night that a large army of giants is assembling on the other side of the Bifrost Bridge. We don't know why they are there, but we must presume it is to avenge the deaths of the mason and his colleagues. I will be sending Thor, Tyr, and Freyja later this morning to the watchtower and I would like as many warriors and maids as possible to accompany them. Be warned however, there may be bloodshed."

Odin's caution had the desired effect. Far from diminishing the warriors' appetite, the prospect of bloodshed fuelled a feeding frenzy, with each girl fighting to stake her claim for a place in the party. Valkyries lived for war and fighting was their favourite pastime. Eventually, arguments about who should go became so heated that Freyja had to intervene. They would draw lots later to decide who would go and who would stay.

When things finally calmed down, Odin spoke once more. "Unfortunately, there's one more problem, and this is one so serious that I and the other gods may be forced to leave Asgard altogether."

Where a brief moment ago there had been chaos, a deathly silence descended upon the gathering. What trouble could possibly be so awful as to eject Odin from the world he adored?

"Loki did more than just kidnap Cole the other evening," Odin began, with palpable distress in his voice. "He took Idun as well. Without her there are no apples, and without the apples we gods cannot survive."

It took several minutes for this terrible truth to sink in. It was well known that the gods were old beyond their years, and that they visited Odin's garden each day to eat the apples left by Idun. They also knew that these apples stopped them from aging, just as the mead from Valhalla did for the Valkyries. Now, however, faced with this harsh reality, the situation seemed bizarre. *How could the gods depend on just one person?* This seemed an extraordinary blunder.

"How did this happen?" Ruby broke the prolonged silence with the question that hung impatiently on all their lips.

"We don't know exactly. We suspect Loki must have shape-shifted and lured her away somehow. Exactly how he did it is irrelevant; what matters now is there are no apples and we gods will die if we stay here without them."

Kat pricked up her ears—*shape-shifting?* An idea had already begun to form inside her head.

"But why would he do that?" Juliet enquired. "Loki must need the apples, too, so stealing Idun must hurt him as much as it hurts the rest of you?"

"Leverage," Odin replied emphatically, deciding to share the horrible thoughts he had had about the matter during his sleepless night. "He has almost certainly taken refuge in Niflheim with his ghastly daughter. I believe he will return soon and propose a deal, one so vile that it is truly unthinkable…" His voice trailed off.

"Yes, and?" Clearly whatever Loki's intended deal would be, Juliet hadn't grasped as yet.

"Hel," Odin sighed resignedly. He had hoped not to utter Loki's daughter's hideous name. "He will offer to hand back Idun if Hel can return to Asgard. I cannot do that. I cannot unleash that evil child upon us all again, not after last time. That would be an unimaginable horror."

"Odin, do you have any apples at all?" Kat interrupted. She felt embarrassed to speak out at her first meeting as a Valkyrie warrior, but an idea was bursting inside her head and she needed to know more.

"A few—a basket I keep here in the citadel for emergencies, enough perhaps for Freyja, Balder, Thor, and I to stay here for a week, but certainly no longer than that."

"Then that will be enough!" Kat cried excitedly. If Loki returned with a deal her plan would work, she felt sure of it.

Suddenly and with a loud flapping of wings, Huginn, Odin's raven, landed in the room. Blinking repeatedly, he hopped over to the throne then jumped onto Odin's shoulder and nibbled at his earlobe.

"You see, Odin, if you could—"

Kat wasn't allowed to finish. Odin waved his hand at her to shush as he focused intently on Huginn's nuzzling. This went on for several minutes. When at last his raven finished, Odin got up unexpectedly from the throne and beckoned for everybody's attention again.

"I'm so sorry, but I'll have to call an immediate end to this meeting. Events have overtaken us; Loki has returned. Even as we speak, he is holding court in Gladsheim and demanding to speak with me—" he paused, barely able to finish his sentence he felt so indignant, "—immediately!"

Odin's face filled with disgust. *How dare the precocious upstart behave so arrogantly?*

"Wait, please," Kat implored, desperate to catch Odin before he waved his hand over his ring. "Please, my lord, don't make any promises to Loki until I get there."

"Why not?" Odin's hand froze in mid air.

"Because I have an idea which might just get Idun back. All I need is a few minutes to get ready and to borrow Freyja. Would that be possible?"

"Of course, my dear Sangrid," Odin replied and then grimaced. It felt odd using the word 'dear' in the same sentence as 'Sangrid,' and it would definitely take some getting used to.

"Oh, and one other thing: may I have some apples, please?" If Kat was going to complete her plan, she might as well go the whole nine yards.

"And how many would you like?" Odin offered as his hand hovered over the basket.

"All of them."

4

A Shot in the Dark

"ello, Marcus."

Jess began with a warm smile as she extended her hand to greet him. It was great to see him again and she could feel the attraction of his soul much more powerfully than on previous occasions.

Under normal circumstances, Marcus would have enjoyed shaking hands with such an attractive woman, but today was far from normal—and he saw red. He had already unholstered his gun.

"WHAT THE HELL HAVE YOU DONE WITH ANNA?" he screamed hysterically, levelling the pistol at her chest and releasing its safety. Marcus wasn't fooling around. Anna should be there and if she wasn't, it could only mean one thing: she was dead and Jess had killed her.

"Who?" she enquired innocently.

"My fucking wife—that's who! Where the FUCK is she?" The tip of Marcus's gun quivered with his rage—and fear.

"Oh, that's what her name is! I'm so sorry, Marcus, she did tell me but I'd forgotten. She's gone out to get some extra shopping. She'll be back soon, so please don't worry and do please put that silly little gun away."

Marcus stared intently into Jessica's eyes but he knew that they would tell him nothing. She had tricked him before, many months ago when they'd first met, but that wasn't going to happen again. Deep down he still believed that she was a good person, but so much had happened since their last meeting, he couldn't trust her.

He felt confused. He needed answers and he needed them fast.

BANG!

Marcus squeezed the trigger without thinking. It was a reflex, a subconscious urge that bypassed his brain and forced his body to do its bidding. He felt the pressure of his finger on the trigger, but he couldn't stop himself from squeezing it.

He had to shoot Jess. It was the right thing to do—the only thing to do—if he wanted the truth behind the Valkyries.

Although Marcus was no marksman, at that range anyone would have been a crack shot. The bullet entered Jess's body just above her left nipple, fragmenting as it nicked a rib. The shattered metal debris fanned out into a lethal, instantaneous shower that ripped through her heart.

Convulsing with the sudden violent impact of Marcus's bullet, for a moment Jess's face held the briefest expression of surprise. Then it was all over. Her lifeless body recoiled backward into the settee before toppling slowly to one side. Jess collapsed limply like a puppet, her flaccid, useless muscles unable to stop her fall.

Marcus stood still, hypnotised by the horror of what he'd just done. He could count on the fingers of one hand the number of times he had fired his gun in anger, and he'd never shot a woman. This just wasn't him.

However, he knew he had to pull the trigger. He had to know the truth.

With agonising slowness, Marcus inched over to the sofa and crouched down beside her body. Either he had just made the most brilliant decision of his life, or he had booked himself a very long stretch behind bars. There was no in-between, no middle ground, no arguments of diminished responsibility. This was a black and white moment, a moment that would define his life.

He stared intently at her eyes once more. *Did an eyelid just flutter, or was that his imagination?*

Cordite drifted lazily from his gun as a pool of blood seeped slowly into Jess's blouse, forming a crimson lake that was growing steadily larger.

Marcus jumped. He should have had a heart attack.

A lifeless eye had just opened wide and swivelled round to stare at him. Gaping with shock, his jaw hit the ground. *Dr. Nyran had been right!*

"Oooh, you didn't have to do that," Jess grimaced as she gingerly righted her aching body. "But I guess I deserved it. Are we even now?" she enquired as she extended her hand once more. Marcus shook this limply without saying a word. He was way beyond devastated.

"Would you be an angel and fetch my handbag?" Jess continued politely, sucking in a painful gulp of air as she indicated toward the hall. Dazed and confused, Marcus obliged. He still couldn't speak. For the moment, shock had robbed him of his senses.

"Aaah, that feels better," Jess sighed gratefully after she'd gulped down a long draft of mead. Wiping her mouth with the back of her hand, she returned the worn leather flask carefully to her handbag.

"Who are you, I mean—what are you?" Marcus croaked, grateful that at last the power of speech had finally returned.

Everything in his life had been turned upside-down. As Woods had said, he didn't believe in ghosts, vampires, zombies, or any manner of other make-believe hocus-pocus and yet here, right before his very eyes, he had witnessed the impossible: a woman survive a fatal gunshot, a woman who was now sitting and smiling in front of him. *He had to tell Woods about this.*

The rulebook on the Valkyries would have to be rewritten. This *thing* sitting before him was way weirder than anything they could possibly have imagined.

"Ah, yes. What am I? At last, that dreaded question." Jess smiled and chuckled as she invitingly patted the seat beside her. "That could take some time to answer, so why don't you come and sit down here beside me? You look as though you need to. You might want to grab another beer as well. Oh, and while you're at it, could you get one for me, too, please?"

Marcus nodded and started toward the kitchen, but he didn't get there. The sound of keys jangling in the front door stopped him dead in his tracks. With a grating, twisting metallic clunk, the lock's tumblers turned the first time. *How did Anna do that?*

"Hi, darling!" his wife called out expectantly.

Never had a voice sounded more welcoming. Leaping down the corridor, Marcus squeezed her tightly. The familiarity of her body soothed his frazzled nerves, gently easing him back toward his comfort zone.

"Oi, you," Anna poked him playfully after she'd finished hugging and kissing her in a frenzied embrace. "I've got a bone to pick with you. Why didn't you tell me your cousin was coming to stay?"

5

Horse Trading

"**H**iya, Odin, my old mate! Come over here and grab a pew," Loki grinned maliciously as he patted the throne next to his. He was going to have some fun with 'his lordship' today.

Odin clenched his knuckles so tightly that his fingernails dug spitefully into the palms of his hands. It was an outrage to see Loki sprawled across his throne and being so disrespectful. Luckily, he hadn't brought Gungnir with him, a deliberate and wise precaution given the circumstances. A major earthquake was definitely not needed today.

Forcing a pained smile, he walked over and sat down beside Loki, furtively glancing at the chest before him. *Had Hel honoured their agreement?*

"Don't worry, you old skinflint," Loki sneered as he followed Odin's gaze. "It's all there, just as it always is. Hel's a good girl—she's never let you down, has she?"

Odin guffawed loudly. He couldn't help himself. Only Loki could use 'Hel' and 'good' in the same sentence.

"Thank you. I guess we've got some talking to do." Odin gestured toward the chest before setting their negotiations in motion.

"Look, Odin," Loki began, grinning so vilely that it was all Odin could do not to punch him in the face. "I'm a busy man and I can't be bothered with beating about the bush. These are my terms and they're nonnegotiable. Fenrir for Cole, Idun for Hel. Oh, and one more thing: Hel comes back as a Valkyrie."

"I couldn't care less about Cole," Odin began tersely. "He's stuck in Niflheim out of harm's way and, quite frankly, he can rot there along with your stinking daughter. As regards that cursed child, you know I can't agree to make her a Valkyrie again and besides, there are nine Valkyries already. I can't make a tenth. Those are the rules, plain and simple."

Odin sat back and folded his arms tightly across his chest. For now he wasn't going to budge.

"Hey, Odin—like I give a damn about your rules. Get rid of one of the other girls or, better still, maybe get rid of Freyja and make Hel the queen. It makes no difference to me. Hel wants to come back and she wants to be a Valkyrie. All you have to do is to make it happen. That seems pretty fair to me."

Loki finished with an emphatic flourish before sinking his chin onto his upturned hand. He stared long and hard at Odin with that same, beastly, I'm-holding-all-the-cards grin glued impishly to his face.

"I'm sorry, I can't do that. She's evil, and you know what happened last time. Why can't you just be patient? We have our agreement and Ragnarok is nearly upon us." Odin tried to reason with Loki, reminding him of a deal struck long, long ago.

"I know, I know, but she's had enough. She can't wait anymore and I'm fed up of fobbing her off. You say she's evil—I say she's misunderstood. What's in a name, anyway? Sangrid wants to come home and to come home now. Either Hel becomes a Valkyrie again—or you all die."

Loki snarled the last words as the expression on his face hardened. He had all the aces and Odin's face told him that he knew this as well.

"Loki, it just might have escaped your notice, but without Idun you can't eat any apples either. Your stupid kidnapping will hurt you just as much as it hurts the rest of us."

Odin wasn't going to go down without a fight. Besides, Sangrid had told him to wait until she got there. He needed to play for time and hope that her plan was a good one.

"I know, I know. Yadda, yadda, yadda. We'll all have to leave Asgard and so on and so forth. I don't care, I can accept that. The question is: can you?" Loki intimated, stabbing his finger crudely in Odin's face.

"Loki, there has to be another way! Why can't you see that kidnapping Idun helps no one? I don't understand it. Hel can't come back as the Valkyrie Sangrid—I won't allow it." Odin was losing their negotiations and if Kat didn't turn up soon he would have to give ground. Fortunately, his luck was about to change.

"Did somebody mention my name?" Kat's voice echoed cheerily around the hall as she bounced merrily through the door looking as though she didn't have a care in the world.

"Why, hello, Loki. I've got a bone to pick with you," she continued, deciding not to waste any time on the usual pleasantries as she walked briskly over toward him.

Loki rose hastily. "Congratulations, fairest Kat, on your success in the tournament. May I have the honour of knowing the name of the beautiful Valkyrie whose hand I now kiss?"

Loki bowed flamboyantly as he took hold of her hand. She looked gorgeous, a warrior truly worthy of the finest of Valkyrie names.

"You may indeed. I am the Valkyrie Sangrid and I have someone with me who would like to have a word with you."

Loki froze in mid kiss, his lips glued to Kat's hand.

"Sangrid?" He looked up at Odin, and then at Kat. This had to be a joke. The sweet and kindly Kat taking on the curse of his daughter's name—*impossible.*

Odin smiled. The expression on Loki's face was priceless. "Mimir has spoken and Kat's destiny has been revealed," he replied smugly.

A wicked smile crept slowly across Loki's face. Suddenly he had a lot more in common with the beautiful but rather insipid Kat. He was just about to speak again when Kat clapped her hands loudly together. Another woman crept quietly through the door. Tears streamed down her face and in her hands she was holding a wicker basket crammed full of golden apples.

Idun's apples.

Loki's jaw dropped in amazement as Odin gasped, too. *By his blessed beard, the woman carrying the basket WAS Idun!*

"Loki, this is Nidun, Idun's twin sister. She wants to know when you are going to bring her sister back," Kat declared before pouting and fixing her gaze petulantly on him.

Arriving timidly by her side, Nidun nestled her head on Kat's shoulder. Kat gave the girl a gentle caress and as she did so, Nidun let out a loud wail.

"There, there, shush. It'll be alright. Loki's a nice man, really. I'm sure he'll help you find your sister." Kat kissed Nidun's forehead sweetly before taking the basket from her.

"Here, would you like an apple?" she tossed one casually to Loki and then added, "Actually, why don't you take them all? We've got so many and they'll only go rotten if they aren't eaten. Why don't you give some to your daughter, too, as a special treat perhaps?"

Kat handed the basket over to the speechless Loki. The whites of his eyes were showing, they had opened so wide.

"You, you, you—you never said Idun had a sister!" Loki exploded in bewilderment. "You, you—" he continued stuttering helplessly, lost for once for words.

"Well, come now, Loki. I'm hardly going to tell you ALL my little secrets, am I?" Odin replied with a smirk. "As Sangrid has said, take the basket. We have more than we can eat." He decided to play along with her plan.

Loki scratched his head and bit deeply into an apple. It was definitely from Idun's orchard, no doubt about it. Reluctantly he had to face reality. Neither Idun nor Cole had any value as hostages anymore, and Odin didn't even want Cole back.

He sighed deeply. His daughter definitely wouldn't be pleased.

"Will you bring her sister back soon, please?" Kat asked, fluttering her eyes like a puppy dog. "I'm sorry Nidun can't speak for herself, she's just too distraught."

Bang on cue, Nidun let out another loud wail before burying her face in Kat's shoulder once more. The girl seemed in agony.

Loki paused and stroked his beard thoughtfully for a long while. He looked at Odin, then at Kat, and then at Odin once more. Finally he let out a loud guffaw as he slapped his thigh loudly.

"Odin, you are a sly old dog! I thought I had you all figured out and there you go and surprise me once more. You wily old fox, you."

Kat watched his hand as it passed slowly over his ring. In a dazzling flash of light, Loki was gone, returned to Niflheim for an awkward chat with his crazy daughter. Crossing her fingers tightly, Kat prayed that her wild gamble would pay off. Looking hopefully at Odin, she held up her hands. He did likewise. All four fingers were crossed.

Odin sank back into his throne and shook his head slowly from side to side. *Wow! What madness.* All his apples gone in a single, desperate roll of the dice. He just hoped Sangrid knew what she was doing. Gobsmacked by this extraordinary turn of events, he gazed intently at Kat—and Nidun.

"Where in Asgard did you find this woman?" Odin whispered breathlessly, overwhelmed by her incredible similarity to Idun.

"Ah," Kat beamed broadly. "That, my lord, is my secret."

6

The Harem

Cole pushed tentatively against the heavy, rusting iron doors which stood imposingly before him. They towered high above him and he knew it was forbidden to pass through them. Unfortunately, curiosity and the need to break rules always got the better of him. For reasons he didn't quite understand, he felt compelled to explore the cavern that lay beyond.

Cole had been in Hel for some time. He wasn't sure exactly how long because there were no clocks or calendars. The hours passed by in an endless procession of twilight, the eerie gloom outside supplemented only by the torches and candles inside. There was no night or day because the sun, if you could call it that, hung still and lifeless in the sky without ever moving. For all he knew, time itself had ceased to exist. He had been asleep twice since his arrival, so he guessed this must be his third 'day' in Hel.

For a confirmed atheist who hadn't expected anything other than endless nothingness, an afterlife had come as something of a pleasant surprise. He knew that he could never get to heaven, but so far, Hell—or Hel, as they insisted on spelling it here—hadn't been so bad. He had also managed to learn a great many things since his arrival and some of these might come in handy. His criminal guile was a definite advantage down here. The ability to find subtle weaknesses in the prison around him could be useful, hence his need to test the solid doors in front of him.

The name of the vast network of caverns and tunnels in his new home was the palace of Eljudnir and, to his surprise, he had arrived there as a favoured guest.

His quarters were in the 'harem,' which lay close to the royal suite where Hel herself lived. He shared these quarters with some twenty or so other men of all different shapes and sizes. Most of them were from Earth—or Midgard, as they were supposed to call it. Apparently, corpses from there were Hel's biggest contract.

Hel had a special nickname for the group of men which Cole had joined. She referred to them as her 'little girls' and this left Cole confused at first as to what exactly their purpose was. After asking around, he quickly discovered that they existed only to entertain and pleasure her. This was why their quarters were called the 'harem.'

At first sight, and bearing in mind how damn sexy Hel looked, this should have been a very sweet proposal for Cole. Unfortunately, however, his dreams of a sexual paradise with the girl were rudely dashed by the other men around him.

Hel worked hard—but liked to play harder. Not for her the gentle caresses of a loving and caring relationship. No, Hel liked her sex rough and dirty—and the kinkier the better. There was nothing she liked more than an orgy, and that usually meant her writhing around with two, three, or more of her little girls. She had to be the focus of their attention and she was always in charge. They would be expected to perform sexual acts and fantasies, and role play amongst themselves for her amusement, no matter how depraved these amusements might be.

This chilled Cole to the bone. He took pride in being a womanising love machine and was fiercely homophobic. The thought of getting involved in a bit of man-on-man action for Hel's entertainment was an absolute no-no.

When Cole first arrived, after his brief and painfully slapped introduction to Hel, he'd been whisked away to his quarters. These were comfortable rather than luxurious, as was the food and facilities— adequate rather than exceptional. Unfortunately, he hadn't seen much of the fit-as-fuck hottie since then, other than in the distance. She seemed to spend most of her time busy on the other side of the doors before him, which was where she probably was right now.

If he pressed his ear against the door he could hear the sound of a waterfall as it cascaded into a shallow pool below. He had caught glimpses of Hel in this vaulted cavern before. Through the twilit gloom he had seen her wading through countless corpses scattered around the banks of the pool; this was the beach of corpses, or 'Nastrond,' as it was known. She would stand there with her two trusty servants, dragging out the dead as they cascaded down the waterfall from the worlds around them.

In what seemed a surprising twist for Cole, Hel was admired and respected by most of the inhabitants of her realm. Before her arrival, Niflheim had been an anarchic shambles, a lawless wilderness riddled with crime, pestilence, and starvation. Hel had changed all that. She had brilliant business acumen and a talent for organisation and leadership. This could have made her an exceptional queen if it wasn't for one tiny flaw: her sadistic cruelty.

Other than the first vicious slap, Cole hadn't yet experienced her cruelty firsthand and he wasn't in a hurry to do so, either. Calling the men's quarters 'the harem' and referring to them as her 'little girls' left him under no illusion as to the contempt she felt for her subjects. She wasn't a man-hater—far from it. It was just that when you were a monarch with absolute power over everything around you, everyone becomes disposable. They were all just playthings which she could easily tire of. Teasing and humiliating her little girls was just a part of this game, a desperate attempt to find some relief from the crushing boredom of her captivity.

Despite Hel's abuses of the men around him, what Cole had to remember was that they were, in fact, close to the very top of the social pecking order. Beneath them came the soldiers of her Berserker army, and below them were the miners and other slave castes. These lowest castes toiled deep inside the planet and on the dying surface of the sun. Apparently they mined the planet for 'dwarf gold' and the sun for a much rarer and heavier metal called 'Hellinium.' Cole had no idea what these metals were, or for whom they were intended. However, he made a careful note of their names just in case.

BOOM!

The loud resonance of a heavy bronze gong reminded him that everyone near the gates needed to stand clear and avert their eyes.

Cole stood back and peeked through his fingers as the heavy iron doors shuddered begrudgingly open. They did this as regularly as clockwork, every hour on the hour—if that was how time was measured here. Cautiously he checked inside the darkened cavern to see if he could spot Hel. For once he couldn't see her splashing around in the water, but he could just make out an identical door on the opposite side of the pool. This was also opening.

Out of the corner of his eye, Cole followed the progress of large timber cart hauled by ten stout slaves as it trundled noisily past him. It was brimming over with corpses, some clearly recognisable as people and others simply in bits. It was the same every time the doors opened, and probably the same on the other side of the pool—with one notable exception.

On the far side it was one of her trusted servants who would escort the laden carts to the dark face of the planet, the frozen side which lay in perpetual night. The men around him referred to this side of the planet as 'Old Niflheim.' This was where the souls of people who had died from disease or old age were laid to rest. Theirs was a peaceful and honourable grave, one frozen for all eternity in a dark and frigid wilderness.

Only the evil dead passed through the gates to this the illuminated side of the planet, to Hel, the scorched and flaming fire pit. This, he presumed, was the reason why he was here, too.

According to the men, Hel had four main servants—the Guardians of Niflheim—although he had met only two of them. The other pair were kept locked away separately behind two dark and heavily-barred doors. No one had ever seen them and no one was allowed to go near their rooms.

With his habitual disrespect for rules and regulations, Cole had pressed his ear to both these doors. In one he could hear quiet scratching, buzzing, and gnawing sounds; in the other, nothing. The inhabitants of these rooms were a mystery, and one probably best left alone. Cole suspected they were locked away for a very good reason and he was loath to risk his life in finding out why.

Of the two servants he had met, one was a thin, frail, stooped old man called Ganglati. He wore a wonderfully smart, traditional English butler's uniform and walked unbelievably slowly. Hel shouted and abused him a lot, as she did Ganglot, her female servant. She was the antithesis of Ganglati. Where he was thin she was fat, where he was old she was young, and where he dressed smartly she was an out and out slob. Despite her youth, they did have one thing in common: sloth. Ganglot was every bit as slow as Ganglati was.

Ganglati was old but seemed in reasonably good health. However, the same couldn't be said for Ganglot. Her hair appeared to be prematurely thinning and a perpetual, barking cough emanated from her throat. With her face covered in boils and cold sores visible around her chapped lips, she looked a complete mess, and the rest of her body presented little better.

Her right arm was riddled with arthritis but at least it was whole, unlike her left. This had suffered a partial amputation from the elbow downward. Ganglot's legs, too, were in a shocking state, with swollen ankles and open, pus-filled, gangrenous ulcers on her calves which stank to high heaven. Ganglot reeked of neglect, disease, and incontinence, while Ganglati looked like death warmed up.

For Cole, it was impossible to understand how two such train wrecks could hold such important positions. The pair seemed woefully incompetent, and if the state of their locked up companions matched their own then it begged an obvious question: just who were the Guardians of Niflheim? This was an intriguing issue.

One other similarity between the two servants had also struck Cole as peculiarly odd. They both wore gloves and did so all the time. Ganglati's were smart and white whereas Ganglot's single glove looked filthy and tattered, like some old knitted gardening sock. He didn't as yet know why they wore them, but he guessed it was just another mystery to add to his growing list.

As he turned to make his way back down the hall, Ganglati signalled him with his hands.

Cole walked over inquisitively.

"Her majesty would like to see you," Ganglati began in a thin and quavering voice. "Would you follow me, please," he continued, after clearing his throat with a polite little cough.

Slowly, and at a speed that made Cole want to scream, they walked toward the reception room where he had first arrived. As they approached its door, a young woman with long, fair hair emerged in a hurry. She was wailing and had a bloodsoaked towel pressed tightly against her face. A slave was escorting her hastily toward the royal quarters.

Cole didn't get a chance to see her properly, but he suspected that she was probably quite pretty. With a shock, he suddenly realised that other than Ganglot and Hel, this was the first woman he had encountered since his arrival.

With some hesitancy, Ganglati knocked quietly on the dark, oak-panelled door.

"ENTER!" Hel's unmistakable voice yelled piercingly from inside.

7

Nidun

Kat and Nidun chatted and laughed merrily as they hurried back to the castle from Gladsheim. They were both in excellent spirits and believed their little performance had gone down exceedingly well. As they walked, they felt the ground shake gently beneath their feet. It was Jess, off on her mission to Midgard.

Nearing the castle, they paused briefly to follow the noisy flight of four swans as they sped away from the courtyard. These were the Valkyries Goll, Prima, Skogul, and Mist on their way to war. The swans whooped loudly as they passed close overhead and Kat felt a sudden pang of longing to be with them, a desperate urge to put on her cloak of feathers and give chase. The warriors were en route to Heimdall's watchtower and she knew they would be ready to fight the instant their feet touched the ground.

Their mission was simple: to defend the Bifrost Bridge at all costs, holding any invading giants at bay until reinforcements could arrive. Watching them leave, the thrill of bloodlust rose swiftly inside her. Kat was torn, the desire to return to Midgard being matched by her thirst to wage war. This craving sent shivers down her spine.

In the courtyard Thor, Tyr, Freyja, and the remaining maids were making final preparations to leave. Thor waved his hammer cheerily at Kat and let out a loud bellow. The maids responded with a chorus of penetrating war cries. Kat had to look away; a tear was forming in the corner of her eye. She yearned so much to go with her sisters. The atmosphere all around them was one of frenzied excitement, a vibrant carnival rejoicing in the call to arms.

35

Freyja, too, was going to the watchtower. She would lead the war party in her glorious chariot. Dressed in a beautiful white leather bodice with matching leggings and carrying her silver falcon's helmet, cloak, and shield, she looked every inch their magnificent warrior queen, the leader of the Valkyrie elite.

Freyja's regal splendour cut a stark contrast to Thor's squat and swarthy form and their chariots echoed these differences. Thor's battered affair was pulled by two enchanted but somewhat pathetic-looking goats, who bleated periodically as they munched diligently on mouthfuls of hay and straw.

Freyja's magnificent, gilded war machine was very different, being drawn by a pair of magnificent sleek panthers whose bright yellow eyes and white teeth flashed menacingly as they prowled impatiently up and down in the watery autumn sunshine.

With a final thunderous cheer and a ferocious clattering of hooves (and paws) on the cobbled courtyard, the party departed at a brisk trot. With luck, they would arrive at the watchtower by dusk.

As the party left, Kat and Nidun cheered ecstatically before retiring inside. They both felt a heaviness in their chests as they walked slowly up the twisting stone staircase to Kat's chambers. Closing the door behind them, their despondency soon lifted. At last they were alone together and could celebrate their charade.

Holding hands, giggling, and hugging each other, Nidun slowly began to change form—the shapely, hourglass figure of a slender young maiden gave way to the muscular physique of Freyr, the handsome, shape-shifting, fertility god.

Shape-shifting and mimicry had been the inspiration behind Kat's scheme. *What better way to trick a trickster than by beating him at his own game?*

With a frock and a little bit of makeup, Freyr's transformation had been complete. Even Idun's mother couldn't have told the two of them apart. Everything seemed to have worked to perfection, and the two were jubilant.

"I do hope I didn't hurt you too much," Kat laughed as she sympathetically stroked Freyr's thigh.

"No, but you did draw blood."

Freyr laughed too, and then tossed a string of onions to the floor. These had provided the tears and the red, grief-stricken eyes of Nidun. As for her wails of anguish—these had been only too genuine. Kat had jabbed a well-aimed fork into his thigh to elicit these.

All in all, they both agreed that they couldn't have done a better job and congratulated themselves heartily on their little escapade. If they succeeded and Idun were returned to Odin, then they would have a real feather in their caps. To outsmart a weasel like Loki would be no mean achievement.

"Was it difficult to hide all this?" Kat enquired coyly as she ran her fingers slowly and provocatively down Freyr's stomach and across his groin. Her bloodlust needed satisfying and although his bulging manhood looked a little comical beneath a linen frock, it still inflamed her passion.

"Hmmm, so-so," Freyr smiled, enjoying the touch of her hand. He guessed what she had in mind. "I thought you had a tea party with Frigg to get to?"

"Yes, but that's much later in the afternoon and we have hours to go yet."

Removing her hands from his body, Kat strutted seductively across the room and, after checking outside her door, she closed it and turned the lock. Freyr was her prisoner and he wouldn't be released until she was done. Her needs were lust in its purest form.

"Would you like to go to Odin's garden?" he offered casually.

"Well, with the castle almost deserted and this big room all to ourselves," Kat teased, taking him by the hand and pulling him purposefully over to the bed. Pushing him down roughly, she loosened her dress and allowed it to fall to the floor. Naked, she straddled his hips before flipping his frock up to expose his manhood, which was already swelling toward its full, magnificent strength.

"I thought you might need a little relief after all your hard work this morning," she cooed, tracing her fingernails along his thickness.

Freyr chuckled as he shook his head. He really did like Kat. She was a fun and sexy Valkyrie, entertaining and witty with a wicked streak that was as naughty as it was discreet. Although his job as a fertility god meant he lay with a lot of women, she was right up there with the best of them. With her beautiful soft, clear skin; pert, firm breasts; taut waist; and a petite muscular bottom which had already started to grind rhythmically against his thighs, life was looking good—life was looking very good indeed.

"If a situation ever becomes vacant as a fertility goddess, I might just let you know," he chuckled as he pulled her toward him, kissing and nuzzling her breasts passionately.

Kat smirked. Now that really was an offer worth thinking about.

8

Rules of Attraction

"So you're telling me I'm going to die soon?"

"Yes, but I'll be here to rescue your soul and take you to Valhalla. Isn't that exciting?" Jess exclaimed with a broad smile on her face.

Marcus slumped back into his chair and sipped thoughtfully at his cup of tea. Exciting wasn't exactly the first word that had sprung to mind.

After Anna had arrived home, the evening passed quickly and in a state of comical unreality. Not surprisingly, Anna was shocked by the injury to Jess's chest, but Jess's ludicrous explanation seemed to satisfy her curiosity.

According to Jess's story, she had heard a loud bang somewhere on their floor in the apartment block. Having hurried outside to take a look, she'd realised that she didn't have a key to the front door. Hurling herself against the door as it closed, she had become impaled upon the latch. This was the cause of her rather vicious chest injury.

"You poor thing," Anna muttered as she fussed and flapped over the wound, eventually offering Jess a plaster to stem the bleeding. Marcus had to laugh. The absurdity of a using a band-aid to patch up a gunshot wound was so ridiculous you simply couldn't have made it up.

First aid completed, life at the Finches' quickly settled back into its established weekday routine. Wednesday night was spaghetti

Bolognese night, and they settled down to eat this with some beers. Anna and Jess prattled away happily together, talking about Marcus's family as they dined.

"Jessica Perry," it turned out, was his second cousin and had come to New York to look for a job in IT. As the story unfolded, Marcus became increasingly impressed by the research Jess had done into his family background. As the women chatted, little things that she didn't know Jess would make up on the fly or guess from clues as suggested by Anna. She was a typical woman: capable of lying with absolute conviction and bluffing with equal aplomb. It was a pleasure to watch.

As the beers turned to wine and the family albums came out, Marcus almost forgot that she wasn't really his cousin at all. They laughed and joked together in a manner that felt completely comfortable and natural. It was as if they had known each other all their lives. When at last it was time for bed, he slept soundly, not caring that the woman lying in the room next to theirs was a complete stranger, an accomplished liar, and a cold-blooded serial killer.

The next morning, they all arose looking very much the worse for wear. Too many beers and too much wine had taken its toll.

After a hurried breakfast and nursing a king-size hangover, Marcus offered to show Jess the way to the job centre. Walking briskly together in the pale March sunshine, they travelled a couple of blocks before ducking into a dingy, truck driver-style café for a coffee and a more intimate chat.

Jess looked fabulous as he knew she would. Dressed casually but elegantly in a loose cream sweater, expensive leather jacket, and an emerald green skirt, she turned heads from passersby as they walked. Jess was the kind of woman who gave a man a real high—and Marcus was no exception. His attraction to her when they first met many months before had been no passing fancy, and she was even more desirable now.

He knew he should be calling Woods and arresting her for the suspected murders of Dr. Neal and Mickey Warren—but he didn't. For now, he wanted to learn more.

The Valkyrie 'Jess' was an extraordinary woman and this opportunity was simply too good to miss. He had a hunch that using a softly-softly approach would produce far more information than going in all guns blazing. Cult members were tough and unyielding, force being met with force.

"So what are you?"

Marcus posed the question once more. This had gone unanswered yesterday due to Anna's untimely interruption. He didn't need to ask who she was, because he already knew. He had done some research, too.

Jessica wasn't, in fact, Police Officer Jessica O'Brien nor was she his cousin Jessica Perry. She was born Jessica Anne Louise Marie Sullivan on the second of May, 1946 in a small town in Northern Ireland. Her parents were Patrick and Doreen, and her mother was still alive and living in the house where she had grown up. Doreen was frail and nearly ninety now. Her father, 'Paddy,' served with the British Army in the Second World War and had lost his right arm when the tank he was commanding blew up. She had an older brother, Sean, who had died the previous year from lung cancer. Marcus suspected she didn't know this yet.

The original Jessica Sullivan had joined the British Army after school and had risen quickly to the rank of lieutenant. Unfortunately, she was long departed, having died on September 25, 1972 at the tender age of 26. Her death had been horrific: having been viciously tortured before her brutal murder by the IRA.

Jessica Sullivan had died a very courageous woman, working deep undercover as an informant for the British Army. She was highly decorated posthumously for her outstanding bravery. Had the original Jessica not been killed, he would now be sitting and looking at a sixty-three-year-old woman, not someone who was a ravishing twenty-something.

Hence his question, *What are you?*

"I am a Valkyrie, Marcus, but I suspect you already know that." She smiled provocatively in a way that was totally disarming.

"Yes, but what exactly does that mean? How could you survive being shot through the heart, and why don't you look sixty-three?"

"I can tell you much, Marcus, but first you must promise me something," reaching out, she placed her hand gently on top of his. "You won't shoot me or arrest me again?" She laughed once more. Her voice was as beautiful as a lark.

"Okay, but what you say must be the truth. No more lies now, please. Do you promise?"

Jess crossed her heart with an exaggerated gesture and then began her story.

"I am undead, Marcus, so I can't be killed. Valkyries drink special mead that comes from Valhalla; this stops us aging and heals any wounds." She levered her leather flask up so that it peeped out of her handbag as she spoke.

"I have come from Asgard for two reasons. The first you already know. We need to recover the knife left behind by my sister, Herja. I believe you know where this is?"

Marcus nodded. He wanted to know more. "Where or what is Asgard?"

"It's the world where we live. I'm not exactly sure where it is in the universe, but it is a beautiful place." Jess's eyes sparkled as she spoke. Momentarily, she was back on her stallion galloping across the plains of Ida, a warm wind flowing deliciously through her carefree hair as a hot summer sun beat fiercely down upon her back. *Aah...paradise.*

"Did you know your mother is still alive and very ill?" Marcus enquired, deciding to test one of Wood's pet theories about the cult.

"Doreen? Are you sure?" For a brief moment the sunshine faded from Jess's eyes and Marcus knew instantly that she couldn't be a clone. She had to be the original Jessica Sullivan; it was all too evident in the sadness of her face.

"Uh huh. Have you ever visited her?" He asked, curious to see her reaction.

"No, that would be nice, but I can't. The shock might kill her and besides, there would be too many questions and complications." Jess had recovered her composure and rejected the brief, momentary fantasy of a reunion with her family.

"And the second reason you're here?" Marcus had almost forgotten that Jess was back on Earth for something else besides the knife.

"I'm here for you, Marcus. You're a hero and I've come to save your soul when it's your turn to die."

Marcus sat back, stunned. "Are you saying you're going to kill me?"

"No, no. Don't be so silly," Jess laughed again. "But you are going to be killed and when you are, I'll be here to rescue your soul and take you to Valhalla."

From anyone else, this bizarre statement would have sounded like a lunatic booking his ticket to the funny farm. However, coming from Jess, it all sounded frighteningly real and horribly urgent. Marcus felt he ought to be terrified, but somehow he wasn't. Maybe he was in a state of denial, or maybe the calm and matter of fact way in which she spoke about his impending demise filled him with confidence.

"Do you know how or when I'm going to die? Can you stop it?"

"No, and that's why you can't arrest me because if you do, I won't be around to save you!" she finished with a triumphant flourish before going back to sipping her coffee. After a brief lull, Jess spoke again, staring intently into his eyes as she did so. "By the way, do you feel the attraction?"

Jess's stare burned holes in his eyes and Marcus knew he was going to blush. *He was a married man for God's sake!*

"Well, yes, yes—of course I do. You're a beautiful woman. It wouldn't be normal if I—I—I didn't feel turned on," he stammered, tripping hopelessly over his tongue and blustering like a nervous schoolboy once again. How he hated that feeling.

"No, no. It's not just that, silly! There's an even more powerful attraction between us, which is how I know you're my hero. It's growing stronger, too, and will continue to do so until the time is right for you to die. Oh, do tell me that you feel it!" she finished excitedly, squeezing his hand hard.

Dear God! Marcus was in trouble and he knew it. He was married and had always been faithful to Anna, but the most gorgeous woman he had ever met had just confessed that she was attracted to him. This was too much, a temptation worthy of Christ himself. He had to change the subject and fast. "So you're telling me I'm going to die soon?"

"Yes, but not today. So come on, let's get on and enjoy ourselves." Jess finished her coffee before smiling at him once more. "So, Detective Marcus Finch," she teased. "Where would you like to take me for our first date?"

Marcus looked up as his face turned crimson.

Squealing gleefully, Jess squeezed his hand once more. His handsome, boyish blush was definitely a 'Kodak' moment.

9

How High?

"**H**ello, gorgeous. How are you enjoying things so far?" Hel purred as she indicated for Cole to take a seat at her large oak table.

The room hadn't changed since his arrival, other than for a fresh bouquet of black poppies which had been attractively arranged on the table. These made the air even more oppressive with an aroma that was way too pungent for Cole's liking, although it was still preferable to the constant stench of rotten, sulphurous eggs that pervaded every other nook and cranny in the palace.

"It's cool," Cole replied as he took a seat and made a half grin at her. He wasn't really sure what to expect from the little vixen at this meeting.

"Are my other little girls looking after you?" she teased as she walked slowly behind him and massaged his shoulders firmly, kissing him on the top of his head as she did so.

"They're good, sugar. It's all good." Cole nodded slowly.

"I'm sorry I haven't spent much time with you," she cooed, bending down and nibbling at his earlobe, "but I promise I'll make that up to you soon." Hel kissed him delicately on the cheek before standing up and marching briskly around the table. It was time to get down to business.

"Cole, do you think my kingdom is well run?"

Cole nodded his agreement. It certainly seemed that way.

"Good. It was a disaster before I got here and I changed all that. Would you like to know how?"

Cole grinned but said nothing; the hottie was going to tell him anyway.

"Because there are rules, Cole—my rules, and nobody breaks them." Hel's seductive cooing and sugary sweet smile vanished as swiftly as a moonbeam. "And the easiest way to explain why nobody breaks my rules is with a practical demonstration, don't you think?" She inquired, staring icily—before breaking abruptly into a smile once more.

Christ! She was a changeable bitch.

Suspicions aroused, Cole suddenly became aware of two identical black knives on the table, both with intricately carved handles. He had initially thought they were steak knives but now, well...

"Oh, these," Hel had followed his line of sight. "Do you like them? Go on, pick one up, have a closer look." Hel motioned and he cautiously did as she suggested. They were much heavier than he'd expected, and had a wickedly sharp and slightly curved, serrated blade. One thing was certain: they definitely weren't steak knives.

After a few moments of casual inspection and feigned interest, he put the knife back down on the table.

"Now Cole, show me your sword hand." Hel commanded, holding out her hands as he placed his right one obediently in hers. Examining it studiously, she turned it over and over.

"Come quickly!" She suddenly waved excitedly, beckoning to Ganglati to take a look. Her servant shuffled stiffly forward, shaking as he did so. "Feel how soft and gentle his hand is. Look! It's like a little girl's!"

Ganglati went to take hold of Cole's right hand and to his surprise Hel's servant had removed his white gloves. Cole glanced nervously at the wizened, bony hands. They looked old, very old, but to his relief they seemed otherwise normal. Ganglati took Cole's hand gently in his.

Fuck! It felt as though he'd been gripped by a vise. Cole tried to raise his left arm from beneath the table but all the strength in his body was gone. He felt drained and as weak as a kitten. The weakness and frailty of old age—so visible in Ganglati—had been transferred to him.

THUD!

"JESUS H. CHRIST—YOU MOTHER FUCKIN'—!" Cole didn't get to complete his curse. He couldn't. Swooning with the terrible pain that blitzed his brain, he'd been so distracted by Ganglati that he hadn't noticed Hel pick up a knife and in a single, fluid motion, stab it violently through his right hand, pinning this to the table. The hand was pouring blood and the pain was excruciating.

"Oh, dear. Poor Cole," Hel mocked, as a twisted and cruel smile curled across her lips. "You really shouldn't have sworn, now should you? That was a very stupid thing to do. If Odin won't tolerate swearing, do you honestly think I will?"

Picking up the other knife on the table, she twirled it menacingly in her hands. "If my rules say no poking around doors to my servants' rooms and my palace gateway, then that means no poking—EVER. Do you understand?"

Cole nodded weakly. She was bringing the other knife perilously near to the fingers of his skewered and helpless right hand.

"Which one do you reckon?" Crowing with laughter, Hel glanced at Ganglati as she started to play Eeny, Meeny, Miny, Moe with Cole's fingers.

"Oh, that one, mi'lady, that one will be splendid," Ganglati chuckled enthusiastically as he agreed with her eventual selection.

"YOU FUCKIN' BITCH, DON'T YOU DARE—"

"Oh, dear me, Cole. Do you really want to lose TWO fingers?" Hel interrupted his outburst with a stern warning. She was completely unruffled by Cole's anguish, but extremely annoyed by yet another profanity.

Paying no attention to his garbled pleading, Hel deliberately and theatrically positioned the blade of the knife on the second joint of his index finger before pressing down slowly but firmly. Bones started to separate as cartilage plates crunched delicately, grazed by the kiss of her blade as it slipped easily between them.

The knife's razor sharp journey was as merciless as it was inexorable; blood pumping in arterial squirts as it arrived at its agonising destination. Cole's finger had been amputated and it lay on the table before him, severed from its bleeding stump.

He blacked out.

"Come on, come on. Breathe, breathe—there's a good little girl."

Hel was holding a poppy beneath his nose and encouraging him to inhale deeply. Cole did so gladly, each gulped breath slightly dimming the unbelievable pain which now torched the nerves of his right arm. He knew he had blacked out, because his impaled hand was now freed from the table and Ganglati had let go of his left.

Slowly, very slowly, he could feel his strength returning.

"Jeez—" Cole stopped immediately. He couldn't handle losing another finger. This was her show and he had no choice. For the first time he had to accept a woman as his master.

"Now, Cole, if I wanted to, I could stick this finger back on," she waggled his severed fingertip like a new toy beneath his nose. "And cut it off again and again and again—forever. Do you get where I'm coming from? The pain you've just experienced could go on and on for ALL eternity."

Cole nodded weakly. The pool of blood around his hand was dripping onto the floor and he desperately needed to stem the loss.

"Now do you understand why nobody breaks my rules?"

Cole nodded weakly once more.

"If I tell you to jump, I only want to hear one thing, don't I?" Hel teased, running her fingers through the blood before daubing his face with it. "What do I want to hear, Cole?"

"How high?" he muttered in a coarse whisper.

"Sorry, I didn't hear you." She enquired, salaciously licking his blood from her fingers.

"How high?" he tried to speak louder.

"Sorry?"

Finally, Cole's voice rose to a weak and agonised scream. "HOW HIGH—YOUR MAJESTY!"

"Good girl! You see, Ganglati? I told you Odin's starter of Ragnarok would be a fast learner. Now take her away and get her cleaned up. Oh, and Cole—I'll be seeing you again later."

Hel blew him a seductive kiss as Ganglati, with his white gloves now firmly back in place, escorted him slowly from the room. Reaching the door, Cole took one last, lingering look at Hel.

He hated the bitch like he'd never hated anyone before. For now he knew he could do nothing about it, but if the time came when he could repay her, he would do so—and with interest. He would fuck her hard first, of course, and then cut her up nice and slow, piece by bloody piece. She would die an agonising death; he would make sure of that.

Oh, yes, that time would definitely come. And when it did, he would be ready.

"DADDY!" Hel suddenly exclaimed excitedly as her father unexpectedly entered the room.

Loki glanced briefly at Cole's blood-soaked hand and shrugged sympathetically. There was nothing he could do—Hel had clearly been having some fun today.

"I do hope you have good news for me," she cried as she ran over and embraced him warmly.

10

Billing's Daughter

"Ladies, would you all please be upstanding and drink a toast to the Valkyrie Sangrid."

"HAIL, SANGRID!"

Everybody raised their glasses and after drinking a deep toast, a ripple of enthusiastic applause echoed warmly around the hall of Fensalir.

Kat felt completely overwhelmed by the generous reception she was receiving at Frigg's afternoon tea party, and totally underwhelmed by the state of her attire. Compared to the dozen or so ladies in the room, her clothes seemed so dowdy.

Frigg, as usual, looked absolutely fabulous. She had arrived at the castle about an hour after Freyr had left, wearing the most beautiful ensemble Kat had ever seen: a salmon pink dress with elegant matching accessories. "Dior," Frigg enthusiastically informed her, her outfit having been purchased recently in Paris, her favourite place in the whole universe—or universes, as the case may be.

Frigg's usually straight hair had also been curled and fashioned with a side parting which accentuated her vertiginously high cheekbones, and she delighted in showing Kat the highlights that had been done at the same time. Gossiping away merrily, Kat prayed that their girly chitchat would be a wonderfully girly start to what would turn out to be a wonderfully girly afternoon.

Before Kat arrived at Fensalir, she had been concerned that her Valkyrie name would upset many of Frigg's friends. That fear now seemed unfounded. Everybody expressed delight at meeting her, and she was frankly embarrassed by the effort Frigg had put into making her feel so welcome.

Okay, if she was being picky then perhaps some of the food in the buffet was a little passé. Pineapple chunks and cheese on sticks, sausage rolls, vol-au-vents filled with salmon mousse, and tiny cucumber sandwiches. These somewhat naff nibbles didn't really matter. What mattered was the thought behind them. Frigg genuinely seemed to care about her.

You also couldn't ignore the other, more fabulous, delicacies on display: caviar, smoked salmon, the finest of champagnes, and some wonderful fresh cream pastries that looked as though they had been made only this morning in some chic Parisian café on the Champs-Élysées.

Frigg oozed money, taste, and style in bundles, and Kat reaffirmed her opinion that Frigg's cosy little apartment was the nicest place in all of Asgard.

Right from the outset of the party, Kat was determined to mingle with as many of the goddesses as possible. However, before she could do so, she had to compliment Hod, the only man in the room. Frigg had obviously thought of him, too, during her recent shopping trip to Midgard, and he looked transformed.

Wearing a navy bespoke two-piece suit and an expensive open-necked silk shirt, he looked positively dapper. Gone was the scarf he wore about his head as a blindfold; being replaced by a pair of designer sunglasses that screamed 'handsome, playboy lover.'

Damn! Maybe she shouldn't dismiss him yet as a lover?

Kat hugged him warmly as she greeted him, playfully squeezing his bottom. Caught off guard, he jumped, spilling his champagne. She should have apologised, but she knew he didn't mind. His blush and self-conscious smile said it all. Her show of affection had made his day.

"Who's that lady over there?" Kat asked before immediately apologising. She still forgot sometimes that Hod was blind. "I mean the beautiful lady wearing a wig made from something that looks like gold?" she continued.

"Oh, that's Sif. She's stunning, isn't she?" Hod began. "She's Thor's wife."

Wow! Kat was amazed. How could Thor have such a beautiful wife? He was a noble and muscular fellow but not the finest-looking of gods by any means.

"Why does she wear a golden wig?" she asked inquisitively.

Hod chuckled. "She doesn't have to anymore, but she enjoys wearing it. It makes quite an impact, don't you think? She's such an extrovert and oh, by the way, the wig is actually made of pure gold. Isn't that incredible?"

Kat agreed; it was the most beautiful hairpiece she'd ever seen.

"There's a really great story behind it," Hod continued. "Maybe Thor will tell you about it one day. It was all Loki's fault, but the story is very funny and it's a tale with a happy ending."

Kat was about to beg him to tell her more but Frigg interrupted, dragging her away by the arm. She was insistent on introducing Kat to some of her other guests.

"Stop hogging her, Hodikins," Frigg scolded her son with mock indignation.

"It's a pity Freyja can't be here," Kat started and then stopped; this was yet another faux pas. "I'm so sorry, I keep forgetting."

"Oh, don't worry," Frigg patted her arm reassuringly. "Once upon a time we were really the best of friends. In fact, we made quite a happy foursome—Freyja, me, Odin, and Od."

"Od?" Kat inquired.

"Yes, her husband. Very sad about him, poor fellow. This was how her affair with Odin all started," she looked around conspiratorially before dropping her voice.

"Od went on a journey to Midgard many years ago and never came back. Vanished completely! Freyja was so devastated. Odin tried to help her, spending many long years looking for him without success. This kind of forced the two of them together, partners in adversity and all that rubbish. Well, one thing led to another and before you knew it, they became lovers. It was stupid, really. Incidentally, did you know that this is the reason why Odin chooses Valkyries from Midgard?"

Kat shook her head. Frigg was always so chatty and such a font of knowledge. Kat urged her to say more.

"Well, during his search for Od, he came across a young maiden in Midgard and fell madly in love with her. I can't remember her name, but she was the daughter of Billing, a shipbuilder in a small village in Norway. Odin pursued her for many weeks, buying her fine gifts, writing poems, and generally making a lovesick ass of himself."

They both laughed loudly at this point and heads turned inquisitively in their direction. With a flourish of her hand, Frigg waved the nosy onlookers away. Their cosy chat was private and not really of interest to anybody else. As soon as conversations around them picked up once more, she went back to her story.

"Anyway, as I was saying, he pursued her and she played hard to get. She didn't exactly say 'No' nor did she say 'Yes' to his amorous advances. She just kept him dangling, as we ladies so often do."

Frigg paused tellingly, and Kat nodded that she understood. This was a barely-veiled reference to the way she was treating Hod, and she hoped she wasn't going to confirm her guilt with a blush. Fortunately, Frigg was too engrossed in her storytelling to read Kat's obvious discomfort.

"Well, one night she told Odin to come to her room when everybody else had gone to sleep. She promised she would give him an answer to his weeks of courtship. Overcome with excitement, Odin slipped past her sleeping father and brothers and tiptoed up to her bedroom. Stripping off his clothes, he sneaked into her bed and started to cuddle up beside her and—"

Frigg broke off laughing hysterically. The punch line was just too funny for her to continue.

"Go on, please," Kat implored. She, too, was now eager to hear the joke.

Flapping her hand wildly in front of her mouth, Frigg endeavoured to finish the story. "He put his arm around her and, and—" she giggled once more. "Instead of receiving a kiss from a shapely girl, he got a snarl from a dog! She had tied her bitch up in the bed! The poor fool was about to embrace her mutt in his arms!" With this revelation, they both dissolved into laughter.

"Apparently, he ran away like the wind. He never went back, ever!" Frigg creased up once more.

"Anyway," Frigg continued, wiping tears of laughter from her eyes, "he was so impressed by her rejection that he vowed he would always choose his Valkyries from Midgard. The women there were strong in both mind and in virtue."

When they eventually finished giggling, Kat offered Frigg her sympathies once more as regards Odin's affair.

"Oh, don't worry about that. If the boys can play…" Frigg gave Kat a knowing and mischievous wink, one that suggested she was more than capable of seeking solace elsewhere. Kat wanted to delve deeper and catch the gossip, but before she could open her mouth Frigg hastily excused herself before deftly removing a glass of champagne from a very unsteady-looking guest who was tottering by.

"Please excuse Saga," she nodded toward the goddess who had turned and was already weaving her way back toward the mini bar.

"She has a bit of a drink problem and gets awfully rowdy when she has too much."

Kat chuckled. It was nice to see that goddesses had a vulnerable side, too.

"Thank you so much for making me so welcome," Kat offered as she was introduced to Balder's wife, Nanna. "You've all been so good to me, particularly as my Valkyrie name has such a dreadful past."

"Oh, don't worry about that," Nanna exclaimed as she gave her a friendly hug. "We all remember Hel from when she was a little girl. She grew up with us all."

Kat looked surprised; she'd forgotten that the first Sangrid was once a goddess.

"Yes, she was quite sweet when she was little, awfully pretty," Frigg joined in the conversation. "She was Hod's playmate back then, which probably explains some of his problems now."

Frigg sighed and exchanged a look with Nanna. Kat encouraged them to say more—her curiosity was inflamed. She had no idea that Hod knew Hel, let alone that they had grown up together.

"Well, she was always a bit strange, very dominant," Nanna began, and Frigg nodded in agreement. "When she played doctors and nurses with Hod, she would always insist on being the doctor."

"And make-believe marriages," Frigg interrupted. "She would always make Hod wear the dress and be the wife. He used to get ever so upset."

Nanna and Frigg chuckled as they reminisced together.

"But surely she can't be as bad as people say she is?" Kat asked nosily, seizing the opportunity to learn a little bit more about her namesake.

"How would you describe her, Nanna?" Frigg inquired.

Nanna thought for a moment. "I would say she's a bit like a scorpion, the one in the story with the fox in it." Kat looked puzzled, so she continued. "There was once a flood and a scorpion begged a fox to let it ride on his head when he swam across the river to escape the rising water. The scorpion promised the fox that it wouldn't sting him."

Frigg nodded her head.

"The fox reluctantly agreed because he was a kind and caring sort of fox. Anyway, when they are about halfway across the river, the scorpion stung him."

"But that doesn't make any sense!" Kat exclaimed. "They would both drown."

"Exactly," Nanna continued. "'Why did you do that?' the fox asked the scorpion. 'Now we will both die.'"

"And?" Kat interrupted, eager to hear the end of the tale.

"The scorpion simply said, 'Because I'm a scorpion.'"

Kat's face looked a bit puzzled; it still didn't make any sense.

"You see, Kat," Frigg spoke sombrely once more, "Hel can't help herself. It's in her nature to be naughty or evil, just like the scorpion in the tale. Even when she wants to be nice, or has to be nice, she slips up. She can't help herself. She was devastated when Odin banished her to Niflheim, poor thing. It was such a shame. She really didn't deserve such a terrible fate; she was still only a teenager."

Both Nanna and Frigg grimaced at this point. Niflheim was such an ugly place and Hel's punishment had been cruel and unprecedented. Frigg immediately decided that they should speak no more about this or any other unsavoury topics that afternoon. Taking Kat firmly by the hand, she marched her away across the room and began to introduce her to some of the other guests.

As the afternoon passed merrily by, Kat met many more goddesses and forgot nearly as many names. The good company and champagne flowed like an endless fountain. It was an afternoon that could be filled with many pleasurable memories, provided, of course, she didn't get too hammered.

Amongst the few names that she did remember was Snotra. She was a plain but apparently extremely clever goddess. She also remembered Eir, who was a goddess of healing. Eir was fascinated by Kat's past as a doctor and would have loved to chat for many hours. Unfortunately, Frigg had decided by this time that it was appropriate for them to share some quality moments on their own. Whisking her away to a quiet corner of the room, Frigg poured them both a couple of glasses of bubbly and then sat down. It was time for some intimacy.

Taking a pack of elegant French Gauloises cigarettes from her handbag, Frigg offered Kat one. Kat declined—she'd been a doctor once upon a time. Placing her cigarette in an old-fashioned ivory holder, Frigg lit it and inhaled deeply. At last she could give Kat her undivided attention.

"Now, let me see. What has the beautiful and talented young Kitty Kat been up to?" she purred contentedly as she half-closed her eyes and stared intently at Kat.

Kat knew immediately what Frigg was doing. The goddess was rummaging through her thoughts just as her mother used to go through her handbag. Kat found this vaguely irritating and somewhat annoying. Just like her handbag or the texts on her cell phone, her mind was 'private property' and should be out of bounds. Unfortunately, she couldn't do anything about it.

"Don't get attached to Freyr," Frigg looked up suddenly and Kat blushed. "It's his job to make women happy and give them satisfaction."

"I know," Kat murmured with embarrassment as she looked down at the floor. *Ouch!*

"Now what has Odin been telling you? Good girl, you have learnt a lot," Frigg paused, her eyebrows beginning to rise with surprise. "But why didn't he tell you about the third part of the prophecy?" Frigg stared at Kat, who didn't reply.

"Oh, well," she continued, "I suppose he had his reasons. Oh, very good—you've fathomed out Mimir's well. Now that is very well done indeed. You are a clever thing." She patted Kat affectionately on her head before leaning forward and kissing her on her cheek.

Despite not sounding too obviously under the influence, the alcohol was clearly getting the better of Frigg. As she made to kiss Kat, her handbag slipped off her lap and its contents scattered on the floor around them. Apologising profusely, Frigg helped Kat as she started to gather up her belongings.

"What's this?" Kat enquired curiously as she picked up an unusually heavy, black metal knife. This was definitely not the kind of thing you would expect in a couture bag. The knife was intricately designed and styled in a manner similar to Kat's Valkyrie blade. The handle was beautifully carved, but unlike hers which was fashioned into the form of a graceful swan, this was fashioned into something much more sinister.

The handle was shaped into the elongated form of a mouth screaming, with hands pressed on either cheek. The image was striking, and reminiscent of a famous Midgard painting, 'The Scream' by Edvard Munch. It was a chilling caricature, and Kat shuddered as she returned the disturbing effigy to Frigg's hands.

"Oh that? That's just a paper knife, a souvenir from a friend long ago." Frigg dismissed her suspicious looks with a casual wave of her hand. Kat could sense that this wasn't the whole story, but if Frigg chose not to say any more about it then wild horses wouldn't drag the truth from her mouth. Besides, something else had just struck her.

"Have you ever tried to read Mimir's mind?" This question suddenly seemed so obvious that Kat could have kicked herself for not thinking of it sooner. Everybody feared Ragnarok—the war that would end all worlds—and the one person who knew all about it was the decapitated Mimir. If Frigg could read his mind, then they would all have the answers they so desperately needed.

"Yes, I've tried, but there are many problems," Frigg sighed as she inhaled another fix of nicotine. "Odin doesn't like me going up to his citadel and Mimir hates me peering into his mind. Besides, there's an even bigger problem."

Kat looked at her expectantly.

"Because of the state he's in, his brain has suffered a lot of trauma. It's a mess, a bit like a giant jigsaw puzzle which has been thrown into the air. All the pieces—past, present, and future—are jumbled up into an impossible tangle. Sadly, only he can understand the muddle. This task is beyond me, I'm afraid. Believe me, if I could solve the puzzles of Ragnarok I would. We all have so much to lose."

Frigg paused, and for several minutes they sat quietly together in silence; Frigg puffing elegantly at her cigarette with her eyes closed while Kat sipped not so elegantly at her champagne. Eventually, Frigg opened her eyes and smiled. She seemed pleased and there was a hint of satisfaction in her beautiful blue eyes. She'd been rummaging through Kat's mind again.

"Now tell me, my dearest Kat, who is this Henry Fox you're so anxious to see?"

11

Duvet Day

After leaving the café, Marcus phoned the office and told them he was too sick to come to work. He had hardly ever thrown a 'sickie' before, so he didn't feel too guilty about the little white lie. Dave would be there, and he would be more than capable of handling any problems that arose.

Along with this decision, Marcus made a mental note to have words with Anna at some point. Jess, a complete stranger, had somehow convinced her that she was his cousin and talked her way into their home with absolutely no identification at all. This was an unbelievably stupid thing for Anna to have done, and something he found hard to comprehend.

Gratefully, he thanked God that Jess wasn't the monster he had once thought her to be, and more discreetly he thanked God for Anna's gullibility. Because of this, he was going to spend a day in the company of one of the most beautiful women in New York. He felt about ten feet tall.

At first, Marcus was at a loss as to what to do, but Jess proved to be a vivacious and easy guest to accompany. There was so much she wanted to see. Taking the Staten Island Ferry to Battery Park, they visited the Statue of Liberty—something which Marcus hadn't done since childhood. After visiting Ellis Island, the pair then headed toward Fifth Avenue and the imposing façade of the New York Public Library. They chatted incessantly and Marcus forgot all about his work, Valkyries, and the fact that he was married.

Jess was intoxicating; her infectious smile and beautiful melodic voice made his heart sing with joy. Marcus felt ten years younger and ten times happier than he normally did on a Thursday morning.

The trip to the library was very important for Jess and the one sober moment of their day. She wanted him to show her how to go online and find her mother's address. After teaching her how to Google (she was amazed), they studied the images of the village she had grown up in as a little girl. They even found the house where she used to live and where her mother still lived. She watched with amazement as Marcus unearthed her family tree and discovered nieces and nephews that she never knew existed. Finally, Marcus cuddled her and offered her his hankie as tears streamed from her eyes. They had found the obituary for her brother.

There were pictures, too: photographs of her mother and other family members at the funeral. It was a moving moment and Marcus felt tears welling in his own eyes. It hurt him deeply to see the unflappable Jess so distraught by a world that she'd forgotten, and one which had now forgotten her.

After a very pleasant lunch, Jess decided to change the tempo for the afternoon. No more tears.

Taking Marcus by the arm, she proudly informed him that they were going shopping: Fifth Avenue beckoned and she wasn't going to miss this opportunity. Jess was determined to buy him some decent clothes. Money no object.

At first, Marcus declined her generosity, but after watching a demonstration of her spending power, he relaxed and allowed her to pamper him. The platinum credit card in her purse seemed to have no limit, just like the purse itself. All Jess had to do was to say the amount of money as she opened it and the money was available—no credit checks and no hassle. Surreptitiously, Marcus made a note of the name on the card, O Dragza. The name sounded familiar, but for the moment he couldn't quite place it.

Getting bored with men's ties, shirts, pinstriped suits, and handmade leather shoes, they turned to an altogether more pleasurable line of shopping. Watching Jess try on and occasionally buy the most fabulous and expensive designer gowns the city could offer. It was a voyeur's paradise and Marcus found her growing more irresistible by the minute.

RING—RING!

Damn! Trust his mobile to interrupt their bliss.

"Hello, Finch here," Marcus answered curtly.

"Afternoon, Finch." Taking Marcus by surprise, Agent Woods was on the line. "I hear you're feeling unwell today. Nothing too serious, I trust?"

"No, just a chesty cold." Marcus forced a pathetic impression of a dry cough and then a slightly more convincing snivel to emphasis his ill health.

"What's that noise?" Woods inquired casually.

"Oh, nothing. Just slipped out to the pharmacist to get something for the tickle." Waving his hand frantically at Jess to shush, he tried to move to a quieter part of the street where the background noise was a little less pronounced.

Shit! He hoped his bogus illness hadn't been exposed.

"Any news on the Valkyrie cult?" Woods volunteered.

"No, nothing. How about you?" Marcus replied, looking at Jess as he spoke. His lie was blatant but he didn't care. Jess was a part of him now and he couldn't betray her.

"No, nothing either. Still, keep your eyes open, Finch. They're as likely to come after you as they are me. Do keep in touch." Woods paused for an extended moment before eventually hanging up. Marcus felt uneasy. This was the first time Woods had contacted him about the cult and the man didn't do anything without a reason.

Why the call?

The question bugged Marcus and his face betrayed his vexation. With a reassuring squeeze of the hand and a kiss, Jess smiled cheekily as she dragged him off to yet another boutique. She certainly wasn't going to let some silly call spoil their lovely afternoon. Laughing and chatting merrily, Jess eased Marcus gently back into Fifth Avenue fever. There were so many frocks, and so little time.

Slowly Marcus's fears subsided as he allowed himself to submerge once more in the rapture of her company.

"I can see you two have had a busy day," Anna snapped sarcastically when Marcus and Jess eventually breezed through the door to their apartment. "I could have done with you home hours ago," she added crossly. "Mum's not well and I've got to go and see her tonight."

Marcus looked at the large suitcase in the hall. This time it was Anna's suitcase, and he realised soberly that this wasn't a joke. "I'm so sorry. Just give me a few minutes and I can pack and come with you. I'm sure you'll be alright for a few days on your own, won't you, Jess?"

Jess nodded.

"That won't be necessary and, besides, it would be rude to ignore your cousin. My sister Philippa phoned earlier and Liz'beth is confused and in hospital. Looks like an infection or a mini stroke or something. It's not life-threatening, but I need to be there just in case. I shouldn't be gone too long, I hope. Please stay and keep Jess company, there's an angel." Anna smiled and to Marcus's surprise, she hugged him and prepared to go.

Marcus scratched his head. This was out of character. Normally Anna was jealously possessive. *How strange.*

"Well, at least let me help you down to the car," Marcus offered and Anna accepted. As he picked up her suitcase and followed her out the door he stared quizzically at Jess. This all seemed horribly convenient: Jess arriving and Anna's mum being taken ill. It was the sort of coincidence that he just didn't buy.

Jess shrugged; she'd read his thoughts. Anna's phone call didn't have anything to do with her.

"Be good," Anna cautioned, kissing him on the lips as she got into the car. "And remember, I love you and trust you, okay?"

"Don't be so silly," Marcus scolded as she reversed out of the parking space. Blowing her a kiss, he followed the taillights as they receded up the steep ramp and out onto the road ahead. Turning contemplatively, he made his way slowly back upstairs.

Wow! He had goosebumps.

He was alone with Jess—and the whole night lay ahead.

12
Traitor

RAITOR!"

Loki dodged the well-aimed—but well-telegraphed—vase of black poppies as it hurtled across the room and smashed harmlessly against the oak-panelled wall behind him. For once he didn't mind Hel's fury because he shared that emotion.

Although he may have laughed and smiled with Odin when he left Asgard, deep inside he was fuming. Nobody outsmarted Loki, especially not his vile nemesis.

Frankly, Loki had been shocked by Odin's attitude to Cole, but he could understand his reasons. In a rather stupid miscalculation, he had give Odin 'two for the price of one.' Fenrir was now bound and he had unwittingly removed Cole from making mischief in Asgard. That had been a silly mistake.

Hel could let the starter of Ragnarok go, but then again, she might as well keep him here. Apart from his obvious benefits as a sex toy, she might also find out more about the prophecy. This could be an advantage to them both. Either way, Cole wasn't the reason for her outrage. Nidun had loused their plans up good and proper.

How could he have been so stupid as to think Odin wouldn't have a backup in case something happened to Idun?

Odin could be careless, but he wasn't a fool.

Nidun's presence was a bitter blow, and made Idun worthless now as a hostage. With Nidun still able to supply Odin and the other gods with golden apples, the only loser was himself—and Loki didn't like losing. It was going to be tough to convince Hel to release Idun, but luckily he had a backup plan, the Plan B he always had if things went pear-shaped.

Loki cast his mind back briefly to a conversation he had overheard many years ago.

At the time, he had been masquerading as an old washer woman around the castle, looking for juicy titbits of gossip he could have some fun with. Frigg had been talking confidentially to Freyja about Balder and his enchantment. Apparently, he was immune from death or injury from any object native to Asgard.

The key word here was 'native.'

For many months afterward, Loki had travelled the realm looking for anything which might have been introduced to the kingdom from outside. Although this might at first sound strange, Odin was a sucker for bringing back odd plants and animals from his adventures that caught his fancy. These took root and often flourished. Rabbits and daffodils were two such items, although you probably couldn't kill anyone with either of these.

Loki's quest had taken months, but eventually he was rewarded by tracking down something that might be useful. He could still remember what it was.

Plan B was therefore rather simple: kill Balder and bring him to Hel.

Deciding that discretion was the better part of valour, Loki chose not to tell his daughter about this scheme just yet, just in case he failed once more. He didn't want to risk another tantrum on the scale of her current one.

Gradually, between screams and the hurling of ornaments, Loki managed to convince Hel that releasing Idun was the best thing to do. He was helped in this task by his revelation about her namesake, the new Valkyrie Sangrid. This news intrigued Hel, and she slowly became curious about Kat and what she had done since arriving in Asgard.

Wasting no time, Loki quickly filled her in, giving her plenty of cuddles and kisses as he did so. His strategy worked. Like a petulant child, her rage slowly succumbed to sulking before eventually perking into a healthy interest. Hel couldn't help herself; she was a curious child and she always wanted more, more, more.

Finally, when Loki had finished, Hel plucked one more apple from the basket that Kat had given him. Reluctantly, she gave in. The apples were real and she would have to let Idun go.

"Daddy," she started coyly after a long silence, "you won't be cross if I tell you something, will you?"

"No, darling, of course not. Um, what is it?"

"I've been a bit of a naughty girl, I'm afraid. I'm really very sorry but I just couldn't help myself."

"What have you done?" Loki inquired, feeling a sinking feeling in his heart. Confessions from his daughter were never good news.

"Well, you know how much I hate pretty girls?" she began tentatively.

Oh, sweet Odin—the idiot!

"What have you done with Idun? I told you to keep her safe!"

This time it was Loki getting angry, and he feared the worst. Hel was incredibly vain and had to be the centre of attention. The only thing worse for a person than dying and coming to Niflheim was if the person dying happened to be a pretty young girl and coming to Niflheim. Hel couldn't stand rivals, so these hapless women would always end up disfigured or hacked to pieces. The only women Hel allowed in her realm were either old or hags, and preferably both. Beautiful women were never, ever tolerated.

"Ah, but Daddy, you didn't say anything about harming her. You only said to keep her safe—and she is safe, I promise."

It was Hel's turn now to wriggle out of Loki's fermenting wrath.

"What have you done dear?" Loki asked, counting slowly to ten; he didn't want to explode. That would be a recipe for disaster.

"Just a teensy-weensy, itsy-bitsy, tiny little bit of cosmetic surgery," Hel giggled nervously as she held up thumb and index finger to demonstrate how little she thought she'd done.

"What?" Loki yelled, and then immediately regretted it. "I'm so sorry, darling, I shouldn't have shouted." He tried to control his anxiety. "Please be a good girl. Please tell Daddy exactly what you've done. Please? Pretty please?"

"I've cut off her nose, Daddy. I think she looks better without it, honestly I do. And if she wears a veil no one will even notice, I swear," Hel finished, toying nervously with her fingers. She could see her father's eyes beginning to flash all the colours of the rainbow and this always alarmed her.

"Have you still got it—the nose, I mean?" he enquired pessimistically. Unfortunately, these sorts of titbits had a habit of getting eaten.

"I'm not exactly sure. I can get Ganglot to go and have a look if you like. It might take a while; there are a lot of noses down there."

Loki nodded and Hel went out. Shouting in a loud voice, she ordered Ganglot to move her 'fat arse' and start looking. True to form, Ganglot ambled off in the direction of the stores at a pace that would have embarrassed a snail. She farted noisily as she shuffled away.

"Well, I suppose at least you haven't thrown it away or sent it to your kitchens. I guess we should be grateful for some small mercies."

Loki sighed as he sat down, indicating to Ganglati to fill his glass with some more wine. As Ganglati shuffled slowly past Hel, she gave him a hard and well-aimed kick. He yelped loudly. She couldn't get mad at her father, so the servant would have to be her punching bag instead.

Loki took a sip of wine and sat back. Hel's storeroom was huge and it would take several hours for Ganglot to find anything that resembled Idun's nose. It might be quicker if he went there and looked himself but sifting through bits of bodies wasn't a task he relished, unlike his daughter.

Hel had a passion for collecting such things, bits and pieces from the dead that either caught her fancy or that she thought might be useful when patching up injured Berserkers from her army. With the power of the scent from the black poppies and an atmosphere heavy with hydrogen sulphide, human tissue didn't rot or decay. Once detached from a body, all the arms, legs, and even noses stayed nice and fresh in Hel's store until she needed them—which was surprisingly often.

Hel had many hobbies but one was particularly gruesome: stitching together body parts into grotesque and contorted monsters, creatures Loki found impossible to imagine even in his worst nightmares. Humans, dwarves, giants, and trolls—she would mix and match their body parts and delight in the terrible creations she had made.

"Brides for my Berserkers," she would scoff mischievously. The hobby disgusted him, but if it kept Hel happy he put up with it—just.

Eventually, after what felt like several hours had passed, Ganglot returned with a nose that looked vaguely human. Loki was certain it wasn't Idun's, but he wasn't going to send her off to look again. Hel would have to stick it back on and they would have to hope for the best. Odin would be furious, but there wasn't much more he could do.

Loki was anxious and distracted now by other things. He needed to get back to Asgard and put Plan B into motion.

Night had almost fallen when the main party of Thor, Freyja, Tyr, and the Valkyrie maids eventually reached the watchtower.

From quite a distance they could hear the steady thud, thud, thud of drums beating out an incessant rhythm of war. This sound was mixed with the metallic clinking of sword against sword and axe against sword such that at first the party panicked, believing that the battle had begun. After sending a scout scurrying urgently on ahead, he returned with the comforting news that it was only the giants sparring.

The men from Jotunheim were still on the far side of the Bifrost Bridge.

Goll, Prima, Skogul, and Mist had arrived at the tower many hours before, but fortunately, after returning to human form, the hardest thing they had had to do was to remain standing on their feet. The snaking path and bridges that crossed the treacherous glacier were still incredibly slippery and dangerous; melting by day and freezing into treacherous, icy death-traps by night.

Drawing close to the watchtower, the party discovered yet more good news. Carmel was standing on its steps, waving and calling cheerfully to them.

"Gunnr will be furious that she's missing all this fun," she teased wickedly as the maids formed a joyous crowd around her. Fortunately, her disappointment at losing the tournament seemed to have worn off and Carmel was back to her usual perky and gossipy self.

She had had a difficult few days since storming out of the castle. Carmel had left with little idea of where she was going and what she might do. Wandering randomly, she drifted, almost by accident, to Heimdall's watchtower. Somewhere in the back of her mind she probably had a vague notion to cross over into Jotunheim and take out her frustrations on any unfortunate giants she came across. However, the sight of the growing army camped across the glacier quickly put an end to that flight of fancy.

Heimdall was grateful for her company when she showed up and, indeed, the sight of a Valkyrie at the watchtower may well have saved the realm. The giants wouldn't have expected to see a warrior there so soon and her presence most probably delayed their invasion plans.

There was lots of catching up to do, and the party enjoyed a slap-up feast in the safety and comfort of the tower. This lasted several hours but eventually, when the eating was over, they trickled upstairs to the rooftop to gaze out at the giants' encampment.

After pouring themselves mead, ale, or wine, the girls settled down to study the sights and sounds that drifted across the glacier.

Thrym, the last of the great frost giants and king of the giants' realm, was in his element. Surrounded by leaders of the many clans that made up his kingdom, he had at last united them in a common cause: the desire to destroy Odin for the death and destruction he had wreaked upon their homes and kinsmen.

Giants were both quarrelsome and tribal, and spread thinly throughout the high mountain ranges that lay to the west of Asgard. It had been no mean feat for Thrym to unite them, and he was particularly pleased to see the giantess Skadi sitting around his enormous campfire. She was the warrior queen of Thrymheim, the highest realm in Jotunheim. Her father, Thiazi, had been killed by Odin many centuries before and her thirst for revenge matched Thrym's own. She brought with her a magnificent contingent of warriors, all of whom were heavily armed and battle hardened.

All in all, the total number of giants now at Thrym's disposal was in excess of three hundred. Supply chains had been set up and food, weapons, and siege materials were plentiful. There had never been a better time to attack Asgard, nor a better equipped and motivated army.

With great pride, Thrym sat back and admired the force he had assembled. He was confident that this time the giants would tear down the walls of Asgard and bring Odin to his knees.

Closest to the fire sat the chieftains and elder women of the giant clans. Gullveig the black witch sat sporadically with them, although she was equally likely at any moment to jump up and dance around the fire, screaming and chanting foul curses in the direction of the watchtower. Before they ate, she worked herself into a trance and cast sacred runes. She also read the entrails of a young fawn caught and ceremoniously killed especially for this purpose. Both of these rituals produced omens favourable to Thrym's campaign.

Beyond the chieftains sat soldiers and their womenfolk. They were squatted around the other fires that littered the encampment. Here, meals were prepared and weapons sharpened on grindstones that turned in endless circles. Farther out, on the very edge of the sprawling encampment, were Thrym's pride and joy: three massive war mammoths brought especially from Utgard.

The huge creatures dwarfed all those around them. With their monstrous tusks and heavily-armoured heads, their role was to punch holes in any defences the gods and the Valkyries dared to erect. They looked indestructible and their terrible, deep, trumpeted roars reverberated around the crevasses of the glacier, rippling through the twilight toward the watchtower.

Thrym knew that four Valkyrie warriors had arrived that day. A sharp-eyed sentry spotted them flying low over the plain as they approached the watchtower. Thrym also knew that Thor and Freyja had just arrived—a fading shaft of sunlight glistening from Freyja's gilded chariot heralded their approach as they journeyed the last few kilometres.

He smiled contentedly. It was good to see that Odin was taking his threat seriously.

With some considerable reluctance, Thrym decided to offer Thor one last chance to accept his challenge. Secretly, he hoped the god would refuse his offer of a duel. It would be such a pity to deny his mighty giant army the opportunity of crushing the gods and the cursed Valkyries once and for all.

13

Strange Bedfellows

ole wasn't sure if he'd been properly asleep or just dozing, but he was surprised when a soft knock on his bedroom door was followed by the slow entry of Ganglati. Hel's servant was shakily carrying a large candelabrum of bright new candles and a vase of fresh black poppies.

Cole was particularly grateful for the latter. The stump of his severed finger had stopped bleeding but it still ached terribly. Inhaling deeply, he let the rich aroma of the flowers do their work; his pain all but disappeared.

Barely had Ganglati left the room than there was a second, much louder knock on his door. This time the visitor didn't wait for a reply. She waltzed straight in. It was Hel, but not as he had ever seen her before.

"Hi, Cole," she began coyly, sidling slowly across the floor with her hands behind her back. She looked every inch a naughty schoolgirl, which was exactly how she was dressed: pleated tartan miniskirt, high heels, fishnet stockings, and the obligatory striped tie crudely knotted and hanging at half-mast around her neck. Even her hair matched her attire: two large, scruffy ponytails, one on either side of her head, both tied with flamboyant crimson bows.

If it hadn't been Hel dressed up in this crazy uniform, Cole would have laughed out loud. As it was, he just gulped—nervously. *She was one seriously crazy, fucked-up bitch.*

"I've come to say I'm sorry." Arriving meekly by Cole's bed, she brought out the objects that she'd been hiding behind her back.

"Sweet." Cole's eyes lit up. There was a bottle of Jack D, two glasses, a mirror, and a snuff box which he hoped would contain his favourite treat. Hel also produced a thick black leather belt which she placed prominently on the bed as well. Cole glanced cautiously at this. *Hmmmm, interesting...*

Carefully, Hel took a small amount of white powder from the snuff box and after transferring it to the mirror, she expertly cut two lines. Taking a $100 bill from the pocket of her white blouse, she rolled it up and snorted her share. Grinning mischievously, she sniffed, rubbed her nose, and then offered Cole the other line, which he gratefully accepted. He didn't know, or care, how Hel had managed to get hold of booze and coke but things were definitely on the up.

"I've been a bit of a naughty girl, haven't I?" Hel offered, pouting coquettishly before looking up and fluttering her eyelids. Holding Cole's mutilated hand in hers, she gently kissed the stump of his severed finger. "I really ought to be punished, don't you think?" she suggested devilishly, flinging herself over Cole's knees and arching her bottom high in the air.

"Beat me, Cole!" she sobbed, between poorly-suppressed giggles.

"Yeah, babe. Whatever you say."

Cole picked up the belt and toyed with it in his hands. He still wasn't sure if Hel was just messing about. She was so fickle—one false move and he could lose something a lot more valuable than a finger. He watched as she hitched up her skirt and then half-heartedly gave her a couple of gentle smacks. He wasn't taking any chances.

"Now, did that help?" she cooed saucily before standing up.

"Sure, that was great, babe."

"You see, Cole," Hel remarked as she walked slowly into the middle of the room before stopping, "I know everything about you. I know what you like—and what you don't like." She straightened her legs and, after parting them slightly, she planted her feet firmly on the floor. With the seductive skill of an experienced stripper, she wriggled her underwear down to her knees.

Cole's eyes grew wider.

"If you stick around," she added, bending forward provocatively and flipping her skirt up as she did so, "I will take you places you haven't even begun to imagine yet. I will push your limits so far you'll be begging me for pain and pleasure."

Hel slid her hands slowly down her legs and stopped when they reached her ankles. Gripping these firmly, she held her position—bottom arched and tautly stretched. Her pert behind glistened invitingly in the flickering, mellow candlelight.

Turning her head, Hel stared at Cole, white teeth flashing in a fiendish grin. "Now, I know you can spank me harder than that," she chastised. "So come on, Cole, make me SCREAM!"

For the first time Marcus felt nervous, and he knew that Jess felt the same way too. Being 'home alone' for the evening meant anything might happen and most probably would. It was one thing to fantasise about such a situation occurring, but another when it actually happened. He'd been married a long time and was way out of his comfort zone. Marcus felt terrified and clueless.

At first, they chatted cautiously and spent some time deliberating over what to eat for supper. Eventually they settled on a home delivery pizza. After eating that and sharing a few beers and a laugh together, the tension began to melt. Settling down comfortably, they watched an old movie on TV and polished off a rather decent bottle of wine. By the time the film had reached its expected conclusion, any residual unease had definitely left the building.

Lying blissfully together, they were both sprawled carefree across Marcus's rickety, old settee. Jess dozed with her head upon his chest while Marcus toyed idly with her luxuriant hair. Being with Jess felt the most natural and comfortable thing in the world and Marcus relished every minute of it.

When eventually the time came to say goodnight, Marcus felt a deep pang of sadness. It somehow didn't feel right to be going to separate beds.

With the awkward clumsiness of teenagers, they tried to kiss each other goodnight on the cheek, but their lips became locked in an accidental embrace. It felt good, so they let this linger for far longer than was usually acceptable between friends. With a final, reluctant wave 'goodnight,' Marcus closed his door behind him and climbed into his cold and lonely bed.

Begrudgingly, he hoped Anna would appreciate his faithfulness tonight.

Marcus wasn't really sure why he awoke in the small hours of the night. There had been no loud noises and he certainly hadn't had a nightmare. Something had changed in the bedroom and turning over, he realised exactly what that was. Jess was lying beside him.

She must have crept in silently while he'd been sleeping.

Propping his head up quietly on an elbow, he watched her as she slept. A shaft of light from the street below must have crept stealthily into the bedroom with her, and this now silhouetted her shapely body.

Marcus smiled. It was hard to describe the thrill of seeing Jess lying there so peacefully beside him, her chest gently rising and falling as her fragrant breath drifted in waves across the pillows.

Wow! She was so incredibly beautiful.

Gorgeous locks of tousled hair cascaded around her head, forming a lush carpet that glistened in the slender, luminous rays.

Marcus didn't know for how long he'd been watching her or for how long Jess must have been awake. All he knew was that when she reached over and pulled his head toward her, their embrace was magical. He wanted her with an urgency he had never felt before. The attraction was impossible to resist.

"No regrets," Jess breathed between passionate kisses. "I'm your future now—not Anna."

"I can't believe it's so quiet here!" Jess exclaimed happily as she stared out of the window.

Marcus glanced at his alarm clock. It was just after seven in the morning. He wasn't sure if they'd slept at all during the night, and for once he didn't care.

They seemed to have made love on and off continually in an endless sequence of spine-tingling naked entanglements that ended in powerful, arching climaxes, each one more ecstatic than the last. It had been a wonderful night of passion and he felt totally at ease with himself.

He had no regrets. Jess really was his future.

He was as certain of that fact as he was that the street should be a horrible, noisy jamboree this morning. It was always a constant snarl of taxis, dustcarts, delivery vans, and motorcycles, each jockeying for position on the double-parked and heavily congested road.

An alarm bell went off, clanging noisily somewhere inside his head. *It was too quiet.*

"I'm going to have a quick shower if that's okay," Jess murmured as she knelt on the bed, kissing him warmly before making her way to the bathroom.

Marcus sat up. Something wasn't right; he could feel it in his bones. Hastily he pulled on his dressing gown and tiptoed over to the window. He peered out.

The road was empty. No vans, no taxis—and no people.

Cautiously, he craned his neck and pressed his face tightly against the glass. There were police barriers and yellow and black tape cordoning off the end of the street.

He listened intently. *Was that the whir of helicopter blades hovering overhead?*

Something big was going down on the street this morning, he was sure of that. A major police raid of some sort had to be in progress. Sitting down quickly on the sofa, he urgently rubbed the sleep out of his eyes. He had to think and collect his groggy thoughts.

The phone call from Woods?

Anna conveniently out of town?

Jess at his flat?

Slowly, and with a horrible sinking sensation in his heart, it all began to make sense. Somehow, Woods had joined up the dots. He and Jess were the 'something big.'

14

Insults and Negotiations

hile Jess and Marcus were joyously making love in Midgard, Silk and Balder were bickering away angrily in Asgard. Balder had been awoken yet again by his hellish nightmare, and he and Silk were now standing by their window. They were arguing in terse whispers.

Tensions in the castle had mounted steadily the day before. All the warriors who had been left behind—Ruby, Kat, Silk, and Jameela—were feeling disgruntled. Somebody had to stay and guard the castle, but why them?

Jameela was the least distressed of those left behind. She was devoted to Ben and she knew that tonight would be their last night together for some time. The next morning he would depart for Valhalla. Ben had already stayed too long in Asgard and that made Odin nervous. He didn't like his heroes getting overly attached to the pleasant little realm. They were needed for his army and that need was growing ever more urgent.

Ragnarok was coming faster than a winter's storm.

Both Silk and Balder understood Odin's reasons for keeping them at the castle. If Balder's dream was of his death, then it was a near certainty that his life would end at the watchtower. Unfortunately, avoiding danger didn't mix well with a warrior's blood. Staying at home felt like cowardice, and neither Silk nor Balder were cowards. They had to go and join their friends, even though Odin had forbidden it.

Drawing closer to each other and kissing as they talked more calmly, Silk and Balder made a pact. After Ben left for Valhalla, they too would leave the castle and make haste to Heimdall's watchtower. Odin would be furious, but they would take their chances. After all, what good was it being the son of a god if you couldn't break the rules now and again?

"Thor, you are a cheat and a coward!"

"Thrym, you are a lazy old fool," Thor smirked and then added for good measure, "and your mother was a whore!"

It wasn't unusual for negotiations with giants to begin with lengthy exchanges of hurled insults. These were now being traded between Thor and Thrym as they stood and shouted at each other across the centre of the Bifrost Bridge. It was a form of one-upmanship and Thor enjoyed it nearly as much as the giants did.

The total width of the glacier at the watchtower was about two thousand metres across and of this, the centre section of a thousand metres was the most perilous. It was here, swaying precariously on the makeshift rope and wooden bridges, that Thrym and Thor had finally met.

Behind Thrym, and standing on the firmer ground of Jotunheim, stood his mighty host. His giants were bare-chested and daubed in woad. They dwarfed the tiny band of Valkyrie warriors and maids who opposed them.

Size, however, could be deceptive.

The only way for the men of Jotunheim to reach Asgard was via the narrow sequence of bridges and paths which crisscrossed their way over the glacier's maze of crevasses. This treacherous route could be defended by a tiny handful of skilled warriors, even against an army ten times the size of Thrym's. This was the ace in the hole for Thor and well he knew it. It would not be easy for Thrym's stout fellows to gain a foothold in the realm.

"Tell me, Thor, if you are such a big hero, why did you go all yellow-livered and not take up my challenge?" Thrym hollered.

"Thrym, you fat braggart, what challenge?" Thor retorted gleefully.

"The challenge that vile, half-witted son of Farbauti delivered." Thrym didn't like repeating himself.

"Thrym, your addled mind plays tricks on you. The vile, half-witted son of Farbauti delivered no such challenge."

Thor chuckled loudly. He didn't have a clue what Thrym was going on about, but he took great delight in referring to Loki as a halfwit. Still, this latest exchange of insults must have given Thrym pause for thought. He had temporarily stopped trading insults and was now gesturing to the band of leaders behind him. It was a twist in their conversation which he obviously hadn't expected. Eventually, after several minutes had passed, Thrym beckoned with his arm for Thor to cross the bridge and talk more quietly and sensibly.

Leaving the warriors behind, and reassured by the presence of Mjollnir tucked securely into his thick leather belt, Thor carefully traversed the few hundred metres that separated them.

The conversation between the two leaders seemed to last an age and, as they waited, the girls huddled together and chatted amongst themselves. For once, their beautiful cloaks of swans' feathers provided warmth rather than flight.

Although it was still September, the weather was definitely on the change. The sky was covered in unforgiving sheets of grey clouds and a chill wind blew down from the mountains, angrily giving chase to their puffy forms. Occasional flurries of snow scurried amongst the warriors. These arrived in brief showers, providing a tantalising glimpse of the harsh winter that lay ahead.

It could, of course, have just been a coincidence, but one of the prophecies of Ragnarok was that the war would be accompanied by a bitter, early winter which would continue without pause for two frozen years. Few knew of this omen, but if Odin had been present, the presence of such early snow showers would have surely sent him into a spin.

Finally, when the girls had just decided that a quick return to the watchtower for a glass of mulled wine was in order, Thor began his precarious walk back toward them. Even from a distance they could tell that he was smiling. He was looking very pleased with himself.

"That Thrym really is a dimwit," he began with a chuckle when he finally reached his huddled Valkyries. "He's challenged me to fight with his champion, Hrungnir, winner take all. If he wins, Thrym takes you, Freyja, to be his wife. If I win, all the giants will depart in peace and not trouble Asgard for as long as the old codger lives."

Everybody looked expectantly at Thor. There was one crucial detail to the challenge that was missing, and this stuck out more obviously than a dagger embedded in a giant's swollen belly.

"And Mjollnir?" Mist raised the glaring omission.

Thor threw his head back and roared with laughter. "He didn't mention it! The challenge is just me against Hrungnir. That silly old fool, I can't believe he didn't ban me from using my hammer!"

There was a moment of stunned silence before the group erupted into whoops of victorious delight. With the enchanted Mjollnir in his hands, Thor could probably smash Thrym's entire army and still be home in time for tea. It seemed too good to be true.

The giant army would be defeated without a battle and peace would last for many years. This unexpected good news called for serious celebrations, and the jubilant party headed swiftly back to the watchtower. The duel was scheduled for noon the following day, so they had at least twenty-four hours of drinking and partying ahead of them.

All in all, it had been a very successful morning's work.

Thrym watched and heard the party celebrating as they negotiated their way back across the bridge. He could hear their laughter and knew that this would be about Thor's mighty hammer. He could imagine the insults they would be hurling about his feeble, addled, giant's brain.

Chuckling, he called over to Gullveig who looked up from her cauldron. She was busy chanting and brewing yet more potions for Hrungnir and his troops.

For Thrym, noon tomorrow couldn't come soon enough. *Thor's mighty hammer be hanged!* Of course he hadn't forgotten it. With Gullveig and her magic on his side, he knew he would have the last laugh.

Let the Valkyries make merry today because tomorrow Thor and his band of cursed, arrogant, warrior women would drown in their own blood.

15

The Great Sea

orns blew and drums were beaten, but it was a pale reflection of the normal send-off that a hero bound for Valhalla would receive. Not that Ben noticed or even cared as he waited patiently on the stone jetty. He was cuddled up next to Jameela, and they only had eyes for each other.

Since his arrival in Asgard they had been inseparable, spending all their days and nights together. The bond that had formed between Jameela and her hero was as close as any the warriors could remember and everybody agreed it would be a terrible wrench to see them part. Odin had already agreed that Jameela could go to Valhalla in due course, but there was still the 'small' matter of recovering her Valkyrie dagger. This had to be attended to first.

Ben had begged to stay on longer in Asgard, too. He offered to go with the other warriors and maids to the watchtower but, unfortunately, Odin declined his request. His need for Ben was too great now Ragnarok was drawing close. Besides, he was simply too unskilled in the art of hand-to-hand warfare to be of any use in Asgard.

Ben's performance in the arena had been the cause of some merriment. The girls had chuckled as they watched him sparring with Jameela. Ben was brave and strong, but his strength was no match for an agile Valkyrie. Jameela had toyed gently with him, determined not to humiliate her hero before the nosy crowds of spectators. Training in the arenas was a public spectacle and the townsfolk would drift by most days, congregating at the arena which held the greatest interest. To see one of Odin's heroes in action was guaranteed to be a big draw.

Ben tried hard, but it was like watching a frustrated dog snapping at a lynx. He couldn't get close to laying a blow on Jameela.

From early dawn a wind had picked up, sending blustery gusts swirling in from the Great Sea. The weather was on the change, with a patchwork of clouds hurrying across a windswept sky. Each wore a different shade of grey and promised rain, sleet, hail, and even snow. The sea before them, too, had a murky, wintery swell to it. Foaming waves broke in a relentless, ragged frenzy on the shore that stretched far away to the west of where Ben and Jameela were standing now.

The stone jetty lay immediately to the north of the castle and down a steep stairway of rough-hewn steps that had been carved long ago into the jagged cliffs. The jetty wasn't big and it curved sharply as it jutted tentatively out into the chilly waters of the Great Sea. It formed a small harbour, one with just enough room to provide shelter for the handful of fishing vessels that lay huddled there this morning.

The cliffs at the base of the castle rose sharply from the eastern end of a long, sandy beach which stretched away to the distant horizon. This was where the warriors and their maids would often ride their horses, splashing excitedly through the refreshing surf during the long, hot days of summer. Apart from the staircase leading down from the castle, a much wider and gentler route wound round the hill from the arenas. This allowed access to the beach for the people of Asgard. A small group of serfs and peasants were standing there now with them today.

With so many Valkyries at the watchtower and the townsfolk fearful of war, the crowd that had come to bid farewell to Ben was pitifully sparse. Odin, Balder, Silk, Ruby, and Kat were the only inhabitants of the castle available for the ceremony. Despite their small number, they decided to make up for this by being especially loud and noisy, clapping and cheering as hard as they could as Odin sang Ben's praises in his farewell speech. Eventually, when he had presented Ben with a golden wreath of oak leaves, all eyes turned toward the distant horizon and the tiny, glimmering speck which had been slowly growing larger.

This was the long boat from Valhalla.

Since her arrival in Asgard, Kat had heard a great deal about Odin's paradise and the final journey all heroes and warriors would take one day. She had never witnessed such an occasion before, but the vessel that was slowly coming into view more than exceeded her expectations.

Skidbladnir was a large boat, heavily gilded from stem to stern with a thick coat of finest gold. She had a single, large, central mast, but today her sail lay furled and unused. Along the sides of either flank rested a row of ornate golden shields, but there were no oars.

Neither was there a captain nor a crew.

Enchanted by ancient magic, Skidbladnir moved calmly through the waves churning all around her. Neither pitching nor yawing, she glided effortlessly toward them like an albatross soaring on the slightest of summer breezes.

Toward the stern of the vessel stood an opulent gazebo. The curtains, cushions, and chairs were fashioned from a rich burgundy fabric, which was probably a heavy silk. This area was carpeted with a scattering of red, pink, and white rose petals and even from a distance Kat could imagine their wonderful fragrance.

The long boat screamed of wealth, as did its occupants.

In the middle of the vessel sat a small group of musicians whose soothing music could be caught in brief spasms over the clamour of the waves as they crashed against the shore. Kat could already make out the gleaming golden wig of Sif, and she was certain that she could see Frigg and Nana among the ladies on the vessel. Hod, too, was present, looking relaxed and resplendent in his shades, cream trousers, and an expensive navy blue polo shirt.

Hod had chosen to spend a few days in Valhalla with his mother, and Kat had mixed feelings about his absence from her life. She had grown used to his familiar presence and the pleasure of his friendship. She did have feelings for him, strong feelings, feelings that were possibly now tipping in favour of love—but this was causing a terrible conflict.

She was beginning to hate herself. Hod was kind and gentle and sincere, and yet was far removed from Kat's image of hunky perfection. Was it really so shallow and wrong to yearn for a more manly lover? She always seemed to end up with a geek, and for once she begged for a change. Freyr would have been ideal but, sadly, he belonged to everybody.

She cursed herself—and Hod—for causing such a commotion in her heart, before hastily turning her attention back to the remaining inhabitant on the boat. She wasn't sure that Frigg's mindreading skills stretched this far and she didn't want to push her luck, just in case.

Kat had also recognised the last passenger. This was one of the ladies in waiting to Frigg whom she had seen at the tea party in Fensalir the day before. Although she couldn't remember their names (Lin,

Fulla, and Gna), one of them was now busy preparing pillows and refreshments for their honoured guest.

Finally, and to rapturous cheering, the boat drew alongside the small jetty and rested motionlessly beside it. The vessel looked surreal with her calm, unmoving deck surrounded by grey, frothing waves that bobbed violently up and down.

Frigg and Sif got off the boat and, after greeting Odin, they both shook hands with Ben before hugging him enthusiastically. Kat smirked when she saw Ben bow stiffly. She knew he couldn't help it; they were just dressed so regally and looked so magnificent. His unwitting gesture reminded her of her first meeting with Odin in Gladsheim on the fateful day when she had made her pledge to join his Valkyrie elite.

It was almost time to go, but the gathering hushed as Odin made ready for the final part of the ceremony that would allow Ben to join his army in Valhalla. Signalling for him to kneel, Jameela assisted her hero as he got to his knees and bared his chest.

He was ready to be marked.

With a wail from a single high-pitched horn, Odin raised Gungnir and, using the tip of his mighty spear, he expertly carved the letter 'V' into Hod's flesh. He did this just above the left breast, over his heart. This letter confirmed him as a hero and deserving of a place in Valhalla.

For a brief moment Jameela looked crestfallen. Had she not lost her knife, she would have had the honour of doing this. It was a bitter moment, an opportunity missed to mark Ben as her own.

The crowd cheered and whistled loudly when Odin finished, and with a last tearful, lingering kiss goodbye, Ben bade farewell to the woman he loved. It was a rare sight to see a Valkyrie cry, but for once the usually quiet and reserved Herja couldn't hold back. Fresh tears ran in rivulets down her already tearstained cheeks. Silk, Ruby, and Kat all comforted her as Ben slipped reluctantly from her arms and onto the barge. Sitting down beside Frigg, warm blankets were wrapped around him for the journey ahead. Frigg's maid made a terrible fuss over him, plumping his pillows and plying him with drinks as she strove to make him feel comfortable.

With a final flourish of horns, and a rousing cheer from the assembled crowd, Skidbladnir slipped slowly away from the jetty and began her journey home. The crowd clapped and waved enthusiastically and continued to do so long after the shapes of the occupants had blurred into one and the vessel itself had faded into a shapeless, distant mass on the horizon.

Gradually, Kat became aware that the crowd was waiting for a moment, the moment that would herald the true departure of the boat to Valhalla. With a final triumphant cheer and wild beating of drums, a brilliant flash of golden light illuminated the sky. It flared for just a few brief seconds and when it eventually subsided, Skidbladnir had gone.

Just as the bright rainbow in the sky heralded the arrival of people from Midgard, the brilliant golden sunburst marked the passage of heroes to the realm of Valhalla.

Odin beckoned to Kat and Jameela as the small crowd on the shore quickly dispersed. He wanted to see them in his citadel at noon. Their departure to Midgard must take place as soon as possible.

Kat suddenly felt like a bag of nerves. Desperate though she was to return to Midgard, the thought of passing through Mimir's well filled her with dread. She had always had a problem with motion sickness and she knew the journey would be most unpleasant.

"Greetings, my lady Sangrid." Sif slapped Kat cheerfully and unexpectedly on the back as they climbed the winding staircase back toward the castle. Kat hadn't noticed that she had stayed behind on the jetty when the boat departed.

"Greetings, gracious lady," Kat replied politely, bowing respect-fully. Sif was a goddess whom Kat barely knew and her months in Asgard had taught her the importance of courteous introductions.

"Oh, do please call me Sif," she laughed cheerily. "Do you like my hair?" Sif had noticed Kat eyeing it closely yesterday and she offered Kat the opportunity to run her fingers through the fine, golden locks. Kat did so, gasping in amazement at their touch. Each strand had been spun to an impossible fineness such that the whole wig was woven into a wondrous skein whose softness and delicacy rivalled any woman's hair.

"Where in Asgard did you find craftsmen skilled enough to create this?" Kat exclaimed as she reluctantly let the beautiful golden tresses slip from her envious fingers.

"Not Asgard—Nidavellir. The story's long, but it's a good one," Sif smiled as they reached the entrance to the castle. "Do you have time?"

Kat paused and looked at Jameela who by now had joined them. She knew Odin was in a hurry for them to depart, but the opportunity to hear so fine a tale was one she dearly didn't want to miss.

"Come on," Jameela replied grabbing Kat's hand excitedly.

"Why don't we all go into the hall and share a jug of ale together? I need cheering up and would love to hear the story. I'm sure Odin won't mind a small delay."

16

Treasures of the Gods

Sif, Kat, and Jameela sat down in the castle hall and, after pouring them large horns of ale, Sif began her tale.

Long ago, when Asgard was a world still in its infancy and she and Thor had not long been married, Loki had stolen as silently as a fox into their marital chambers. It was early in the morning and Thor had already gone out hunting. Sif was deeply asleep, apparently snoring peacefully in their large four-poster bed.

Tiptoeing carefully up to her pillow, Loki took a razor-sharp knife from his belt and expertly began to cut the long, golden locks of hair from her head. He did this so skillfully that she didn't wake up, even when he had cropped her hair so tightly that only stubble remained. Grinning wickedly at his handiwork, he held her soft tresses in his hands before scattering them gaily around their bed. When Loki had finished with his fun, he quietly closed the door behind him and hurried away from the castle.

Not long afterward, Thor returned. He heard Sif crying loudly and when he saw the state of her head he went berserk. The roaring of his voice shook their normally tranquil castle like an earthquake.

"It was only a joke, honestly," Loki begged and pleaded when Thor eventually caught up with him and dangled him in the air by his throat. Loki's legs paddled furiously as Thor shook him hard.

No one knew if it really was intended as a joke, but Sif had her own ideas. Thor was actually her second husband, and both he and Loki had courted her aggressively before Thor eventually won her hand in marriage. Thor didn't win because he was the most handsome; he won because she could trust him. Loki was fickle and flighty and she needed someone much more stable with whom to raise a family and to be a good stepfather to her son, Ull.

Enraged by her choice, Loki then proved why Sif had chosen correctly; spreading malicious rumours that she had been his mistress and that he had bedded her many times, even after her marriage to Thor. No one knew whether these tales were true and Sif still denied them to this day.

"So, what are you going to do about my wife's shaven head?" Thor demanded as he shook Loki harder.

Pleading with Thor for mercy was no use, so eventually Loki agreed to replace her hair with a suitable alternative. He would find craftsmen who would weave the finest skein of hair that had ever been made. Knowing he would not find such skilled folk among the Aesir and Vanir, Loki travelled to the one place he knew he could find them: the deepest caves in Nidavellir, the kingdom of the dwarves.

Loki headed immediately to the fine hall of Ivaldi, where he approached the two sons with a deal. If they could make him a magnificent wig, he would offer them the friendship and protection of the gods. Both brothers agreed immediately to this offer.

In those days, rivalry and civil war among the various dwarf fiefdoms was rife and the whole realm was under attack, both from the dark elves beneath and the giants above. Such an alliance would preserve the wealth they had amassed—and their lives. Such was the greed of dwarves this was, in fact, the correct order of importance to them: money coming first.

The two Ivaldi brothers set to work immediately, melting down a whole bar of solid gold. They worked with extraordinary speed, and before the day was finished they had produced a skein of hair so fine and soft that it took Loki's breath away.

"Seems a pity to waste the rest of the gold," Loki hinted as he greedily eyed the remaining ingots of molten metal in their furnace. The brothers exchanged glances, and then agreed. With a similar amount of skill and speed they fashioned a spear from the remaining gold. It was the most slender and strongest spear Loki had ever seen and the dwarves told him that its name was Gungnir. It was also enchanted. With some reluctance, Loki agreed to take it as a gift to Odin. He wanted the weapon for himself because the Ivaldis had told him that once thrown, the spear never missed its target.

Any sensible person would have taken these beautiful gifts and returned straight to Asgard, but not Loki. He could sense a cunning plan to gain more favours from his fellow gods and goddesses. Fortified by several horns of mead, he marched around to the halls of Brokk and Eitri, bitter rivals of the hall of Ivaldi.

"Bet you can't make gifts as magnificent as these," bragged a very cocky (and very drunk) Loki to the two dwarves. They were both enviously fingering the treasures which Loki had laid before them.

"Bet we can," said Eitri.

"And finer, too," added Brokk.

"I bet you can't and I'll stake my head on it." Loki laid down his challenge with scant regard, as usual, for what he was saying.

Now, contrary to what Loki imagined, he was not well-liked amongst the dwarves. His mischief-making had often caused them to suffer and had brought them into conflict with Odin and the rest of the gods on many an occasion. Brokk and Eigri saw this wager as too fine an opportunity to miss. The price of a bar of gold and a few days' labour could bring about the death of a hated enemy.

They summoned colleagues to bring a fine feast for Loki and plenty more mead. Then, as he sat down to eat and drink, they set about creating their rival gifts. It took a long time and Brokk almost fell asleep as he pumped the pigskin bellows that kept the furnace at the correct temperature. It didn't help either that he was bothered by an annoying wasp that buzzed around him incessantly as he toiled. Finally, their first gift was completed: a beautiful, heavy armband for Odin. It was intricately fashioned and enchanted in much the same manner as the hair for Sif.

On the ninth night and every ninth night thereafter, while Odin slept, it would divide in two, giving birth to an identical band of gold. Blessed by a powerful magic, it would repeat this process forever more.

Loki's mouth opened wide at such a fabulous prize.

"Ah, but Ivaldi's sons made two gifts," he bragged proudly, hoping against hope that they might create another masterpiece.

Brokk and Eitri deliberated in hushed whispers for some time, and then came to a decision. They had used up all the melted gold, so they cast a block of iron into the furnace and set to work fashioning their second gift. As Brokk toiled away at the heavy bellows, his tiredness grew once more. To make matters worse, the wretched wasp was back and buzzing around him closer than ever. Seizing its opportunity when it thought Brokk had drifted off to sleep, the evil pest alighted between his eyebrows and stung him viciously. How Brokk hollered as he clutched at his swollen face!

For several vital minutes he stopped pumping the bellows, and when at last he remembered them, he prayed that their labours hadn't been in vain. To his and Eitri's immense relief, the hammer they eventually pulled from the furnace was perfect in all but one tiny detail. Its handle was a bit short.

"That doesn't look like much," Loki scoffed when the dwarves eventually showed him the iron hammer. They had named it 'Mjollnir' but it looked pretty much like any other boring hammer that Loki had seen—apart from the stunted handle, that is. Proudly the dwarves explained that the hammer was magical and was intended as a gift for Thor. It would grow in size and power when he used it and nothing could withstand its crushing blows. Better still, when it wasn't in use it could shrink to a size which he could hide about his person.

Feeling a little more impressed now he understood the true value of the hammer, Loki set off back to Asgard with Brokk accompanying him. Brokk wanted to ensure fair play when the gods and goddesses chose the finest gift, and to claim Loki's head should one of their gifts prove the winner.

At first, when Loki presented these wonders, there was a frosty atmosphere in the hall of Gladsheim. Sif had to attend with a scarf wrapped tightly around her shaven head and Thor was still furious at Loki's prank. His hand twitched eagerly on the handle of his axe. He was dying for the slightest excuse to dispatch Loki to his doom.

One by one the fabulous gifts were presented, and the gods quickly warmed to their magical beauty and power. When at last all the gifts had been displayed, they voted on their favourite and their decision was unanimous. Thor's hammer had stolen the day.

"Off with his head, off with his head!" screamed the victorious and jubilant Brokk, pointing excitedly in Loki's direction.

Loki needed no further invitation. He turned tail and bolted.

Loki was a good runner and quickly put many kilometres between him and the castle. Unfortunately, he had forgotten about one small thing: Thor's new and enchanted hammer. Chasing after Loki, Thor eventually caught sight of him in the distance and threw it at him. Mjollnir struck Loki on the head and he fell to the ground prostrate, dazed, and confused. Grabbing the rogue by the scruff of his neck, Thor dragged him back to the other gods who were waiting expectantly in the hall.

The mood now amongst the gods and the townsfolk was frenzied. Everybody secretly liked Loki and enjoyed most of his mischievous pranks, but unfortunately a deal was a deal and honour was at stake. Unless there was a miracle, Brokk would take his head.

"Wait!" cried Loki as Thor held him firmly down on a chopping block. A freshly sharpened axe was already in Brokk's eager hands and he was holding it high above his head. In a matter of moments, Loki's life would have been over.

"All right, Brokk, I agree you have won your wager fair and square," Loki began with a flash of inspired brilliance. "You may take my head, but not one inch of my neck."

A silence fell as the gods absorbed his words of genius.

Slowly, one by one, they began to clap and cheer until eventually they broke into rapturous applause. It was impossible for Brokk to sever Loki's head from his body without taking at least some of his neck, so the wager couldn't be settled.

Furious at his humiliation, Brokk took a needle and thread from his breeches and sewed Loki's irresponsible and malicious lips together. Then he left, a cloud of dust billowing from the hooves of his pony as he galloped angrily away.

Loki had been saved from his doom, but it would take him many painful days to unpick the spiteful stitches from his mouth.

"So—there you have it!"

Sif finished with a flourish as she lowered her third flagon of ale. "That explains many things: how Loki's lips are slightly crooked when he smiles, how Thor came upon such a powerful weapon, and how I...," she paused, proudly shaking her golden hair, "...came to own such a fabulous wig."

Kat and Jameela joined her in a long and carefree fit of laughter. Sif had proved to be an excellent storyteller, and although Kat took some of the tale with a pinch of salt, she felt she'd learnt a little bit more about the gods of Asgard.

"Right, my dear Valkyries," Sif stood up, stretched, and motioned for them to do likewise as she continued, "Odin awaits and it is unwise even for goddesses and warriors to test his patience any longer."

Kat and Jameela agreed, and they embraced her in turn as they said their goodbyes. Sif wished them luck and Kat thanked her for her lovely tale.

With the end of the story, Kat's nervousness returned. She hastily ran upstairs and picked up the few items she knew she would need for the journey ahead. A few moments later, she took her place beside Jameela outside the black door at the bottom of Odin's citadel. Without any further delay, the door opened slowly and quietly before them.

Odin was definitely in a hurry today.

17

Use It

"Would you like a cup of tea?" Marcus called out loudly to Jess as he hurried over to the TV and switched it on, cranking the volume up as loud as was socially acceptable for seven o'clock in the morning.

Jess didn't reply; she was in the shower. Marcus turned the kettle on and tiptoed as quickly and as quietly as he could to join her in the bathroom. If his suspicions were correct, then time was precious, incredibly precious.

"Shush!" He put his finger to his lips as he opened the door to the cubicle. Jess hugged him enthusiastically. Making love in a cascade of deliciously warm water would be a fabulous way to start the day.

"I think the flat is bugged and we're about to be raided by the Feds," Marcus murmured in a barely audible whisper. He quickly explained his thoughts about the phone call from Woods, Anna leaving last night, and the street being cordoned off this morning. There could be no other possible explanation for the quietness outside, and to his relief Jess agreed. *If the hat fits...*

Quickly Jess analysed the situation. She could probably get away, but that would risk being separated from Marcus, her reason for being there in the first place. Capture was not ideal as that would allow Woods to get his hands on more Valkyrie relics. He already had Herja's knife and any more could put them all at risk. If that happened, there was a distinct possibility that Woods might discover the truth about the Valkyries, and their secrets.

93

"Do you have a bottle of red wine and some old coins lying about?" Jess whispered quietly in Marcus's ear. He nodded, made to leave, and then stopped abruptly. He had turned pale and his face had dropped.

"Is—is—is this it?" he stuttered, nervously.

Jess could hear his voice faltering and had already guessed the question that was hanging on his lips.

"Is it—today?" Marcus gulped, turning an even ghostlier shade of pale.

"Oh, sweetie!" Jess pulled him close and kissed him passionately on the lips. "No. There will be no fighting today and no, you're not going to die."

"Are you sure?" A wave of relief had already begun to spread across Marcus's taut face, but he had to be sure.

"Of course I am, you idiot," she replied, hugging him close and patting his back reassuringly. For a brief moment she was a loving mother, a role she had never, and would never, experience. "I can tell. The attraction is strong but not quite ready yet."

With a huge sigh of relief and an even huger smile on his face, Marcus left the bathroom. He wasn't a coward, but he preferred not to know the moment of his death.

For the next few minutes, the two of them worked quickly and industriously, all the while chatting about news items, what they wanted spread on their toast, and the weather. It was all trivial and pointless conversation, meaningless chatter to mask their true activities. Marcus found a bottle of red wine and a shiny old coin, and Jess—taking a huge leap of faith—pressed her Valkyrie knife, her gold coin, and credit card into Marcus's hands.

"Guard these with your life," she breathed softly into his ear. "My fate is in your hands."

THUD—THUD!

There was a heavy and menacing knock on the door which made them both jump. They had expected it, but the loud blows still managed to catch them unawares. Jess hastily looked in the mirror, brushed her hair, and then put on some lipstick.

THUD—THUD!

"Open up, Finch, I know she's there." It was Agent Woods and he didn't sound happy. "I don't want to have to break this door down," he continued malevolently.

Marcus could practically sense the sneer on Wood's lips.

"I am so looking forward to meeting you...," Woods continued, pausing as he deliberated over what name to use for the Valkyrie, "...Brynhildr."

Neither Marcus nor Jess replied, but with a curt nod to each other they indicated that they were ready. Marcus undid the chain and turned the levers to the lock. Slowly and calmly he opened the door.

"Finch, I'm disappointed in you, very disappointed indeed." Wasting no time, Woods avoided Marcus's handshake as he marched straight past without waiting for an invitation to come in. "I thought we had a friendship, a trust," he continued angrily.

Marcus went to speak, but Woods raised his hand to silence him. He didn't have time for lame excuses. "Ah, the lovely Valkyrie Brynhildr."

Woods had spied Jess and held out his hand. She shook it firmly.

Marcus chuckled; at least Woods had got one thing right. Jess did look lovely this morning. Somehow amongst their myriad tasks, she had managed to throw on a pair of black drainpipe jeans, leather boots, a loose-fitting T-shirt, and a leather bomber jacket. She had tied her hair back in a rough ponytail and even managed to apply the slightest hint of eye shadow. She looked amazing.

"I presume you must be Agent Woods?" Jess spoke calmly, the soft Irish lilt of her voice making Marcus's heart skip a beat.

Christ! He was going to miss her.

Woods nodded and held his hand out expectantly. Jess obliged by offering him her handbag. With an ease that went with many years of practice, Woods thumbed through its contents. Satisfied that he had what he was looking for, he motioned for Jess to follow him out of the flat.

"May I please say goodbye to my excellent host?" Jess enquired, flashing Woods one of her dazzling and disarming smiles. He nodded that she could.

"Thank you so much Detective Finch, for your marvellous hospitality," Jess took his hand and pulled Marcus toward her, kissing him lovingly and open-mouthed on the lips. She let her kiss linger, wanting Woods to know that their relationship was so much more than friendship. Ending their embrace with a final, heartfelt hug, Jess patted Marcus firmly on his bottom.

"Use it," she mouthed inaudibly. Letting him go reluctantly, Jess turned to face Woods. "Now, Agent Woods, where would you like to take me on this fine March morning?"

Farewells over, Jess took Woods firmly by the arm and marched him out of the front door. As they began to walk away down the corridor, she turned briefly and blew Marcus a kiss. He returned the gesture, and then wished he hadn't. Anna had been standing amongst the agents and SWAT team crouched awkwardly at the end of the corridor, and she was beginning to walk menacingly toward him.

Marcus gulped.

She had a face like thunder and body language that told him she wasn't the least bit impressed.

"Hi, darling," he began hesitantly as Anna stormed angrily by.

Closing the door behind him, he followed her into the flat.

"WELL, DID YOU FUCK HER?" Anna screamed, lips trembling as she spoke. She was trying to be brave, but in reality she was close to tears.

"No, of course not, my darling. Of course I didn't. I wouldn't do that." Marcus began, denying everything just as all the best 'Manuals for Men' would have told him to.

"Liar, I fucking heard you—you BASTARD!" Anna was having none of it. Marcus was right, the flat had been bugged.

Slapping him hard across the face, she flounced into their bedroom, slamming the door forcefully behind her. Her message was unequivocal. She was furious and didn't want to be disturbed.

Marcus stood silently in the sitting room and took stock of his situation. The sound of cars, vans, and motorcycles driving up and down the street had begun to drift up once more from the kerbside. Life around them was beginning to return to normal, but that couldn't hide an ugly truth.

Could his and Anna's lives ever do the same?

He knew he had deserved her slap and that he should feel horribly guilty about breaking their wedding vows. Unfortunately, to his surprise, he didn't. All he could see was Jess's smile and all he could think of was how on earth could he now rescue her?

As the seriousness of her situation began to dawn upon him, Marcus began to feel terribly small and insignificant. Jess had entrusted him with her faith and her most treasured possessions, believing that somehow he could storm her prison fortress and save her. It was a responsibility that weighed heavily on his fragile shoulders.

He felt such a fraud. *He wasn't a hero, surely?*

Suddenly he remembered Jess's provocative pat on his bottom. He could feel something there now, hard and firm, nestling in his back pocket. Reaching into it with his hand, he withdrew a slim mobile phone. Her phone.

"Use it." That's what she'd said.

With more than a little excitement, Marcus began to search for her list of telephone contacts.

"Good morning, may I speak to the Contessa?'"

With Jess already handcuffed and sitting in his car ready for transport to Washington, Woods had walked a few yards away and was now standing out of earshot in a partially secluded doorway. He had to make an important phone call, one he didn't want overheard.

"Who may I say is calling?" came a polite reply.

"Agent Woods."

He didn't know where the Contessa's office was, but he had guessed some time ago by the wonderful West Indian accents of the receptionists that it had to be somewhere in the Caribbean. He suspected it was located on a small island, one of those offshore tax havens for the filthy rich and famous.

"I'm just putting you through now. Have a nice day," she continued cheerily. Woods held.

"Good morning, I'm so sorry, the Contessa can't take your call at the moment."

Woods knew by the time delay and faint echo of the voice down the phone line that his call had been transferred to somewhere on the other side of the world. He half-recognised the voice of the Contessa's assistant, too. She had the slightest hint of a German or Scandinavian accent.

"When would be good time to call again?" he enquired. "I have important news that I'm sure she'll want to hear."

Woods felt a little deflated. The Contessa was the only person he could tell about his capture of a Valkyrie and, particularly, one complete with all her artifacts. He knew she would be delighted to hear this news, so what the hell could the Contessa be doing that was so important as to prevent her taking his call? He decided to ask as such, but phrased the question a little more politely to her assistant.

"She's at a charity function with the French president and is going on to the opera later this evening. I'm sure, however, that she would be happy to take your call tomorrow morning."

Woods grunted that it would have to do and hung up. *Charity function, my arse!*

He glanced at his watch. She must be in Paris and that was some five, six hours ahead of East Coast time. He bet she was actually out shopping or making love with one of her countless boy toys.

Jesus Christ! The life of the idle rich. Reluctantly, he pocketed his phone and headed back to the car.

Oh, well. It was the Contessa's loss if she had to wait another day to hear about his capture of Brynhildr.

18
Fresh Meat

Hel awoke after a decent enough nap and in an extremely good mood. She could definitely feel a spring to her step after her session with Cole.

In an unusual move, she decided to dispense with her familiar attire of black leather trousers and matching bodice and go for an altogether different look. Humming cheerfully, she rifled messily through the extensive wardrobes in her royal suite.

Apart from vast sums of money, grateful deities would also send Hel trinkets and tokens of appreciation for her services. These included clothes, jewellery, makeup, electrical goods, and, of course, drugs and booze. The reason why her chambers were strictly out of bounds was partly due to the obscene opulence that oozed from every corner. She had so much and yet, confined as she was to Niflheim, she had so very little. Wealth makes a poor substitute for freedom and nowhere was this divide felt more acutely than here.

Perhaps these extremes—obscene wealth and eternal incarceration—helped explain her outrageous mood swings.

Happy with her eventual selection, Hel hurried off down the corridor to make her usual rounds. She had chosen a very short, pleated miniskirt, a tight crop top, some expensive thigh-length boots, and most importantly, no underwear.

As she walked past the many mirrors that adorned the rooms and corridors, she paused and hitched her skirt up, purring with delight as she did so. Cole's handiwork was indeed impressive. Copious red and purple welts covered the cheeks of her well-toned bottom, making it tingle erotically. The exquisite pain lingered seductively in her mind.

With a little coaxing, Cole had eventually thrashed her hard, though not quite hard enough to make her scream. Just as she was addicted to sex, alcohol, and drugs, Hel was hooked on pain. She had an incredibly high threshold and would often cut herself deliberately when stressed. Cole had tried hard to force her tears, even using the heavy buckled end of the belt, but he eventually tired before she succumbed to the pain.

Still, he had done well and exceeded her expectations. It would soon be time for the starter of Ragnarok to graduate and join the rest of her little girls. Hel's mouth watered at this tempting prospect.

Passing the reception room, the harem, and her servants' quarters, she reached the first of many heavily-bolted iron doors. A slave bobbed a quick bow and nervously opened the door as fast as he could. Hel was never patient and had no time for tardiness. There were no second chances if you failed to please.

"Anything interesting?" she enquired hopefully, popping her head around the first side door in the corridor beyond. The masked woman shook her head woefully from side to side. "Pity," Hel muttered as she studied her *Book of Punishments.*

Hel had dubbed this area of her palace the 'VIP' quarters because it was reserved for guests who required 'Very Important Punishments.' These had to be administered according to the specifications of the god or deity who had sent the victim for eternal damnation.

Unfortunately, exotic and unusual curses for punishments had been in decline for some time now. What had once been a fun part of her job was, frankly, becoming a bit of a chore. Countless bolted rooms spread out into the distance and thuds and screams could be heard coming from all of them. The Fallen Angels were hard at work, inflicting endless rounds of torture and agony upon the most unfortunate of Hel's guests.

The list of the damned was long and detailed and would have made for an interesting read, one full of infamous names and more than a few surprises. However, Hel considered this information confidential and would never disclose its details nor allow the book to leave these quarters.

For a moment, Hel reminisced on the fun and innovation she had known in the past. The satisfaction in organising a curse that involved a snake dripping venom onto the face of its hapless victim, and the one where she trained an eagle to endlessly peck out somebody's gizzard.

Ah, bliss—such happy days!

Now the best curse she could hope for was 'May you burn in Hell,' and it infuriated her that they always managed to spell her name incorrectly. Frankly, the bonfires and furnaces were becoming so overcrowded it was getting to be a hazard. It was almost a Health and Safety issue, if ever such things could exist in Niflheim.

With a sigh, she said her goodbyes and continued along the main corridor. Temporarily deflated, her high spirits returned as she neared her favourite place in the whole of Eljudnir—her kennels.

"And how are all my lovely babies?" Hel cooed eagerly as she got down on her knees and became quickly enveloped in a frenzied sea of black fur, furious tail-wagging, and ecstatic barking.

Hel's hounds were one of the achievements she was most proud of, and her kennels were the one place where she felt most relaxed. Stripped of the need to be anything other than her true self, here was the real Hel, happy and at peace with creatures she adored.

When Odin had first exiled her to Niflheim, Hel had pleaded to be allowed to bring a companion with her. At first he refused, but eventually he made a small concession. She could take a puppy.

As the countless years rolled by, she had asked her father to bring more puppies, usually on the pretence that the previous one had died. Gradually she had built up a kennel of dogs and began to crossbreed them. By suggesting different types of puppies for him to bring, she had managed eventually to create a unique and terrifying breed.

Her dogs were as big as Irish wolf hounds, with the musculature of a mastiff and the pelt of a black Labrador. Their teeth and bright yellow eyes were more wolf-like than hound, and their sharply-pointed ears and short, stubby tails were reminiscent of a Doberman. The hounds had short tempers and tremendous strength. They could tear a man to pieces and frequently did so. They were her pride and joy, and the dogs repaid Hel for her love and devotion with their absolute and undivided loyalty. They would die for her, and she knew it. Hel had named them all, and only she could tell them apart.

After much petting, hugging, and kissing, Hel finally stood up and strode over to a tray of raw human meat. Picking her way carefully through the offal, she selected half a dozen tempting treats. However, just as she was bending down to feed them to her beloved hounds, she paused and gave them a sniff.

"Is this meat fresh?" she demanded quizzically of the slaves who tended her pack.

"Yes, your majesty," mumbled the four female slaves, who were all lined up, dressed in coarse, shapeless sacking, and bobbing their curtsies.

Each girl had deformed features, the end products of Hel's obsession to remain the fairest woman in all of Niflheim. One had her nose cut off, another had her lips removed, and a third had lost both her ears. The fourth was spared the agony of Hel's surgical fumblings courtesy of being born with a cleft palate.

"Are you sure?" Hel enquired menacingly. She sniffed at the meats once more and glared angrily at the girls. Her eyes flashed a violent orange colour for a split second, a trait she'd inherited from her father.

"Oh, yes, your majesty. We got them from the kitchen just, just, recently…I think," the tall girl in the middle stammered defensively before ending lamely.

To Hel's immense satisfaction, a small puddle was beginning to form beneath this slave's legs. She had wet herself. This wasn't an uncommon event. Hel could elicit incontinence in both male and female slaves when they knew she was displeased. Her wrath was terrible and the extreme depth of their fear was well founded.

"ARE YOU DELIBERATELY TRYING TO POISON MY BABIES?" Hel screamed furiously, chucking the offal at the slaves who were now falling to their knees and wringing their hands. Her hounds, too, were becoming excited. They could smell the maids' fear and started to form a ring around them, snarling, barking, and baring their teeth as they did so.

If you angered their mistress, you angered them, too.

"If I tell you to feed my babies fresh meat, I mean exactly that—FRESH MEAT! Here, let me show you what that is." Hel clicked her fingers and pointed at two of the slaves.

The excited hounds needed no further invitation. With a tremendous din of howling and barking, the dogs leapt upon the hapless girls, sinking their razor-sharp fangs deep into their flesh. Within minutes it was all over. The desperate screams of the women turned quickly to blood-choked gargles before fading rapidly into a deathly silence.

The dogs tore their bodies apart with the ease of a child dismembering a jelly baby, snarling ferociously as they fought over the choicest cuts.

"Ah, my precious babies, do you feel better now?" Hel knelt once more and spread her arms open to hug her happy family. The dogs reciprocated, barking and competing with each other to be chosen to walk with their mistress today.

After she had picked a pair of mighty beasts, the two lucky and oh-so-grateful-to-be-alive slaves attached heavy studded collars and leads to their necks. They handed these quickly to Hel, their hands still trembling violently. With a final cheery wave and a farewell kiss to her hounds, Hel left the kennels and headed deeper into her underground palace.

Before returning to the Nastrond, she had one last stop to make and she was looking forward to it. It was her regular chat with Lucifer, the new general in charge of her Berserker army and the brightest rising star in Niflheim.

She quickened her step once more as the hounds strained eagerly at their leashes, her stilettoed footsteps echoing eerily as she trotted away down the gloomy, winding corridor.

It was always a pleasure to chat with 'Louis,' as she had nicknamed him, even if she still didn't know exactly who he was.

19

Yellow Pages

The second thing Kat did after arriving at Dulles airport in Washington was to hire a car. The first thing she did was to throw up.

It was her first journey to Midgard through the well and the experience was far worse than she'd expected. She ached all over and her head swam in a sickening fashion.

By sheer good fortune, the wormhole had landed them in one of the ladies toilets in the main arrivals hall—and on the right side of customs, too. Her initial fear, that they would arrive naked, was immediately laid to rest. She was extremely relieved to find herself wearing a pair of jeans, a T-shirt, a New York Giants' baseball jacket, and the most comfortable pair of trainers she could ever remember putting on.

Kat looked the perfect tourist, which was in stark contrast to Jameela, whose mission was to recover her knife which Odin believed to be secreted somewhere inside FBI headquarters. Dressed in a navy blue suit with elegant pencil skirt and damson silk blouse, she looked the perfect secretary, one that the Feds would be proud to hire. They both laughed at the designer glasses the well had added as a finishing flourish, and admired the elegant French tuck it had devised for her hair.

All in all, they felt they were probably the oddest pair of friends to leave the terminal buildings that day.

Kat and Jameela's journey had begun in Odin's citadel, where at first he had been a little annoyed by their late arrival. After muttering briefly about their lack of punctuality, he had hugged Kat enthusiastically. Idun had been returned and he was delighted that Kat's clever scheme had outsmarted Loki. He was furious, too, that Idun's face had been butchered by Hel, but at least she was alive and otherwise in one piece. Idun had always been a shy goddess, and Hel's shoddy attempt at cosmetic surgery certainly wouldn't help this. Still, as she spent almost all her time in either her orchard or his garden, it probably would affect her less than most.

Odin had other reasons for being irritable, and he beckoned Kat over to one of his telescopes. Adjusting the eyepiece and panning the instrument just a little, she quickly picked up another cause for his ire.

There, with his long golden locks streaming in the wind behind him and trailed by a cloud of dust, was the figure of a man galloping away on a beautiful, dapple grey stallion. The man, of course, was Balder, and the beautiful steed he was riding was none other than Odin's favourite stallion, Sleipnir, the fastest horse in the realm.

Kat had already predicted that this might be what he was looking at. As she and Jameela had made their way to the citadel, they heard the loud flapping of wings and ecstatic whooping of a swan as it circled the castle before flying away fast and low in the direction of the watchtower. The swan had to be Silk on her way to the battlefront. Both Kat and Jameela knew that Balder wouldn't be far behind, galloping hard to get there first.

Kat patted Odin's shoulder sympathetically as they exchanged glances. She understood his anguish; Balder was his favourite son and his determination to go to the watchtower and fight probably meant he was now riding to his doom.

Despite his obvious annoyance, Kat caught something else in Odin's eye: pride.

The look was unmistakable, a joyous respect for his son's disobedience. Had Silk and Balder stayed in Asgard, they would have been branded cowards frightened into staying at home by some silly nightmare. If death were to be his fate, it was far better Balder die a hero rather than hiding behind the tresses of his Valkyrie lover. To disobey the order to stay at the castle was the right decision and both Odin and Kat knew it.

Silk and Balder were warriors. To deny them the right to wage war was to condemn them to a dishonourable death. Swiftly Kat prayed that, by Odin's grace, the two of them would return safe and sound when the battle was done.

"Now, dear Sangrid, it's time to choose your alias," Odin chuckled as he reached beneath his throne to retrieve a worn yellow book. "You must look under the letter A," he continued as he handed it to her.

To Kat's great surprise, the book turned out to be a telephone directory, the *Yellow Pages* no less, and as Jameela joined her, they began to thumb through the faded sheets.

By tradition, the warriors changed their alias every time they returned to Midgard. They usually kept their Midgard first name but changed their surnames which would correspond with the number of journeys they had made.

As this was to be Kat's first mission, she would start with a surname beginning with the letter A. She chose 'Adams,' as this seemed to go nicely with Kat. Jameela took her time and chose more studiously. She had been Masood on her last trip and this time she chose the surname 'Nagra'—only two letters behind Jessica Perry.

The warriors were fiercely competitive in all things, and missions to Midgard were no exception. Like carving notches for sexual conquests on a teenager's headboard or painting kills on a fighter jet, the girls would flaunt their aliases with pride. The further along the alphabet they were, the greater their accomplishments.

There was, of course, only one true winner in this friendly competition, and that was Ruby. Seemingly immune to the lure of paradise, she had been through the alphabet on missions at least three times and was acknowledged as being in a league of her own. No one would ever match her tally, as the hunger to make the final journey to Valhalla consumed the Valkyries one by one.

This was now Jameela's case. One last mission and she would have her desire: to leave Asgard forever and join her beloved Ben.

Surnames chosen, Odin carefully outlined what he expected from each girl. For Kat this was a quick affair: assist Jameela and keep out of trouble. Jameela's mission was difficult and Odin didn't want to lose his latest warrior on her first assignment. Kat was to be the tour guide and nothing else.

Odin spent considerably longer with Jameela and most of their conversation was held in private. There was a lot to discuss and organise, and it was a good hour before they all finally descended to the Chamber of the Valkyries. Kat felt a bag of nerves, but Odin did his best to keep her calm. In the absence of Freyja he would operate the well himself.

As they took their places, Kat couldn't help but glance at the defiled figure of her evil predecessor. The statue of the first Sangrid stood silent, headless, and daubed with crimson paint. Kat shivered, silently re-affirming her vow. There was no way she would ever tread the path of Hel, no matter what Mimir had foretold. It would never happen, of that she was certain.

With incantations chanted and two brilliant flashes of purest white light, Kat and Jameela were gone.

The clock was ticking.

Marcus left for work with that horrible feeling in his pants—the squirming sensation you get when you know you've done something wrong and are minutes away from retribution.

After Woods had departed with Jess, other than Anna's first, vicious slap, Marcus hadn't exchanged a single word with his wife. He had dressed hastily and then begun a tortured journey to work. He stopped once, making one small but important detour on his usual route. Going to the post office, he mailed a small package. Other than that, he followed his usual routine and feared the worst.

Harbouring a murderer and fugitive from the law was a serious offence. At the very least, he would lose his job and most likely be looking at a year or two behind bars.

Arriving at his desk, he waited expectantly for the phone call to come. He hoped his superior officers would be discrete, sparing him the ignominy of being dragged, handcuffed, from his desk. As time slipped by, his imagination ran riot, each scenario becoming more outrageous and ghoulish than the last. His nerves felt paper thin and his hands trembled as he tried to concentrate on work, which was a pointless lesson in futility.

He couldn't focus on anything but his stupidity and impending fall from grace. With excruciating slowness, the minutes ticked into hours and the hours eventually dragged exhaustedly past midday. With his umpteenth stare at the clock, Marcus finally realised that it was one in the afternoon and nothing had happened.

Glancing surreptitiously at one of the many television screens dotted around the station, he caught a snippet of news. It was a report of the dawn raid on his flat and the capture of a possible terrorist suspect. No names were mentioned and no familiar faces flashed across the screen.

Marcus had to pinch himself hard just to be sure—it looked as though he was off the hook. For reasons best known only to Woods, a whitewash had been arranged. For now at least, Marcus was in the clear: his reputation and job intact.

In stark contrast to the morning, the afternoon floated by for Marcus. He left the office feeling elated and it was only the cold, unwelcoming emptiness of his flat that finally brought him down to earth. The world may not know of his role in this terrorist arrest, but Anna did. She wasn't a forgiving woman and had left a simple but curt note: 'Gone to mother's, will call when ready to talk, A.'

No hugs, no kisses, and no invitation for him to join her there. The hostile silence of their flat screamed at his desecration of their wedding vows. Their marriage was in tatters, betrayed by his night of infidelity. *Did he wish he could turn back time?*

Probably not, Marcus eventually decided. His marriage to Anna had been a good one, but if he truly believed what Jess had said to be true, then it would soon be over. He was a dead man walking and Jess's presence here on earth seemed to confirm this fact.

It was odd, but the thought of dying still didn't scare him; it was all just that little bit too weird.

He was thirty-one, reasonably fit, and with a job that seldom put him in the firing line. With Jess no longer there, her talk about death and her role as his saviour now seemed surreal. The bleak future she had been so certain of was beginning to fade. Only the things she had so hastily given him reminded him of a future he would rather not know.

As this jumble of self-pity, guilt, and morbid speculation drifted through his mind, he remembered Jess's phone. Casually he took it from his pocket and read the names of her contacts again: Herja, Sangrid, and Emergency.

He pressed the autodial button for Emergency and waited patiently for the phone to connect. If this wasn't an emergency then he didn't know what was. He could hear the phone ringing, once, twice, three times, four—

"Good evening, Dragza Corporation. How may I help you?"

Stunned, Marcus hung up. It was definitely not what he'd been expecting.

The sweet and businesslike voice had a heavy Caribbean accent and sounded quite unlike any emergency number he could remember. For a moment he suspected the phone might have misdialled, but even if it hadn't, what on earth was he going to say? *Who should he ask for?*

The person at the other end of the phone sounded like the receptionist of a large and busy company. He could hardly say 'Hi, this is Jess's phone,' and expect anyone there to know who the hell he was talking about.

Getting up slowly from the sofa, he made his way over to the kitchen. What he needed was a nice cold beer and a think. He had to do something to help Jess—that went without question. However, before dialling any of the numbers again, he needed to focus on what he was actually going to say.

RING-RING, RING-RING

The sound of a phone ringing cut through the flat like a knife. Marcus froze. It was coming from the coffee table in the sitting room. It was coming from Jess's phone.

He didn't have to worry anymore about who he was going to call or what he was going to say because someone had beaten him to it. That someone was now calling Jess.

20

Thor's Duel

At about the same time as Jameela was saying her tearful farewells to Ben, the party of warriors at Heimdall's watchtower were sitting down to enjoy a late breakfast. They were in excellent spirits and excitement was mounting. Thor's fight with Hrungnir was going to be a horribly one-sided affair and, with any luck, they would all be back in Asgard before the day was out.

It seemed a pity that only Thor would see some action, but no one was actually complaining.

The same sullen and blustery autumn weather that was whipping the Great Sea into a frothing lather had deposited the first dustings of snow onto the Bifrost Bridge. With temperatures falling, from now on the passage across its maze of slippery bridges would become much easier and safer. Fortunately for the party, the deteriorating weather didn't seem to have dampened Thor's enthusiasm for a fight. Any day was a good day for giant bashing and Thor twirled his hammer impatiently at the girls.

He was as keen as mustard to get on and batter Hrungnir into the dust.

The site chosen for the contest was a few hundred metres from the giant encampment and also on Jotunheim soil. Heimdall believed it would be better for the Asgard party to cross into giant territory rather than vice versa. No one wanted a host of angry giants making mischief in Asgard, particularly if—or rather, when—Hrungnir lost. Besides, the chosen site, the 'Stone Fence House,' was a sacred giant monument that the warriors and maids were keen to see.

Many years past, back in the time when Asgard was still young and before a huge glacier divided the realms, a large stone house had stood in a clearing in a vast, ancient forest. It was inhabited by generations of frost giants, the ancient ancestors of the host that now stood before them.

As times changed and the glacier began to creep down from the mountains above, the river that nourished the mighty trees around the house dried up. The plentiful supply of fish and beasts moved elsewhere and so, too, did its giant inhabitants. The house was abandoned and the lush pine trees in the surrounding forest withered slowly and eventually died. One by one, their huge, dying trunks splintered and fell crashing to the ground below. Starved of water, the arid soil couldn't rot the ancient trunks, so instead their huge remains slowly petrified and turned to stone. This extraordinary maze of giant, broken trunks, some erect and some lain flat, seemed to form a fence-like ring around the tumbled ancient building, hence its name.

It was rumoured that the ruins were haunted at night and no one dared to sleep amongst their cold and hostile shapes. The men from Jotunheim were a particularly fearful and superstitious crowd. They lived in terror of their monstrous, ghostly ancestors, the dead giants who awoke each night in this frozen, barren reminder of a time long gone.

"Where's my prize, Thor, you overgrown dwarf?" It was Thrym who started the insult hurling when at last the party of warriors assembled on the sacred site.

"Look above you. Are you as blind as you are dim-witted?" Thor shouted as he pointed to the sky above. Thrym looked up. There, circling high above soared a huge eagle. Suspicious of foul play, Freyja had donned her cloak of falcons' feathers and taken to the air. She didn't trust the giants and she was certain that they had a trick or two up their sleeves today.

"Meet your widowmaker, Thor. Meet the god-slayer and mighty killer of the braggart and cowardly Thor!" Thrym bellowed these words and the whole ground shook as his mighty host roared their approval. They then parted, letting his champion through.

Hrungnir was indeed a mighty opponent.

He must have stood well over three metres high and was head and shoulders taller than his nearest warring comrade. Had Thor stood next to him and raised himself to his full height, he would still barely have measured higher than his waist. Hrungnir was as muscular as he was tall, and his huge shield, spear, and axe seemed bigger than all the weapons of the Valkyries put together.

Thrym's caustic taunt that Thor was little more than an overgrown dwarf suddenly didn't seem so cruel after all.

"Where is he, where is this mighty Thor? Will someone show him to me?" Hrungnir continued the giants' mockery as he spoke. Raising his hand to his heavily furrowed brow, he looked all around. He was deliberately pretending he couldn't see Thor and the giants roared with laughter. This was excellent comedy and the kind of slapstick humour they found the most entertaining.

"Ah, there you are, my little fellow," he sneered at last when he finally pretended to spy Thor. "Would you like to strike the first blow?" Bending forward, he offered his helmeted head as a target.

Thor chuckled heartily and rubbed his eyes. He couldn't believe his luck. The giants had definitely taken leave of their senses.

Putting on his chain mail gloves, he began to swing Mjollnir above his head. Faster and faster he swung until he was ready to unleash a mighty blow. Just one more swing would do it—one blow of his enchanted hammer and this lunatic giant would be blasted into his afterlife.

Thor brought his hammer down with all his force on Hrungnir's helmet. The Valkyries cringed and braced themselves for impact.

"Ting!"

It sounded like a table knife tapping gently on a pewter goblet, the kind of pathetic blow that might be struck by a small child.

Thor staggered back, his eyes and mouth wide open with amazement. He stared blankly at his hammer. *What trickery could have robbed Mjollnir of its strength?*

Hrungnir roared with laughter. "Come now, my valiant little one, you can hit harder than that." He leant forward once more, offering the other side of his head as a target.

Once more Thor swung his hammer around his head and with a tremendous roar he brought it down upon Hrungnir's skull.

"Ting!"

This blow sounded even feebler than the first, like a tiny pebble bouncing on a slab of stone.

Thor shook his head. His face was bright red, crimson with exertion and embarrassment. He looked in anguish at the watching warriors. *What in Asgard would they think of him now?*

The giant host howled once more with laughter and began to shuffle forward. Perhaps the mighty Thor had had his day and they need fear his hammer no more. Things were beginning to look bad, a sight not missed by Freyja high above them. Flapping her wings, she began to spiral lower. There had to be magic and witchcraft in this, but where was it coming from? Urgently she scanned the ground below her.

"Would you like one last chance, my little gnome of a friend?" Hrungnir's taunts were becoming unbearable. Snarling through clenched teeth, Thor wound his hammer up for one last blow.

Faster and faster Mjollnir spun above his head until its shape was lost in a blur of motion. Finally, with one last mighty roar, Thor brought the weapon crashing down upon the head of Hrungnir. He brought his hammer down with such force that both Thor's legs leapt high into the air.

"Ting!"

Instead of shattering the giant into a thousand pieces, the blow barely made a sound. It seemed as though a mere wren had alighted on Hrungnir's helmet.

Thor slumped backwards gasping for air, exhausted by his efforts.

"Now, you pathetic little god, it's my turn." A wicked smile flashed from Hrungnir's twisted lips as he raised his axe high above his head.

Thor looked in desperation toward the warriors. He'd been so confident in Mjollnir's power that he hadn't even brought a shield. Mika came to his rescue, tossing him hers as Hrungnir swung his mighty axe. Turning immediately, Thor raised his arm and held her shield high above him.

THUMP!

The ground shook with the force of the mighty blow, and the Valkyries screwed their eyes up, wincing at its impact. Miraculously, Thor was somehow still on his legs but he seemed to have shrunk by several inches. Such was his huge strength, only he in all of Asgard could withstand such a meaty blow.

"Bravely done, my midget foe, but I'm just getting started." Hrungnir raised his axe once more and Thor, thinking more wisely at last, decided to dodge the swinging axe that flew predictably through the air like a pregnant sow. Even he didn't fancy being on the receiving end of another one of Hrungnir's hearty blows.

"COWARD!" Hrungnir roared as he missed.

The giant host echoed his disapproval at Thor's dainty dodge. It was clear they expected him to stand his ground and trade blow for blow until one of them prevailed.

For the first time in his life, Thor knew what if felt like to be a failure. He was being humiliated in front of Odin's Valkyries and their most detested enemy. It was agony. If Hel had opened the gates of Niflheim before him he would gladly have leapt to his doom, such was his embarrassment.

Fortunately, things were about to change.

With a mighty screech Freyja plummeted toward the ground, disappearing behind a cluster of boulders as she did so. A sudden silence enveloped the gathering and even Hrungnir and Thor paused in their battle. Everybody was intrigued by this unusual turn of events.

"AARGH!"

With an equally piercing shriek, the cloaked figure of an old woman emerged from behind the rocks, waving her hands frantically in the air as she ran. It was Gullveig, and it was her evil incantations that had blocked the power of Mjollnir.

With a gleam of victory in his eye, Thor picked up his hammer once more. Gullveig's chanting had ceased and with that her evil curse was broken. He could feel the throb of power in his hands and Hrungnir's skull lay in his sights.

For a giant, Hrungnir thought and acted swiftly. Knowing that his luck had ended, he raised his axe once more and struck at the base of one of the huge stone tree trunks. It shattered and as it toppled lazily down to the ground, Hrungnir pushed it toward Thor.

"Look out!" cried Carmel, lurching forward to push Thor out of harm's way. With a sickening thud, the stone trunk landed heavily on the frozen ground.

Thor hollered.

Carmel had saved his life, but not his legs—one of them was now trapped beneath the hefty trunk. Worse, he had dropped his hammer and it lay tantalisingly out of reach.

"Quick—release me!" Thor yelled as Carmel and the other warriors and maids formed a defensive ring around him. They began to work together, straining and heaving at the heavy trunk.

Events began to accelerate.

Seeing Thor trapped and helpless, Hrungnir lumbered off in the direction of Freyja. She stood some two hundred metres away and was already engaging giants in combat.

With enviable elegance and power that belied her forty years of age, she wheeled her blade left and right, ducking and weaving as she slashed and thrust at her foes. Had these giants been the same as the poorly armed and unskilled masons, no doubt a dozen or so would have fallen beneath her powerful blade.

Sadly for Freyja, the hefty fellows weren't novices. These giants were well-trained soldiers heavily armed with stout shields, swords, axes, and thick metal breastplates. It was slow work, wearing them down and searching for chinks in their armour where she could strike a fatal blow. Their sheer numbers were too great, and as the girls struggled feverishly to release Thor, Freyja became more and more isolated. From afar, it looked as though she was drowning in a sea foaming with muscle and hair.

The Valkyries were strong, but the fallen log was extremely heavy. Caught between the need to defend Thor from the surrounding throng of giants and their attempts to wrestle him free, the girls were getting nowhere. The situation was looking bleaker by the minute. Hrungnir had arrived at the mob surrounding Freyja and she was moments from capture. Thrym, too, had mounted his mighty stallion Gold Mane and was cantering toward her. His prize was almost within his loathsome grasp.

It was Carmel who had a flash of inspiration. "Quickly—get me Hrungnir's spear."

Lara threw it over to her and after digging it under the trunk, she placed a boulder beneath its shaft. Carmel beckoned to Vicki, Maya, and Alex to help her bear down on the other end. She had made a lever with the boulder as its fulcrum. With a tremendous yell, the maids bore down on the spear with all their might. Slowly, creaking and groaning in protest, the trunk began to move.

Thor saw his opportunity and took it. Dragging himself free, he stood up. Miraculously, neither of his legs had been broken. With lightning speed he retrieved his hammer and swung it wildly once more above his head.

The giant army paused in their attack and then backed slowly away from the Valkyries. No one wanted to be the first to taste Mjollnir's ferocious power.

With a mighty cry Thor hurled the hammer in the direction of Hrungnir. It sped through the air like an unstoppable arrow. Hrungnir raised his stone shield and held it up before him.

CRUNCH!

The shield was useless, and it splintered into a thousand pieces, its shards flying like deadly shrapnel into the giants all around him. One particular piece whistled through the air and hit Thor squarely between the eyes. He didn't flinch. He barely even noticed the fragment as it embedded itself deep within his forehead.

Undeterred by Hrungnir's shield, Mjollnir continued in its deadly flight. With a sickening thud it struck Hrungnir on his helmet—splitting it in two before killing him instantly. Just like a mighty tree, the giant toppled over and crashed into the dusting of powdered snow beneath him.

Gullveig, who had sneaked back toward the fight, began to loudly chant a strange and evil incantation that rippled through the air. Mjollnir lay still and lifeless on the floor instead of returning to Thor's hand as it should. Gullveig had blocked its enchanted escape.

Seizing the initiative, Thrym dismounted from his horse and raised the hammer triumphantly above his head. For the moment he had forgotten about Freyja and the key to Mimir's well. For now he held a far more intoxicating prize in his hands. Without Thor's hammer, Asgard lay defenceless, impotent against Thrym's mighty host.

"Kill them all—we march on Asgard!" he yelled as he rallied his army. Thor was furious and made to chase after him but Prima and Skogul held him back. Thrym had already mounted Gold Mane and was spurring him to gallop away in the direction of Utgard, the capital of his realm.

To give chase would be a hopeless folly, and one that would separate the party further.

Once more the giants turned and began to descend upon Freyja and Thor. Now, with Mjollnir removed from the battlefield, the fight really did seem lost. The warriors and maids raised their shields and swords with heavy hearts.

They would fight to the death and kill many times their number, but with so many giants surrounding them their fate seemed ultimately hopeless. Each girl knew that ballads would be sung about this battle for many generations to come. Their Valkyrie pride simply wouldn't allow them to fade meekly into the night. The gates of Valhalla beckoned and each woman raised her voice in a growing cacophony of bloodcurdling war cries, each clamouring for death with glory.

In the briefest of moments before the two sides engaged, a beautiful but solitary swan glided low across over the battlefield and alighted in the middle of the Valkyrie ring. Without pausing for breath, Silk emerged from the brilliant flash of light.

"Valkyries, we have our queen to defend!" she cried loudly and with authority. "Skogul, do you have the umbrella shield?" she barked urgently and Zara nodded that she did.

Raising her sword high above her head, Silk yelled her command with an almighty roar.

"WHEEL!"

21

Louis

*L*ooking a little blood-spattered after her trip to the kennels and with two eager hounds barking and straining at their leashes beside her, Hel headed deeper into her palace. She was keen to get back to the Nastrond but before she did so, she was anxious to see 'Louis' and find out how he was getting on with the task of remodelling her Berserker army.

Louis—or 'Lucifer,' as she should correctly call him—was a bit of an enigma. He was a rising star who, in a very short space of time, had risen to command her army of the damned. He was a lucky find, one of the few bodies from Midgard she was genuinely pleased to have plucked from the Nastrond.

It had all started in such an ordinary way.

Hel had been busy as usual fishing corpses from the beach with Ganglati and Ganglot, when she came across his body floating face down in the inky waters. He was from Midgard and was nothing exceptional to look at: a bit chubby but otherwise intact and healthy—that is, if you excluded the obvious wound which had dispatched him to his afterlife.

The body wasn't obviously tagged as being that of a wrongdoer and by rights she should have sent his soul to rest in peace in the frozen wastes of Old Niflheim. Unfortunately, Hel hated to see the 'healthy' dead go to waste. So, breaking all the rules (as she so often did), she resuscitated his body and promptly stole it for her army.

In many ways it was lucky for Hel that the gods of Midgard were pretty slack about keeping track of her activities. They were simply

too busy squabbling amongst themselves and sorting out messes in
their universe to care about what she got up to. Out of sight, out of
mind—that was their attitude. They paid Hel handsomely to take care
of their dead and, in return, they turned a blind eye to her more
unsavoury activities. So long as there weren't any complaints, they
wouldn't interfere.

This situation suited Hel down to the ground.

Unfortunately, having pulled her find out of the waters and turned
his body over, she had had to send him to the mines. He was wearing
a crucifix and was obviously a Christian. Hel had nothing against this
deity's followers as such, it was just they made poor soldiers.
Although they were often incredibly brave and strong, they seemed to
have a bit of an attitude about taking up arms against others. They
also quarrelled with soldiers of other Midgard religions, the followers
of Mohammed in particular. Hel simply couldn't understand why they
all didn't just get along together. After all, they were dead already so
what was their problem?

Anyway, this decision was where her difficulties really began.

Clearly unhappy with the way he and his fellow slaves were being
treated, the man had organised a rebellion against her rule. This was not
especially unusual as there were always complaints and disturbances
amongst the slaves. Their wages (death if they didn't work) and hours
(twenty-four hours a day, seven days a week) were common gripes.
What made this uprising different, however, was how effective it had
been and how close the rebels had come to entering her royal chambers.
The other slaves followed him with a loyalty she had seldom seen.

He also had an inspired flair for tactics.

Her elite guards, the Fallen Angels, were strong and well trained
but they lacked imagination. Time and again he had foiled their
attempts to crush him. Indeed, she stopped to admire a charred scorch
mark on the wall of the tunnel; he had even managed to fashion a
crude, hand-held incendiary device which his troops had used most
effectively against the Angels.

Eventually, and only after her personal intervention, the rebellion
had been crushed and Louis was dragged in chains before her. The
usual fate for such defiance should have been a ferocious whipping
followed by being hung, drawn, and quartered, but in his case Hel
decided to act differently.

One of her many gifts was the ability to identify and respect talent
when she saw it, and the man clearly had this in spades. She decided
to offer him a pardon, but did he accept?

No—the ungrateful so-and-so didn't. He instead begged her to kill him and put an end to his misery. He went further, vowing he would rise up against her again and again until she eventually was forced to execute him. He wanted death, a blissful nothingness to release him from the torment of his inner demons. At this point, the man pushed an unusual button for Hel. His suffering and desire for oblivion intrigued her.

Making some paltry concessions to the slaves in the mines, Hel spent some time delving into his problems and pampering his wounded ego. Gradually he mellowed, and in the end they reached an agreement. Lucifer, as he decided he wanted to be called, would become her faithful servant if she delivered those who had brought about his premature demise. It was this burning, passionate hatred for the people responsible for killing him that now made him such a strong and obedient ally.

Once their deal had been struck, Louis had changed immediately.

Loyal and polite, she found his gentle manners beguiling and his pent-up rage a source of endless fascination. Both of these qualities turned her on, although she would never admit as much. It was unusual for Hel to feel anything other than contempt for those around her, but in Louis she made an exception.

It was just such a pity that he always kept his face hidden. Apparently it had been badly burnt in the fighting and he wouldn't reveal it until he was ready to do so. Hel didn't know when this would be and she wished she could remember what he had looked like when she first fished him from the Nastrond. 'Chubby' was the only word that sprang to mind, which wasn't terribly helpful.

Pity. She would probably seduce him if he would only let her sort out a decent face.

"No, you useless idiots. Not like that—like this!"

Hel paused and watched with admiration as Louis chastised the soldiers around him. He was working hard to fashion an army she could be proud of, but it wasn't an easy job. At the moment, he appeared to be trying to teach them the art of an organised retreat.

Hel stifled a laugh. It would probably be easier to teach her hounds to do this. Berserkers fought as fearless, drug-crazed zombies which was what made them so terrifying. Getting them to work together as a united force was about as unlikely as getting them to eat with table manners. Still, at least Louis was trying, and they were all wearing her new armour that had been specially coated with Hellinium to give it extra strength.

"Hi, Louis. How's it going?"

Lucifer stopped abruptly and turned around. He hadn't noticed Hel arrive and he was clearly flummoxed by her unexpected presence. "Your majesty." He bowed low. "Please forgive my lack of respect."

"Oh, don't worry about that," Hel interrupted, waving her hand dismissively. "And how is my darling Louis getting on today?" she continued.

"Oh, um—well, ma'am—not so good, I'm afraid," Louis stuttered apologetically. Hel loved to see him fluster. She knew he was blushing, even though she couldn't see his face.

"And my armour?" she scraped her fingernails provocatively down his breastplate and heard him gulp with embarrassment.

"Excellent, ma'am. Very impressive indeed, your majesty." Louis backed away awkwardly. Hel was a beautiful woman and he really didn't want to be distracted by her, not now. Briefly he remembered another beauty back in Midgard. He'd died because of her, the vicious, heartless, scheming bitch.

"May I be allowed to return to their training, ma'am?" he enquired, bobbing a small bow. His anger at her memory felt good and he desperately wanted to channel the rage back into his work.

"Well, if you must, then I suppose you must. Have fun—toodles!" Hel kissed a finger before planting it firmly on Louis's masked cheek. Waving goodbye with her fingertips, she strutted slowly away, her two hounds baying at her heels. She knew his eyes were following her and that gave her such a wicked thrill. She could sense he was attracted to her and she knew that he was desperately fighting to resist it.

For Hel, his conflict was like a red flag. She desperately wanted to flirt with him and coax him out of his emotional straightjacket. It would be such fun to have him drooling and begging at her feet. She hadn't felt a challenge quite like this since being a child in Asgard, a teenage girl heavily infatuated with the dashingly handsome but oh-so-out-of-reach Balder.

"Come along, babies." She pulled irritably at her hounds' leads. *Damn you, Louis!*

It was frustrating to be distracted by such wicked urges when she should be getting on with her work. Hel had planned to go to the Nastrond and get down to business, but that would have to take a raincheck for now. Louis had put her in mind of other pleasures.

She needed to get to her harem straight away.

Ganglati knocked, and then gently pushed open the bright red door for Cole. It was the first time Cole had entered Hel's 'playroom' and to be truthful, he didn't quite know what to expect. He had been summoned there at Hel's request and he knew from the other men that this was where the seriously kinky stuff went down.

To be honest, that didn't bother him. He had a broad mind and had spent more time in bars and clubs than most other guys he knew. So long as there was booze, coke, and some fine ass to fuck, then that would be just 'sweet.'

Cole entered the room and paused, letting his eyes adjust to the dim lighting inside. He had to admit that at first viewing, the playroom definitely lived up to its sleazy reputation. The décor was admirably tacky and gaudy, heavy on reds and pinks, and splashed with copious amounts of bling and glitter.

Hel, he quickly discovered, was already there, centre stage and reclining naked on a velvet chaise-longue. She was hard at it, writhing rhythmically with one hand tightly clasping the head of a 'girl' kneeling between her thighs. Her other hand was massaging the testicles of the owner of the phallus that lay buried inside her mouth. A third 'girl' was squatting beside her, caressing her breasts firmly with his mouth and hands.

Hel hadn't noticed Cole's arrival.

Taking a few cautious steps deeper into the room, Cole became aware of two other men standing in a corner of the room. They were both naked and engaged in heavy petting. Seeing Cole, they walked over and began to disrobe him, stroking his body lustfully with their hands as they did so.

"Get lost!" Cole hissed loudly as he pushed them angrily away. He was a ladies' man, not some bisexual freak. He could tolerate homosexuality, which was cool if it was your thing, but it definitely wasn't his scene.

"Colleen!" Hel's voice called out abruptly. She had heard his heated outburst and temporarily stopped what she was doing. A wicked smile curled across her lips. She gave each of the men in her harem a girl's name and this seemed to be the perfect one for Cole.

"Naughty, naughty." She stood up, wagging her finger in a mock scolding sort of way as she strolled leisurely over to him. "That wasn't a very nice thing to do to, to...," she paused deliberately. "What did you say your name was?"

"Diana, your majesty," the man replied, bowing his head.

Hel knew his name, of course, but it just gave her such a delicious thrill to hear the men use their girls' names. It was so degrading—she loved it.

"You really should say 'sorry' to Diana, now shouldn't you, Colleen?"

"Sorry," Cole murmured quickly, his severed digit being a permanent reminder not to piss the bitch off.

"I think you can do a little better than that," she cooed, flicking a finger playfully under his chin. "I think you should make it up to Diana, show her a bit of...love. Perhaps, I don't know...give her a little...satisfaction? Just for me?" She fluttered her eyelids teasingly as she walked her fingertips suggestively along Diana's manhood.

Oh, shit!

Cole's eyes widened. *Hel wanted him to give the freak a blow job!*

He froze. This was too much, a line in the sand he couldn't and wouldn't cross.

Without thinking what he was doing, Cole pushed Diana roughly out of his way and stormed toward the door. He could hear Hel laughing hysterically behind him, the sound fading to a harsh cackle as it followed him out of the room and down the corridor beyond. He dreaded what she would do to him, but he would be damned if he would take a walk on the queer side simply for her amusement.

"Oh, my poor dear little Diana," Hel mocked sarcastically before giving the man a fake, sympathetic air kiss. Chuckling, she returned to her seat. Hel wasn't angry with Colleen. In fact, she was far from it. Cole had just revealed his worst nightmare and that was a huge mistake. This suddenly became a cherished prize, a target for Hel to shoot at.

Oh yes, Hel mused as she returned to her sex games. *Cole's number was up.*

22

Connections

$\mathfrak{C}$rowded, smelly, rude.

These were the unfortunate words that swirled around Kat's head as they set out from Dulles airport and headed toward the centre of Washington. She had been away from Midgard—or 'Earth,' as she must get used to calling it again—for a little over three months, but it felt like many lifetimes ago.

It was such a pity. She had expected to cry with joy when she saw twenty-first century humanity again, but instead her heart had wept with sorrow. There were too many people, the air was filthy, and the constant foul language hurt her ears. She felt ashamed to think that she had once used the F-word as frequently as 'please' or 'thank you.' It was disgusting.

How could anyone doubt climate change?

This beggared belief. It was so obvious now, seeing the world as an outsider. Midgard (she had decided to stick with that name because it sounded so much friendlier) was dying and humans were to blame. She had an irresistible urge to scream this at the top of her voice to every passerby.

Kat and Jameela exchanged looks as they drove away from the airport. No words were spoken, but Kat knew she felt the same way, too. Midgard's treatment was a crime and it wouldn't go unpunished for long. 'Give someone enough rope and they'll hang themselves' was a phrase that seemed to sum it up nicely. The gods were watching, and they definitely wouldn't be pleased.

Kat took her time and drove carefully at first. The minutes ticked by and Jameela watched with a mixture of fascination and terror as Kat wheeled and dealed in the treacherous traffic. Indicating, swerving, braking, and accelerating—and then Kat did it all over again, a thousand times more.

Eventually they arrived in central Washington and found a decent but not ostentatious hotel. It was a reasonable walk from the J. Edgar Hoover Building but close enough for their needs. Booking a shared room, they decided to familiarise themselves with their surroundings. It was late afternoon when they started walking and the hours seemed to roll by without them getting very far.

The streets were immense. A single avenue would swallow the town of Asgard with room to spare. They had to begrudgingly admit that the scale of human endeavour was remarkable, with the decadent glitz and bling of the bustling shopping malls holding a particularly seductive allure.

By early evening they were famished and it was time to choose a place to eat. This was something Kat had been looking forward to: the endless choice of food. Pizzas, burgers, fried chicken, Chinese, Indian—the list went on and on. After an age, the girls settled on a pizza with Jameela being particularly keen to get back to a vegetarian lifestyle. At first, this seemed an excellent pick, but they quickly regretted their choice. The pizza tasted bland and processed; it was lacking in the richness of flavour and textures of the fresh food that was served daily in Asgard.

Kat chastised herself soundly. She must stop comparing the two worlds and be grateful for the opportunity to be here again. Three months before, she'd been a corpse in a refrigerator. Now she was alive and breathing, and fitter than ever.

They did a little shopping together during their walk about and after eating they produced their credit cards once more and settled the bill. It seemed that the credit of O. Dragza was good everywhere they went, although it bugged Kat that she couldn't put her finger on the name. The irritation didn't last long. They had far more important things to worry about.

As they began to walk back toward their hotel, Kat's mind drifted to Jess. She knew she was only a matter of hours away in New York and her fingers hovered lovingly over her number on her mobile. She was so tempted to call, but decided she mustn't. It was an unwritten rule that other than for emergencies, the Valkyries didn't disturb each other when on missions in Midgard. Odin had been most insistent about this during her briefing. Oh, well. She guessed Jess would be okay, especially if she were in the arms of her hero.

Finally she turned her thoughts to her old school friend, Henry Fox.

For Kat, meeting up with him was the most important and secret part of this trip to Midgard. Hod's words on their hunting trip back in Asgard had been seared into her mind. As soon as she dropped Jameela at the FBI headquarters tomorrow, she would head out to meet him. She knew more or less where he was and it was only a few hours' drive from Washington.

She felt certain he could give the answers to questions that plagued her—provided, of course, he could survive the shock of seeing her returned from the dead.

"Brynhildr—how awfully sweet of you to call."

Marcus was momentarily speechless. The voice of the woman who had rung Jess's phone sounded so melodiously rich and aristocratic.

"Brynhildr—are you there?" The wonderful voice now held a hint of concern. With a start, Marcus realised he had been silent for some time.

"Uh, yes. Hi. My, my name is Marcus, Detective Marcus Finch. Brynhildr isn't here at the moment."

God! he cringed. *He sounded so lame!*

"Can you please tell me what exactly you are doing with her phone?" The woman's voice was now frosty and authoritative. She was clearly comfortable with being in charge and concerned about Jess. "Didn't you just try to contact me?" she continued, her more tentative, questioning tone of voice searching hopefully for an answer.

"Yes, thank god, yes!" Marcus exploded excitedly. At last the phone call was going somewhere. *The woman not only knew Jess but had used her Valkyrie name Brynhildr!* The charmingly polite West Indian receptionist must have passed on the message that a call had been received from her phone.

"Look," Marcus continued hurriedly, blurting out the whole story in an unprepared and garbled monologue that must have gone on for at least three minutes. The stranger at the other end listened silently without interrupting, not once.

"By the way," he added almost apologetically as he neared the end of his dissertation, "I didn't catch your name?"

The woman paused and Marcus could hear her take in a deep breath. She was clearly choosing her answer carefully. "Please call me Fran. Thank you so much, Detective Finch, for your kind and very detailed explanation. I'm afraid I'm a little tied up at the moment, but if you can give me twenty-four hours I could come and meet you. Are there any other numbers on Brynhildr's phone?"

"Yes, two: Herja and Sangrid."

"Ah, that's good. Look, if you feel you can't wait for me or if any other problems develop, do please call one of those numbers. They should be closer to you." She paused once more. "I suspect Sangrid would be the more helpful in that eventuality."

Marcus confirmed that he understood, and then asked her where she was exactly. He noted she ignored his question when she next spoke. "Thank you so much for being such a good friend to Brynhildr. I'm sure we all owe you a big debt of gratitude. I will see you tomorrow, Detective Finch. Au revoir for now."

Fran hung up abruptly without giving him time to say goodbye. Marcus didn't care. He sat down, relieved that at last he was getting somewhere. Whoever this Fran person was, she clearly knew the Valkyries and was in a position to help them, thank god.

He ran through the three numbers on the phone once more and his finger wavered over Sangrid's name. He was so tempted to call, yet he knew he ought to wait. Unless something new came up, he would do as Fran suggested. Give her twenty-four hours. If she didn't show after that, he would definitely call Sangrid.

Interestingly, the name Herja sounded familiar. He had heard it before. She was the Valkyrie whose knife now lay in Woods' hands. Sangrid, on the other hand, was a completely new name to him.

For a brief moment, he wondered what she might look like…

"Do you like this one?"

Ottar asked his question in English heavily laced with a German accent. His shaggy, model's mop of mousy hair cascaded around his perfectly-chiselled cheeks and stubbled chin. He stood a metre ninety tall, and every centimetre was honed to perfection. At twenty-two, he was a top fashion model throughout Europe.

"Yes, darling, of course. Now please choose anything you like quickly so I can settle the bill. Something has cropped up and we really do have to get going."

The Contessa Francesca Dragza handed her platinum credit card over the counter and into the eager hands of the sales assistant.

The expensively discreet *Boutique pour Les Hommes* was situated on a secluded side street set back from the Champs-Élysées, and it had been closed for her private and exclusive use all afternoon. Suits, ties, shirts, and shoes—the final tally of knick-knacks she purchased for her latest, disposable boy toy was enough to make any sales assistant drool. The cost, of course, was peanuts to the Contessa and she tried desperately to hide her impatience and annoyance as they waited for her limousine to draw up outside.

She wasn't cross with the 'delicious-but-dim' Ottar; she was cross with herself. *What had she been thinking of, organising a few days shopping and R & R in Paris instead of going to Princeton straight away?*

She could slap herself, and others quite probably would, if she didn't sort out their little problem before the Valkyries beat her to it. She wasn't sure how damaging it could be, but the problem posed a risk and one they could ill afford to take. Besides, if she got there first, the 'problem' just might be useful to them.

Curse those wretched Valkyries! They had arrived in Midgard far sooner than she'd anticipated. Clearly, others were speeding up their agendas, too.

Settling immediately into the back seat, she instructed the driver to make his way to Charles de Gaulle airport as quickly as possible. She also instructed him to contact her pilot and have the jet fuelled and ready for takeoff the moment they arrived. To hell with booking take-off slots and aeroplane stacks. She didn't care how much it cost—just make sure the plane was ready to fly as soon as they arrived.

The Contessa sat back and lit a Gauloises cigarette. Its nicotine soothed her aching head as she inhaled deeply. She had one more call to make.

Her conversation with Detective Finch had given her yet another headache, although thankfully this could be settled much more quickly. Hard cash could buy you practically anything these days. She was aware that Woods had called, too. Her personal assistant had kindly fielded that nuisance for her. She was in absolutely no hurry to talk with that obsessive and annoying little man just yet.

Gratefully, she accepted the glass of chilled champagne Ottar had so thoughtfully poured for her. He really was a darling. After a wonderfully refreshing sip or two, she pulled his head toward her and kissed him delicately on the lips.

The Parisian traffic was always atrocious at this time of day and she desperately needed something to ease her tension. She lazily flicked a switch and the smoked glass screen glided silently up. Relaxing a little, she let Ottar's persistent caresses begin to work their usual magic. Slowly she guided his lips toward her ample breasts, and then down toward her toned stomach.

Ottar looked up with an expectant smile upon his thick, Cupid's bow lips.

Fran smiled knowingly before sinking deeper into the luxurious leather seat. Pushing his head lower still, she let out a moan of pleasure when his kisses finally reached her sweetness. They really did have plenty of time, and his unusually long and energetic tongue was wonderfully satisfying.

23

The Jaws of Defeat

HEEL!"

Silk's urgent command spurred the warriors and maids into decisive action.

Smoothly and with a skill honed by years of practice, they formed a ring around the wounded Thor. He was dazed and confused, with a huge chunk of rock lying deeply embedded in the middle of his forehead. Blood gushed in arterial spurts, blinding his eyes and forming broad streams which cascaded down his cheeks. Despite this terrible wound, he still had the strength to fight and was eager to help the Valkyries as best he could. He clumsily obeyed Silk's orders and when her words didn't suffice, a timely push was all he needed.

The wheel was a defensive formation used by generations of Valkyries in their battles against giants, dwarves, and other marauding foes. It allowed a small band of warriors to penetrate deep inside an enemy's defence and return with minimal loss. When done well, it was mesmerising in both its speed and fluidity of movement.

The girls quickly formed two concentric rings around Silk with the outer ring being formed by the maids. They stood shoulder to shoulder with their brightly painted shields raised high and overlapping. It was an impenetrable defence from which only their long spears protruded, ready to repel anyone foolish enough to draw near.

Within this outer ring stood Skogul, Goll, and Prima. Their bows were strung with arrows which were always ready to be loosed. Their role was simple: to plough a deadly furrow through enemy ranks with a continuous volley of arrows.

In the centre of the formation stood Silk with Thor by her side. It was her role to call the orders that would guide the direction of the swirling wheel. Thor held aloft the protective umbrella shield which provided cover for the warriors from aerial bombardment.

Like some primitive medieval armoured tank, the outer ring of girls crouched low and began to briskly walk, crab-like, in a circle, sometimes moving to the left and sometimes to the right. The whole formation spun gracefully, wheeling left and right in a constantly changing, zigzag path that was impossible to predict. For the giants it was like having a prickly porcupine rampaging through their ranks. They became confused and momentarily rendered impotent in battling the warriors.

At first, faced with such a mighty and well-armed host, the wheel made slow progress as it spun its way toward the stranded Freyja. Skogul, Goll, and Prima unleashed arrow after arrow which made little impact on the seething mass of heavily-armoured giants around them. The giants' shields, helmets, and breastplates were just too thick and tightly packed for their arrows to be anything more than an unpleasant nuisance. This changed rapidly after a helpful, tersely whispered suggestion by Mist.

"Aim for their legs!" she cried hoarsely.

Aiming lower, the archers soon found their sweet spot: the poorly defended thighs and groins of their giant foes. Now wherever the archers aimed their bows, the giants' ranks melted away like springtime snow, each being anxious to avoid a crippling injury. Thighs and groins made for particularly painful and vulnerable targets.

Progress became rapid and, like a hot knife through freshly-churned butter, the girls quickly arrived at the beleaguered Freyja. She had stood her ground heroically, battling ferociously against wave after wave of charging giants. Each foe would chance his hand at felling the mighty Valkyrie queen, but each would find only disappointment or death at the tip of her majestic sword. At least ten lay dead or dying beneath her feet, their pitiful moans a final testament to the awesome power of her hands. She would have liked to stay longer and killed more, but by the time the Valkyrie wheel arrived she was grateful for salvation. In truth, she was exhausted. Her body and armour was drenched with sweat and soaked in the blood of her enemies.

With their queen safely inside the wheel, the girls turned once more and headed back toward the Bifrost Bridge. Realizing their new direction, the giants redoubled their efforts to stop the wheel's progress, throwing an endless barrage of massive rocks and boulders to crash down upon the Valkyrie formation. For once, Silk was grateful that Thor's massive arms were holding the umbrella shield aloft. Only he had the strength to defend them from such a monstrous onslaught.

Slowly but surely the giants gave way once more and the wheel spun quicker still as it twisted and turned inexorably toward the sanctuary of the bridge.

Although giants weren't stupid, they were slow thinkers. This was why negotiations took such a long time and why they hurled insults. It gave them time to think.

For giants, waging war was an ancient and cumbersome affair, one steeped in tradition that had changed little down the centuries. They were poor archers and had little time for spears, which were used only as thrusting weapons, bayonets on which to impale their enemies. The giants' favourite mode of fighting was to stand an arm-span apart and trade blows. They exchanged one massive clubbing blow of an axe or sword with another until the exhausted loser lowered his shield. This simple and primitive form of combat had served them well through countless generations of tribal feuds.

Unfortunately, fighting the agile and creative Valkyries required markedly different tactics and improvisation. It wasn't until the wheel was well on its way toward the bridge that the giants finally realised they had the perfect weapon to destroy this formation. And better still, it lay close at hand.

With a frantic chorus of loud trumpeting and the pounding of feet, the giants unleashed one of their massive war mammoths. He was an awesome sight: his heavily armoured head swayed from side to side as the enraged animal charged toward the girls. Infuriated by the constant jabs of the giants' spears, the creature was being funnelled between them and toward the Valkyrie formation. Their tiny arrows and spears would be useless against such a massive creature. The beast would crush them as easily as a man might squash a beetle.

This point wasn't lost on Silk.

With a frantic yell and an exhortation for one last mighty push, the girls redoubled their efforts. They had fifty metres to go but arrows were running low. It was a race they couldn't afford to lose, and yet one they couldn't win. With each passing moment, the mammoth was gaining on them. He would smash their wheel long before they reached safety.

Just when all seemed lost, the sound of Gjall rang loud and clear across the battlefield. The steady tone of the horn rose high above the clamour of war. The warriors looked up. To their great relief, Heimdall, Tyr, and Balder were charging across the final roped section of the Bifrost Bridge.

Within moments the trio had arrived in Jotunheim and were taking aim with their heavier bows and arrows. As one, they unleashed a hail of flaming arrows that arched high into the air and then gathered speed as they hurtled down toward the rampaging monster.

All animals fear fire and this beast was no exception.

The flaming shafts landed inches from his trunk and the terrified creature veered sharply away from his chosen course. With fearful yells, the first ranks of giants collapsed, bulldozed beneath his massive armoured tusks. The unstoppable, lumbering behemoth then ploughed effortlessly through their rapidly fragmenting ranks.

With whoops, yells, and piercing cries of triumph, the girls broke formation and charged the last few metres to the bridge. The gods fought frantically, the swords of Balder, Tyr, and Heimdall flashing like exploding fireworks as they held the last of the giant army at bay.

One by one, the warriors crossed the delicate rope bridge. It swayed alarmingly, threatening to overturn at any moment and tip its luckless travellers into the yawning crevasse below. The giants pressed closer and continued to hurl huge boulders at them. Some landed heavily on the bridge, shattering wooden planks and fraying the stout ropes which held the structure in place.

It was a desperate and excruciating dash, but at last all the warriors and maids had made it to the safety of the first icy spur. Finally, when he was certain everybody was out of harm's way, Balder inched his way back across the bridge.

The giants were not going to release the warriors from their clutches easily. Three hefty fellows followed Balder. They were undeterred by the deadly rain of arrows fired by the waiting Valkyries. The giants lunged at him with their spears and swords, with Balder ducking and weaving as he evaded their deadly blows.

Finally, when at last he reached the icy spur, he slashed one more time with his sword. This time it wasn't at the bodies of their foes; this time it was to sever the stays of the bridge. With a mighty crack, the ropes gave way and the bridge collapsed. Plunging into the murky depths of the crevasse below, the bridge convulsed repeatedly, scattering the giants like confetti as they fell to their doom. For a while, the party could hear the terrible moans of their fallen foes crying out for help as they drew their last breaths in their icy tomb. Eventually, their tormented screams faded into an eerie and chilling silence.

Totally exhausted, the small party headed toward the inviting lights of the watchtower. With the bridge now broken, the only link to Jotunheim had been destroyed. Asgard was safe, but there were no wild and jubilant celebrations amongst the bloodied party. None of their number had been killed, but there had been no victory in their salvation.

They had barely survived and their survival had been bought at a price that might just prove too great.

Thor's hammer was lost and without Mjollnir's awesome power, Asgard lay naked and helpless. The fearless Valkyries would defend its borders to the death, but they numbered just nine warriors and eight maids. News of Thrym's capture of Mjollnir would spread quickly. What had been an army of hundreds would swell rapidly to many thousands in the days and weeks ahead. Sheer weight of numbers would numb the giants' fear of Odin's mighty warrior women.

Mjollnir, now heading toward the giant stronghold of Utgard, seemed impossibly out of reach with the only route by land now severed. Somehow the warriors had to think of a plan to get Thor's hammer back, and they had to think fast.

The giants would quickly repair and strengthen the bridge over the glacier and Mjollnir had to be back in Thor's hands before the giants completed that task. If the Valkyries failed in this endeavour, the giants' war machine would surely conquer Asgard.

24

M Theory

t might have seemed a little harsh, but drastic times called for drastic measures.

Placing a slender leg on either side of the man who was lying on the floor beneath her, Kat leant forward and carefully emptied a jug of ice cold water over his head. Coughing and spluttering, Henry finally came to his senses.

At last Kat had got his attention.

After saying goodbye to Jameela and dropping her a discreet distance from FBI headquarters, Kat had made for the freeway. It was a few hours' drive to the Institute for Advanced Studies in Princeton and this gave her plenty of time to collect her thoughts. She needed to work out exactly what questions she wanted Henry to answer for her, which was going to be a tough call. There were just so many tangled unknowns in her head.

As if to emphasize this point, one of her hands drifted subconsciously to her absent pulse.

The Institute for Advanced Studies had been established in the 1930s and was the first such place of its kind in the world. It was an inspired idea: to create a secluded campus where the finest minds on the planet could meet and chat without interference. The place was a hotbed of creativity and networking, and over the years it had spawned many fruitful collaborations and successful theories. Einstein himself had been one of the first great intellects to spend time in the relaxed and manicured campus grounds. It was a 'zoo for geniuses' as Kat had once dubbed it because of its brilliant and exclusive clientele.

Admittance to this hallowed club was based purely on intellectual prowess, backed up by a rigorous selection process. If you were brilliant enough—and lucky—you might just be invited to stay for a year's sabbatical. For Henry Fox, one of the genius-calibre chosen few, the place was heaven and he had taken to it like the proverbial duck to water.

Henry had been a colleague of Kat's and they had grown up together, living a few streets apart and attending the same high school. He was the consummate nerd and Kat was certain he wouldn't have changed. Tall, geeky, and bespectacled, he had had absolutely no sense of fashion whatsoever. You could expect to find him dressed in corduroy flares, a lilac shirt, and a striped knitted tank top or any other such tasteless combination. He tended to faint at the slightest provocation, and while an acne-infested teenager he continually took iron supplements for anaemia.

Kat and Henry hadn't been close at school, though they used to sit together in physics. She had flirted with him to get help with her homework but that was about it. Kat was an A-list hottie, a prom queen contender, while Henry was a Z-list nobody. He was the sort of boy who only made headlines for winning academic prizes, chess tournaments, and acne. It would have been social suicide for Kat to be seen mixing with him or any of his friends.

Kat now rather wished she had got to know him better when they were younger. Like so many of the nerds pretty girls write off, he had been really good fun to talk to and had a wonderfully dry sense of humour. She did remember him well enough, however, to know that he was driven by one thing, a simple obsession: before Henry died, he wanted to know 'the meaning of life, the universe, and everything,' to quote from a Monty Python film that was one of his favourites.

When Henry finally came around from his faint, Kat helped him over to the settee and then made them both a mug of sweet tea. He really did look as white as a sheet.

She was touched that he had been to her funeral and she shed a few tears when he told her about her parents. Memories that seemed so distant suddenly came flooding back, and Kat struggled with the impulsive urge to race home screaming, 'I'm alive!' before throwing herself into the sobbing arms of her parents.

That, however, could never be. She could never visit them; it would be a fatal mistake. Odin had made her swear on oath never to do it, not just for her sake but for theirs. It was a taboo for the warriors: never visit family or friends. Never, ever, ever.

It was therefore kind of ironic that Kat was breaking this sacred rule on her first trip by visiting Henry. Still, she had her reasons and they were good ones.

As they sipped their tea, Kat poured her heart out, sparing him nothing. She began at the moment when Jess first bumped into her and she ended with her description as to how she'd got lost using the Sat Nav on her way to meeting him that morning. By the time she had finished, well over an hour had passed and lunch was seriously overdue.

Henry listened intently, making a few hasty notes as she spoke. He hardly interrupted, asking questions only when he needed clarification on technical points which she did her best to help him with.

When she had finally finished, he stood up, stretched, and walked over to a wipe board. Scribbling frantically, he covered the board with strange, elegant, post-graduate mathematical symbols. Some of these he would circle; with some he made grand, sweeping links to others; while yet others he would cross out with a staccatoed 'tut' of annoyance. It all looked terribly impressive, but Kat didn't have a clue as to what the symbols meant.

Eventually, Henry turned around and gave her one of those heart-warming, boyish grins she had loved so much back at school. He hadn't changed.

"You know, Kat, you really are an excellent storyteller," he began, grinning cheekily, "but a lousy scientist. You are asking all the wrong questions. Instead of asking how, you really should be asking why."

Kat looked surprised. Henry had shot her down in flames. She felt mortified.

"Don't worry," he laughed, reading her expression as he held out his hand. "What we need is to go shopping for a sandwich or something. We also need to buy a nice loaf of sliced bread," he paused, "and a roll of grease-proof paper."

Kat took his hand and stood up. It was all too clear now. Henry had lost his marbles.

Sliced bread, grease-proof paper—what in Odin's name was the idiot-genius on about?

Jameela needn't have bothered turning up to work at the J. Edgar Hoover Building. And she really shouldn't have unpacked her pencil, pad, and other secretarial bits at the impressive workstation they'd arranged for her. Instead, she should have walked straight over to the reception desk and held her wrists out to be hand-cuffed.

She was a marked criminal even before she entered the building.

Her name, Jameela, had triggered Woods' computer the moment her employment details were registered. Regardless of surname, Jameela was a name linked as a Valkyrie alias and Woods began investigating immediately.

The Valkyries must have thought he was daft not to recognise her empty paperwork for what it was. Just like police officer Jessica O'Brien, it was all in order but flat and two dimensional. Scratch just that little bit deeper and it was instantly apparent that the person the forms related to had to be a fake. By midmorning, Woods was certain that the beautiful new Indian secretary was the same Jameela who had evaded the soldiers in Afghanistan. He studied her curiously on the CCTV. *Surely she must know that he would recognise her?*

This had to be a game of bluff and double bluff, but he couldn't quite fathom out what to do next. If he arrested her, would he be playing into her hands? Or were the Valkyries really that naïve and stupid?

Eventually, when her movements suggested that she was going on her lunch break, Woods sprang into action. Throwing caution to the wind, he made his way to the secretarial pool and with two burly agents in tow he took her into custody. She didn't resist and, unfortunately, the look in her eyes told him that he had done exactly what she'd expected him to do.

Damn it! he thought irritably as he checked the contents of her handbag. *What games were they playing with him now?*

Initial dismay turned quickly to exultation as his cursory rummage through her belongings revealed the flask of mead and a battered leather purse. If the Valkyries were calling his bluff, they hadn't done a very good job of it.

The mead, the purse, and the gold coin all seemed genuine, unlike the shoddy imitations he had recovered from Jess's bag. Clearly, Jess and Marcus had had time to hide her original items and Woods had already arranged a follow-up raid to turn his flat upside down. He might even arrest Marcus if that was what it took to get what he was after.

One way or another, he would have his artifacts as well as the Valkyrie women. He had waited ten years for this moment of triumph, and he wasn't going to be denied.

When he phoned the Contessa again, she would have no choice but to answer his call. She had promised to reward him if he delivered and she would damn well have to honour that agreement now. If what they believed to be the truth behind these extraordinary women was correct, then their reward would be truly exceptional.

Success would give them the ultimate prize—the Holy Grail—for the chosen few.

Henry spent some time proudly setting up his little demonstration.

After they returned from lunch, he carefully opened the loaf of sliced bread and then took a while placing pieces of grease-proof paper between each slice. He built a small stack of these on the coffee table.

Kat was convinced he was crazy—and he seemed to be just about ready to let her into his tiny little world of insanity.

"Now, Kat, it's my turn to talk," he began confidently. "Like I said, you need to start asking the question Why rather than What or How. Hopefully, I can explain some of the What or How questions which you have raised, but I must admit I'm no expert. There is one thing you are definitely right about: Odin and the other gods are from a highly advanced civilization, a race millennia ahead of our own. I can make educated guesses at some of their marvels, but as to the details—it's a bit like asking a monkey to explain the workings of a motor car. It's way beyond my comprehension."

He paused, and Kat indicated for him to go on. *So far, so good.*

"Part of what you have said about Mimir's well is correct but part probably isn't. If Asgard is indeed in a parallel universe, then a wormhole might not be able to connect our universe to it. Wormholes will connect different places within the same universe but not two different universes. Each has different physics. It is like these slices of bread here. Imagine each one is a separate universe. We are here on Earth in this one."

He paused, and buttered one side of a slice of bread to make his point.

"Your friends in Asgard are on this other piece of bread here," he explained as he proceeded to spread jam on that slice.

Kat was impressed, and so far she was keeping up. She was the butter and Odin was the jam—easy!

With an impressive 'slop,' Henry squashed the two slices of bread together, making sure a piece of grease-proof paper lay between the butter and jam. He began to rub them against each other, smearing the paper as he did so.

"You see, the two universes could be so close together that we could almost reach out and touch each other. But because each has different physics—the butter and the jam—the two can never meet."

He carefully separated the two slices of bread and held up the grease-proof paper. He was right: one side of the paper was coated with jam and the other with butter, but there was no mixing.

"What Odin has done, and this really is the fantastic bit," he continued excitedly as he picked up a small pin he had strategically placed on the coffee table, "is to create a connection."

Carefully he made a small pin prick in the grease-proof paper before placing it once more between the two slices of bread.

"Wow!" Kat almost purred her appreciation of Henry's genius. "Did you just think that up yourself?" She was truly impressed.

"No, no. I—I didn't, unfortunately," Henry blushed, ruing the fact that he couldn't take the credit. "It's called M Theory, one of the latest variations in string theory. It helps explain our universe by making the assumption that it is just one of countless, infinite, random universes—like the slices of bread in this stack."

"How has he made this connection?" This seemed a logical question to Kat.

"I don't really know. The power source may be a black hole as you suggested, but it could be a monopole, a super string, or some other even more exotic creation. What I can say with absolute certainty— and this is the really, really exciting bit—" he paused, enjoying a spot of showmanship, "is that there absolutely has to be another well here on Earth for this connection to work."

Kat looked up in astonishment. *Why hadn't she thought of that?* It seemed so obvious now that he had said it, but she would never have thought of it, never in a million years. "How can you be so sure?" she asked hurriedly.

"Coding and decoding. The only things that can travel from one universe to another are gravitons. These are tiny, theoretical particles that transmit the force of gravity. Everything else, even light itself, is trapped in just one universe. Just like the butter and the jam are stuck to their particular slices of bread, light too is stuck and can never leave. Mimir's well not only turns your body into the pure energy of light, it then converts it into a graviton wave and beams this out from

Odin's universe. You have to have another machine somewhere else to reverse this process—to receive the graviton wave, convert it back into energy, and then condense that energy back into matter."

Kat was impressed. Henry's proposed method of travelling between universes was even better than the *Star Trek*-style transporter she had imagined. She had travelled as a wave of gravity, something which sounded extremely posh and way cleverer.

"But there's another thing, and this is really important," Henry continued. Kat looked up expectantly. "There is an imbalance between the wells," he added.

"How can you be so sure?" Kat enquired, looking bemused.

"Because of the tremors you feel when both wells are open. I don't believe either of the wells is unstable as you originally thought, Kat, because you don't experience tremors when only the Asgard well is being used. It's only when someone travels between the two universes that tremors occur and there can be only one possible explanation for that. One of the wells has to be stronger than the other and it's trying the suck the other into it. This is why the wells are never opened more than a few millimetres—the destructive forces would be too great."

"What would happen if you opened one of the wells right up?" Kat wasn't sure if he could answer that question, but she hoped he could.

"That's actually quite easy. The weaker of the two wells would implode, the opposite of an explosion. It would suck in everything close to it and then disappear—poof—in a relatively small bang." Henry waved his arms in the air at this point, pretending that he was a magician making something disappear in a cloud of smoke.

"Is that it? A poof, a small explosion, and nothing more?" Kat was dubious. There had to be a catch somewhere; there was always a catch.

"Not quite." Henry began, confirming her suspicions. "Unfortunately, what would happen at the other end of the connection is a lot more serious. What implodes in at one end must explode out the other. The resulting sudden release of incompatible matter would cause a cataclysmic explosion, quite possibly destroying the other universe in a big bang."

Kat sat bolt upright. Her secret daydream that one day she might be able to shut down the connection between Asgard and Midgard had taken a decidedly nasty turn for the worse.

"I'm afraid, dear Kat, you won't be able to have your cake and eat it." Henry had read her thoughts.

"If you want to shut down the connection between the two worlds, you will have to choose carefully. The end you close will suffer little harm, but the other end will be completely destroyed. At some point you will have to decide either to save Earth, or to save Asgard. You won't be able to save both. One will survive and one will be completely destroyed. I'm afraid it's as simple as that."

Kat got up and took in a deep breath. The cup of tea they had drunk earlier now seemed a little inadequate. "Do you have any brandy?" she asked breathlessly, feeling more than a little overwhelmed.

Henry nodded as he pointed toward his small drinks cabinet.

"I think we're both going to need this."

25

A Poisoned Chalice

T he kiss was soft and moist, and the lipstick sticky and fragrant, as firm lips lingered tenderly for a while and then parted slowly from his. Her breath smelt sweet and warm upon his cheek and her strong perfume screamed with the invitation of sex, sex, sex.

Fucking hell! Cole awoke from his slumber with a fright.

It was indeed Hel who had just kissed him and he jolted hard from the shock of her unexpected visit. Opening his eyes, he could see that yet again she was naked. Hel, it seemed, was completely at ease wandering around her royal quarters, the reception room, and her harem dressed only in her birthday suit.

Still, with a perfect body like hers, Cole couldn't exactly blame her. She was drop dead gorgeous, and didn't she just know it.

"You really were a very naughty girl in my playroom, weren't you Colleen, don't you think?" Hel frowned sombrely as he nodded slowly in agreement.

Fuck! He was for it now.

"I really should be very, very angry with you, shouldn't I?" she continued ominously. "In fact, I really should punish you most horribly, shouldn't I...," Hel paused for added dramatic effect, "...Colleen?"

Cole nodded even more slowly this time. Oh dear, this was it, the moment he had expected. Farewell to his manhood—or worse.

"But look." Hel stood up abruptly. "Look at me—I'm not going to punish you! In fact, I've decided instead to be generous and kind and loving and forgiving. I've even brought you a lovely, lovely, little present. Look."

Cole glanced anxiously over at the table beside his bed. True enough: a glossy black box, about the size of an ordinary shoe box, sat upon it. The present was beautifully wrapped, complete with a red ribbon tied at the top in a flamboyant bow.

"Now, Colleen," Hel began as she sat down beside him once more, letting her fingers drift lazily toward his groin. Finding his manhood, she started to stroke it teasingly, encouraging a firmness he really wished he wasn't getting. "I can be nice and I really want to be ever so nice to you."

Hel ran her tongue suggestively down his stomach before taking his manhood gently in her mouth. Slowly, she swallowed him down to the hilt, choking as she did so. He really was fabulously endowed, right up there with the biggest of her girls.

Cole clenched his teeth as he grasped the sides of the bed, knuckles bleaching white as he did so. *Dear god!* he begged, *don't bite!*

Hel didn't; she was enjoying herself far too much. Rhythmically she worked at his manhood, moving him back and forward in her mouth, coaxing his passion with every stroke. Eventually, when she felt his breathing change and his groin beginning to move in strengthening jerks, she released him and looked up.

She had judged the moment to perfection, taking him to the point of no return and then leaving him high and dry. Like a ship stranded on a sand bank, all he needed was one more push to set him free.

"You see, Colleen, if you accept my little gift and come to me with it…," she smiled that devilish, mischievous smile once more, her eyes flashing red with the wickedness in her mind, "…I can give you so much more."

Moving her lips back to his manhood, she planted the tiniest and most tantalising of kisses on its begging tip. "I might even…," she ran her tongue delicately around the rim of his firmness before tugging hard with her hand one last time, "…finish you off."

She paused, clenching his strength firmly in her grasp for a moment longer. Letting go, Hel suddenly stood up. Their encounter was over.

"Until then, you will just have to use your imagination—and your hands."

Cackling loudly, she strutted toward the door. Turning as she opened it, she paused for one last quip. "Do let Ganglati know when you have come to your decision. Oh, and Colleen," she smirked horribly, "tick-tock." Hel waggled her finger mischievously from side to side like a musician's metronome. "Don't make me wait too long. I can get so frightfully bored."

With the tiniest wave of her fingertips, she blew him a kiss before departing. He could hear her crowing wildly as she skipped away down the corridor. *What had that crazy, fucked up little minx in mind for him now?*

"Damn you!" Cole shouted, angrily slamming his fists frustratedly into the mattress beneath him. No woman had ever left him like this before, ever.

He got up, furious that his manhood was standing proud and erect and begging for his attention. He wasn't going to play with himself, not for her, not for anybody.

Cole looked nervously over to the box by the bed. He knew he had to open it, curiosity killing the cat and all that crap. Sitting back down, he cautiously untied the ribbon. This was it, his moment of truth.

Pausing, he deliberated for a moment longer and then took the plunge. In one rapid movement he ripped the lid off.

Jesus Christ! The fucking bitch!

Cole recognised Hel's present immediately and knew exactly what she had in mind. He was broadminded, very broadminded, but he wasn't ready for that kinky gift, not by a long shot.

"Oh, shit!" he exhaled loudly, falling backwards onto his bed. He wished he knew what she had in mind when he turned her 'lovely' gift down.

26

The Question Why

Kat put her foot down on her way back to Washington. As she drove she tried to phone Jameela to let her know that she was going to be late. There was no reply. This annoyed her slightly, and made her more than a little concerned as well.

She had stayed far longer with Henry than she had intended to. His shocking revelation about the well had dwarfed everything they discussed afterwards. He could of course be wrong, but what he said felt right intuitively.

There simply had to be two wells. One was in Asgard and the other here, with the tremors only occurring when someone travelled to or from Midgard. When the gods used their rings in Asgard there was never a problem, no juddering or shaking. They must only be using the well there.

At first hearing, what Henry had said next sounded easy.

Open both wells, then open one a little bit wider, and 'poof'—to use his own words—problem solved. Both wells would be destroyed. Except, of course, they weren't. She didn't have a clue how to operate either one of them and had absolutely no idea where in Midgard the second well could be located. It might look identical to the first, or be disguised as something completely different. Finding it would be like looking for a needle in a haystack—or several haystacks, come to think of it.

Her head was beginning to ache as she struggled with this nightmare so she tried to sort through the many other fascinating suggestions Henry had come up with instead. He really was a genius. She just wished she'd brought a pen and paper and taken some notes.

Why had Jess bumped into her?

Henry had pointed out that she might have deliberately delayed Kat so she would stumble across Mickey in that fateful alleyway. Kat had always thought Jess had tried to prevent the encounter; but what if the reverse were true? *Where did that leave her and Jess?* This thought upset her more than she could bear so she moved quickly on to other questions he'd raised.

Why did Odin choose his Valkyries from Midgard?

Kat thought she knew the answer to this one and had proudly recited the tale of Billing's daughter. Unfortunately, this hadn't cut any ice with Henry. It was a carefully contrived fairytale, nothing more. His proposal was much more plausible: Odin was gathering intelligence about Earth.

The facts seemed to fit this notion. When she first arrived in Asgard, Odin had spent many long hours asking her all manner of questions. He also visited Midgard frequently, as did Frigg. If he were indeed gathering information, this led to another awkward question: why?

Why was Odin so interested in Midgard?

There seemed no obvious answer to this and they both drew a blank. Another question also had them stumped, too.

Why was Odin still recruiting heroes from Midgard?

This made no sense to Henry. Modern soldiers were trained to fight modern wars with modern weapons. Odin's army in Valhalla was destined to fight Ragnarok in Asgard. This would be a medieval battle fought with medieval weapons. It made far more sense for Odin to recruit or train heroes from Asgard rather than taking them from Midgard now. Again, there was no easy answer.

Why was Odin so strict about Valkyries not visiting Valhalla?

This was an absolute rule, but one that defied logic. What harm would a weekend trip do now and again? When Henry put it like that, Kat had struggled to come up with a sensible reason as to why not.

The answer to this and so many other questions always seemed to end in Valhalla. Henry suggested that if she could get a peek into that realm she would probably find many answers. Kat knew this was a possibility. She could use and abuse Hod again.

She thought of him briefly. In his own peculiar way he was very like Henry—an Asgard geek. They seemed to be attracted to her like moths to a flame. She liked Henry, but not in the same way that he was so obviously infatuated with her. Time and again during the after-noon she would deliberately excuse herself to make a cup of tea or use the toilet. After each occasion, as soon as she sat back down on the sofa Henry would cosy up nice and close to her again. It was awk-ward, but Kat was determined not to give him the wrong signals as she had for Hod.

One infatuated geek in either universe was more than enough.

At one point much later in the afternoon, Henry managed to make her angry. It was when they got on to the topic of her Valkyrie knife, which to his jaw-dropping astonishment (and gratitude) she let him hold.

Henry was absolutely, unshakable certain that she wasn't the same Kat as the girl he had grown up with at school. Yes, she had the same looks, the same thoughts, and the same memories, but she wasn't the self-same flesh and blood. He had attended the funeral where the body of the original Kat had been cremated, so she simply couldn't be.

At that point she felt like showing him some of her warrior skills by punching him in the face. *How dare he suggest she wasn't Dr. Katarina Neal?*

Unfortunately, as she listened to his reasons, his argument pre-sented an unpleasant and disturbing truth.

All that her Valkyrie knife needed to recreate a perfect copy of Dr. Katarina Neal was a sample of her DNA, her memories, and the wir-ing map of her brain. The knife could sample blood when it stabbed her body and the warmth in the handle could be the heat from a com-puter chip as it learned the wiring pattern of the cells inside her head. Henry hadn't a clue as to how it accessed the memories, but then he wasn't from the same advanced civilization as Odin.

Send all this information through the wells to Asgard, mix them up with a bit of energy—shaken, not stirred—and abracadabra: a physi-cal copy of Kat comes out the other end of the Rainbow Bridge. An exact replica, perfect in every detail right up to the moment of the original Dr. Neal's death.

Once Henry came up with this idea, he wandered off on a tangent for a while, speculating wildly about the possibility of making other copies of Kat or her having endless deaths and reincarnations. It was all possible, but Kat really didn't want to know what Henry might do with his own personal, perfectly formed clone. That was way too much information and besides, there had been other important ques-tions that still needed answering.

Why didn't she have a pulse and yet she ate, breathed, and felt warm to the touch?

As a former doctor she felt she should have worked this one out already. Once again, however, it was Henry's lateral thinking that came up with an elegant solution. The answer lay in the mead the Valkyries drank.

Henry's solution was as ingenious as it was intriguing. Something in the mead altered their body metabolism. This was definitely true; they recovered far more rapidly from injuries and didn't age. However, he speculated, what if it did more?

What if it freed the cells of the body from their need for oxygen?

Remove this requirement and the heart served no useful purpose. At first it seemed like a crazy notion until Henry reminded her that insects didn't have hearts or circulatory systems. If the gods could create beams of gravitons that blasted her from one universe to another, then they would hardly break a sweat designing a drug that messed around with her metabolism.

Kat was very impressed by Henry's ideas. It reminded her of her concerns when she was in the forest with Hod back in Asgard—her fear that Odin used the mead to control them. It might even alter their minds, accounting for changes that went far beyond the bloodlust the warriors experienced. This chain of thought left one idea hanging tantalisingly in the air.

What if she stopped drinking the mead? Would she feel different? And, more importantly, *Would her heart restart?*

She wished she had the nerve to try it out, but her current mission was too important to risk an experiment right now.

Downing one last mug of tea and scoffing one last delicious chocolate biscuit, she said her goodbyes to Henry, kissing him on the cheek and holding him close for a while. They were friends, and for once she didn't mind his hands sliding down her slender waist, past her thick, leather belt and clutching at her denim-clad behind. He was so like Hod she could cry—hopelessly unskilled in the art of subtle seduction.

She would forgive his fumblings just this once. He was a sweet guy and a bit of an old woman, too, insisting that she call him when she arrived safely back in Washington.

RING-RING, RING-RING

The sound of her mobile phone jolted Kat back to the freeway and away from her thoughts. To her great surprise, the caller was Frigg who was also in a car and driving.

"Beverly Hills, darling—you simply must find the time to come shopping with me," Frigg purred in her delightfully chatty and aristocratic way.

To Kat's surprise, Frigg was very interested in exactly where she was in Midgard—most insistent, actually. Observing another one of Odin's rules, Kat deliberately kept her location as vague as possible. When pressed for an answer she lied, stating that she was in New York and had just nipped out to buy some groceries. This was a sensible precaution. It was never wise to say too much about what you were doing, just in case.

Frigg hung up after some other small talk and Kat tried Jameela's number once again. It was after six in the evening and still no reply. Surely she must have finished work by now? *Where in Midgard was she?*

Barely had she hung up than her phone rang again. It was like a telephone exchange that night. She could tell from the display that the caller was Jess, and with scarcely containable excitement she pressed the answer button. She felt like singing for joy in spite of Henry's concerns.

Kat missed her friend, her lover, and her sister so very, very much.

"Sangrid, is that you?"

To her shock, the voice on the line was that of a man and someone she didn't recognise. It sounded as though he was outdoors, breathless, and more than a little flustered.

"Sangrid, it's me, Marcus Finch, Brynhildr's friend. She's been captured, but that isn't why I'm calling you. Fran knows all about that and she's taking care of it." Marcus paused to catch his breath.

Who in Odin's name was Fran? The thought spun crazily through Kat's mind, but Marcus didn't give her time to ask any questions. He was in way too much of a hurry. "You have to come and help me right away. Someone is trying to kill me."

Kat slammed on the brakes and pulled over. Her plans had changed. Jess was captured, Jameela wasn't answering her phone (and was quite probably captured as well), and the hero Jess had been sent to rescue was fighting for his life. Suddenly she was no longer the tour guide—she was the only one left on the job.

Scribbling down a few quick notes, she drew up a hasty plan. Washington was no longer her destination; she had to get to New York, her primary goal being now all too obvious.

She had to save Marcus.

27

A Private Celebration

*I*t was in the dead of the night when Balder and Silk finally made love. Their passion was driven by happiness, a desire to share in the joy of a very private victory. They did this secretively, long after the battle was over, the sun had set, and the other warriors had wined and dined and gone to bed.

Their lustful union was the only celebration to take place after the bloody day of fighting.

Balder had fought like a tiger, holding the Bifrost Bridge with Tyr and Heimdall until all the exhausted warriors had returned to safety. He had fought without regard for his life and emerged unscathed. The dream that had foretold his death seemed conquered, its curse broken, and he felt reborn at last. His destiny had been rewritten.

Silk shared his triumphant mood and desperately wanted to reward his success. Unfortunately, with so many warriors, gods, and maids staying at the watchtower, privacy was at a premium. There were separate dormitories for the men, the warriors, and the maids, but no rooms to spare for couples.

Intimacy required ingenuity.

With mounting excitement in their hearts, they climbed the spiral staircase to the rooftop and persuaded Heimdall that a warming horn of mead was what he needed to stave off the chill of the autumn air. At first he was reluctant to leave his post, but after assurances that they would keep a good eye out for trouble, he went downstairs. It seemed an odd request to make of him, but he wasn't going to refuse the favourite son of Odin.

Heimdall was an unusual god because he never slept. That was why he had been chosen as the guardian of the watchtower. He was lean and tall, with the eyesight of an eagle and the hearing of a bat. His other distinctive feature was that all his teeth had been crowned in gold. The reason for this was unknown, and would probably remain so because he wasn't one for gossiping or small talk. He was a retiring man by nature, and found the company of so many gods and warriors overwhelming. Night-time was his time, the time when he could relax and enjoy the solitude of his own company.

After watching him descend out of sight, Balder and Silk gazed out across the glacier that was now hidden from view in the inky darkness of a moonless night.

Standing close together, Balder behind Silk, they pressed themselves tightly against the stone parapet which encircled the top of the watchtower. Balder caressed her neck as Silk ran her hands lustfully through his hair and then down the sides of his body. It would have taken a keen eye to notice that Silk's warrior skirt had become upturned and that the top of Balder's trousers were unbuttoned.

Swaying gently together, their bodies were coupled tightly as one.

Furtive, tentative thrusts of hips swiftly gave way to faster, more powerful jerks with Balder holding Silk firmly against his groin. Spurred on by the cold and the seductive allure of discovery, they raced with ever longer, deeper movements toward their final, triumphant caress. When this at last came, they shared the warmth and tightness of their embrace with Silk locking him there, his thickness buried deep inside her belly. Together they savoured their passion until Balder eventually lost his strength.

When Heimdall finally returned, they bid him good night with unusually warm and contented smiles. Their celebration had ended just in time.

Dawn broke to squalls of icy rain that beat viciously against the watchtower, driven in their ferocity by gales that billowed down from the jagged peaks of Jotunheim. Unfortunately, the unpleasant weather hadn't dampened the spirits of their enemy.

At first light, the giants repaired the broken section of the bridge and a raiding party of four heavily-armed fellows crept across the glacier in an attempt to establish a bridge head. Goll and Alex were on duty and they returned heavily spattered in blood. They were both in an exuberant mood.

The giants had fought ferociously but were no match for the two beautiful and powerful Valkyries. The women's bravery and skill was too great and they had killed all four intruders, dismembering their fallen bodies when the fight was finally done. Decapitating each in turn, they piled the headless corpses onto the bridge as a barricade before skewering the severed heads with the giants' own spears. They had then planted these upright in the ground.

It was a horrific message—a grisly warning against others foolish enough to chance their hand. Asgard belonged to the Valkyries.

The warriors' actions were gruesome, but they had to be. With such a large and aggressive army pitted against them, anything less would have been seen as weakness. For the moment, the giants feared and respected the might of the Valkyries. This brutal slaughter and aftermath would reaffirm their fears. No further raiding parties followed.

Changing their tactics, the giants decided to turn to another, more industrious, invasion strategy. Throughout the day the girls could hear the sound of heavy axes chopping at wood, the crack of splintering trunks, and the reverberating thuds of monstrous trees as they fell crashing to the ground.

With the colder weather, the icy spurs of the glacier were becoming stronger and more stable. The giants had decided to build a new, stronger, and wider bridge across the treacherous chasms. It would take many days, but eventually the giants would succeed in building a massive highway, one strong enough to bear the weight of their mighty force.

The need for a plan to recover Thor's hammer was becoming more urgent by the hour. Mjollnir was the only thing that could thwart the giants, and it lay in the hands of Thrym who was safe and secure in his hall in Utgard with his giant army blocking the only route to his stronghold.

At first sight, the task to recover the hammer seemed impossible, but throughout the morning a series of clandestine meetings took place in and around the stable block, with Carmel taking the lead. She had an idea, and discussions were held with those who might be able to assist in her audacious plan.

Freyja, the first to be consulted, nodded and shook her head politely. Carmel's plan seemed crazy, but it might just work. Even if it didn't, it was the only proposal on the table so they would have to chance it. Prima was dispatched to fly with great urgency back to Asgard. There were items which Carmel needed and Prima had to return to the tower before nightfall.

Finally, with preparations underway, Thor was consulted. He listened intently, raising his eyebrows and studying Carmel's face incredulously at one point. He shook his head slowly before tugging at his beard, and then with a final guffaw he slapped her heartily on the back.

"If you say you must then you must," he chuckled loudly as he reluctantly agreed to this particular part of her plan. To be truthful, he was feeling in no mood to argue. The large fragment of stone embedded in his forehead was stuck fast and making his head hurt. Heimdall had sent for a local soothsayer, Groa, who tried for several hours to charm the jagged lump from his brow. She chanted and rubbed potions around the block but all to no avail. Growing bored of her attentions and her failure, Thor stomped off irritably to the foundry next to the stables.

For the next several hours he banged and hammered at molten lumps of iron he withdrew from the furnace. He was hard at work, concentrating on building something to Carmel's instructions. She popped in frequently, encouraging him when he got things right and scolding him soundly when others were wrong. She knew what she wanted and wouldn't accept anything less, not even from him. Carmel made for a tough and unforgiving mistress, but Thor didn't mind. He felt at home in the forge and her bossing helped him forget his pounding headache.

To their delight, Prima returned shortly before nightfall, sooner than expected. She had flown to Asgard and managed to obtain everything that Carmel had requested, and without rest had returned at the gallop on the fastest horse remaining in the castle stables. Prima was exhausted, but her endeavours were greatly appreciated.

Armed with the items and veiled by a shroud of secrecy, Thor, Carmel, Silk, and Freyja vanished into a thicket of trees not far from the tower. Although they were concealed from view, the frequent outbursts of laughter which drifted toward the watchtower suggested that at least this part of the plan was lightening the sombre mood.

As the sun began to set and an even thicker band of clouds descended from the mountains, the little group of conspirators emerged cheerfully from the cover of the trees. Carmel was in particularly high spirits. The only thing better than a good plan coming together was when that plan happened to be hers.

Freyja had decided to set her scheme in motion and the moonless sky above was just what she needed.

28

Bored

Hod sat quietly at one of the many empty tables in the great feasting hall of the castle. Before him, sitting on the table, was an empty pewter flagon.

Feeling for the handle, he casually twirled it with his hands, listening and counting slowly as the flagon spun round and round on its rim. Finally it came to rest. He had lost track of how many times he had done this, but his longest spin, he guessed, had lasted about twenty-five seconds. He was horribly fed up, and the sound of the spinning flagon echoed drearily around the deserted hall.

The castle was empty and he was bored out of his head.

Hod had returned from Valhalla at the same time his mother had headed off to Midgard on one of her many shopping trips. He'd just missed Kat's departure and this hurt him deeply. He'd been so looking forward to seeing her, spending some intimate time together, building on the fragile hope that love could blossom from their budding friendship.

Their solitary night of passion had been magical for him. Yes, of course he knew that Kat had been drunk, but the pleasure he'd given her was real—he'd felt it as she writhed uncontrollably beneath his kisses. Those wonderfully sweet moans of satisfaction were genuine, not faked. Her warmth, too, at his mother's tea party, the suggestive squeeze of his bottom, and the tone of her voice left him in no doubt now that her heart was slowly melting. She could love him—and she would love him—if they only had the chance.

Damn! Why had he let his mother talk him into staying on in Valhalla? He was such an idiot.

"Hello!" Hod called out frustratedly, but only empty echoes returned.

Everyone was at the watchtower, leaving only him and Ruby in charge of the castle. Ruby was desperately busy maintaining discipline amongst the arena prisoners, and when she wasn't at work she made for sullen and atrocious company. She hated being left behind and was like a boar with a sore head, snapping viciously at him in a manner that was quite terrifying.

Hod felt useless, a complete waste of space. Without sight, he knew he would be a hindrance if he followed the Valkyries to the watchtower. They would welcome him and be kind to him but he would be a liability, a god requiring a nanny to watch over him. He felt so ashamed, reduced to needing a babysitter. He could hardly bear his misfortune.

"Hiya, Hoddy, my old mate!"

The doors to the hall swung open with a resounding thud, causing Hod to almost jump out of his skin.

"What a splendid day this is!"

The air was suddenly filled with the sound of Loki's voice, full of beans and cocky as ever. Pouring two fresh flagons of ale, Loki swaggered over to Hod's slumped figure and slapped him heartily on the back. He sat down.

"Pining for the fair Kat? Or should I say, lusting after the mighty warrior Sangrid?" he jibed. "By the way, where is that magnificent Valkyrie of yours, anyway?"

Hod blew Loki a loud raspberry; the trickster was deliberately poking fun at him and delighting in rubbing salt into his wounds. Loki knew only too well that his relationship with Kat was heavily one-sided, with Hod having to content himself with second or possibly third best when it came to her affections. Hod suffered his lowly status in silence, but to have Loki spell it out to him was not only hurtful but compounded his misery. He felt totally wretched.

"Why aren't you at the watchtower fighting with everybody else?" Hod enquired, changing the conversation.

"What, me?" Loki exclaimed with mock consternation in his voice. "And tell me, dear Hod, exactly which side would you like me to fight on, hey?"

Hod hadn't thought of that. With both Loki's parents being giants of royal descent and his heart lying here with Carmel, he really couldn't pick a side to fight on. If he did, the other side would feel betrayed and that betrayal wouldn't be easily forgiven.

"Why don't you come and join me in a spot of hunting?" Loki suggested.

"Durrr!" Hod scoffed sarcastically, pressing his finger to his lower lip. "In case you haven't noticed, I'm blind. Can't you see?" Lifting his tankard, he threw it angrily at Loki, who ducked and laughed as it clattered harmlessly against the wall behind him.

"Actually, that wasn't a bad shot," Loki conceded unexpectedly. "Look, why don't you let me be your eyes? I'll tell you where the deer or wild boar are and you can shoot them with your bow. I'll give you their location and range and you can do the rest. You were a fine archer once and could be again." Loki paused. He could see that Hod was listening.

"Trust me. We have plenty of time to practice and I'm sure you'll get pretty good. Don't you think it would impress the beautiful Sangrid on her return, hey? Definitely get you between her sheets—and her legs—I shouldn't wonder."

Hod lashed out a fist at Loki, missed, and then spun round, toppling as he did so.

"Hey, steady on there, Hoddy. You don't want to go hurting yourself, do you?" Loki chortled as he held out his arms to catch him. Hod struggled angrily for a few moments before giving up and sitting down.

Several flagons of mead and a few sarcastic exchanges later, Loki's crazy notion didn't seem quite as harebrained as it had first sounded. With nothing better to do, Hod decided to give it a go. Taking Loki's arm, the unlikely pair set out for the stables.

Whatever happened on their hunting expedition, it was going to be a damn sight more exciting than listening to a flagon spinning endlessly round and round.

Ruby was fed up, too.

She had just finished whipping her fourth prisoner of the day and was barely halfway round the cells. News of the troubles besetting Asgard travelled fast, as did the obvious absence of the warriors and maids. Without this constant reminder of their worthless state, the prisoners became uppity and disrespectful, usually toward the younger female serfs who gave them food and water. The prisoners were the lowest of the low, beneath even the lowliest serf or eunuch slave. They had to know their place and the current unrest wasn't helping this.

Ruby took her responsibilities seriously.

She resented being left at the castle, but as the last Valkyrie she would stay at her post—unlike the rebellious Gunnr and Balder who had already upped and gone. Her job was to keep order, and that was exactly what she would do even if she had to whip, castrate, or execute every last prisoner in the cells. If one of these was disrespectful he would be strung up and whipped until the person, usually a lowly female serf, felt satisfied. Second offences were rare, immediate castration being their fate.

It was a strange truth, but the younger and more insignificant the serf, the crueller the punishment they wanted administered. Some clearly revelled in it: their moment of glory, ogling as prisoners endured being whipped or emasculated at their behest.

Ruby didn't care. This was her job and she did it well. What annoyed her most was that these constant punishments were distracting her from her real duty—guarding the castle and the Chamber of the Valkyries. These were now vulnerable targets which their enemies could easily attack. She was determined that the treasures of Asgard wouldn't be stolen or ransacked on her watch. That would be unthinkable.

As she toured the castle grounds and the dank, miserable cells, Ruby's mind reflected restlessly on her past, a past that she usually kept deeply buried.

Elijah featured strongly in these contemplations. Other than Joe, he was the one man she had truly fallen for. *If only she could have prevented his death.* Saying a little prayer, she hoped that wherever he was, Elijah's soul was resting in peace. He deserved that at least.

Ruby's memories of Joe were more clouded. She could barely remember his handsome face anymore. They had grown up as slaves together in the early nineteenth century, the property of a colonial sugar plantation in the Caribbean. They had nothing, and even the fledgling love that sparked briefly between them had been viciously stubbed out.

She could remember Joe still, lying face down in a pool of blood, his back beaten into a bloody mess and his throat cut. It was all because he had dared to court her, dared to chance his luck with the pretty Negro slave who had caught the landowner's lustful eye. She had been whipped long and hard, too; the overseer had seen to that.

Then began a life filled with endless rapes and forced abortions. Her owner wanted her for sex, but not for their bastard, picaninny offspring. She had lost count of the number of times he had forced himself upon her, sometimes in private, and sometimes as sport to entertain his perverted guests. For a while the owner lived the life of a god, until Ruby reaped her terrible vengeance.

The memory of it still made her smile. It was because of it that she had been saved by Odin's Valkyries.

Ruby had led a rebellion, killing the owner and his overseer with her own bare hands, beating and strangling them before a rapturous audience of slaves. Her moment of triumph had been glorious but short-lived. Soldiers came and squashed their insignificant act of defiance and she'd been put to death shortly thereafter, hanged from the yardarm in old Kingston town.

Ruby shuddered violently at the memory of her death before turning her thoughts once more to Asgard. It was this need to find a true love which kept her from Valhalla. Until she felt complete, until she found the someone who would make her whole, she would remain a Valkyrie.

She sighed as she made her way toward the next depressing arena. If only things had worked out differently with Elijah. He could so easily have been the one.

Elijah could have been her salvation.

Hod and Loki arrived back at the castle just before dusk. They were in a jubilant mood and had hunted deep into the forests around the castle. Hod felt exhilarated riding behind Loki with the wind in his face, and stalking quietly through the undergrowth until the moment came for them to pounce. They hadn't caught anything, but they had come close, he was certain of that.

Dismounting together, they crossed the courtyard from the stables to the castle carrying some slender, green shoots between them. The stems of these saplings were slim and supple, with leaves sprouting in pairs and adorned with sticky, white berries at their base.

Loki believed that the longbow would prove too hard for Hod to master quickly, and had suggested he try using a shorter, stubbier crossbow. This was a weapon favoured by dwarves for close-range use. It seemed like a good idea and Hod was as keen as Loki to get inside and start fashioning some darts from the saplings they had collected.

Finding them had been hard work. They could have made it home a lot sooner, but Loki had been most insistent about the type of wood they collected for the darts. The wood had to come from one particular type of shrub, a plant that was as rare as it was unique; living its life high in the forest canopy feasting on the sap of mighty oak trees. They seemed to have wasted a lot of time searching until they found precisely what Loki was looking for.

Hod didn't mind. For the first time in weeks he was enjoying himself and not missing Kat.

With a horn brimming with mead, he whistled cheerily as he set to work whittling the shaft for his first new dart.

29

Blasts from the Past

Marcus hadn't slept well. The flat seemed empty and ghostly without Anna, and she hadn't called. The double bed was vast and cold, like an ice rink after the skaters had gone. He was glad when dawn eventually broke. Gulping down a hasty mug of coffee, he set off early to work. At least there his thoughts could be distracted from Anna, Anna, Anna.

The day passed well enough.

Marcus had a golden rule: never bring his troubles to work. It helped; although in this instance it felt as though hell itself had exploded inside his heart. By gritting his teeth and smiling politely through the agony, he carried on as if nothing had happened, immersing himself in discussing other peoples' petty problems and not his own. There was nothing more guaranteed to break his spirit than the constant niggling of 'Are you alright, honey?' or 'If there's anything I can do to help…'

By the time he finished at around five, Marcus left the station in a good humour. There was still no phone call from Anna, so he didn't need to hurry home. Changing his usual route, Marcus decided to head for a bar he had frequented as a bachelor. He fancied a drink and—*hey*—who was going to stop him? Temporarily single, he could get rat-arsed and nobody would give a damn.

It was while he was contemplating an evening of solitary entertainment that the attack happened. It caught him completely unawares.

Marcus had just bought a newspaper and was casually flipping through the pages when a flurry of sounds pattered eerily around him.

They were soft and gentle, a surreal 'phut-phut- phut' that tore through his paper, shattered concrete from the wall behind him, and punched a hole through a polystyrene cup filled with steaming coffee on the newsagent's stand.

It took Marcus an extraordinarily long time to make the connection that the sounds were shots fired from a gun with a silencer. As lights flickered on inside his head, Marcus looked around without any fear or sense of immediate danger. *Who on earth would be firing random shots here and at this time in the evening?*

There was no obvious bank or security guards with cash boxes around, so the bullets simply didn't make sense. He had almost convinced himself that the shattered cup and shredded paper were figments of his imagination, when he caught sight of the gunman. The shooter was sitting upright, riding pillion on a motorcycle, and his pistol was raised once more.

It was aimed directly at him.

Marcus hit the floor just in time and felt the shockwave of one of the bullets as it whistled millimetres from his ear. Crawling forward on his belly, he reached shelter behind the kiosk just as the third and final spray of bullets ricocheted off the pavement where he had first lain. It was a close call.

People around him began to notice what was going on and they started to scream and dive for cover as well. Miraculously, no one was hit. The whole incident seemed to last for hours, but in reality it was over in a matter of seconds.

The gunman didn't have time to let loose a fourth, fatal burst of bullets. A traffic cop had blown his whistle and was drawing his gun as he made his way at a half jog down the street toward the scene. Taking flight, the driver of the bike sped off, weaving frantically this way and that through the rush hour traffic.

Marcus stood up but he didn't get the license plate nor did he get at good look at the helmeted gunman, either. All he knew, and all he needed to know, was that he had been the intended target.

A crowd began to form as sirens wailed. Marcus should have stayed, taken charge, and secured the crime scene. Instead, he slunk away, carefully extracting himself as others vied for the spotlight. To a spectator it seemed a random, meaningless attack and he was happy for it to be reported as such. Marcus's name and the reason behind the attack were really unimportant, particularly as no one had been injured.

Picking up speed, Marcus hurried several blocks from the shooting. He began to shake uncontrollably. His assailant could double back and take another potshot at him, or there could be others waiting to finish him off.

Suddenly Jess's prophetic words, 'I'm here for you, Marcus,' took on a chillingly new and sinister meaning. His imminent death, such an improbability only a few days before, now seemed a certainty. The thought scared him, shocking him into an unreality: a world crowded with faceless gunmen hell-bent on his annihilation.

Panicking, he decided to call the one person who might just save him from his deathly predicament. A Valkyrie.

This was the moment when Marcus called Sangrid. His breathless, worried conversation that had her screaming to a halt before changing direction and heading toward him here in New York.

He was waiting for Sangrid now, in a busy restaurant that they had both agreed upon. She seemed to know this part of New York quite well, which came as a surprise to Marcus. Her name was that of a Valkyrie, but she had the definite twang of a native New Yorker. This observation was noteworthy but he hadn't dwelt on it, other matters being far more pressing.

After his frantic phone call he hadn't gone straight to the restaurant and waited. He walked about, keeping to busy streets and joining shoppers in the most crowded department stores. He decided not to return to his flat, and instead withdrew several hundred dollars from a cash point. Credit cards left a digital trail and it seemed like a good idea for him to vanish for a while.

As it turned out, this was an extremely wise move for Marcus.

Under the instruction of Woods, the FBI had ransacked his flat earlier in the day, gutting it completely. They had also posted plainclothed agents both there and on the streets surrounding it. Their intention was clear: to quietly pick him up when he returned home from work. Woods didn't want a drama. His work with the Valkyries needed to stay below the radar and not draw unwelcome police or media attention.

Marcus would be arrested discretely, with a message left at the police station that he was away on sudden and unexpected compassionate leave. There wouldn't be any fuss as Woods carefully tied up the loose ends.

Marcus had just taken his first, refreshing sip of chilled beer when the second shock of the evening happened. It was just after ten when

Kat eventually arrived at the restaurant and she didn't have a clue as to what 'Marcus Finch' might look like. Fortunately, she needn't have worried. Marcus knew exactly who she was the minute she stepped through the door. Her face was unforgettable, just as his ashen expression was becoming now.

Kat had no difficulty in spotting the single, handsome gentleman sitting alone at a table for two because he was the person who was very obviously beginning to sweat and turning a particularly ghastly shade of white.

Swaying slightly, Marcus quickly bent forward and put his head between his legs. He felt he was about to faint, but knew he mustn't. He couldn't afford to draw attention to himself.

"Hi, are you…," Kat hesitated, "…are you Marcus?"

His gaze was buried in the floor, but he could see the trainers and snug-fitting jeans of the beautiful woman now introducing himself.

"Yes, yes," he mumbled, trying to recover his composure. "You—you must be Sangrid."

Marcus slowly sat up. His eyes inched their way past the curves of her hips and her slender waist, and carried on past the 'I ♡ New York' T-shirt and upward toward her breast-length, sunstreaked, blond hair. Finally he looked at her face, a face he had last seen lying cold and grey on a mortuary slab.

The Valkyrie Sangrid was Dr. Katarina Neal, the woman whose murdered corpse had led him to the Valkyries all those months ago. The thought was shocking.

"Hey, I'm sorry—you don't look well, like you've seen a ghost or something." Kat sat down, taking his hand in hers. Her prophetic words prompted a weak smile from Marcus's lips. *If only she knew!*

This was definitely a day Marcus wasn't going to forget.

Introductions over, they ordered food and began to talk. Sangrid seemed very charming and ordinary, just as he had imagined her to be from the lifeless body he once examined. She preferred to be called Kat and Marcus felt it prudent not to tell her of their former meeting, the one she remembered nothing about. At first, he did most of the talking.

Kat was keen to learn all she could about Jess, Agent Woods, the FBI, and the artifacts they now had in their possession. She was delighted to learn of his clever idea to mail the genuine articles to himself. They should arrive at his private numbered box the next morning. It was a box he used to hide presents he bought for Anna—and his small stash of porn. They both agreed that they should find a cheap hotel somewhere close by and stay the night in New York. That way, they could pick up the packet tomorrow before heading off to Washington.

Kat was especially interested to hear about Fran, the person at the end of the Emergencies telephone number. It seemed bizarre that someone in Midgard would know all about the Valkyries and be there as a last-ditch backup should things go wrong. Odin had never mentioned such a person to her and she was sure he hadn't mentioned it to the others, either.

Intrigued, she dialled the Emergency number on her own phone and heard the same, lilting Caribbean receptionist enquire, "Hello, Dragza Corporation, how may I help you?" before she, too, hung up. Putting the phone down, Kat became excited. She pulled a credit card from her purse and thrust it knowingly under Marcus's nose.

Sure enough, there was that name again: O Dragza.

It was a name they both infuriatingly felt they ought to recognise, but couldn't quite place. This became their second resolution of the evening: to Google it tomorrow and see if that would help them piece together the connections between Fran, the Dragza Corporation, and Odin's Valkyries.

The link was there, right under their noses, but they just couldn't see it.

Neither Marcus nor Kat ate very much; food wasn't high on their agenda tonight. Meal finished, they split the bill and paid in cash. Standing up, Marcus chivalrously helped Kat put on her baseball jacket. Standing so close to him, Kat suddenly became aware of the attraction of 'a hero.'

It was exactly as the warriors had described: a dull ache in her chest, a sense of desire, and a need to be with him. For Kat the feeling wasn't quite sex; it was more like a deep, deep schoolgirl crush on the boy in the year above, the boy she would always fancy but who remained tantalisingly out of reach.

"Kat!"

She recognised the voice immediately and turned instinctively. Kat knew she shouldn't have done so, but the reflex was too strong. *Of all the restaurants and bars in New York, how in Odin's name could Suzy choose this one—tonight of all nights?*

Rooted to the spot, Kat stood there, unable to speak or think as to what to do next. It was a nightmare moment: the instant when you freeze and stare as your world comes crashing down around your head.

Suzy was shaken, too; terrified almost. She looked as if she was about to speak, but Marcus beat her to it.

"Hi. You're Suzy, right? We met once before, do you remember? I'm Detective Finch." Marcus held out his hand, but Suzy didn't shake it. She didn't look at him, either. All she could do was stare dumbstruck at the silent Kat, scrutinising every inch of her face in microscopic detail.

"We met when I was investigating the death of your friend, Dr. Neal. You must remember me, surely?" Marcus continued, desperately trying to drag her attention away from Kat.

At last it seemed to work. Suzy finally pulled her eyes away and nodded that she did indeed recognise him. She still didn't shake his outstretched hand.

"It is you, isn't it, Kat? It's you, Kat, I'm sure of it. Hey everybody, look! Look, it's Kat—she isn't dead. Look—IT'S KAT!"

Suzy's voice was raising excitedly and drawing attention from the people around them. Tables were falling silent as one by one the gossip-loving New Yorkers switched their attention to the activities at table seven, Marcus's table. He had to sort this out and quickly. He could see that Kat was paralysed, unable to think or even move.

"Oh, do forgive my rudeness. I haven't introduced you. Suzy, this is Sangrid. Sangrid, this is Suzy." Marcus nudged Kat forcefully, and with a mumbled "Yeah," she held out her hand and limply shook Suzy's.

Suzy didn't let go.

"Sangrid's my new au pair. Sangrid, er…Sangrid Asgard. She comes from Sweden and doesn't speak any English," Marcus continued, frantically trying to concoct a credible story on the fly.

Suzy craned her neck forward, screwing her eyes up tightly. She was searching desperately for any telltale moles or scars that might just give Marcus's explanation some plausibility.

There weren't any. This woman was Kat, not Sangrid. She was certain of it.

Marcus knew they had to get out of there fast and with a theatrical flourish of his arm he brandished his watch. "Christ! Is that the time already? We really should be going. It was lovely to meet you again, Suzy, and your friends, too. Do keep in touch."

Snatching Suzy's hand from Kat's, Marcus shook it firmly before speedily putting his arm around Kat's shoulders and hustling her urgently toward the door. With a final, hurried, overly exaggerated wave goodbye, he bundled her out into the street.

"Come on!" Hissing urgently, Marcus grabbed Kat's hand and towed her along behind him, dragging her swiftly away from the restaurant. They had gone at least fifty metres before Kat finally came around and could talk once more. Marcus understood her shock and he put a protective arm around her as they turned a corner.

Finally, the blast from her past disappeared from view.

"How do you know Suzy?" Kat began falteringly, her voice still trembling with the shock of their unnerving encounter.

"We met briefly, when I was investigating...," Marcus's voice trailed off. He didn't want to say the words that had to follow.

"Investigating my murder," Kat prompted, finishing his sentence for him. "You were the detective, weren't you? That's why you went so grey when you first saw me." Kat stopped as she pulled him round to face her. It was her turn now to look pale and drawn. "How did I look, you know, how did I look when I was...dead?"

Kat suddenly burst into tears and Marcus held her close, hugging her gently and stroking her hair. Her chest heaved as she sobbed quietly into his shoulder. There was no need for words; her question had been rhetorical.

Marcus held Kat for what seemed an age but was in reality only a few minutes. Snivelling when at last she pushed him away, she dried her eyes and wiped her nose with the tissue he offered.

"I need to make a few phone calls," Kat insisted as she pulled her phone from her pocket and urged Marcus to stay put while she moved out of earshot. She had forgotten to call Henry and she suddenly felt the need to talk to him again. His homely voice would calm her nerves and besides, she'd promised she would ring.

Henry's phone rang and rang but there was no reply. *Where in Odin's name was he?* Cutting eventually to his messaging service, she left a terse, irritated message and then wished him well.

Scrolling through the call log on her phone, Kat pressed the return call button. She wanted to try Frigg's number. She desperately wanted to talk to someone familiar, anyone who could take her mind away from the nightmare image of her own dead body. The ghostly, sunken, greying corpse that now filled her thoughts.

There was no reply from Frigg, either. Her phone was switched off and she couldn't even leave a message. With Jess and Jameela also unable to answer their phones, Kat suddenly felt the loneliest person in the world. She turned slowly before walking back toward Marcus. Solving this mess was now down to her and Marcus, just the two of them.

Taking his arm in hers, they began to walk sombrely toward a street where they knew they would find a cheap hotel for the night.

Tomorrow looked set to be a very busy day.

30

Mission Impossible

Carmel waited for several hours after supper before leading the small party some distance away from the watchtower. They didn't carry torches, and no goodbyes were said. They walked carefully, trying to avoid making too much noise as they headed into the dense undergrowth that lay a few hundred metres from the watchtower. They didn't want their presence seen or heard by anyone.

Thor and Carmel hugged their silent goodbyes to Freyja, Silk, and Balder, and then Carmel put on Freyja's cherished Brisings necklace. Just as Kat had once done when she was a maid, Carmel chanted along with the group and, in a flash of brilliant white light, she was transformed into a beautiful white swan who now graced the undergrowth. Turning to Thor, she honked encouragement. He, too, had changed. After putting on Freyja's cloak of falcons' feathers, he had turned into a very large and somewhat ungainly eagle.

This was what had caused the merriment yesterday in the clearing in the woods: Thor and Carmel's first clumsy attempts at flying.

Clutching the heavy iron cage in his beak, the one he had slaved over making the day before, the two of them took off. It was a nerve-wracking moment and the party held their breath. Surrounded by tall trees, there was no margin for error. Charging down the tiny runway and flapping wildly, they cleared the treetops at the end of the woodland glade with just centimetres to spare. They then headed east away from the glacier and Jotunheim and after a short distance they banked before heading west once more, swooping low over the glacier some distance from the watchtower and the giants' camp.

It was a perilous journey, the heavy cage almost proving too much for even Thor's mighty wing flaps. Twice he nearly let it fall, once over the chasms of the glacier and once again over the fringe of the ever-widening encampment.

Carmel had hoped they would remain airborne for some time, putting as much distance between themselves and the giants as possible but, unfortunately, the burden of the cage proved too much. Thor's muscles were tiring badly, and he was now clipping the tops of the mighty fir trees. With one last effort he forced himself a few hundred metres farther, and then that was it. Instead of gliding elegantly, his exhausted body plummeted to the forest floor below.

He landed heavily, the cage bouncing noisily from his beak and rolling, clattering, and clanking across the carpet of brush and pine needles that had cushioned its fall.

Carmel landed close beside. Unburdened by the cage, her return to solid ground was altogether more accomplished and graceful, one befitting a Valkyrie warrior.

Dusting themselves down as best they could in the darkness, they quickly realised the noise of their landing had attracted the attention of a small patrol of giants. They had heard the clattering of the cage and were now heading in their direction, torches raised high and grunting loudly amongst themselves. Thor and Carmel fell to the floor and pressed their faces deep into the musty, forest carpet. They held their breath.

The giants drew closer, moving inexorably toward the disturbance they had heard. Giants had very good hearing and an excellent sense of smell. Carmel and Thor could hear them sniffing at the air, their noses upturned like wild dogs, sampling the many scents of the still, night air. Thor didn't know if they were downwind or upwind of their foe, but soon it wouldn't matter anyway. The men from Jotunheim were now so close that their torches had begun to illuminate their flattened bodies. They would be discovered any second.

A yearling buck, startled by the closeness of the giants, suddenly broke cover and bounded noisily away through the trees. His nervy escape saved their bacon; the giants stopped and then moved away once more. They were satisfied that the noise they had heard must have been made by the immature beast.

Thor and Carmel waited face down and motionless for a long time after the torchlight faded from view. The encounter had been too close.

Cautiously, they began a fingertip search, groping around themselves in ever-widening circles until they located the iron cage. To Thor's touch it seemed intact, thank Odin. Whispering almost inaudibly between themselves, they decided to try to push on with their journey on foot.

Unfortunately, the moonless, starless night which had been so helpful in hiding their flight across the glacier now proved their undoing. They could barely tiptoe five paces without stumbling over some roots or fallen branches. It was suicide to carry on; each trip or bump running the risk of alerting more nosy giants or causing themselves injury. Reluctantly, they both agreed to settle down for the night and restart their journey just before dawn.

The air on the forest floor around them was cold and still; high above, the branches of the trees creaked and groaned as a gentle breeze caressed the heavy boughs into waves of languid motion.

Carmel and Thor nestled close to each another. Wrapped in their feathered cloaks they snuggled up warm and cosy for the long hours ahead. They weren't going to take any chances, so as an extra precaution, Thor spread Odin's beloved blue cape across them as well. This hid them from view, making them safe at last from the prying eyes of watchful patrols.

As they tried to catch a few hours of uncomfortable sleep, they silently congratulated each other. So far so good: the first stage of Carmel's impossible mission had been accomplished. They had landed with the cage in Jotunheim without injury or detection.

The long road to Utgard lay ahead and it was a path they would now be travelling on foot.

31

An Early Christmas

Henry would have dearly loved to answer Kat's call.

His phone rang noisily beside him as he lay restlessly on his bed. Unfortunately for Kat, he was a little tied up.

He was rather busy dying at that moment, being suffocated by his pillow. His body was struggling ever more weakly as he laid pinned beneath the arms of a beautiful woman—a stranger, someone he had just met.

This same woman was kneeling elegantly on top of him with her legs bent on either side of his chest and an attractive, black silk dress hitched up high around her waist. Her long alabaster arms were stretched out, firmly pressing the pillow against his semi-conscious face. Leaning forward, she let all the weight of her body bear down upon him.

In a matter of minutes, it would all be over for young Henry Fox.

The Contessa had arrived at Dulles airport late in the afternoon feeling somewhat refreshed. She had managed to grab a few hours' sleep on the tedious flight across the Atlantic, relaxed as she had been by a few stiff drinks and the erotic bliss of Ottar's tongue. Whilst she slept, her personal assistant had been hard at work hiring a car and tracking down the exact location of her quarry. In both of these endeavours she had been successful, a fact which pleased the Contessa greatly. Showering when she awoke, the Contessa changed into a revealing, figure-hugging dress. Elegant without being ostentatious, it was still more than enough to turn heads. She put on a short matching jacket, too; the air in Washington could be chilly at this time of year.

By the time the private jet touched down, everything was ready.

Placing a lingering kiss on Ottar's obedient lips, she traded her plane for a hired silver SL600 Mercedes roadster and hit the road. The trip to Princeton was one she would be making on her own, no chauffeur required.

When Henry opened his door about two hours after Kat had left, he must have felt Christmas had arrived early this year. Not one, but two beautiful women were gracing his doorstep that day.

This second beauty was a stranger, a mature woman comfortably in her early forties. She was fuller figured than Kat, but her voluptuous breasts, straight blond hair, and crystal clear skin stretched tight over high cheekbones made her an easy equal in looks. She was one of those frightening ladies, the type who become more attractive as they grow older, prising handsome men from the clutches of younger, less experienced women. Her obvious wealth helped, too; her melodious, aristocratic voice purring with all the sophistication and class that money could buy.

Henry was smitten instantly. He barely heard her introduce herself as Dr. Francesca Dragza and claim that she was lost. She had been desperately looking for her apartment for over an hour now and would he please, pretty please, possibly help her?

This was like a red flag to a bull. His manly instincts, already super-charged by Kat, sprung immediately into hyper-drive. He was help personified; the god of help if such a thing existed. He studied her map studiously and even offered to drive her to her apartment.

'Dr. Fran,' as she begged him to call her, was delighted, so much so that she asked if he knew a good restaurant nearby. She was famished and would be delighted to repay his kindness by treating him to an all-expenses-paid meal. Thanking God for his incredible good fortune, Henry walked elatedly beside her to the restaurant. His enormous grin and the persistently annoying bulge in his trousers didn't pass unnoticed by the Contessa. She was in her element, reeling him in like a fish.

He had swallowed her hook and her line, and in a very short while he'd be swallowing her sinker.

When Henry had first opened the door to Francesca, she too had been startled, almost jumping out of her skin. Unlike Henry, it wasn't his looks that had rocked her world. No, it was the blast from his powerful intellect that almost bowled her clean off her feet.

It was truly astonishing. His fabulous mind was like a museum: the Metropolitan, the Tate, or even the Louvre in Paris. There were endless tidy corridors leading to countless numbered rooms, each of which was filled to bursting with priceless thoughts and all of these were beautifully stored, immaculately catalogued, and studiously cross-referenced.

She could see instantly why he was so important and she was furious with herself for allowing the Valkyries to get to him first. Kat had beaten her to this cherished prize and the memory of their encounter was already stored in a darkened basement area. This particular little room was labelled 'Private' and lay at the end of a somewhat tatty and narrow corridor, dimly lit with a red light and covered by a well-worn carpet. She didn't pry further; she could tell that the images of herself were already being filed in a drawer there, too. *The naughty boy!*

The Chinese meal she bought for them was excellent by any standards and with consummate skill she encouraged him to talk about his work rather than let him ask too many awkward questions about her paper-thin disguise. She rode her luck well, helped by his hopeless, drooling eyes that wandered time and again to her breasts and inviting cleavage. When at last he excused himself and went to the toilet, she discretely emptied some GHB (gamma hydroxybutyrate) into his glass. This was a powerful sedative and would deliver him like a lamb to her slaughter.

Within twenty minutes of finishing his wine, Henry was kaput.

Frigg had to help him stagger back to his digs, propping him up and prompting him to put one foot in front of the other. He apologised profusely for his wayward behaviour. He didn't usually get so badly drunk, or drunk so badly.

After struggling through the front door, she placed him on the bed and took off his shoes. It was the least she could do for him. Studying his innocent, boyish face for a while, she climbed on top of him and then placed a pillow over his drowsy head.

This was where they were now, with Henry straddled between her thighs as she slowly suffocated the life from his body.

With a frantic, final, uncoordinated effort, Henry struggled to grab one last desperate gulp of air. Taking one hand off the pillow, Fran hitched her dress higher, and then shuffled farther up his chest to get a better grip. As she did so her silken hem rose to just above her hip, just high enough to reveal a sexy thong and a small tattoo of a flower at the top of her left buttock. It was a poppy, jet black in colour with a bright scarlet centre.

Francesca bore down on his head once more, glancing casually at her jewel-encrusted watch as she did so. She was crushing the life out of him, but it was becoming a little tedious. He was taking an annoyingly long time to die.

At last, Henry stopped wriggling and his arms fell limply from her behind. He had clung on to this to the last, clawing his fingers deep into her bottom in a final desperate bid to unseat her.

With Henry's resistance gone, she was almost done. Shuffling forward, the Contessa repositioned her knees such that they now pressed down upon the pillow. With hands now freed, she twisted sideways and pulled a cigarette from her handbag. She lit up and then smoked it slowly. She wanted to be absolutely certain that the boy buried beneath her thighs was well and truly dead.

Finally, when she had finished and stubbed out her cigarette on his bedside table, she stood up. The heavy black knife she withdrew from her elegant designer bag seemed strangely incongruous. In a flowing and practiced move, she raised it high above her head before plunging it deep into his heart. The handle glowed warmly in her hand and a brilliant flash of red light shone briefly before disappearing, imploding into itself.

Her job was done and she replaced the blade into its sheath. The Contessa Francesca Dragza had served her mistress well. The Queen of Niflheim would be well pleased with her catch tonight.

Frigg—the Contessa Francesca Dragza—and mightiest of all Hel's Angels, had just provided her mistress with a very important soul.

32

Dodging Giants

Carmel and Thor woke early in the dim grey twilight just before dawn. Neither had slept well. They were both stiff and irritable, and the damp ground had chilled them to the bone, even through the insulating warmth of their feathered cloaks.

Thor got up first, shaking himself violently to get the circulation flowing once more in his massive limbs. He stretched lazily and was about to speak when he suddenly froze and then crouched down, finger pressed tightly against his lips.

Carmel sat up and peered out through the undergrowth.

The spot where they had landed and made camp for the night was within a stone's throw of a cluster of giants' yurts on the edge of the sprawling encampment. The smoke from their fires could already be seen rising lazily from somewhere amongst them.

Yurts were the temporary shelters used by giants when hunting, fishing, or gathering berries from the forests. They were large, round structures made from wooden staves and covered with animal hides loosely stitched together. Each yurt had a wide, low door and the centre of the roof was open to the sky. This allowed a small fire to be built for cooking and to provide warmth. They were very cosy shelters, easy to erect and transport. If ever they needed to be repaired, the only materials required were wood and animal pelts, items plentiful in the forested slopes of Jotunheim.

Some yurts became more permanent dwellings, and these would be brightly painted with crude symbols to ward off evil spirits and prayers asking their gods for good hunting.

Having been warned by Thor, Carmel got up far more cautiously and sipped frugally at her mead. She hoped she had enough to last the duration of their journey. Gently raising the heavy iron cage upon his immense shoulders, Thor quietly tiptoed with Carmel away from the yurts, the thick carpet of pine needles helping to mask their footfalls.

At first they headed directly up the mountain slope, but when they were sure they were out of sight and earshot, they traversed across the incline looking for the well marked trail that led to Utgard. It wasn't long before they found it; the heavy traffic of carts and giants travelling to and from the camp had made the path rutted, muddy, and easy to see. It would have been much easier going if they could have used the path as it snaked gently left and right, weaving its way upwards through the trees, but unfortunately that wasn't possible. For now, their journey required secrecy.

Reluctantly, they resigned themselves to following the course of the track but travelling fifty to a hundred metres away from it. This made their journey arduous. Great roots, boulders, and fallen boughs thick with cones slowing their progress at every turn.

As the greyness of dawn gave way to morning, which in turn grew into the afternoon, the number of giants and carts using the trail steadily increased. Time and again, Thor and Carmel were forced to dodge behind the trunk of a massive tree or bury themselves in the thick carpet of pine needles and fungi. On each occasion Carmel would hug Thor tightly and he would envelope them both in Odin's cloak. On many an occasion they could hear the men from Jotunheim sniffing the air suspiciously. The giants could smell the scent of human flesh, but they couldn't see them.

Unlike their hearing and sense of smell, giants' eyesight was much more limited, a weakness the Valkyries exploited to the full. If you were standing straight in front of a giant then he would be able to see you very well, possibly in greater detail than a human eye could discern. However, move slowly to one side and you would quickly disappear from view. This was their weakness. They had poor peripheral vision, making their eyesight blinkered such that they viewed the world as though looking down a tunnel.

When fighting with giants, the Valkyries would exploit this limitation by darting sideways. Momentarily lost from view, the warriors could launch a deadly assault from the side, striking at the flanks of their bewildered foe. It was a strategy that worked well in battle and served Carmel and Thor with equal success as they climbed ever higher into the mountains, their progress remaining undiscovered despite so many close encounters.

The pair toiled hard all day, not stopping to eat and pausing only briefly to drink from the occasional spring they came across. Thor had a small amount of dried biscuits and pemmican in his knapsack, but because of the heavy weight of the birdcage, the quantity he was carrying was very limited. Carmel carried their flasks for water and her small knapsack held Freyja's priceless but heavy necklace. Food had not seemed a priority earlier, but as dusk started to fall both their empty stomachs began to growl pleadingly.

In spite of what seemed like painfully slow progress, by nightfall they had reached their objective: the high pass that opened out onto the great plateau. Carmel calculated that it would take them at least one, possibly two, days to cross and then it would be a half day's journey down through the forest glades to Utgard, Thrym's seat of power.

Satisfied that they were back on target, they agreed to pitch camp in the shelter and seclusion of the forest's edge. Walking far enough away from the trail to be out of sight, they worked quickly to fashion a passable shelter from fallen boughs, bracken, and clumps of heather which they scavenged from the moorland edge of the mountain plateau. When they finished, their creation looked a far cosier place to spend the night then the previous one.

Unable to risk a fire, they settled down together and nibbled at dry, salty oat biscuits and chewed on tough but tasty pemmican rounds. These latter were made from strips of dried, lean meats which had been pounded into a paste and then mixed with melted fat and berries before being pressed into small cakes. It may not have looked like much, but it felt like a magnificent feast for the starving pair. With the hunger from their aching bellies staved, they made ready for the night ahead. Carmel snuggled up close to Thor once more, the warmth of his mighty body comforting her as she drifted rapidly into a dreamless sleep. With his massive arms around her, Carmel felt secure, invulnerable to the savage beasts which roamed the forests throughout the night.

The nerves of Heimdall, Silk, Balder, and Freyja were stretched to breaking point as they struggled through the busy morning at the watchtower. They were the only ones who knew the details of Carmel's dangerous plan and they strained their eyes and ears for telltale signs that the two had been discovered.

By mid afternoon they began to relax. There had been no indication, no triumphant whooping or beating of drums, to suggest that either had been captured or killed. It was a good start and each silently prayed for Odin to make their journey a successful one. All their lives depended on it.

During the day, the giants finished the first section of their new route across the glacier and began to prepare the second bridge. After testing the first's strength, they found it could easily bear the weight of a war mammoth, a point not lost on the occupants of the watchtower. Mammoths would make short work of hauling the heavy timbers for each of the bridges, and the fact that they could travel back and forth lumbering the heavy loads meant a dramatic reduction in the time needed to build a new causeway.

Freyja now felt they would complete this task within a week.

This was sobering news and the watchtower quickly became a hive of activity. There were many comings and goings as cartloads of provisions arrived to be stockpiled and craftsmen were drafted in to make arrows and spears. Swords and axes, too, were sharpened in the small forge, and a constant whirr came from the grindstones as they sent cascades of sparks flying in all directions. Edges of weapons were ground to razor sharpness.

Many local men—sons of farmers, peasants, and serfs alike—came to the castle and offered their services as soldiers to stand alongside the warriors and gods. Few were turned away, although the peace-loving Vanir usually made poor soldiers. They were unskilled in even the most basic disciplines of fighting, unlike the more warlike Aesir who lived closer to the town of Asgard.

Taking it in turns, the Valkyries kitted them out with swords, spears, and shields, and then started the painstaking task of training them in the art of warfare. The attempts of the young men were often pitiful; wielding their weapons as though they were pitchforks and scythes.

In more normal times the maids would have laughed and sent them packing back to their fields, but these days were far from normal. No matter how poor their fighting skills, every man and boy prepared to stand his ground against the giant foe was gratefully welcomed. They could assist in guard duties and building barricades, adding layers of additional defences around the thick walls of the watchtower. In the event of invasion, the longer the Valkyries repulsed the enemy force, the better the chances that Asgard would be saved.

Everyone had to work on the basis that Thor's mighty hammer was lost forever. No one could afford the luxury of relaxing in the hope that Carmel's journey would end successfully. For now, they couldn't have too many arrows, spears, swords, and soldiers at the tower, nor could they have too many ditches and stakes defending it.

By early evening, as the light began to fade from the cloudy, sun-less sky, things began to feel a little more secure and organised. They could watch the progress of the giants and compare this with the building of their own defences. They had done well, but late in the afternoon two enormous iron cages arrived in the giant encampment. Their arrival caused an intense buzz of excitement and curiosity on both sides of the glacier.

The contents of these cages were shrouded from view by thick swathes of blackened sacking. Their size looked ominous and the wide detours given by the giants as they made their way around the objects gave Heimdall cause for alarm. He had never seen cages like these before, and he suspected their mysterious contents would make for very unpleasant viewing.

33

Meet the Dragzas

"That's her, that's definitely her!"

Marcus nodded his head enthusiastically, stuck his thumb up, and mouthed the words excitedly to Kat as they both tried to listen in to the conversation on her mobile phone. It was an unexpected return call, Frigg apologising for missing Kat's from the night before. She had been having dinner with a very important new friend, and had forgotten to switch her mobile back on after the meal had finished.

Kat mouthed her thanks to Marcus, and then continued to explain her current predicament to Frigg: two Valkyries captured and a hero under attack.

"My dear Sangrid, of course I'll help!" These were Frigg's reassuring words as she agreed to return to Asgard immediately and inform Odin of the situation. She was delighted to learn that Marcus was safe and well and insisted that Kat didn't let him out of her sight. One last thing she made Kat promise: absolutely no attempts to rescue Jess and Jameela until she returned. After wishing her luck and apologising once more for not being able to help the night before, Frigg hung up.

Conversation over, Kat turned to Marcus with a look of relief on her face. At least now the mystery as to who 'Fran' was had been cleared up. Fran, the Contessa, and Frigg were all one and the same person.

They both returned to the computer screen and continued looking at it with renewed intent. The *Wikipedia* entry for the Dragza Corporation made for very interesting reading.

The morning had started well for Kat and Marcus. A clear blue sky had dawned over New York, delicately laced with a hint of frostiness that hung persistently in the languid March air. The breakfast at their hotel had been, well, rubbish, but they gobbled it down just the same. With a great deal of relief, Marcus collected the artifacts from his mailbox and Kat ditched her hired car in a nearby car park. They then organised a new vehicle; this time paying cash to a grubby, no-questions-asked, second hand dealer, who was as anxious to know as little about them as they were about the car they were buying.

Marcus marvelled at her wonderful purse. Fake identity, driving license, cash—almost anything could be persuaded to come from it as she mouthed her requirements over its 'no problem' jaws. He could have retired years ago if he had had one of these, he quipped, as their car ate up the kilometres. They were speeding swiftly toward Washington with Kat at the wheel. She had always been a fast driver and she was now back in the swing of things with her old 'skills' returning quickly. Driving was just like riding a bike: a habit, once learned, you never forgot. Even if the habits, in Kat's case, were pretty bad.

Arriving on the outskirts of Washington in a fraction of the time it would have taken had Marcus been driving, they stopped for lunch at an Internet café. This was where they were now, both perched before an anonymous computer screen. Every task they undertook was being done using cash and fake identities. They didn't want to leave an easy trail for Woods or an assassin to follow.

After Frigg's fortuitous interruption, they continued with their reading.

The Dragza Corporation was founded in Milan in 1940 in war-torn Europe. It was a company created by Oswald and Flavia Dragza. Oswald was of German descent and his wife was Italian. The company was a munitions manufacturer and grew rapidly with the strong demand for weapons driven by the Nazi war machine. Oswald had opened up plants in Germany and Norway, and become heavily involved in the research and development of the V2 rocket, as well as the production of heavy-water in Hitler's failed attempt to build an atomic bomb. In 1943, in recognition of his heroic war efforts, the ill-fated Italian leader, Mussolini, had bestowed on the Dragzas the coveted title of Count and Contessa.

The names tickled Kat. In true Valkyrie style, Odin and Frigg had assumed aliases which related to their true identities. A single, faded, black and white photo of the couple existed and this had been pasted into their entry. Odin's eye patch could be clearly seen, even though his other features were hazy and out of focus.

It seemed odd to Kat that he had chosen to throw in his lot with the monstrous Nazis—the losing side—but perhaps sentimentality had made him pick the side closest to his historic roots in Midgard

World War II came to its eventual end and Oswald and Flavia followed the path of so many war criminals who were pioneers in rocket research. They were offered pardons and eagerly snapped up by the Americans, who were anxious to exploit the couple's scientific expertise.

The Dragzas were clearly allowed to bring substantial assets to the USA, because within a decade their company was up and flourishing once more. In fact, throughout the 1960s, 1970s, and onward to the present day, the company enjoyed spectacular growth and success. It was involved in all aspects of weapons manufacture and research, computers, the space program, and telecommunications. No lucrative market ripe for exploitation seemed beyond their reach.

At some point during the 1980s, the aging and reclusive Count and Contessa were tragically killed in a car crash whilst holidaying in Monaco. Control of the company then passed to their grandchild, Count Oliver Dragza. He apparently married a British socialite who then became the Contessa Francesca Dragza. The Count—or 'Ollie,' as he preferred to be called—remained highly reclusive and no known photographs of him existed. Strangely, like his grandfather before him, he had lost an eye, too. Oswald lost his eye in a factory incident in Italy, whereas the youthful grandson Ollie had lost his in a hunting accident.

Kat squealed with delight at this point. The ease with which Odin and Frigg managed to create such fake identities beggared belief. They were all rubbish, but totally believable. Disguised and hidden from public view, Odin had managed to steer all the emergent technologies of the late twentieth century in the direction he wanted. To Kat, his motive was transparent. He was trying to speed up humanity's progress toward becoming an advanced civilization, a civilization which emulated his own.

Kat read on. There were only three paragraphs left in the entry.

Unlike Ollie, the Contessa revelled in the spotlight. She was a consummate socialite, and her elegant photographs could be seen adorning many glossy magazines around the globe. Undoubtedly this was why the name had seemed so familiar to Kat.

In a moment of inspiration, Kat grabbed a pen and paper and nudged Marcus to look at what she was doing. She began to write the letters of their surname in large capitals and in reverse order.

A Z G A R D

If you replaced the 'Z' with an 'S,' the surname leapt off the page and slapped you in the face.

Odin was mocking the world, flaunting their secret identity in full view. His weapons, satellites, and planes flew around the world with the truth proudly displayed as banners and trademarks, right under the noses of the rich and powerful. It was extraordinary brilliance, hiding his identity in plain sight where everybody could see. Kat clapped her hands with delight; Odin's audacity was lunacy at its most creative.

The final two paragraphs made for the most useful, and disturbing, reading.

The company had bought a large Caribbean island in the late 1980s which was currently their global headquarters. They had received a large grant from the World Health Organisation around the time, so at the dawn of the twenty-first century the company entered the increasingly lucrative world of genetically modified crops. Its expertise was in the development of new strains of apples, ostensibly intended to ease poverty and hunger in third world countries—hence the grant.

With a sudden urgency, Kat asked Marcus to find the island on Google Earth. The pictures were of low resolution, but there was sufficient detail to confirm her worst suspicions. There, in all their fuzzy glory, stood row after row of carefully manicured orchards: thousands of trees producing millions of apples.

If—and she knew she was right about this—the apples Odin was cultivating were the same golden apples as those Idun grew in her garden, it begged two questions: Why the charade back in Asgard about not having any apples? And why did he need so many of them here? It seemed that just as one mystery closed, another opened.

Kat did, however, have one last piece of good news. She would bet her sword and shield that the second well, the one that Henry had been so sure of, was located on the island. She knew that at some point she would have to visit the place.

Finishing her research on the computer, she tried to call Jameela one more time. There was still no reply. Jameela's capture was now a certainty and Marcus agreed that this could be the only logical conclusion. She would have already contacted them otherwise.

Kat and Marcus left the café a little over an hour after they had entered it. So far, the day had been particularly fruitful with only one major question remaining unanswered: who had tried to kill Marcus?

There were many criminals in New York who bore him grudges, but the timing of the attempt on his life seemed too much of a coincidence to be related to any of these. The assassination attempt had to be linked to the Valkyries. Woods and the FBI seemed unlikely suspects because they wanted him alive. With 'Fran' now confirmed as Frigg, and very much part of the Valkyrie family, she was ruled out, too.

They were both stumped. Without an idea as to who the assassin might be, they would have to keep a very low profile indeed. They just hoped that Frigg would return quickly with help from Odin.

Frigg put her mobile phone down with a cheerful smile upon her face. Sangrid was the only Valkyrie Frigg actually enjoyed talking to and she had just given her an opportunity for an even greater pleasure, the opportunity to return to Asgard with bad news for Odin. He always took his troubles so badly.

With any luck, he would be forced to send more of his wretched 'Choosers of the Slain' to Midgard, weakening his defences still further.

Frigg lit a cigarette and allowed herself to bask momentarily in her triumph.

For as long as she could remember, she had used and abused her position of trust with Odin, gleaning information from him in pillow talk and using it to frustrate and thwart his plans whenever she could. She was careful, very careful, taking great care to ensure her machinations went undetected. It was a shame that the hit man she'd organised hadn't killed Marcus, but in the broader picture, it didn't really matter.

Marcus would become just one more hero for poor, sad, angst-ridden Odin.

It was her friendship now with dear Kat which was proving the most productive. Kat's trust and naivety had led to the marvellous lapse back at Frigg's tea party in Fensalir which had provided the identity of Henry Fox, quite possibly the most important person she had ever sent to Hel.

It was now clearer than ever to Frigg that Kat hadn't been named Sangrid by accident. Mimir wouldn't have made a mistake like that. It was only going to be a matter of time before she became like her predecessor—and then the fun would really begin.

Someday, somehow, Frigg knew that Kat would join forces with the first Sangrid, the mistress whom she now served in Hel.

34

Smilodons

"**S**milodons!" Heimdall hissed urgently as he hurried down the warriors' dormitory, shaking each one awake as he did so. "Two of them—in the stable block—now!"

It was well after midnight, the time of night when they were most deeply asleep and Silk struggled hard to wake from her exhausted slumber. Her head felt like mush.

"From the cages?" she yawned loudly as she stretched.

"Yes, got to be. The giants must have opened them and sent them across. They're hungry—and high."

Struggling to rid the grogginess of sleep from their minds, the girls got dressed as quickly as they could. Silk took charge as usual. She asked Heimdall to wake Tyr and Balder and the maids as well. They would need plenty of firepower if they were going to get rid of these dangerous beasts.

Smilodons (sabre-toothed tigers) were one of the biggest and most ferocious beasts in the whole of Asgard. They lived exclusively in Jotunheim and very few warriors or maids had ever seen one. Their ferocious reputation was well deserved. They were at least twice the size of great white tigers, the only other big cats that roamed high in the mountains. The fear they instilled in humans and giants alike was in part due to their size and in part due to the way they slaughtered their prey. They were solitary beasts who killed their quarry by slashing their necks with their two, huge canine teeth. This was unique; most other carnivores killing their victims by suffocation, smothering their muzzles with their mouths.

The necks of the tigers were strong and lithe, too. They could wield their deadly fangs with a speed and dexterity which matched or probably bettered a Valkyrie's blade. To complete their lethal ensemble of weaponry, the tigers' paws were immense, the size of dinner plates, and featured long, curved, razor-sharp claws. With one casual swipe, a smilodon could eviscerate a warrior or break her back, depending on where the heavy blow fell.

Within five minutes the party had assembled in the hall at the foot of the spiral stairs. They were whispering noisily in a rising crescendo of nerves that spread among them like an infectious disease. Silk ordered a round of Valhalla mead to calm the mood and prepare them in event of injury. Each warrior carried a shield, sword, and spear, and some carried bows with quivers jammed with arrows. They lit torches, lots of torches. They knew they would need these. Fire was the universal fear of all beasts and smilodons were no exception.

As the party gulped down the mead, Silk discussed strategy with the warriors Skogul and Mist. The problem was tricky and it had to be tackled properly.

It wasn't going to be easy to kill the tigers. Out in the open and vulnerable to a hail of arrows and spears, the pair could be dispatched with confidence and without risk of injury. Unfortunately, the beasts were confined and firmly entrenched in the stables, chowing down on whatever was left of the horses. In a way it was lucky that they had gone there first. If they had travelled farther to the east of the watchtower, they would have run into the small cluster of tents where the Vanir soldiers were billeted. That would have created pandemonium, shattering their fledgling confidence in their warrior skills. Tackling the animals in the stables and disturbing the cornered beasts as they ate would be about as dangerous as it gets. The cramped confines of the stables would definitely give the tigers the upper hand. At such close quarters, the girls would be well within their slashing and clawing range.

There was another problem, too.

In an ideal world, they needed to return at least one of the vicious animals to the giant encampment. This would create havoc, and the giants would think twice about repeating this kind of attack. The last thing the warriors needed was a run of disturbed nights chasing enraged smilodons or cave bears around the watchtower. What was required was a well organised and co-ordinated assault, one that the warriors could execute with the minimum amount of shouting and screaming. It had to appear like business as usual, routing furious tigers being a chore that was hardly worth getting up for.

Clearly no pressure, then, for Silk to come up with a daring plan!

In the end, they all agreed on a sensible line of attack. The stables stood to the north of the watchtower and had two entrances, one at the western end nearest the Bifrost Bridge and the other at the eastern end. A small group of warriors with Tyr and Balder would enter the block from the east and disturb the beasts. Using torches, they would flush them out of the stables through the western door. Here a funnel of blazing torches laid on the ground would shepherd the animals back toward the first section of the Bifrost Bridge. The maids would be standing behind the torches encouraging the animals along the route with their spears. In the event of a tiger breaking out of this cordon, two archers would be stationed at the top of the watchtower. The maids Yuko and Priya were chosen, as they were the most skilled with the bow.

It seemed a good idea and the stage was set. The girls formed a circle and placed their hands one on top of the other. With a hushed chorus of "Hail Valour! Hail War! Hail Odin!" Heimdall opened the heavy wooden doors to the watchtower. It was time to face the monsters.

Whilst the maids began to lay the torches, Silk, Balder, Tyr, and the other warriors made for the stable block. They could hear the tigers inside, growling and smacking their lips noisily as they feasted on the dismembered remains of the horses.

Outside the block lay the grisly aftermath of one, or possibly both, of the Vanir guards—it was impossible to be sure. All that remained was a bloody mess of limbs, entrails, and shattered bones which glistened fiendishly in the flickering torchlight. It was a grim reminder of what might lie in store.

The night was moonless once more, with a low cloud enveloping them in an eerie fog which was slowly growing in thickness. There was a chill to the air, too, which made the girls shiver and worsened their already jangling nerves.

Taking the lead, Silk entered the stables first, quickly followed by Balder and Zara. The darkness inside was almost impenetrable, but at least some of the horses were still alive. They whinnied and reared loudly as the party crept in, the whites of their eyes clearly visible, rolling wildly in fear as the torchlight danced around the shadows of their stalls.

Near the western entrance, exactly as Silk had predicted, they could just make out the heaving shadows of the two giant beasts. They were clearly fractious and irritable: a combination of starvation and being fed a tiny morsel of meat by the giants, a juicy titbit heavily laced with bog myrtle. This was the same psychedelic plant that was used to enrage Berserkers before a battle.

Heimdall had been right. The poor beasts were as high as kites.

The tigers detected their human scent as soon as the party entered the stables, and they let out a chorus of low, blood-curdling snarls. It was the clearest of warnings that they didn't want to be disturbed. The noise echoed round and round the stables, driving jagged icicles of fear deep into the warriors' hearts.

Silk crept forward first, half crouching and gliding as silently as a cat. Reaching the stall where the first tiger was feasting, she crouched lower still and peered around the corner. Even in the dimness of the torchlight, she could make out the tiger's huge white fangs. They flashed as they jerked this way and that, tearing strips from a haunch of meat it held lovingly in its giant paws, the tiger's huge tongue slavering as he licked at his midnight feast.

Becoming slowly aware of Silk's presence, the tiger's pupils gradually changed shape, transforming from relaxed, contented ovals to narrow, malignant slits. Pinning his ears back and curling his lips, he opened his massive jaws. A deep growl echoed like thunder all around her. This was his final warning.

Two rows of dagger-shaped teeth glistened menacingly in the darkness: his promise to tear her apart should she venture any nearer. It was decision time.

Valkyries lead by example and this was just such an occasion. Rising up, Silk raised her shield high and with a ferocious battle cry, she charged forward, plunging her spear down with all her force. It glanced off the beast's shoulder as he twisted violently sideways, evading her blow.

Now it was his turn. With a mighty roar, the enraged tiger reared up and lunged forward, lashing out with a giant paw as he did so. His blow was as powerful as it was accurate. With claws open wide, he dealt Silk's shield a glancing blow, ripping it like a toy from a child's hand. She stifled an agonised scream—her arm had been broken by its impact as she spun dizzily to the floor.

Balder sprung into action. Without a moment's hesitation, he charged forward. With a mighty battle yell he lunged at the exposed chest of the beast with his spear, running the animal through like a stuck pig. It was a fatal blow, but the tiger didn't know it yet. Rearing up once more, he shattered the shaft of the spear. With a roar that shook the stable to its foundations, the tiger pounced forward, knocking Balder to the floor. Squirming in a desperate attempt to get away, Balder was soon trapped, pinned to the ground beneath a mighty paw.

Bleeding heavily, and with the spear lodged in his heart, the tiger began to lash drunkenly at him. Its huge fangs slashed this way and that, slicing through Balder's arm and chest like a branding iron through freshly fallen snow. Tiring rapidly as his ruptured heart began to fail, the mighty beast began to collapse sideways, his hindquarters crashing heavily onto Silk's outstretched legs. She, too, was now imprisoned against the floor. The giant cat thrashed angrily at the air with his fangs and paws, trying desperately to dislodge the remains of the spear, its splintered shaft still protruding from his chest.

Zara and Mika pressed forward, spearing the animal repeatedly as they hastened him to his death.

Startled by the commotion, the second tiger rose to her feet and roared loudly. Her voice resonated with anger and hate. Silk and Balder were alive but out of the fight, buried beneath the corpse of the first, massive creature. With a piercing chorus of high-pitched war cries, Zara, Eve, Mika, and Juliet formed a barricade in front of their fallen colleagues. They crouched low with shields raised high and overlapping, spears poking out threateningly between them.

The tigress rolled her eyes and squared off to face them. She crouched and unsheathed her claws, snarling and thrashing her massive jaws from side to side. It was a standoff, neither side wanting to make the first move nor show any sign of fear.

The Valkyries struck first. Chanting loudly in unison and drumming the shafts of their spears against the tops of their shields, their voices rose swiftly to become a deafening cry. The monotonous beat of their spears against their shields filled them with courage as they began to inch forward, daring the tigress to pounce.

This was a bold and audacious move, and one that was richly rewarded.

Still snarling, and pawing at the girls with her viciously curved claws, the tigress gave ground, shuffling slowly backward toward the stable door. She desperately wanted to strike, the rage and frustration being all too visible in her slit-like eyes as thick rivulets of saliva drooled freely from her foaming jaws. The tigress thirsted for revenge, but she could see her fallen mate lying still and prone behind the warriors and instinctively understood that any such retaliation could bring about her own death, too. Finally reaching the door, she turned tail and, with one giant leap, bounded outside. The warriors followed close behind, their shields still locked tightly in formation.

The torches outside blazed brightly, temporarily dazzling the tigress as she stopped dead in her tracks, growling and snarling with fear and rage. Desperately she thrashed her head left and right, searching for a path along which she could safely take flight. Behind the torches she could make out the shapes of the jeering maids crouched with their shields raised and spears pointed at her. Torchlight flickered wildly from the deadly metal tips of the spears and the metallic tracery of their shields. These weaved in bewildering patterns, suggesting an enemy far greater in number than they actually were.

With a final prod of encouragement from Zara's spear, the tigress bounded down the funnel and disappeared across the swaying, twisted frame of the rope bridge. The girls cheered loudly and followed her progress with elation. The noise that erupted from the giant camp when the tigress reached the far side was tumultuous.

The Valkyries had been victorious, and the giants scattered in panic before the marauding beast. It would be many hours before peace would finally descend upon their camp again.

With both tigers now dealt with, the girls returned to the stables and heaved the remaining beast off Silk and Balder. They were both alive but seriously injured.

Silk was furious, not only with herself but more so with the stricken Balder. Her foolish lover had once again thrown caution to the winds and put his life at risk in a heroic but stupid attempt to save hers. She loved him dearly for his suicidal bravery, but to offer fate a second chance to fulfil its deadly spectre was just too much.

Odin's horse, Sleipnir, had survived the tigers' onslaught, and Silk vowed silently that Balder would be on its back and heading toward Asgard just as soon as he was able to sit again. Silk couldn't risk another act of madness from Balder; she loved him far too much for that.

She had no wish yet to light his funeral pyre nor weep anguished tears as a long boat bore his burning corpse slowly out to sea.

35

An Experiment

$\mathcal{A}$gent Woods chewed worriedly at his fingernails as he stood in his office deliberating on the past and contemplating what to do next.

He was surrounded by an embarrassment of riches and should have been feeling like a pig in the proverbial. Unfortunately, with two Valkyries locked up in FBI headquarters and his safe crammed with artifacts, he felt anything but.

So much activity could draw unwelcome attention from his superiors, attention he could do without. He was desperate to move both Brynhildr and Herja to the Contessa's private Caribbean island as soon as possible, his paper trail ending with them being rendered there for more intensive interrogation.

To get his 'terrorist suspects' out of the limelight was now an urgent priority, before too many questions were asked. He was on the brink of realising his dream and he didn't want any last-minute foul-ups to snatch this prize from his grasp.

To this end, he was becoming increasingly annoyed with the Contessa. She had been particularly evasive over the last few days, and he had managed to get hold of her only once since Brynhildr's capture. She was, of course, her usual sophisticated and charming self, lavishing him with extravagant words of praise, but that was all they were—just words. What he needed now was action, her permission to move the two women to her secluded island. Without it, he was stuck.

Quite frankly, he was surprised by her procrastination. He would have thought she would be as excited as he was to finally taste the 'Ambrosia of the Gods,' as she had once so eloquently described it.

Woods was a pragmatic man. He had risen as high as he was ever going to in the ranks of the FBI and his job and pension were secure and adequate. He could coast through work for the next twenty years or so, watching his hair go grey and belly sag as he succumbed to Old Father Time. He had watched so many fine men do this over the years: their youthful minds and vitality dying while their bodies carried on living, each of the agents fading into shadows of their former selves.

It was a destiny he had almost resigned himself to before he met the Contessa Francesca Dragza. This had happened a decade ago and shortly after he had become interested in the activities of the Valkyries.

Their meeting hadn't been a lucky coincidence. They shared a mutual fascination with these mysterious women and she had sought him out, not the other way round. Apparently, she, too, had been secretly tracking their activities, and she had suggested that they pool their resources: his clout with her considerable wealth.

The Contessa was convinced of two things: that the Valkyries were not of this earth and that they held the key to immortality.

Woods hadn't believed her crazy fantasy at first. His interest was in bringing to book the murderous women who came and killed as they pleased, living their lives while flicking two fingers at the law. Even now, he could still vividly remember the occasion when his disbelief had changed—the moment when he, too, had become a believer.

His first encounter with a Valkyrie was with Ruby—or Prudr, as she called herself—and it had almost cost him his life. Nine years ago he had her cornered and at his mercy, but she refused to surrender. He emptied four rounds from his revolver into her chest and she repaid him handsomely for this act, stabbing him repeatedly with a kitchen knife before leaving him for dead. As he lay haemorrhaging on the floor, senses slowly fading, he remembered her muttering strange words and vanishing along with the soul of the other victim in the room. He still bore the scars, both from her knife wounds and the hours of emergency surgery that had saved his life.

Woods had converted immediately, convinced on the spot that the extraordinary theory of the Contessa was true. His theatrical act in front of Dr. Nyran and Marcus had been just that: a carefully staged drama to distract them from the unholy truth. Now at last, the quest he and the Contessa had begun a decade ago was nearing its fruition.

Woods wasn't remotely interested in Brynhildr or Herja, nor in their knives, ancient coins, and tatty purses. His crock of gold was the liquid they carried with them, the 'Mead of Valhalla' as the Contessa believed it to be called. This was their ambrosia, the nectar that gave them the power to defy death, reappearing time and again down the years unmarked by the ravages of time.

He had tasted the mead from both of the flasks he had confiscated and he could dismiss the liquid in Brynhildr's immediately. It smelt and tasted like the cheap, red bottle of plonk that it so obviously was. It wasn't even worth the bother of analysing.

Herja's, on the other hand, seemed the real deal. It had a full, aromatic bouquet and a sweet richness of taste that he had never experienced before. The liquid sent a wave of intense warmth radiating to each and every extremity of his body. The sensation was hard to describe—one sip and he felt reborn. He desperately wanted to drink more, to feel its warmth over and over again. The mead was the most addictive substance he had ever tried: one mouthful two days ago and he already begged for more. Unfortunately, he knew he had to control this urge and wait. Once the mead had been analysed and the Contessa confirmed that she could replicate it, then would he be able to drink his fill and slake the thirst.

This was why he was now feeling so excited and so frustrated.

His deal with the Contessa had been simple. He would capture the Valkyries and bring them, and the mead, to her. She would throw her money, her scientists, and her privacy at unlocking its unholy secret. If they succeeded, then they would both share the fruits of their endeavours, living lives of everlasting health and luxury funded by her obscene fortune. He didn't know or care what she did with the women; his interest was in the mead, only the mead.

They had both agreed that secrecy was vital. The knowledge of its miraculous properties would be far too shocking to share with a world locked in the remorseless cycle of birth and death. He could scarcely imagine what he could do, or what he would see, with countless years of perfect immortality stretching endlessly before him.

When they first met, he had prayed for a relationship with the Contessa. She was a magnificent woman, a few years older than himself but with a timeless and breathtaking beauty. Indeed, she seemed to have aged a mere ten days since they first met, while his body had been devoured by ten long years. This fantasy of a relationship hadn't lasted long and their alliance had become more strained and moody with the passing of years. His initial flirtations had been casually rejected, his amorous attentions turned down with the gracious lightness of a feather falling from the sky. The fabulously rich and aristocratic had a flair for wounding those less fortunate. It was a skill that allowed them to stab and twist the knife of misfortune without you noticing its exquisite pain, at least not until long after they had gone.

The phone on Woods' desk began to buzz quietly, interrupting his daydreaming. He pressed a button and put the call to speaker phone. "Yes?" he answered with characteristic brevity.

"There are two special agents here to see you, sir. Were you expecting them?"

"No." This definitely wasn't on his agenda for the day. "Who are they?"

"They are special agents Smith and, er, Smith, sir. They're brothers—twins actually. Would you like me to send them up?" the receptionist added almost apologetically.

Woods muttered as such before ending the call. *Who in the devil were they and what did they want with him today?*

Whilst he waited impatiently for their arrival, Woods' thoughts wandered back to the women in his custody. He was a cautious man by nature and, true to form, he had been running a little experiment with his two Valkyrie guinea pigs downstairs. He wanted to be absolutely certain that the liquid in Herja's flask was indeed the fabled mead from Valhalla.

He was holding both women in solitary confinement, isolated from each other. One was receiving a mouthful of mead each day, and the other wasn't. Once he had finished with Agents Smith and Smith, he would pop down and see how things were getting on. So far, his little experiment had yielded some extraordinary results, quite scarily so.

36
Lost

The damp and annoying fog that enveloped the watchtower became much more unpleasant and cold as it clung to the slopes higher up the mountains. There it formed a thick, freezing blanket, chilling all who were caught in its frozen embrace.

Dawn broke and its arrival came as an unwelcome surprise for Carmel and Thor.

Pushing back the fallen boughs and brush wood that covered their cosy shelter, they discovered that it was snowing. Not the delicate, lacy picture postcard flakes of Christmas, but a fine mist of tiny, icy shards that had already coated the ground in a layer of fresh snow about a centimetre deep. Looking around them, they could follow the whiteness of the ground as it disappeared into, and merged with, the whiteness of the sky above them. Visibility was dreadful, reduced to a few tens of metres or less.

It was a white-out, their worst possible nightmare.

With some urgency, they discussed their situation, wolfing down the remaining biscuits and pemmican as they did so. Mouthfuls of melted snow did little to improve their meal's dryness; their provisions tasted far less appetising for breakfast than for the snack the previous night. Staying put until the cloud lifted was not an option, nor was going back. They had to press on and they decided to pick up the trail to Utgard and walk upon the road itself rather than follow its course from afar. This would mean that they were bound to run into giants at some point, but the risk of such an encounter was less dangerous than the alternative of becoming lost. They would deal with the problem of giants when, or if, it happened. Getting to Utgard as quickly as possible was their priority. Getting lost would be a complete disaster.

Cautiously, they retraced their steps back to the trail which was, luckily, still visible a few hundred metres from where they had pitched camp. The deep ruts and hoof marks created by the endless procession of heavy ox carts had rendered the path easy to see, lifting their spirits.

Gazing appreciatively, they followed the trail as it stretched away before them, gently rising and falling as it curved around small hillocks of powder-coated mountain grasses, lichen, and moss.

Reluctantly shouldering the heavy cage once more, Thor grunted wearily as he fell in behind Carmel. Picking up their pace, they walked quickly—both being anxious to make it across the high plateau in a single day. Neither fancied the thought of spending another night up there, exposed to the elements and the beasts which roamed more freely at night. Apart from the obvious predators—smilodons, wolves, and hyenas—there was a more subtle but equally deadly hazard. It was one that came from the great herds of grazing animals that meandered across the plateau's vastness. Being accidentally trampled to death by musk ox, caribou, or mammoth would be a rather inglorious end for a mighty god and a Valkyrie warrior.

As the day progressed the weather at first seemed to lift. A slight breeze picked up, and its gentle breaths coaxed the low clouds to stir and scurry along. Visibility improved and they could enjoy the ancient scenery unfolding all around them. A large herd of bison grazed close by and smaller groups of caribou scraped at the thin coating of snow, carefully picking and nibbling the tastiest lichens and mosses they uncovered.

At one point in their journey they had to make a detour. A group of woolly rhinoceroses had decided to take a break and were lying across the trail. Neither Thor nor Carmel thought it wise to try to move them. Like their relatives in Midgard, the rhinoceroses were short-tempered and had bad eyesight. It would have made for a particularly black comedy to see either one of the pair being chased by an angry bull.

Within half an hour, they picked up the route once more and their pace quickened again. They were making good progress and they began to talk seriously about the descent on the other side and how close they should try to get to Utgard before turning in for the night. They definitely wouldn't have time for the final stage of Carmel's plan that day, but things were looking up.

"I'm so sorry, darling, but only Sangrid is left. Both Herja and Brynhildr have been captured. I came back especially because I thought you would want to know." Frigg could barely suppress the smile which was begging to burst from the corners of her mouth. Odin's look of frustration was a joy to behold.

Keeping her word to Kat, she had returned immediately to Asgard and was now in Gladsheim discussing the predicament of Odin's warriors in Midgard. She hadn't spared her husband anything, embellishing each problem with flowery descriptions that made matters appear even worse than they actually were. She could see he was worried, very worried, and that delighted her.

"Can't you help at all?" Odin pleaded.

"I'd love to, darling, but you know I have always been useless at that sort of thing. Skulking around and killing people. I could try...," she paused, relishing what she was going to say next, "but I might only make things worse."

Oh bliss! It was like sticking a red hot poker in his eye. She would kiss Sangrid when she next saw her; she had to thank her for this wonderful opportunity to stir his already oh-so-troubled waters.

"I really can't spare any more Valkyries—you know how things are up at the watchtower. I have to keep Ruby here just in case the rotten apple returns. Ragnarok is in the air. I can feel it...it's coming very soon...," Odin's voice trailed off as he became deeply lost in thought.

Shoulders slumped, he sank back into his throne. The unseasonal winter chills the warriors were feeling at the watchtower had spread their icy fingers across the whole of Asgard. It was almost as if autumn had been forgotten and the year was crashing headlong into winter. That was exactly as the omens had predicted: Ragnarok coming when the world was trapped in a winter freeze.

Everything was happening too quickly, far faster than Odin had planned. Ragnarok was inevitable—it was Asgard's fate—but it had to happen when he dictated, and not by happenstance. He still needed more time to complete his preparations, but unfortunately the disk hidden deep inside his pocket sang a very different tune. Time was running out.

Frigg interrupted his melancholy. "Well, I'm so sorry about your little problems, darling—I really am—but I just don't know what more I can say to help you. I'm sure you'll figure something out; you always do. You're just so clever—sometimes I wish I had your brains." Frigg's words sounded sincere, but she was mocking him with every syllable. *The fool!* After all this time he still hadn't discovered her duplicity.

Odin stood up and she hugged and air-kissed him tenderly. To all the world they looked like the perfect couple—a loving husband and his caring wife—but the truth was, so very different.

As Frigg's hand hovered over her ring, she paused for a moment. "By the way, it's so lovely to see how Hod is getting on with Loki, don't you agree? They seem to have patched up their differences at last and Loki is being so thoughtful, encouraging him to hunt once more. They both seem so excited. It really is quite heart-warming."

Odin nodded his agreement and with a wave of her hand she was gone. Thank goodness for Hod's happiness. At least there was one thing going right in his life.

Odin took his hand and brought it up to his ring. Frigg had been right—he always worked things out in the end. He did have a solution to his problems in Midgard, but he really was scraping the very bottom of the barrel. He knew two irritating, interfering busybodies who would love to go to the rescue of the fair and lovely Kat, but the thought of using them made him wince. He hated asking the meddling twosome a favour, knowing how they would crow at his predicament. He also knew they would be completely hopeless at the task. Yet he had no choice.

Odin sighed deeply. At least he could draw some comfort from his decision to ask his brothers for help. Even at their worst, they did have certain abilities which would see them through. Bungling or otherwise, he knew they would be able bring his precious Valkyries home.

By late afternoon Carmel and Thor knew they were in trouble—big trouble.

The wind that had seemed so helpful earlier in the day had gained in strength, bringing a fresh band of low, black clouds above them that were busily unleashing their fury. Snow that had started falling again as delicate, lacy flurries had quickly escalated into a continuous, blinding cascade. Now viciously whipped by a howling wind, these irratic flurries had turned into a ferocious blizzard.

Horizontal blasts of icy pellets blinded them and small drifts of snow swirled angrily around their feet, obscuring the slender path on which so much depended. Around them they could see animals huddling together in tight clusters, their heads lowered and facing inwards. The creatures left their bottoms pointing outwards to confront the bitter storm and these quickly became plastered with the driven snow. Carmel and Thor hadn't seen a giant all day, which was hardly surprising—they were lost and had wandered a long way from the trail to Utgard.

Time and again they strained their ears, desperate to hear the grunts of giants or the creaking of their carts. They heard nothing, only the incessant roar of grains of ice as they hurled themselves violently against their cloaks and hoods.

Carmel felt panicky, becoming convinced that they were walking around and around in circles or heading back toward the bridge. She begged Thor to use his ring and take them to Odin's garden. It seemed like a good idea at first, but ultimately it would be pointless: after visiting the garden the ring would return them to the exact place and time from where he'd used it. Any temporary warmth they would receive would make the bitter cold around them even more unbearable. It might even break their spirits completely.

As dusk began to fall, they had to swallow the bitter truth. They would be spending another night on the plateau.

Carmel was amazed at Thor's stamina. Having struggled all day with his heavy and cumbersome load without complaining, he put on his chain mail gloves and began to dig as deeply as he could into the frozen tundra, fashioning a tiny foxhole in which they could shelter against the storm. It was exhausting work and even with his powerful arms and protective gloves his fingers were bleeding by the time he'd finished.

Carefully lining their den with meagre scraps of moss and heather, Carmel snuggled down for the coldest night of her life. The winds howled incessantly around them as snow continued to fall. Without her mead and Thor's selfless rubbing and cuddling of her freezing hands and feet, she wouldn't have survived the night, being either frozen to death or eaten by the pack of hungry wolves that surrounded them once they eventually fell into a fitful sleep.

Dozing and oblivious to what was going on around them, the blizzard eventually abated and twinkling stars came out to greet the clearing sky. So, too, did the wolves. The ravenous beasts scratched and sniffed frustratingly at the fresh snow around Thor's den. They could smell an appetising meal but couldn't find it. Once again, Odin's cloak had saved them from a gruesome fate.

Having survived the bitterest of nights, Carmel and Thor both awoke early to a splendid dawn marked by a brilliant, yellow sun rising cautiously through a cloudless sky painted the palest and iciest of blues.

It was a beautiful morn, with long golden rays of sunshine fingering their way lazily across the snow-swept plateau, daubing the tops of powder-coated hillocks with their twinkling, golden lustre. On any other day Carmel would have been inspired by their beauty but today the magic was wasted. She felt faint with hunger and half frozen to death. They were horribly lost and the clock was ticking. Every hour counted and it was anybody's guess as to how far they'd strayed from their goal.

Filled with anxiety, the two of them set off once more. They had no idea where they were but, using the sun as their compass, they headed roughly west, a direction which they knew would lead them closer to Utgard. All morning they toiled, trampling and wading through snow that drifted in places to high above their waists. By noon Carmel was exhausted and ready to give up. The effort was simply too great.

Even Thor's optimism and endless stream of encouraging words had dried up. His stomach was growling louder than the volcanoes of Muspellheim and he began to ruminate obsessively about food, pointing out all the beasts he could have slain and cooked if only he had his hammer. Carmel shared in his obsession, her empty stomach gnawing mercilessly at her.

By mid afternoon they were at breaking point. Carmel's footsteps were growing shorter and weaker as the endless drifts of snow seemed certain to defeat them.

"We've made it—look!" Thor suddenly bellowed dramatically, pointing ahead excitedly with an outstretched arm.

Carmel looked up, something she hadn't done for at least an hour. He was right. There on the horizon she could make out the tips of the first stunted pine trees, with taller ones rolling away down a slope beyond. They were at the end of the plateau and they embraced, dancing cheerfully around each other as they made a wonderfully messy ring in the virgin snow.

Within the hour they arrived at the trees and began to descend as quickly as their exhausted legs would carry them. The wintry blanket of snow seemed to lose its grip with every downward pace they took, quickly fading into lonely islands of chalky whiteness on the steep and jagged slope.

Neither of them had a clue as to where they were, but they didn't care. They were alive and heading down from that accursed plateau. As they half walked, half stumbled through the broken rocks they could hear the sound of a stream growing in strength away to their left. They headed toward it, knowing that there must be shelter somewhere along its course.

When at last they reached the waters, the stream had become a torrent, its face broken by worn rocks and grazed by others that lay just beneath. The waters frothed and hissed noisily as they cascaded down steep waterfalls into deep, swirling pools. Thor stared intently at the foaming waters and as he did so, a smile began to form upon his weary face.

"I know this river!" he bellowed excitedly above its roar.

"What?" Carmel yelled.

"This river—it's the River Vimur, I'm sure." Thor waved his hands at the torrent and Carmel drew closer. She could barely hear him.

"See? Look at the water. It has a reddish tinge." Thor crouched down and let his hand trail in the seething, icy water.

Carmel looked and nodded her head. Sure enough, the water had an unusual pinkness, as if the river were gently bleeding as it flowed.

"Loki told me about this river a long time ago. He has a friend, Geirrod, who has a hall not far from its banks. We are saved, Carmel, because Geirrod is a friend of Odin's and a bitter rival of Thrym," Thor announced triumphantly as he stood up once more.

"Are you sure?" Carmel shouted close to his ear. She was shivering violently and her teeth were chattering. The icy chill from the spray had coated her in a dampness that froze her to the bone.

"Absolutely. Loki was certain of this. Apparently he also has two beautiful daughters, always eager to please, if you know what I mean." Thor's grin widened as he gave Carmel a telling wink.

Despite her chill and exhaustion, this was unwelcome news and she let him know it by giving Thor one of her most sullen stares. The thought of two attractive giantesses lavishing their attentions on him didn't please her one little bit.

Carmel was becoming rather fond of her rugged yet ever-so-genteel partner.

37

Shame

There is an interesting fact about people who are forced to live in perpetual darkness or perpetual light for weeks on end: they quickly get into a pattern. Everybody has a natural circadian rhythm, the body clock that tells them when to sleep and when to wake. It does this at regular intervals. For most people kept in perpetual light, this cycle repeats itself approximately every twenty-five hours.

When dealing with a group of people confined together, another remarkable feature becomes apparent: their individual rhythms become synchronised. Without any cues from the feeble sun that hung motionless in the sky over Niflheim, Cole and the other inhabitants of the miserable realm fell into this peculiar quirk of nature. They all tended to sleep, eat, and wake together.

After deciding that he would decline the lovely gift Hel had left for him, Cole waited nervously for two whole cycles of waking and sleeping before he informed Ganglati of his decision. He had postponed the confrontation for as long as he dared, but he took Hel's parting warning of boredom very seriously. He hated her, but he wasn't stupid. He certainly wasn't going to test her patience.

It was with this thought in mind and with some trepidation that he stood now before the glossy red doors to her playroom. Hel was expecting him.

"Colleen!" she squealed excitedly as he entered, clapping her hands as she skipped down the steps from the chaise longue to greet him.

"Well?" she asked breathlessly, barely able to control her excitement. She danced around him like an excited schoolgirl, desperate to hear his answer.

"I'm sorry, sugar—I mean, your majesty," Cole began, bowing low and trying to sound as reverential as he could possibly be. "I just can't dig it. I know it's cool and stuff, but it ain't my scene. I just don't swing both ways." He tried to grin, but his lips felt tense and false as he did so. His strong white teeth gleamed brightly, exaggerating this fact.

"Oh, what a shame," Hel pouted and frowned as she took the box from his outstretched hand. "And I dressed up especially for the occasion. Look!"

Doing a little twirl, Cole had to agree that her outfit was appropriately sleazy and practical: tight, short, leather hot pants and a black, zippered, sleeveless body suit. She looked perfect, absolutely perfect.

"Girls!" Hel announced loudly as she waved her hands to grab the attention of the four other men in the room. "I'm afraid our dear little Colleen is going to be leaving us."

There was a soft, murmured chorus of 'Shame' which sounded even less sincere than Hel's lament. There was considerable rivalry amongst her girls, each desperate not to fall out of favour. One fewer competitor was good news for the rest of them.

"But girls, please," Hel continued, "we mustn't be downhearted. Our brave little Colleen is going to join my courageous army—isn't that wonderful?" There was a moment's silence. No one was sure if they should cheer or not. "So come on, let's all give three cheers and wish our brave little girlfriend all the luck in Niflheim."

Cole waited and listened with growing relief as half-hearted cheers resounded around the circular room. He was delighted that he wasn't going to be sent to the mines or pinned out on the boiling surface of the planet to rot. He considered himself lucky; many others wouldn't have been so fortunate.

"It's a real shame you won't be staying longer." Hel continued, taking both his hands in hers and air-kissing him with grossly exaggerated affection. "Do visit whenever you can."

As Cole started to walk away, Hel took her gift out of the box and toyed lovingly with it. He was almost at the door when she turned abruptly and spoke once more.

"Gosh! Wait a minute girls—how could we be so rude?" she exclaimed loudly. "We haven't given Colleen a leaving present, something to remember us all by."

The men around the room murmured once more. No one was really sure where she was going with this line of conversation, but they giggled politely nonetheless. So long as Hel was being playful, they could relax and feel secure.

"Now, let me see, what in Niflheim can we give her?" Hel pressed her finger to her lower lip and gazed slowly around the room, grinning mischievously. She was toying with Cole and she emphasised this point by deliberately tossing the gift slowly up and down in her hands.

Cole felt a sinking feeling deep inside. He looked nervously at the door which Ganglati had come so close to opening a second before. It was still shut and he had let go of the handle. Worst of all, his gloves were off.

Fuck! He was trapped. Cole wished now that he'd accepted her gift, because it looked as though he was going to get it anyway.

"Why, girls!" Hel exclaimed with mock surprise as she came to a halt. "This would make an absolutely perfect gift, don't you think?" Hel tossed her present high in the air and one of the men caught it. It had unwound during its flight and the identity of the black, rubbery object was now all too horribly obvious.

It was a strap-on, complete with a long, thick, rigid phallus.

Hel snapped her fingers at two of the men and they vanished through a small door behind her chaise longue. Cole hadn't noticed this previously and he guessed now (correctly) that it must be some sort of storeroom for her kinky toys and gadgets.

The men emerged quickly, smirking widely. They were carrying an old-fashioned vaulting horse between them.

"Now come on, girls, will you please show me how to put this on? I swear I've never seen such a funny-looking contraption before." Hel laughed hysterically as two of the men helped fasten the device tightly about her hips. The others bent Cole spread-eagled over the horse, tying his wrists and ankles securely such that his bottom was arched nice and high and looking suitably inviting.

Cole didn't resist. *What was the point?* With Ganglati present, Hel had a cast-iron insurance policy. One touch from his gloveless hands and Cole would be as helpless as a kitten.

What happened next was quite possibly the darkest period of Cole's existence, a memory he would dearly love erased from his mind if only that were possible.

Hel's cheeky laughter quickly turned to cruel cackles as she set about her task with gusto, pounding away relentlessly. When she eventually tired, she let each of her girls have a go at Colleen and they did so with equal vigour.

In some ways, Cole's send-off was quite touching—Hel and her merry band of sycophants trying their damnedest to cure Colleen of his worst nightmare.

Some time later, when they had all finished their fun and Cole was dragged from the room, Hel paused for a moment of satisfied reflection.

Cole was supposed to be the starter of Ragnarok and a man whom Odin feared. By rights, she should keep him close at hand and treat him as an honoured guest. However, now that she had found and exploited his weakness, Cole was yesterday's news. He was conquered and the challenge was gone.

Losing interest as swiftly as a flick of her lustrous hair, Hel was ready to move on to the next prize that tickled her fancy. Sure, Cole had a handsome face and a delicious thickness down below, but there were plenty of girls his equal, with fresh ones arriving every day.

Hel giggled once more. It would really be rather fun now to see what Louis made of him. See if he could whip the 'rotten apple' into some sort of fighting shape. That would be interesting, finding out if Odin's nemesis could live up to his fearsome reputation. Growing bored with thinking about Cole, Hel's mind wandered to other more stimulating matters, and she squealed loudly at the very thought of them.

She had just received a lovely present from Frigg, one she felt particularly excited about. A new playmate had arrived and she had a strange feeling that she would be having a whole lot more fun with her spanking new toy.

38
The Hall of Geirrod

Thor and Carmel barely had to scramble down another fifty metres before they caught sight of a thin trail of smoke. This delicate strand was rising lazily from a chimney that was almost invisible in a small forest clearing.

The camouflaged hall from where the smoke was emanating was built from large logs with layers of moss plugged between them. It had a low roof that was tiled with layers of wooden shingles with grasses and lichens growing amongst these. Had it not been for the telltale sign of an inviting fire, they would probably have missed the dwelling altogether. This hall to be Geirrod's and it held the promise of shelter, warmth, and food.

The building lay a short distance from the far bank of the river, which flowed swift and deep at this point in its course. Carmel was clearly too cold and exhausted to ford the waters safely, so Thor picked her up carefully in his arms and, after raising her high above his head, he stepped into the freezing water.

The rocks were smooth and slippery beneath his feet and invisible to the eye, and he was quickly up to his waist in water that threatened to topple him with every precarious step he took. Looking up, he could just make out the figure of a woman on the opposite bank. She appeared buxom and stood at least two hundred and ten centimetres tall.

"Hey!" cried Thor, feeling certain that she was one of Geirrod's daughters. "Look it's me, Thor."

To his astonishment, the woman picked up a large stone and threw it at him, narrowly missing his head.

"Hey, stop! It's me—Thor. Look, it's me!"

The woman didn't stop, and she threw two larger rocks at him. They splashed noisily around his waist and he lurched sideways, almost dropping his precious load. Clearly, the woman couldn't hear him.

With a great deal of muttering and cursing under his breath, Thor returned to the bank and placed Carmel gently upon it. The crazy woman was still hurling rocks at him, each seeming larger than the last. Her aim was improving, too. Reluctantly, Thor picked up a medium-size boulder and lobbed it at the woman. It hit her squarely on the leg and she hobbled away howling, her voice making a noise that sounded remarkably like that of a wounded dog.

"I'm so sorry about that," he mumbled apologetically to Carmel as he picked her up once more.

"Are you absolutely sure they're friendly?" Carmel inquired warily. Secretly she was quite relieved that the woman, if she was one of Geirrod's daughters, was definitely no beauty.

"Yes, certain. Loki swore they would welcome me any time with open arms."

Thor started across the river once more with Carmel high above his head. She hung on tightly this time. She was beginning to have doubts about her lover; Loki could be playing one of his pranks again.

Spluttering and shaking his head, Thor eventually reached the other side and set Carmel safely down upon the bank. He had taken a ducking on the crossing, but to his pride he hadn't dropped Carmel into the freezing torrent.

"Where in Asgard are you going?" she shouted in amazement as he made his way back into the waters.

"To get the cage!" he bellowed without turning round.

Carmel sat down on the bank and smiled. How he had carried that heavy load across the plain and through all the snow she would never know. He really was the strongest and kindest god in Asgard. Hugging her knees and shivering, she smiled wistfully as she followed his progress through the churning waters. She could see what Sif saw in him now, how safe she must feel with his powerful arms wrapped around her.

Sif was a lucky goddess. That was for sure.

After reaching the bank, Thor picked up the cage and made his way back across the river once more. This was his third trip and his legs and feet were already blue with cold. They were beginning to feel completely numb. The freezing waters had made his muscles stiff, too, making it hard for them to move. As he neared the bank with the cage, he slipped once more and his head ducked beneath the waters. This time he had lost his footing completely.

With a mighty roar, he hurled the cage onto the bank and then began to drift away, flailing his arms wildly in the air as he picked up speed in the current. He shouted loudly, his head spinning from side to side, looking for something, anything, to grab hold of.

Carmel dived into the waters. She didn't hesitate, not even for a second. Thor's life was at stake and she had no thought for her own. She had to save him.

The icy shock of the water as her head went under made her gasp deeply from the reflex caused by the sudden chill upon her face. Choking and spluttering, she too now drifted helplessly downstream. The current was too strong and she was simply too cold and weak to fight it.

Bobbing up and down like a half-drowned rat, Thor saw her desperate struggles. With a final huge effort he reached out an arm and grabbed hold of a rowan tree that hung from the banks. Its roots held firm and he was safe. Stretching out and using every inch of his arm span, he caught hold of Carmel's fingertips. She clutched at his hand, clinging onto it like a limpet.

Coughing and shouting words of encouragement to each other, they hauled themselves onto the rocky bank. They lay there for some minutes, side by side, their chests heaving as they coughed up the water which had so nearly drowned them. Carmel wept as she threw her arms around him. The tears weren't for her. The heartfelt sobs were for Thor. She had so nearly lost her mighty friend. Laughing and shivering as she cried, she wept tears of joy at his salvation.

It had been a very lucky escape and to mark his gratitude, Thor borrowed Carmel's knife to cut a stout staff from the rowan bush. He was a superstitious god, and it had saved his life.

Perhaps it might do so again.

"Thor my, dear friend, that really was a close shave back there!"

Geirrod's words sounded genuine enough as both Thor and Carmel sat in his hall and basked in the warmth of a blazing fire. The hog which was roasting on a spit smelt better than any meal either of them had ever smelt before. Thor was certain he could eat the whole beast in just one sitting.

Contrary to Carmel's expectations, when they eventually arrived at the hall, Geirrod and his not-so-attractive daughters had done their most to make them welcome, apologising profusely for Gjalp's behaviour earlier. Thor had been right. She hadn't recognised him because she was both a little deaf and extremely short-sighted.

To make amends, both she and her sister Greip made a huge fuss of Thor, drying him with towels and warming his body sandwiched between their ample bosoms. They rubbed him down and pressed their bodies against him in such a suggestive manner that it left Carmel feeling sick inside. *The lecherous hags!*

Eventually they all sat down to supper and Thor and Carmel dined so heartily that not a single morsel of hog was left. They even gnawed at the bones until they had stripped off every last piece of meat and all the marrow had been sucked dry. The giantesses continued to shower Thor with their attention, plying him with mead and ale until he swayed with drunkenness in his chair.

Warm, drunk, and with a belly now aching from fullness, Carmel relaxed and got ready for sleep.

Growing bored with Thor receiving all the attention, she got up from the table and spread her body out lazily on a bear skin which lay invitingly close to the roaring fire. Stretching and squirming around like a cat, she eventually found exactly the right spot to be comfortable in.

With a single, wide yawn, Carmel made ready to fall into an exhausted asleep. Just before doing so, she decided to take one last protective look at Thor. The two floozy sisters had finally disappeared and he now lay snoring peacefully, slumped in his chair. He looked so relaxed she decided not to disturb him, but how she wished he were cuddled up next to her in front of the lovely fire.

Thor awoke suddenly in the middle of the night.

He had been having a frightful nightmare that his body was still rocking and swinging from side to side as the raging river Vimur tossed him around once more in its churning waters. To his immense surprise, he found that he was indeed rocking from side to side—his chair was slowly being hoisted into the air.

Thor wanted to shout out loud, but a coarse leather gag had been tied around his mouth and both his arms and legs were loosely bound as well. He was trapped. Looking to either side he could see Gjalp and Greip. Both sisters had an evil glint in their eyes and wicked smiles on their faces. They were the ones raising him aloft.

"Are you ready, sister?" Gjalp whispered coarsely to Greip. She grunted she was.

"On the count of three," Gjalp continued. "One."

Thor's chair rose higher and with a horrible feeling in the pit of his stomach he noticed that the ceiling of the hall was now getting awfully close to his head.

"Two."

Thor's chair rose higher still and his hair brushed against the rafters. He was in deep trouble and the intentions of the daughters were all too obvious. They were going to finish what Hrungnir had started: they were going to smash his head against the ceiling and splatter his brains across the roof of their hall.

"THREE!"

Both girls screeched with delight as they tossed Thor's chair upwards for the third and final time with all their might.

Luckily, just before they did so, Thor had time to collect his addled wits. Luckier still, the women had bound his arms quite loosely and with a weak twine.

Flexing his muscles as the chair came down on the count of two, Thor broke free and, reaching out, he managed to grasp the rowan staff which lay propped against the table. As he hurtled up toward the ceiling for the third and final time, he raised the staff and used it as a wedge, jamming it between the seat of the chair and the wooden rafters closing in above him.

The chair jerked suddenly to a violent halt, stopping abruptly as the staff did its job.

Taken by surprise, the force of the jolt wrenched the chair from the girls' hands and it crashed heavily back to the floor. Gjalp slipped and fell beneath it. The chair crushed her, killing her instantly as her ribs shattered like twigs beneath its heavily-laden mass.

Greip was luckier. She stumbled sideways and escaped its deadly impact.

Looking around, she spied another piece of twine and after wrapping it quickly around Thor's neck, she jerked it tightly backwards.

She was behind him and her hold was good and strong. Raising her knee against the back of the chair, she pulled on the noose with all her might, strangling him with her grip.

Thor couldn't breathe. He couldn't make a sound. His mouth opened and closed like a floundering fish as his face slowly began to turn red, then blue, and then finally purple.

"So you think you can kill my sister and her fiancée, Hrungnir, do you?" Greip hissed malevolently as she strained at the rope around his neck. She was basking in her moment of glory, throttling the life out of the mighty Thor.

Suddenly, to Thor's immense surprise and relief, her hold went limp and he could breathe once more.

"So you think you can strangle my friend and hero, Thor, do you?" Carmel mocked, mimicking Greip's words as she ran her through with her sword, killing her instantly. "Are you alright?" she whispered hoarsely to Thor in a voice that was trembling and threatened tears.

"Yes, but take cover quickly." Thor tore away the last of the twine that had tied him to his chair and nodded urgently in the direction of Geirrod. He, too, was now awake and making his way hurriedly toward the fire. He wouldn't be pleased that they'd killed both his daughters.

"THOR, YOU ARE A FOUL BASTARD!" Geirrod cursed furiously as he picked up some fire tongs and thrust them into the blaze. "I have hated you all my life and it will give me the greatest pleasure to kill you. It will be revenge for the death of my dearest friend, Hrungnir," he bellowed loudly, with a rage that matched the heat of the fire.

Pulling a molten ingot of iron from the hearth, he raised the tongs high above his head and hurled it at Thor. His aim was true, and the heavy blob of metal sizzled and hissed as it sped through the air.

Thor had noticed Geirrod digging in the fire and with tremendous foresight he had already put on his chain mail gloves. With these he was able to easily handle the ingot without harm, and in one fluid movement he caught and then hurled the molten rock back at Geirrod.

Geirrod opened his mouth to say something but his words never escaped it. So hard and fast was Thor's throw that the ingot bore through his chest, smashed through the iron support of the fireplace, and then passed clean through the stone wall behind it, finally embedding itself deep within the soil beyond, smoking and steaming as it did so. Geirrod fell to the floor, his chest hissing like a pit of vipers as the venom of the air inside his lungs slowly escaped. He had joined his daughters in death.

Thor looked at Carmel and Carmel looked at Thor.

"I guess Loki must have made a mistake about these giants," Thor shrugged, and with a loud and reassuring chuckle, he slapped Carmel firmly on her back. "Let's look on the bright side," he smiled and winked as they made their way toward the bear skin in front of the fire, "at least they wined and dined us as a good host should."

Carmel laughed and stretched out once more on the luxurious pelt. This time Thor lay beside her and she wrapped her arms tightly around him.

She wasn't going to let her mighty hero get himself into any more mischief that night.

39

Quantum Blocked

"Now let me see if I've got this right." Woods scratched his head and prayed that a smile didn't spoil his solemn façade. "You are Special Agent Vincent Smith and you, you are Special Agent Victor Smith."

The two men standing before him both nodded their heads enthusiastically and held out their hands to shake his once more. Naturally, their paperwork was in order and their identities were correctly recorded on his computer. However, if they were genuine federal agents he would eat their shiny, black, leather shoes—strip by glossy strip. Special Agents Victor and Vincent Smith had to be the most laughable stooges ever to enter the J. Edgar Hoover Building.

With their polite, flawless accents and quaint mannerisms, it felt as though the fictional detectives Thompson and Thomson had just stepped out of an episode of *Hergé's Adventures of Tintin.*

Although usually not one to waste valuable time, Woods decided to play along with the pair. He had been tipped off by the Contessa that another Valkyrie was coming, but he suspected that even without her phone call he would have sussed these two imbeciles out. Turning up and giving him paperwork demanding the transfer of his two Valkyries into their custody—*dream on!*

The existence of male 'Warriors' had come as a bit of a surprise to Woods; he had been under the impression that all the Valkyries were women. He had been expecting one or possibly two more of those to turn up, and couldn't understand why a couple of warrior men had tipped up in their place. The Contessa had stated that there were nine

Valkyries, *so where were the other seven?* He chuckled silently as he let the pair chat merrily away. If this was the best the Valkyries could do for men then no wonder the women wore the trousers.

The pair were complete muppets.

Unfortunately for Special Agents Smith and Smith, they had tripped themselves up almost as soon as they entered his office. Very few people knew about Brynhildr and Herja's presence in the cells and even fewer knew their Valkyrie names. Woods had been extremely sketchy in reporting the details of their custody. In an ideal world, he wanted them off to the Contessa's island without their presence having been thoroughly documented.

What had clinched the bogus identity of pair was when they described the inscription of Herja's name on the shaft of her dagger. This was minutiae known only to himself and Marcus. He had deliberately not mentioned this in any paperwork, keeping it as a safeguard for an eventuality such as this. No one from the FBI would have been able to confirm this detail; only a Valkyrie could do so.

He had caught them red-handed, but the question now was: *what to do with them?*

"Would you both like a cup of tea?" he enquired, having come to a decision.

"Oh, that would be lovely," replied Vince or Victor. They were identical in every detail and he really couldn't be bothered to look for any telltale moles or scars that would tell them apart.

"Earl Grey?" Woods asked mockingly.

"Oh, that would be splendid," they replied in unison, clearly missing the sarcasm in his voice.

"I'll just buzz down for some then," he added with a sneer. Woods pressed the panic button beneath his desk and then settled back to enjoy the show. A few minutes later he heard the heavy footsteps of security guards making their way along the corridor to his office.

"I think that must be the tea now. Would you like some biscuits?" Woods enquired, enjoying milking the situation to the last.

"Gosh, that was quick. Biscuits would be lovely, wouldn't it, Ve—I mean, Vince?"

Woods turned and pretended to get some from the cabinet behind him. "Come in!" he called out loudly when the footsteps eventually paused outside his door.

Timing his move to perfection, Woods took his revolver from the safe and spun round to level it at the pair just as the two security guards entered the room and did the same with their guns.

"Well, I say. That's a bit of a surprise, isn't it, Vili?" said Ve after a prolonged pause.

"Crikey, yes, I should say so. And I thought we were doing so well, too. Where in Midgard do you think we went wrong?" Vili enquired innocently.

Ve walked slowly around the table separating them from Agent Woods and peered closely at the gun that now lay frozen in his hands. He could have done the same to either of the guards who had entered the door. They, too, were standing still as statues. Even the noisy clock on the wall had stopped ticking.

For a while, Vili and Ve, identical twins and estranged brothers of Odin, bickered about their failure. Each was eager to blame the other. They were clearly disappointed, as they had put a lot of effort into their disguises. Maybe their shoes were too highly polished, or perhaps their suits were the wrong shade of black. Possibly their ties were too thick or the earpieces which they had researched so carefully (and worn so proudly) were in the wrong ear. What neither of them could see was what should have been patently obvious: as undercover agents, they sucked.

"I wonder what happened to the tea?" Vili enquired as he drummed his fingertips on the table.

"I wonder what we should do now?" Ve mused as he posed a much more pertinent question.

For the time being the two gods were safe, their special ability having saved them from immediate capture and incarceration.

Both Vili and Ve shared an important gift: they were able to 'quantum block' a small bubble of space-time around them. This effect allowed them to accelerate time for themselves (and selected friends) to the speed of light, effectively freezing—or blocking—time for everyone else caught within the bubble. The effect was only temporary, lasting only until somebody else entered the bubble or until one of the brothers chose to end it. Interruption by an outside observer would break the enchantment, and time would return to normal once more.

Fortunately for Vili and Ve, the office of Agent Woods was at the end of a small corridor with few passersby. They could probably have drunk their tea (if it had actually been requested), eaten cake, and taken a small nap before anyone would have disturbed their haven of safety.

"I think we should empty the safe," Vili suggested, and Ve agreed.

Carefully he pressed a hand against the steel door to the cabinet and as he did, his hand dissolved into an indistinct, shadowy blur before passing right through it. The peculiar effect of their charm not only accelerated time for the brothers, it also smeared their bodies into massless waves of probability. Each and every one of the atoms in their bodies was no longer a solid particle. They could pretty much travel wherever they wanted to, 'quantum tunnelling' their way through solid walls as though they didn't exist, which was extremely handy in situations such as these.

After feeling around inside the vault, and with a satisfied smile on his face, Vili withdrew the Valkyrie artifacts.

"I'll take them somewhere safe," Vili offered as he waved his hand over his ring, vanishing briefly with the knife, purses, and flasks. When he returned, the artifacts were gone. At least the pair had accomplished the first part of their mission successfully.

"So what do we do now?" enquired Ve, returning the conversation once more to their predicament.

"We don't know where Brynhildr or Herja are, so we can't go and get them," Vili offered, which was true. The cells in which the Valkyries were being held captive could be anywhere in the labyrinthine building.

"And we can't really leave," acknowledged Ve, stating the obvious.

"Then I suppose there's only one thing we can do," Vili sighed as the two brothers looked at each other with wry smiles upon their faces. Words weren't necessary as they held their arms up high in the air.

"WE SURRENDER!" they cried in unison as Ve snapped his fingers.

He had broken the quantum block.

40

Carmel's Kiss

Thor and Carmel set out early from Geirrod's hall. They would have liked to stay longer, wining and dining at his treacherous expense, but time was their enemy. It was the fourth day since they had left the watchtower and they had to get to Utgard today. They urgently needed to have their showdown with Thrym.

The hall of Geirrod was a recognised landmark, and there was a well-marked trail which led them back to the main road to Utgard. It was chilly when they set off, but the sky was clear and blue again and promised fine weather ahead.

Within the hour they were back walking through the woods as they paralleled the main route to Utgard. The road was wide and busy now as it wound down the mountain on the final approach to Thrym's capital. The number of giants on the path grew rapidly in number, seeming to double with every kilometre they travelled. It was tiring work ducking, hiding, and then scrambling forward once more through the heavy brush that carpeted the forest floor.

Finally, when the stone walls of Utgard were clearly visible in the sunlight dazzling from the lake beyond, Carmel suggested that it was time for the next part of her plan. With a shrug of tired resignation, Thor turned and headed once more away from the path. Carmel followed behind him. To her surprise, she was now more nervous than he as they pushed deeper into the woods. Of course, her apprehension was completely understandable, given their extraordinary circumstances.

It wasn't every day a Valkyrie maid got to whip a mighty god of Asgard.

After travelling a good distance from the track, they reached a narrow, steep-sided ravine that gouged a deep cleft in the side of the mountain. A stream bubbled and chattered noisily as it tumbled over worn pebbles at the bottom of the slope. There were trees, too, tall and mature with ancient and sturdy trunks. The location seemed ideal. The valley's steep walls and noisy stream would mask the loud crack of her whip when she eventually set to work on Thor's back.

This was the one part of Carmel's plan which Thor had been most reluctant about, the part where he had raised his eyebrows and given her the strangest of looks. He knew too well of her fiendish reputation with the whip and he didn't relish the opportunity of experiencing its vicious kiss. There had been some discussion about this before he agreed, but in the end he had to admit that Carmel was right. It was the only way she could mark Thor to make Thrym believe there had been a struggle.

Of course she could have tried kicking and punching him, but against Thor's massive frame her blows would have been laughable. Like a small child flailing at her father's legs, they would have left no impression.

Finding a suitable tree, Carmel bound him to the trunk. She tied his arms and legs as tightly as she could, having learned this lesson from the ghastly giant sisters. She couldn't afford to have him struggling free. As an extra precaution, she bound his waist as well. This was Thor, and he could never be too secure.

"Would you like me to gag you? Because I'm afraid it's going to hurt," Carmel offered apologetically, but Thor refused. He was big and strong and she had promised to give him no more than a dozen strokes—just enough to make an impression, and that was all. He was confident he could take such a brief beating from a woman, even if that woman happened to be Carmel.

Carmel stepped back and uncoiled her whip. It was a marvellous creation and she ran its thick, heavily-braided leather lovingly through her hands. She had had it custom made to an exacting specification.

The whip had a heavy, double-plaited belly covered by a thick leather bolster. The overlay was an intricate four-seam braid which tapered delicately as the thong neared the leather fall at its end. This was attached by an intricate snake-head knot. Carmel had given the fall extra weight by adding small, threaded beads of lead; these gave her whip extra speed through the air and a much more vicious bite. In her expert hands the beads acted like a scourge, digging deeply into flesh and then ripping it from the body of her helpless victim.

Cautiously, Carmel tested the whip in the air. It felt good; the balance between the handle and thong was perfect.

Apologising profusely, she delicately delivered two or three gentle strokes across Thor's back. She flinched with each one, just as he did. Even these first tentative blows had raised unpleasant purple welts. She offered to gag him once more and, to her relief, he accepted. She bound it tightly—if he bellowed loudly, she felt sure the noise would carry all the way to Lyr, the hall of Thrym.

Taking her position once more, Carmel was ready. It was time to get the job done. The harder she whipped, the quicker it would be over. She decided to cut loose and get to work.

Time and again Carmel cracked her whip, its leather thong singing sweetly to her as it snaked high above her head, curling, and then lunging forward once more. The lazy swish as it danced overhead thrilled her, as did the sharp crack of its brutal tip as it sank its jaws deep into her victim's back. It was a beautiful song, and one Carmel never grew tired of.

In her hands each lash was an effortless, fluid motion, the whip arcing and carving its way through the air with the supple grace of a ballerina. It became one with her body; both being melded into a single deadly weapon of destruction. Harder and harder she beat him, one vicious stroke after another flowing from her whip with all the force she could muster. She had forgotten her victim was Thor—his faceless, bleeding back looking much the same as any another. She couldn't hear his muffled screams, being lost in the poetry of her craft, revelling in its strength and beauty.

It was the noisy, startled flight of a pheasant taking off close by that probably saved Thor's life. With a terrible shock, Carmel froze. Her hand was raised and the thong of the whip stalled in mid air, before dropping limply beside her.

Sweet Odin! What had she done?

Hardly daring to look, she rushed over to the bleeding mess before her. Thor's body was slumped against the tree and his breathing had changed. He was barely conscious. Shaking with fear, she cut him loose and watched in terror as he collapsed onto the earth at her feet.

"Thor?" she shouted loudly through clenched teeth. She felt sick. Fear twisting her stomach into knots. He didn't reply.

"Thor, are you alright?" she called louder and nudged at him with her foot. Still nothing.

She cursed her vanity and her stupidity.

"Thor!" she cried as tears welled in her eyes. She kicked his body hard, blind terror spurring her on. "For the love of Odin, please don't die on me!"

She kicked him once more with all her force. To her relief, he moaned and grunted. He was alive, but far from happy. Slowly rising to his feet, Thor beckoned with his hand for her to give him her whip. He didn't look at her and Carmel feared the worst.

Now it was going to be her turn.

Trembling violently, she passed it over, his hands tightening like a pair of vises around its handle. He was going to murder her, of that she was certain, as was the fact that she deserved it. After all, she had damn near killed the most powerful god in the realm.

Muttering loudly, Thor turned and half walked, half staggered away toward the stream. He was quickly lost behind some boulders and she could hear him splashing and cursing as he plunged into the icy waters. Carmel slumped against a tree, choking back tears that threatened to flood her eyes. *How could she have become so hypnotised and blind?*

She thanked Odin once more that Thor was alive before cursing herself yet again. She was livid at her stupidity. She should hack her evil hand off, but even that wouldn't be enough. If Thor wanted to take her life she would gladly give it to him, such was her shame. For almost the first time in her life, the vain, cruel, and frequently selfish Carmel felt the terrible pain of remorse. She swallowed hard. Its bitter taste was well deserved.

After what seemed an age, Thor emerged from behind the rocks and to her great surprise he seemed to be in a much better mood. He was in obvious pain but a lot less angry. She wondered if he had visited Odin's garden and eaten some apples beneath the soothing shade of Yggdrasill. Whatever had happened, his calm and confident stride as he climbed up the slope toward her brought a slight smile to her face. He had even washed her whip and coiled it neatly for her.

"Thor, I, I'm so sorry, I—" Carmel started to stutter a heartfelt apology but Thor waved for her to be silent. He didn't want her apology.

Drawing nearer, Thor gave Carmel the biggest and most important surprise of her life. Dropping stiffly to one knee, he reached for her hand and kissed it.

"Thank you, my lady," he spoke gruffly and then looked up, winking, as a mighty grin spread across his lips. "But please—never do that again."

As soon as he was standing once more, Carmel threw her arms around his shoulders and then wrapped her legs tightly around his waist. She squeezed him hard. Half crying, half laughing, she hugged and kissed his face and cheeks, thanking him over and over again.

This was undoubtedly the best moment of her life.

By calling her 'my lady' and kissing her hand, Thor had given Carmel the highest accolade possible. He had bestowed on her the honour reserved for goddesses and the Valkyrie elite. His intention was clear: he had made her a warrior—his equal and a powerful woman he would respect and obey. She couldn't have been happier or prouder.

When at last Carmel released him from her embrace, her world had changed. Thor picked up the heavy cage once more and she led the way back to the road. No longer a maid, she didn't need to seek his permission or offer polite suggestions. She could command and lead, confident that he would follow. It was a wonderful feeling and she pranced ahead of Thor with all the elegance and vigour of a yearling doe.

Thor chuckled as he followed her footsteps, wincing noisily and cursing occasionally under his breath. He had always liked Carmel and admired her strength and determination. His back stung like crazy, but just like the chunk of rock embedded in his forehead, the wounds would quickly heal. If the kisses of her whip left scars he couldn't care less. He would wear them with pride.

For many years he had considered her the finest of the Valkyrie maids, and all he had done that day was bestow upon her an honour that was rightfully hers. She had saved his life in Geirrod's hall and risked her own in the freezing torrent of Vimur. He couldn't have asked for more. She had more than earned his respect and she would need the confidence of a warrior for what surely lay ahead. Thrym's hall beckoned and their reception was bound to be hostile.

The fact that Thor had created a tenth Valkyrie was of little consequence to him. That particular superstition was Odin's problem, not his, and he would deal with this minor inconvenience when—or rather, if—they ever made it home.

41

Hello Stranger

"I'm so sorry, Sangrid, I really am. He just won't do anything. I tried my hardest to persuade him but he simply wouldn't listen. I'm afraid you're on your own now."

Kat could hardly believe her ears when Frigg eventually hung up. Odin wasn't sending anybody to help them, no one at all. *How could he do such a thing?*

She had trusted him and thought that he cared. Everything seemed to be collapsing around her: first Jess captured, then Jameela, and now Odin refusing to send any help. What hurt the most was that she'd bothered to wait. She believed in Odin and he'd abandoned her. The thought was baffling. She and Marcus had wasted over twenty-four hours skulking around, dodging surveillance cameras, and for what?

Absolutely nothing.

It had all been a pointless waste of time, time they could have used rescuing her friends already. She suddenly felt sick.

Frigg's phone call came as a bitter blow because yesterday had been a surprisingly good day, too. She and Marcus had started early, eating breakfast quickly before checking out of their cheap hotel. They were finding lying low tough, especially in urban twenty-first century America with CCTV cameras perched on every street corner and others checking your car as you drove by. Big Brother was watching you, and he was doing it big time.

To minimise detection, they decided that their best option for keeping out of sight was to head out of Washington for the day, travelling through the suburbs to the countryside beyond. They drove for several

233

hours, and if Kat hadn't had other things on her mind then it would have made for a lovely journey, particularly as Marcus was doing the driving.

The first green shoots of spring were bristling on trees and early daffodils clustered in vibrant yellow carpets beside the road. Dirty brown slabs of slushy snow lay in shady ditches, each struggling to hide from the tentacles of sunshine which crept lovingly toward them. Sadly for these slabs, there could be no hope of escape, each snowflake's doom having been sealed the moment it fell from the skies.

Marcus had decided to take Kat to a secluded woodland he had known and loved when he was a boy. There was a good reason for their visit: she needed to learn how to shoot a gun. They had stopped briefly on their way to buy some ammunition and now they were going to put it to good use.

The whole exercise of learning how to shoot came as something of a shock for Kat. She could wield a sword and axe with deadly intent and had killed in the heat of battle, but she had never fired a gun. That definitely hadn't been on the curriculum when she was at med school.

Marcus made a good teacher, even though he wasn't the greatest shot. He taught her how to load the gun, release the safety, and aim correctly. Her posture was good, but at first her technique was lousy. She tended to snatch as she pulled the trigger, tensing up at the expectation of the powerful recoil, which spoilt her accuracy. Slowly she learnt to relax and squeeze, relax and squeeze, just as Marcus had told her. Her aim improved dramatically, as did her confidence. She would still have felt happier with Talwaar in her hand, but taking a sword into FBI headquarters was not really an option.

After lunch at a roadside truck stop, they went for a long and productive walk. They needed a plan and despite turning over countless alternatives, they kept coming back to their first and simplest idea. It was an embarrassment really, and Kat wished she had Silk or Carmel with her. They would have come up with a much more ingenious scheme, something guaranteed to shake the building to its foundations. She felt sure that next to their ideas, hers was both stupid and boring.

The plan was simplicity itself but they couldn't improve on it. Marcus would turn up and ask to see Agent Woods with Kat in (unlocked) handcuffs in tow. After convincing Woods that he had captured a third Valkyrie, the agent would then, ideally, take them up to his office.

Once inside, Kat would miraculously spring free, grab Marcus's gun, and take Woods hostage. For good measure, they had both agreed that Kat should hit Marcus over the head and he would crash 'unconscious' to the floor. From there, he could surreptitiously monitor progress and intervene if Woods managed to turn the tables on her.

With Woods hostage, Kat would force him to retrieve the knife and other artifacts and take her to the cells. After locking him inside, she, Jameela, and Jess would make good their escape.

If the whole scheme sounded a bit familiar then that was because it was. Much of the plan had been borrowed from the one Jess had used to free Ruby, with one exception. Marcus implored Kat not to knock him out as Jess had done. The plan felt weak and fallible, but try as they might, they couldn't come up with anything better.

Getting into the car once more, they headed back toward the sprawling outskirts of Washington. They would stay at a cheap motel some distance from the centre tonight. Neither of them was sure if Woods was trying to track them down, but they weren't going to take any chances. Kat had her suspicions that he probably wasn't. For the moment he held all the cards.

Woods was like a spider in the middle of a web, with two juicy Valkyries all neatly trussed up in silk beside him. He didn't need to come after them, because he knew they had to come to him. She and Marcus would almost certainly be walking into a trap, and that was why Odin's refusal to send a more experienced Valkyrie had been such a crushing blow.

Kat felt doomed, but she couldn't let Marcus sense this. For his sake, she had to show confidence in their plan. It was going to be a nerve-wracking night ahead.

"Are you ready to go?" Marcus asked tentatively as he looked up from his coffee. Kat nodded. It was minutes after Frigg's phone call and she'd been daydreaming. She was still very tired and hadn't slept well during the night. Hour after hour she had tossed and turned, chewing over in her mind all the countless ways their rescue mission might go so horribly wrong.

Settling up their bill, the two of them got into the car. Marcus turned the key and the engine spluttered slowly into action. They were on their way to Washington. It was going to be a one way trip.

Woods had indeed acted exactly as Jameela and Odin expected.

Bang on cue, he arrested her—an arrest that they had anticipated and planned for. Jameela's job was simple: to gain intelligence from the inside and let Jess find her own way into the building. Between them, one on the inside and one on the outside, Odin felt certain that they could retrieve her knife and make it safely back to Asgard.

Because Odin had been so confident of Jameela's capture, they had spent a long time preparing for the eventuality. The captured purse and coin were fakes, as was the mead in her flask. The mead was a good fake, a very, very good fake, because it had to be. Odin had a hunch that this was probably what the FBI was after. He had made some 'Mead from Valhalla' that was lacking the one crucial ingredient: it had no healing or restorative powers. In every other aspect it looked, smelt, and tasted just like the real thing. It delivered the same warm glow and helplessly addictive kick to anyone who drank it.

Odin hadn't sent Jameela in without the genuine items, however. Using material identical to his blue cloak, they had strapped her gold coin and a miniature flask to her leg. The material they used was a meta-material and hidden beneath its veil of invisibility, the items passed undetected during the cursory 'pat down' before her imprisonment.

Jameela was actually taken aback at the brevity of this examination. She had expected a strip search, cavity check, and hours and hours of endless, brutal interrogation and torture. None of this had happened. She was locked in solitary confinement and then pretty much left alone. Woods spent a little time with her and she had answered his very general questions politely and as best she could, but other than a chest X-ray and an electrical reading of her silent heart, nothing else had happened.

If Woods wasn't trying to bore her into breaking down, then the only other explanation for his inactivity must be that he was waiting for something else to happen first. What that might be, she couldn't tell.

She had, however, made one important discovery: her knife was locked up in the safe in his office. He had shown it to her when she first arrived, asking her to confirm that it was indeed her weapon. He had done this very cautiously, with her hands cuffed behind her and standing a long way from his desk. Two burly guards had kept their automatics cocked and pointing at her throughout. Clearly, lessons had been learnt from the debacle when Jess sprang Ruby.

Other than this discovery, the rest of her stay so far had been a crushing bore, being cooped up in a claustrophobic cell for three days and left to count the cracks in the walls. It was day four now and her slender supply of mead was running out. If Jess didn't make her move soon, she would have to use her coin and return to Asgard. There would be no alternative.

"Greetings, my lady!"

Jameela nearly jumped out of her skin. Ve 'tunnelling' his wave-like body through the locked door to her cell was the last thing she could have imagined happening today. It was crazy, and she rubbed her eyes hard, just in case they were playing tricks on her.

"Come on, we need to get you out of here," he cried, pulling excitedly at her arm without giving her time to speak. Meekly she obliged, and then wished she hadn't. In his excitement, he tried to drag her back through the closed door and she bashed her nose hard against it. She was clearly too large and solid to tunnel along behind him.

After a quick debate and some considerable rustling of pockets, Ve re-entered the cell with the guard's keys. After quite a few failed attempts, Jameela finally found the one which turned the lock and then joined the brothers outside. Two quantum-blocked guards stood frozen beside them, and she could make out a door farther along the corridor that had already been opened.

"What in Odin's name are you two doing here?" she hissed crossly at them. She had expected Jess to come and rescue her, not a pair of sweet, well-intentioned, but completely incompetent gods. She had had many dealings with them over the years and they always found a way to mess things up.

The brothers attempted to fill her in, but they kept getting side-tracked. She tried politely to hurry them along and eventually had enough detail to sketch an outline of their story.

They had only just been captured and had quantum blocked the guards as soon as they arrived in the cell block. Fortunately, they'd already recovered her knife (she thanked Odin for that small mercy) and to her immense surprise she learned that Jess had been captured, too, at least a day before she too had been taken prisoner.

"Have you released her yet?" she asked anxiously. The brothers nodded that they had and indicated to the open cell farther up the corridor. "Good. Is she alright?" Jameela enquired casually, just to make sure.

Vili and Ve looked at each other, not really knowing quite what to say. For once Odin's brothers had been rendered speechless.

Marcus and Kat turned the final corner and the J. Edgar Hoover Building loomed ominously ahead of them. They had parked some distance from their destination and walked the last half kilometre or so. Kat was grateful for this; it had helped to steady her nerves. Now, seeing the building's imposing concrete and glass edifice, she crumbled once more.

The coin which would send her back to Asgard was held tightly in her clenched fist and she yearned to chant the words that she knew would take her back home to safety. What they were about to do was madness, but she knew they couldn't stop. She was a Valkyrie warrior and they had to go on. Her sisters were inside and they had to be rescued. She and Marcus were their last and only hope, now that Odin had forsaken them.

Crossing the road, they made their way along the pavement toward the steps outside the building. Drawing closer, Kat's attention was inexplicably drawn toward a grey-haired lady who was just exiting the building. The woman was walking as briskly as she could, but the first cruel blows of old age had begun to take their toll, stiffening her hips and causing her shoulders to hunch and sag. Her hair, however, was still well groomed and lustrous and she retained a slimness of figure that hinted at a much more gracious youth.

The woman continued to hurry away from the building and with a pang of alarm, Kat realised that she was now heading straight toward them. Worse, her arms were opening wide.

"Oh, my dearest darling!" the woman exclaimed loudly and joyfully, hugging and kissing Kat like she was some beloved and long-lost friend. "And you, my precious Marcus," she continued, turning and showering him with similar affection.

Marcus and Kat exchanged hurried glances and shrugged in bewilderment. Neither of them had returned the warmth of her embrace because they shared the same confusion.

Who in Midgard was she?

42

The Lair of Thrym

At last, the final pieces of Carmel's plan were falling into place.

When the road to Utgard was once again within their sight, Thor and Carmel stopped and Thor put on Freyja's cloak of falcons' feathers. Chanting the sacred incantation, with a flash of light he transformed into an eagle once more.

At first, Carmel was shocked. Her whipping, which was intended to make the bird look as though it had been in a struggle, appeared far worse. Its back was practically bald like a vulture's neck. Kissing Thor's beak apologetically, Carmel helped him hop over the threshold of the cage. It was her way of saying 'sorry' and he squawked loudly in return. Carmel didn't understand what he was trying to say, but she hoped it wasn't too rude.

Thor would hate being cooped up but for next few hours there was no alternative. This was the plan and they had to stick to it.

Locking the cage behind him, she half dragged, half rolled it to the roadside. Now all she had to do was wait and hope some suitable help came by. It was mid morning and a lot of people were travelling up and down the trail.

Unfortunately, the first two giants who passed by were less than useless. With a chorus of startled grunts and eyebrows raised high in the air, the pair bounded away into the depths of the forest. They looked like teenagers and were probably farm labourers or woodsmen. The shock of a Valkyrie dressed in full battle tunic was way too much for them to handle.

In complete contrast, the next group to come along was a trio of elderly widows. They were courteous without being friendly, bobbing polite curtsies and then continuing on their way. They weren't afraid, but also were not much use. What Carmel needed was someone who could help her carry the heavy cage to the gates of Utgard.

Fortunately, the next passersby were perfect: a farming family sitting atop an ox-drawn cart laden with livestock, eggs, milk, and fresh vegetables they were taking to the market that morning. If they were surprised at the sight of a magnificent Valkyrie warrior so close to their capital, they didn't show it. After a brief explanation of her situation, the generous couple offered Carmel and the cage a lift on their already-crowded cart. The parents spoke little as they trundled the last few kilometres to Utgard with their young son staring wide-eyed and open-mouthed all the way. He had never seen such a beautiful woman before.

Carmel's treatment at the gateway to the town was pretty much what she'd been expecting. There was a lot of shouting, fear, excitement, and a noisy, mobbing crowd that gathered quickly and bristled with hostility. Drums were beaten and a messenger dispatched to Thrym's hall to inform him of her presence. Tensions escalated quickly as they waited for his reply.

Someone threw a rock at her and then another, and then someone else joined in. Carmel didn't want trouble, but faced with an impromptu stoning, she was compelled to act. Seizing the young son of the couple who had given her the lift, she held him in front of her with her sword at his throat. To her dismay, he became so terrified that he messed his breeches.

Eventually the messenger returned with a guarantee of safe passage to the hall of Lyr. Thrym wanted her bound as a prisoner, but Carmel flatly refused. She would either enter the hall alive and free, or dead and bound as a corpse.

After another small delay, Thrym dropped his condition. He was obviously intrigued to know what a Valkyrie was doing so far from Asgard and the battlefront. Accompanied by a heavily-armoured guard and with the iron cage swinging precariously from a pole stretched between two stout giants, the procession headed toward Thrym's hall.

Crowds gathered along the route. Some cheered and waved, but most booed and jeered. A few threw rotten vegetables, which didn't come as too much of a surprise. Odin and the Valkyries were the most feared and hated enemies of Jotunheim.

After what seemed an age, Carmel finally arrived in the small flag-stone-paved square in front of the hall. With a lump firmly stuck in her throat, she watched as the massive wooden doors to Lyr swung slowly open. Her journey was over.

Finally she would stand before the last great frost giant, the mighty Thrym.

"So, Valkyrie whore, what brings you to your doom?"

Thrym's voice bellowed from a large table that lay before a roaring fire at the far end of the hall. As Carmel's eyes adjusted to the dimness, she could make out his massive frame. He was sitting at the table, hunched over a large plate of vittles as he chain ate and drank his way toward lunchtime. To her great relief, she could see Mjollnir lying beside him, glistening in the flickering firelight. Thor's hammer never left his side—Mjollnir was Thrym's pride and joy, the ultimate symbol of his triumph over the gods. He kept it proudly on display both day and night.

"Do you know who I am?" Carmel asked politely as she moved forward and ushered the giants to put the birdcage down on the floor beside her. She wasn't letting it and its precious cargo out of reach, let alone out of sight.

"Indeed I do, evil wench. You are the vile Valkyrie temptress who has stolen the heart of Loki." Thrym was eager to demonstrate his knowledge of the comings and goings of the court of Asgard.

"Then you know why I am here. I come with a deal for you, great king of Jotunheim." Carmel tried to speak with confidence and reverence. Today was not a day to exchange insults as Thor had done. For the moment, she was negotiating from a position of weakness.

"Speak!" he cried as his fingers curled around Mjollnir's handle. He was expecting a deal that involved Thor's hammer, exactly as Carmel had predicted. "So you've come for this little trinket?" he continued scornfully and without giving Carmel time to reply. He waved Thor's hammer high above his head.

The crowded hall erupted. A chorus of excited grunts, foot stamping, and triumphant jeering resounding from each and every giant who had managed to squeeze into Lyr to witness this spectacle. It had been many a year since a mighty Valkyrie had come to Utgard.

"No, my lord, I care not for Thor nor for his hammer. I come only for my one true love and I come to bargain for his release." Carmel replied once the cacophony had died down. She spoke more softly now, lowering her head respectfully.

Thrym paused and replaced Mjollnir carefully on the table. Carmel's words had taken him by surprise. Loki wasn't his prisoner, but he definitely wasn't going to tell her that yet. He was, however, intrigued by the caged eagle. *Was that what the Valkyrie intended to offer?*

He decided to pose the question. "And what have you brought in trade for the safe release of that bastard son of Farbauti?"

"Great king, I bring you no less than the great queen of the Valkyries. I bring you Freyja herself!"

With an exaggerated bow and flourish of her hand, Carmel presented the cage with the eagle inside. She knew Thrym wasn't holding Loki prisoner, and she also knew that Thrym didn't know her true intent. Loki was the ruse, the red herring to draw his attention away from Thor's hammer.

Carmel knew he would never exchange Mjollnir for Freyja, but the thought of having both Mjollnir and the queen of the Valkyries would be just too tempting an offer for him to resist. This was why only she could complete this daring mission; only she was Loki's besotted lover and desperate for his safe return.

Thrym stood up and came around from behind his table. He carefully picked up the cage and examined the tatty-looking bird inside, muttering coarsely under his breath. Eventually he placed the cage roughly back on the floor.

"How do I know that this eagle is Freyja and not some rabid cockerel that will tear my eyeballs out?" he blustered loudly. Thrym was being cautious, very cautious. The cursed Valkyries were spawned by the devil and renowned for spinning great webs of treachery and deceit.

"Because, my lord, I also come with this." Carmel suddenly took the jewellery box from her knapsack and opened it in front of her. To gasps of admiration, she proudly displayed the fabulous Necklace of the Brisings before the gathered crowd.

"Would the great queen of the Valkyries let me come to you with this if she herself hadn't been forced into this cage?" she challenged angrily.

The crowd grunted loudly, and Thrym nodded his head slowly. There could be no other explanation, but he still didn't trust the beautiful woman before him. He had had too many dealings with Valkyries before.

"What if I take the necklace, kill you, and then throw your mange-infested bird into the fire? What then, hey?" he raged once more. Picking up the cage, Thrym pretended to swing it in the direction of the blazing hearth. Thor squawked loudly and flapped his wings in alarm. This wasn't looking good.

Carmel kept her nerve, flattering Thrym and pampering his ego. "My great king, I know you wouldn't do that. You are far too wise to kill the queen of the Valkyries, the holder of the key to their secret Chamber."

The tactic seemed to work. Much to her relief, he paused and then put the cage back on the floor.

Thrym stared intently at Carmel, bending forward and bringing his face so close to hers that his foetid breath sprayed morsels of half-chewed meat onto her lips. The sensation made her stomach churn.

Still not satisfied that the Valkyrie was telling the truth, Thrym decided that there was only one way the issue could be resolved. Standing up once more, he turned to face the crowded hall with hands raised high above his head.

"WE WILL LEARN THE TRUTH, GIANT-STYLE!" he roared loudly and the crowd responded by beating their chests, grunting, and stamping their feet. This would be spectacle of the highest order, one befitting the mighty hall of Lyr and the last of the great frost kings.

Thrym turned to Carmel and pressed his face close to hers once more. His eyes were open wide and his yellow teeth were visible through a hideous, snarling grin. He spoke quietly, his voice laden with venom as he hissed his poison at her.

"You, my pretty little Valkyrie scorpion, will fight a duel to the death and you will fight this giant-style, do you hear? Then, and only then, will I know if you are truly telling the truth about you and your rotten, mange-infested bird."

"As you wish, my lord, your justice will be done." Carmel stood back and calmly laid her sword and knapsack on the ground. She had never felt so alone or nervous before, but she couldn't show it, not even a hint. She knew what murderous trial Thrym had in store for her, but there was nothing she could do about it now.

It was all or nothing—and she had to succeed.

43

Toys

Hel hated the White Room with a vengeance. She banged at its white door with her fists, rattled the handle hard, and for good measure gave it a damn good kicking.

It wouldn't budge.

For now, the door was firmly locked shut and that was that. It was the only door in the whole of Niflheim that lay beyond her control, hence her anger and frustration.

The White Room, which lay opposite the corridor leading toward her royal chambers, was the place where deities left money and gifts for the services she provided. It was a two-way system. If she needed anything or wanted to place a request, this was where she would leave a note. When the room wasn't in use it was kept locked; the gods only opened the door when they deemed it appropriate for her to enter.

She hated that.

Occasionally, very occasionally, a deity would use the White Room to come to her realm in person. He or she would visit Niflheim, checking that their wishes and instructions for the dead were being carried out. Generally these visits were organised well in advance and Hel would be on her best behaviour. She would wear something white that looked chaste and modest, and would order her finest food and drink to be served in the oak-panelled reception room. The god would make the briefest of inspection tours and then be on his way, usually leaving a nice big bonus for Hel in her next installment of goodies.

Sometimes however, things went spectacularly wrong.

This usually happened when visits were impromptu or arranged through her servants Ganglati and Ganglot. A god would turn up expecting to see the souls of his favourite citizens laid peacefully to rest in Old Niflheim, and what would happen? Hel would give them a guided tour of the mines or her VIP torture chambers instead.

These catastrophes were shocking and, fortunately, rare, but when they did occur Hel somehow always managed to wriggle out of trouble. She was the mistress of excuses, and could always find a way, any way, to appease their wrath, wheeling and dealing until at last they were placated.

Of course, when the deity was gone, things were very different. Hel would let loose, thrashing her useless servants mercilessly as they tottered like a pair of startled turtles down the corridor away from her. They would scream and beg for mercy, but she would have none of it, beating and bullying the pair until they collapsed in a dishevelled heap.

You would have thought that Hel's servants would hate Hel and her constant abuses—and they did—but when the dust eventually settled and her anger abated, they would always remain loyal and faithful.

Along with the two brooding shadows locked in their rooms, Niflheim was their home, and the only one they had ever really known. United as a foursome, the Guardians of Niflheim were powerful, extremely powerful, but separated from their imprisoned friends and with no means of escape, Ganglati and Ganglot were impotent. They were powerless to escape and duty-bound to do Hel's bidding. Good boss or bad boss, they had no alternative but to serve and obey Niflheim's ruler.

Growing bored with the locked door, Hel finally stuck her tongue out at it and then turned and opened the entrance to her chambers. She wasn't really angry. It was just the principle of somewhere or something she couldn't control that ticked her off.

By the time she reached her room, the white door was already forgotten. She was smiling broadly once more and eager to play with her new toy.

Clapping excitedly, she made a bee line for one of her many wardrobes. She wanted to wear something special, something that would drive Frigg's present crazy. Chucking clothes wildly this way and that, she dug deep until she neared the very back of a wardrobe.

At last she found what she wanted.

Purring with delight, she held up an original Victorian corset. It was beautiful, although covered in dust. After giving it a good shake, Hel pranced excitedly around the room, admiring the way its figure-hugging form nestled against her body. The corset was made from heavy silk, black in colour and stiffened with ribs made from whalebone. A wide red ribbon laced all the way down the back of the garment to its bustle. She hadn't worn it in ages, probably not since the great, great grandfather of her latest toy had been alive, but it still felt wonderful to hold and she rushed to put it on. She didn't have time to call Ganglot to tie her in properly, so she clumsily laced it up as best she could.

Pinning her hair up in a loose and tousled manner, she quickly applied rouge, powder, and thick, scarlet lipstick to her mouth. Her technique was crude, trading quantity for quality. Putting on 'slap' was definitely not Hel's greatest talent.

Eventually she was ready. With a big sigh of approval, she admired herself lovingly in a mirror, turning slowly left and right as she did so.

Hel looked incredible: a surreal cross between a fantasy French tart and a Victorian burlesque dancer—and one who had slept in her clothes and makeup the night before. Whatever the image she had hoped to convey, tramp or temptress, in truth it didn't really matter. Her new toy would drool even if she tipped up in a bin bag.

He'd been there only a few days, but he was already a hopelessly devoted fan and she loved it. So much so that she'd moved him into the room next to hers, allowing him unprecedented access to her innermost sanctum. This decision was extraordinary, but so too was Hel's new toy.

Hel's personal chambers were a closely guarded secret. Few had entered her rooms, ostensibly because of the fabulous wealth hidden inside. In truth, however, the reason for her secrecy was far more mundane. Hel's chambers were a disgrace, reminiscent of the shambolic dumping ground of a teenager, and one of the most spoilt variety.

The delicate antique furniture, the exquisite paintings, ornaments, and acres of her vast, four-poster bed were hidden beneath a carpet of discarded trinkets. Clothes, books, DVDs, shoes, handbags, and computer games lay scattered around the room with gay abandon.

Hel's filing system was simple: she didn't have one. Home for any item was where it fell or where it was thrown, depending on her mood.

Apart from money, jewels, alcohol, and drugs, the gods gave Hel goods in exchange for her services. She had a passion for gadgets and electronic toys, especially the kind that crammed the shopping malls of Midgard. On her wall hung a monstrous plasma TV screen and beneath it, buried amongst a mound of cables and remote controls, were a PS3, an iPod, and an Xbox.

Hel would willingly admit to being a bit of a games addict, and could play a mean bout of *Halo* or *Call of Duty*. Her favourite challenge, though, had to be *Grand Theft Auto*. It just sort of hit the right spot. Strangely enough, her favourite game of all time wasn't a computer one at all. It was chess, and she was exceptionally good at it. According to players from Midgard (and she'd played more than a few), she was the equivalent of a Grandmaster—which to Hel sounded pretty darned good.

She loved films, too, being enthralled by Charlie Chaplin and Laurel and Hardy from the era when moving images and 'talkies' first hit the silver screen. Unsurprisingly, her favourite genre was horror, and she often made notes to try things out in her VIP chambers. People in Midgard could be so creative.

However, in spite of the passage of time and the countless movies which had come and gone, her all-time favourite remained unchanged—*Gone with the Wind*. Clark Gable was her perfect man and she had replayed the movie countless times in her head, casting herself in the role of Scarlet with Balder as Rhett. They were characters she could empathise with and she always cried along with Vivien Leigh when she was left weeping and alone in the grand, sweeping, staircase finale.

With a final purr of approval, Hel turned and strutted into the suite next door. She was ready to play.

"So how's my darling little boy today?" Hel cooed lovingly as she flounced unannounced through the door. Sashaying provocatively, she sped across the room to end up sprawled across Henry's knees.

She had caught him by surprise. He was studying the stolen schematics of Mimir's well on a large computer screen on the desk in front of him.

Throwing her arms around his neck, Hel bent forward and planted a huge, exaggerated kiss on his lips. Henry blushed furiously, torn between his two greatest passions: science and a beautiful woman.

"Pretty good. I think I've found what you've been looking for," he eventually replied with a smirk. He knew his loving angel Sangrid would be pleased with this, as indeed she was. Squealing with delight,

Hel ran her fingers passionately through his hair and then down the front of his chest, her tongue and lips roaming freely as she smothered his face in kisses.

"Are you sure?" she purred hopefully.

"Absolutely. Well, I mean—I think so," Henry blustered. The diagrams were extremely complicated and unlike anything he had seen before. However, he had begun to grasp the basics of the well's control system and that was good enough for now.

"I think my lovely little boy deserves a reward," Hel suggested with an impish grin. Standing up, she repositioned herself to straddle his legs, and then sat back down once more. They were now facing each other on her swivelling leather executive chair.

"Do you fancy a game of *Halo?*" Henry suggested naively, oblivious to the sexual innuendo she was flaunting in front of him.

"Oh, my darling little boy, I think we can do so much better than that," Hel breathed as she attacked his face and neck once more with her kisses, grinding her hips suggestively against his as she rocked back and forth on his legs.

Henry finally got the message. "Are we, you know, are we going to—" Henry stuttered, almost too excited to speak.

"Shush, not yet," Hel pressed her finger swiftly against his lips to silence him, looking up furtively toward the ceiling as she did so.

"I haven't got permission from you-know-who yet," Hel mouthed the word 'God' as she spoke. "He gets funny about his angels doing things. You wouldn't want me to end up in…would you?" Hel drew an imaginary line across her neck as she spoke and pointed downwards with her finger, mouthing 'Hel' as she did so.

It was hard for her not to burst out laughing. *The poor, brilliant, besotted idiot!*

She had convinced him that he was in heaven and that she was Sangrid, his personal and oh-so-virginal guardian angel.

"Oh, I'm sorry. I shouldn't have asked. I wouldn't want to get you into any sort of trouble," Henry stammered as he blushed profusely, swallowing every lie that fell from Hel's gorgeous, pouting lips.

"Oh, my pet, don't be down," Hel empathised as she studied his crestfallen face. Just as she admired strong leaders like Louis, Hel had a weakness for intelligent men, particularly those who were naïve and shy. Without realising it, Henry had struck a particularly sensitive nerve.

"I can always help you, you know…"

Placing her arms around his neck, Hel pulled his face toward her chest, burying it deep in her inviting bosom. Gently, she began to thrust her hips against his, grinding them in spasms which gained swiftly in urgency and strength. It wasn't long before they had the desired effect. Henry's gasps and brief spasmodic jerks signalled that he'd definitely enjoyed her reward.

Relaxing back into the chair with a sigh, Hel gradually released her steely grip.

"Better?" she enquired casually before standing up slowly and walked around behind him. Running her hands down his chest once more, she bent forward and nibbled invitingly at an earlobe with her teeth. The temptation to bite was almost unbearable, so she pulled away quickly, slapping herself hard across the face as she did so.

She had vowed to be extra especially nice to Henry, and that was exactly what she was going to do. At least, that is, until he delivered on the well.

"Are you alright?" Henry had heard the slapping noise and looked around innocently.

"Oh, I'm fine—a fly or something. Do you still fancy a game or a film or something?" she suggested hopefully.

Henry's eyes lit up. "*The Grudge?*"

Hel squealed once more, clapping her hands with delight. He really was the bestest playmate she could ever remember having. He loved all the same films that she did and was pretty good at computer games, too.

"Popcorn and beers?" she enquired, eyes sparkling excitedly like a child's. Grabbing Henry's hand, she dragged him quickly away from the computer. Work and the girls in her harem would have to go on hold a while.

For the moment, lounging across Henry, watching a movie, and eating junk food seemed far more appealing.

While Hel settled down to watch a horror movie with her latest toy, an old and discarded one was beating a painful retreat from her harem.

Hel's tongue-in-cheek attempt to convert Colleen to the joys of anal sex hadn't been successful. Cole, assisted now by a gloved Ganglati, was waddling slowly down the corridor in a gait reminiscent of an aging, saddle-sore cowboy.

For the first time he was grateful that he was dead and buried here. As a former gang lord and drug baron, he couldn't have lived with the humiliation of being gang raped by a psychotic, teenage bitch and her faggoty, fairy friends. His arse burned like a furnace and he was glad to be finally getting away from Hel and her lunatic inner sanctum of sycophants.

The Berserker army didn't sound brilliant, but it was the only option on offer and at least it would be a man's world, a place where his physical strength and mental toughness could garner respect and admiration.

After walking some distance downward and passing through two sets of guarded and heavily-bolted iron doors, Cole finally arrived at the entrance to the great cavern.

Inside here was where the Berserkers ate, slept, worked, and trained. It would be the perfect place for him to disappear from Hel's radar and become a statistic for a while in her army of madness. Unknown and starting with a clean sheet, he could work his way into a plan to take revenge on her.

It was with these reassuring thoughts in mind that the final set of iron doors was slowly opened.

Cole would find anonymity here at last.

"COLLEEN!"

A scornful voice bellowed immediately from somewhere in the smoke-filled haziness that shrouded the vast hall. The room was immense, brightly-lit, and larger than several football pitches rolled together. It was heaving with large, sweaty bodies of all different shapes and sizes and they had turned as one to face Cole when the doors finally creaked open.

Cole's arrival had been expected and was anything but discreet.

"I've been looking forward to this moment for a long time." The voice spoke again and seemed to be getting closer, although Cole still couldn't make out which of the countless men was doing the talking. However, an empty space was rapidly forming and the ranks of heavily-armed soldiers were parting swiftly to allow a masked and shadowy figure to emerge.

"Would somebody throw this piece of shit a sword and shield?" the figure barked caustically.

Cole could just about make out the person behind the voice now. He was a black man, medium build and muscular, with his head swathed in a red scarf that left only his deep, chocolate brown eyes visible. He was clearly the leader, but hadn't introduced himself as yet.

His instructions were obeyed swiftly and a sword and shield clattered ominously to the ground in front of Cole. The Berserkers hated the girls of Hel's harem, and the opportunity to humiliate one of them was too good a sport to miss.

Glaring angrily, Louis thumped his sword against his shield and indicated for Cole to pick his weapon up. "Now my little bitch, Colleen, let's see what Odin's rotten apple—the starter of Ragnarok—is really made of."

44

Carmel's Duel

There was no shortage of volunteers in the hall of Lyr willing to fight Carmel. Indeed, there was a considerable delay in the proceedings as one by one the giants stepped forward and staked their claim to be Thrym's champion. In normal circumstances, giants wouldn't be keen to cross swords with a Valkyrie, but these weren't normal circumstances.

They would be fighting a woman on their own turf and on their own terms. In their minds, there was absolutely no question about it: the victor of the duel would be the giant, and everybody wanted to be that person, the giant who slayed the Valkyrie.

Carmel stood back and watched silently as the drama unfolded before her. It was quite comical in some ways. Chests were beaten, biceps flexed and compared, and an occasional giant's fist was thrown. In the end, Thrym picked a short list of six contenders and the right to be his champion was determined by bouts of arm wrestling. Eventually the winner was decided and a space made ready in the middle of the hall for the duel to begin.

All this messing about gave Carmel considerable time to come up with a plan. Fighting a single giant wouldn't usually be a problem—almost as simple as falling off the proverbial log. Normally she would duck, weave, and move around freely in a manner that would confuse and overwhelm the floundering behemoth. The contest would be heavily onesided and the Valkyrie would always emerge victorious.

Unfortunately, fighting a giant in a giant-style duel would be a very different affair, a battle that would heavily favour her opponent.

The pair would be joined at the waist, held together by a length of stout rope that would allow them to move apart only by the arm span of a typical giant—or Thrym, as in this particular case. They would be expected to trade blows and she would have to stand her ground with absolutely no dodging or weaving under any circumstances.

Thrym had been quite clear on this point. Any hint of 'Valkyrie' tactics and the contest would be over. His champion would be declared the victor and she would be hacked to pieces.

The daunting challenge now facing Carmel was that she would have to win not only by beating a giant many times her size and strength, but also by beating him at his own game. It was a tricky ask, but not completely impossible.

Having chosen his champion, Thrym ordered them to be tied together and to choose their weapons. While the knots were being fastened, Carmel had an opportunity to size her opponent up. In some ways she was lucky and in others she wasn't.

She could tell that he was a young giant of average height and clearly not properly trained as a warrior; the best of these were already at the Bifrost Bridge. She reasoned he was probably a local labourer or lumberjack. He looked as strong as an ox and definitely a lot less intelligent, his brains being in his ample biceps and nowhere else. He was a typical 'Ug'—a nickname the Valkyries sometimes unkindly used when talking about the lower castes of giants. His strength and determination would count in his favour, but his size and lack of experience wouldn't. He had already chosen a large, heavy axe as his weapon and this definitely wasn't a good choice. It underlined his lack of warrior know-how.

Carmel herself chose a medium-sized sword and spent a great deal of time sorting out a good shield. After pointing out to Thrym that the shield's brace was much too big for her slender arm, numerous linen towels and a woollen blanket were brought. Carmel wrapped this and as many of the towels as she could around her arm, using them as padding. A single direct blow from her opponent's axe could shatter her arm, and she needed as much protection as possible to absorb its force.

Everything was finally ready and the two squared off to face each other. Carmel looked her opponent coolly in the eye. He was already smirking and grunting with delight, savouring his victory over the feeble woman in front of him.

For a giant, life was simple: black and white with no shades in between. You were either good or bad, and if you fought, you either won or died. They didn't take prisoners and they didn't accept mercy. Men were farmers and soldiers, and women stayed at home to cook and raise the children. This singularly myopic view helped to explain why the giants feared and hated the Valkyries so much: the warriors were women and shouldn't be able to fight. The fact that they did so and were always victorious infuriated them.

As far as the giants could make out, the Valkyries had to be cursed. Odin must have cast some evil spell upon them, one which gave them extra strength and agility to duck, weave, and murder giants in a manner that wasn't really proper fighting at all. This duel should prove that point.

Take away Odin's poison and the Valkyrie would be exposed for the weak and inferior woman that she was. Carmel's death was a foregone conclusion, as certain as the fact that snow would fall in Jotunheim this winter.

With these thoughts in mind, the gathering in the hall began to beat their chests, stamp their feet, and grunt their grunts in unison. The chorus of their cries grew in an ever rising crescendo as their eyebrows rose and fell, flashing the dazzling whites of their eyes against the darkest recesses of their sunken sockets.

Finally, when it felt as though the very rafters of the hall would collapse around their ears, Thrym brought Thor's hammer crashing down upon the table. Silence fell as the last echoes of their war cries faded away, rippling down the streets from the hall.

It was duel time.

Carmel braced herself for the first blow and she wasn't disappointed by its force. The giant raised his axe and brought it down with all his might.

It should have broken Carmel's arm, but it didn't. She had positioned herself cunningly, making sure the blow struck slightly away from the centre of her shield thus deflecting its full force from her slender and vulnerable arm. She hadn't dodged his axe, she merely cushioned its blow in a manner that was imperceptible to the throng around them.

Carmel was determined to show her audience that a woman could take on this hulk of an Ug and beat him fair and square.

Another blow and a third blow came, all struck with equal force and equal conviction. Carmel's shield arm ached, but the padding did its job. Her arm held firm. She allowed the giant to strike five blows and then retaliated with a single stroke of her own. She struck him hard, but not with all her strength. This was being held in reserve for later.

Along with the giant's inexperience, Carmel had one other weapon up her sleeve: the heat of the hall.

Lyr was notoriously warm and with so many giants packed into the hall it was now positively sweltering. Her giant foe was fit and strong, but his bulk would heat up far quicker than her slender body. This would sap his strength, cooking his muscles in the heat they were generating. As soon as she felt him begin to tire, she would counterattack, beating him with her sword with all her might.

This was her strategy in a nutshell: to defend and absorb his blazing attack and, when he was spent, launch a final victorious assault. It was a gamble and it soon paid off.

THUD—THUD—THUD!

The giant struck blow after blow as the pair slowly moved around each other. Carmel stumbled a couple of times, but she didn't allow a single stroke of his axe to miss her shield. Slowly, almost imperceptibly, she could sense her foe tiring.

What had at first been five blows struck to every one of hers gradually became four, then three, two, and eventually one for one. As each stroke delivered by the giant grew weaker and weaker, so each stroke struck by Carmel grew stronger and stronger. The tide was slowly reversing, with Carmel striking two blows, then three and four to each of the giant's blows.

As they fought on, the raucous merriment in the room began to subside. One by one, the giants could sense the impossible was happening. Thrym's champion was failing and the beautiful Valkyrie was winning. This made for a disturbing spectacle.

Finally, as her foe's arms turned to jelly, Carmel's relentless trickle of blows became a torrent. Her opponent's strength was gone and, in a scornful gesture to maximise his humiliation, she threw her shield away. He could barely raise his axe and she set about his shield with gusto, landing one blow after another from a sword which she now gripped with both hands. She taunted him as they fought, rubbing his nose in the disgrace of being defeated by woman.

Left and right, left and right, she pounded until the giant finally collapsed to his knees at her feet. His chest was heaving with exhaustion and he could barely hold his shield above him. His grip had loosened on his axe and in a final, crushing display of contempt, Carmel deftly kicked it from his hands. It was her final insult and a message to all the other giants in the room.

The duel was over and the Valkyrie had reigned victorious.

Carmel held her sword aloft and whooped triumphantly.

The silence around them swiftly ended. With a growing clamour of grunts and foot-stamping, the giants bayed for her to finish the contest. For them a fight was black and white: you either won or lost, and if you lost, you died. Their champion had had his chance and Carmel could only compound the disgrace of being beaten by a woman by shaming him with a pardon. His life was forfeit and the sooner she took it the better.

"Do you yield?" Carmel asked calmly and with authority, standing imperiously over the crumpled figure on the ground before her. To her great relief, he looked up and nodded his capitulation. He was dazed and confused, scarcely able to believe that he had lost to the woman standing over him. The giants around them roared their scorn and spat at his dishonour.

"Will you allow me to give you a quick and honourable death?" she enquired without a flicker of emotion.

The giant looked up once more and gazed into Carmel's face. He had hoped to find compassion there but he found none in her clear, brown eyes. They were cold and distant. He nodded, grunted once more, and then looked down to the floor. He knew he would die at her feet.

Rope and an executioner's wooden block were quickly brought. Carmel tied his arms tightly behind his back and indicated for him to lay his head down. When he had done so, she pressed down hard with her foot upon his head, stretching his neck tightly. For both their sakes, she wanted to take his life quickly with one, swift stroke.

"Are you prepared?" Carmel asked as she took hold of his axe. The giant looked up at her once more, and nodded yes for the last time.

Slowly Carmel turned round and looked at Thrym. His expression told her all she needed to know. He wasn't going to offer his fallen champion a last-minute reprieve from the gallows.

The giant's end came swiftly, just as she had promised.

Without pause or hesitation, Carmel raised the axe high above her head and brought it down in one flowing, powerful movement. She severed his neck with a single blow and his twitching body toppled sideways. A sudden surge of blood gushed from the stump where his head had been, threatening to engulf Carmel's feet. She stepped back hastily.

"You have won fair and square, Valkyrie!" Thrym bellowed loudly above the baying clamour of the giant host, his voice heavily laced with bitterness at her success. "Your words must be true. Open the cage and release the bird so I may gaze upon the fair Valkyrie queen for myself."

Thrym stood back and turned his gaze eagerly toward the bird in the iron cage.

"As you wish, my noble lord." Taking the keys from her knapsack, Carmel opened the cage. The eagle emerged cautiously onto her arm and she set the bird down carefully upon the table. Putting on the Necklace of the Brisings, she quietly chanted the sacred incantation.

As its ending drew near, a broad smile crept across her face.

45

The Truth

rynhildr!"

Kat almost breathed the words in disbelief, her mouth dangling wide open like a Venus flytrap. The penny had finally dropped. The grey-haired lady hugging her and Marcus simply couldn't be anybody else.

"I'm afraid she's gone, dear Kat. It's just me now. Plain, boring Jessica Sullivan. I hope you don't mind?" Jess enquired nervously as she gazed into Kat's incredulous eyes.

Of course she didn't; Kat kissed her ecstatically on the cheeks and then on the lips. She was her sister and one true love, and she thanked Odin that she was alive and free once more.

Jess was about to say something else and then stopped. Something or someone had caught her eye across the street. The sight seemed familiar, but her eyes wouldn't focus properly and the image was blurred and indistinct. She screwed her eyes up tightly and tried to squint, cursing the miseries of advancing age as she did so.

"Are you alright?" Kat had noticed Jess's stare and turned swiftly to try to see whatever it was that had spooked her.

"I'm fine. I thought I saw somebody, someone familiar. Look, it's not safe standing here and we must talk. Please, let's go and find somewhere a little less exposed."

Jess lowered her head and took both of them by the arm. The trio half walked, half trotted about three blocks away from the Hoover Building. They travelled in zigzags, choosing random streets and alleyways until they found what they were looking for: a deserted

café. It was one with a fat owner who was more interested in his television soaps than serving the occasional hungry customer.

Buying three large coffees, they huddled together at a corner table,
their shoulders hunched as they pressed their heads close together to
ensure they couldn't be overheard.

"What's happened, Jess?" Kat asked, but she already knew the
answer: she must have stopped drinking the mead. Henry had been
right.

"It's the mead, Kat, it changes you," Jess began as she glanced
knowingly at Marcus. She took Kat's hands in hers. "I'm so sorry, my
darling," she continued, "but I can't come back with you to Asgard."
Jess stared down at the table, unable to look Kat in the eye.

"What do you mean? Oh, do stop talking nonsense, Jess! You have
to come back—there's a war on. Odin needs you. Your sisters need
you. I need you!" Kat practically shook Jess's arm off as she spoke.
She would have loved to beat this silliness out of her if she could.

"I can't. And even if I could, I wouldn't be of any use. What good
would a sixty-three-year-old woman be, fighting with giants and
defending the world from Ragnarok? Use you sense, Kat—it's over.
My story ends here with you today." Jess stroked Kat's face tenderly
as she spoke, hoping her soft caresses would ease the pain of her
words.

"No, no, NO!" Kat shouted loudly, covering her ears and then
shaking her head in disbelief. Tears were welling in her eyes and she
didn't care. Jess was her best friend and her true love. *How could Jess
desert her now?*

"Oh please, dearest Kat, don't cry—I beg of you. I'm happy, truly I
am. You carry my love with you always." Jess picked up a paper nap-
kin from the tacky, chequered, PVC tablecloth and tenderly dabbed
away Kat's tears. They were falling now with gathering pace, large
salty drops heralding a flood that was sure to follow.

"You can't leave us," Kat continued angrily. "What about your
hero? What about Marcus? Can't you feel him here anymore?" she
hissed, thumping her chest to dramatise her point.

"I'm sorry, Marcus, but I'm afraid I can't. I can't feel you anymore.
But Kat, look—feel this." Jess took her hand excitedly and pressed it
tightly against her chest.

KU-DUMP—KU-DUMP—KU-DUMP

Jess's heart was beating slowly, rhythmically, and powerfully, filled
with its own life and vitality once more. Henry had been right again;

he was such a genius. If he had been with them now, Kat would surely have kissed him.

"I want to stay with you, Jess. I won't go back without you." Grabbing Jess's hands, Kat squeezed them tightly between her own. Her beating heart was a bombshell, and they both knew it. Kat looked at Jess, Jess looked at Kat, and Marcus looked at both of them.

He was lost and bewildered, but he knew that something momentous must have happened.

"You can't, Kat. You have to go back. Odin needs you," Jess began but Kat interrupted her immediately.

"You can't make me! Without you, Asgard means nothing. I'll stop drinking the mead and that way I'll have to stay with you, too."

"I beg of you, Kat, please don't do that," Jess looked frightened now. "Stopping the mead is agony, trust me. Think of the worst time in your life and then double it. Promise me you'll never do that. Please, I beg of you."

For a moment, Jess became lost in the terror of her captivity. Her eyes glazed over as she relived the horror of withdrawal: the terrible cramps, the sweating, the fits, and the hallucinations. Worst of all, she still craved the mead with a desire that virtually tore her soul in two. She prayed to Odin that her addiction would come to an end, and soon.

Kat hung her head and wept once more. Large, silent tears of sorrow poured from her eyes. She felt utterly defeated and lost. Marcus put his arm around her shoulders and Jess cradled Kat's head on hers. She wanted to cry too but she knew she mustn't. For Kat's sake, someone had to keep a brave face.

"Why won't you come back? Please, just give me one good reason. What has Midgard got for you?" Kat finally spoke once more. She couldn't accept age as the only reason for Jess not returning.

Jess looked at Marcus and then back at Kat. She would have to tell her the truth.

"My mother, Doreen, is still alive and she's very ill. She needs me and I've nephews and nieces and grandchildren who've never known me. They've forgotten I ever existed...," Jess's voice trailed off, a lump was growing in her throat, and her voice was beginning to choke with emotion.

"Well, visit them! Stay for a week or two—a month even. But please, please don't leave me." Kat tried one last desperate roll of the dice.

"Oh, Kat, I wish it were that simple. Not only does my mother need me but I need her, too. I need to, to…," Jess paused, uncertain how to put what she was about to say, "…to atone for all the lives I've taken."

"What? They were evil lives! You don't need forgiveness." Kat had her now. She couldn't use killing bad people as an excuse.

"Not all of them," Jess lowered her head shamefully. This was the truth she hoped she wouldn't have to tell. "I've killed so many people, taken so many lives, so many…good lives as well."

"What are you trying to say?" A terrifying truth had begun to dawn in Kat's mind. A nightmare Henry had suggested might just possibly be true.

"What Odin is doing is wrong. It's unnatural. He's asking us to take lives, we're…," Jess hesitated once more before adding softly, "…we're committing a sin—a terrible crime—and one that will send us all to damnation."

Jess stopped abruptly. If she said any more then she'd cross a line that would change their lives forever. Unfortunately, it was too late. Kat had already crossed that line and she asked the one question Jess knew she couldn't answer.

"Do you remember when you bumped into me on the street?" Kat began cautiously, her voice changing in tone as she spoke. Jess nodded.

"Were you trying to stop me from getting into a fight or—?" Kat was standing up now and she didn't finish the question. Jess knew exactly what she was asking, but she couldn't answer, nor could she look up.

"Did you have me killed, Jess?" Kat enquired quietly, her voice trembling with an emotion that reinforced her horror. Still Jess didn't reply.

"Answer me please, Jess. Did you make sure that I died before my time? Did you make sure I was MURDERED—JESS?" Kat shouted the last words, and the café owner glanced up briefly from his television set. Luckily even the M-word couldn't persuade him to step back into reality, and he quickly became engrossed in his soaps once more.

Jess looked up from the table as tears began to run down her face. She didn't need to speak a word. Her look said it all.

"You, you, you—bitch! I hate you, YOU MURDERER!" Kat screamed the words at the top of her voice, and before Marcus could stop her, she had made a bolt for the toilets at the back of the cafe. Marcus went to get up but Jess motioned for him to stay. This was her fault, her mess, and she had to sort it out. Hastily she followed after Kat.

Inside the tiny cloakroom, the door to the solitary toilet was locked firmly shut.

"Please, Kat, open the door. We need to talk." Jess tapped quietly on the door as she spoke.

"No! Leave me alone, I HATE YOU! How could you do that to me? How could you, Jess? How could you have me killed?"

Kat was crying and shouting uncontrollably. She had covered her ears with her hands, wanting to block the world, Jess, and even herself out of her miserable, lonely life. Her worst nightmare had just been realised and there was nothing she or anyone else could do about it. She shouldn't have died and the person she called her friend, her sister, and the love of her life was responsible.

If Kat wasn't already dead, she would have certainly wished she were so.

"Please, Kat. It wasn't like that—you must believe me. Please open the door and let me explain. Please, I beg of you." Jess rattled the door forcefully.

"Go away. I hate you!" Kat spat the words with more venom than she could have ever thought possible. Taking the gold coin from her leather purse, she clenched it tightly in her hand. She couldn't stand being there a moment longer.

"Kat, don't go!" Jess correctly guessed the thoughts that were swirling inside Kat's tortured mind. "Please don't go, not like this. Please give me a chance to explain, I beg of you. I love you, Kat. You'll break my heart if you leave."

"Good. You're a murderer, Jess, and I hope you rot in hell!" Crazed out of her mind with anguish, Kat began to chant the ancient verse.

"Please Kat, I love you—" Jess banged in anguish on the door, her fist tightly clenched.

"MURDERER!" Kat screamed one last, agonised time.

A sudden, blinding flash of brilliant light erupted from behind the toilet door and the room fell deathly silent. Kat was gone, but in the moment of leaving, her last tormented word exploded deep inside Jess's head. *Murderer!*

Feeling utterly devastated and with her heart ripped in two, Jess collapsed onto the floor in a heap.

It hadn't happened like that, but what Kat said was true. Jess was a murderer—a cold-blooded, selfish, heartless murderer, one who had callously killed at Odin's bidding. She had done evil, terrible, wicked things in his name but the devilish, mind-altering mead was to blame, not her.

Jess began to cry and a river of tears cascaded from her eyes as she threw herself prostrate onto the filthy, cloakroom floor. Begging for death, she bawled her tortured heart out.

46

To War

*F*or the brief moment that Thrym remained alive, his face was a picture. His eyebrows raised high in horror as the whites of his eyes flashed wild with terror.

The sight of Thor towering over him with Mjollnir in his hands filled Thrym with an unspeakable fear. His lust for the Valkyrie queen, which had been so visible moments before, was replaced now by a haggard mask of death.

It took only a single blow of Thor's mighty hammer to kill the last of the great frost giants.

Bellowing triumphantly and filled with the joy of his newfound freedom, Thor set about the other giants with relish. Carmel set about them too, although she really needn't have bothered. Thor's hammer seemed to grow with each mighty blow, killing one, two, and sometimes even three giants with a single swing. It was a majestic sight and one which filled the hall with the echoing, dying grunts of terrified giants.

Thor was in his element, engaged in his favourite pastime—giant-bashing. His squat and ungainly body had been transformed into an enraged cave bear. Using his hammer like a paw, he swung Mjollnir this way and that, swatting giants as though they were flies. Even the grim reaper would have paused and watched with admiration. Thor carved his way through the crowded mass as effortlessly as though he was scything a field of ripened corn, the giants falling in great swathes before him.

Within a matter of minutes it was all over and both Carmel and
Thor were standing at the entrance to the hall. Impulsively, Carmel
grabbed Thor by the neck and planted a kiss firmly upon his lips. This
lingered for a second.

"Oh, please forgive my forwardness, my lord," Carmel gasped as
she stepped backward, blushing as she did so. For the briefest of
moments she felt him return the fire of her embrace, and that was
more than she had dared hope for. She made to curtsey, but Thor held
out his hand to stop her.

"My lady, think nothing of it. It's the bloodlust rising. I feel it, too.
Come, we must hurry back to the bridge—there is a battle to be won
and Mjollnir has not yet drunk his fill. HAIL, ODIN!" Thor ended triumphantly as he waved his hammer high above his head.

The streets outside the hall were deserted. The terrified grunts of
the dying giants had already done their job, trumpeting a deadly
warning along the alleyways. No one would prevent them leaving—
Mjollnir was an unstoppable force.

"My lady, please allow me," Thor offered as he crouched by a
horse, forming a stirrup with his hands. Placing her foot in his hands,
Carmel leapt upon the back of the magnificent mount he had chosen.
The creature whinnied impatiently and reared his head. He was Gold
Mane, Thrym's magnificent stallion, second only to Sleipnir for speed
and courage. His coat was magnificent, as smooth as finest silk and
glistening with the colour of rust, its hue resembling the leaves of a
copper beech as they reflected the embers of a dying sun. The stallion's name was apt, too, with his mane long and faded to the colour
of sun-bleached straw. Thor jumped up and sat behind Carmel. Gold
Mane was more than strong enough to carry them both.

"HAIL, VALOUR! HAIL, WAR! HAIL, ODIN!" they both yelled
jubilantly and with a mighty dig of her heels, Carmel spurred Gold
Mane into a gallop. They sped like the wind down the twisting streets
and faster still as they galloped up the gentle slopes away from
Utgard. They rode bareback and Carmel clung onto their steed's lush
mane, feeling the warmth of Thor's powerful arms on either side of
her. He made her feel like a queen, and to her surprise she day-
dreamed that one day he might be her king.

"We could have flown, you know!" she cried as the wind whistled
through their hair.

"Niflheim will freeze over before I put on that wretched feathered
cloak again," Thor grimaced as he gave Carmel's back a knowing
look before gripping her tightly between his arms once more. It was

joy to ride together and the feel of her shapely body so close to his made this pleasure all the more intense. She was a magnificent warrior and it was an honour to hold her in his arms.

Her exquisite kiss still lingered fragrantly upon his lips.

The kilometres flew by and Utgard quickly disappeared into the morning's haze. Gold Mane seemed tireless. They would soon be galloping across the great plateau and by noon they should be at the giants' encampment.

Carmel shuddered at this thought. If they arrived too late, who knew what horrors might greet them there?

Odin paced wearily to and fro in his citadel. His forehead was furrowed and he felt as though great chunks of lead were hanging from his drooping shoulders. For four long days he had endured depressing news from the Bifrost Bridge, news brought to him by his ravens Huginn and Muninn. Each day he crossed his fingers praying for a ray of hope from the battlefront, and each day his dreams of sunshine turned to rain.

It was a depressing tale, but he couldn't blame his warriors. They were fearless and untiring, toiling endless hours to ready the watchtower for invasion. Two great ditches had been dug, filled with tar, and then covered with straw and logs. Behind these fiery death-traps lay concentric rings of sharpened staves packed tightly together. Enough food and water had been stored in the watchtower to last a month, but provisions and defences wouldn't be enough. Thrym's army was now so vast it would take only hours for his giants to stampede their way through even the strongest of barricades.

What Odin needed was a miracle.

What Odin needed was Thor's hammer.

As each of the four days slowly passed, the giants had felled more trees and broken more rocks such that every day they completed a new section of the bridge. One by one, the jagged crevasses had been traversed and the mighty causeway was now only hours from completion. Only one section remained, and it was being laid even now as Odin fretted up and down.

When the third section of the giants' bridge had been laid, the strip of land that lay between the glacier and the watchtower had fallen within their throwing range. Wave after wave of giants had taken it in turns to hurl boulders and logs at the warriors and, at first, the warriors retaliated with elegant soaring flights of arrows and spears, frequently setting these on fire in the hope that they would torch the timber bridge. This proved to be a futile strategy.

Shielded by their war mammoths and heavily-armoured barricades, the volleys from the warriors inflicted little damage. Any fires that briefly erupted were swiftly doused. Trying to match the giants blow for blow was both a dangerous and fruitless task, and it placed a significant drain on their slender resources. Reluctantly, the warriors retreated to the safety of the tower by day, watching with mounting anger and impatience as rocks and timber bounced harmlessly against its thick protective walls. Their inactivity was frustrating and ran counter to their violent instincts. The Valkyries were women of war, not cringing cowards.

By night, the situation changed.

The giants, with their poorer eyesight, retreated to the fires of their camps confident in the progress they had made. In contrast, the warriors and local Vanir would scurry around the castle, digging ditches and felling trees from which they could fashion their barricades. They worked with minimum noise; the less the giants knew of their defences the greater their surprise when they arrived on Asgard soil.

Today was the fifth day and Odin knew that the giants would complete their bridge any hour now. As he paced nervously up and down, fretting on his warriors' fate, a black dot high in the sky above grew rapidly larger until its shape confirmed that it was a raven. It was Huginn and he flew straight through the open window and alighted on Odin's shoulder. Impatiently, he nibbled urgently at Odin's ear.

Slowly the scowl on Odin's face began to melt and an imperceptible smile twitched hesitantly on his lips. *Good news at last!*

Digging deep into a pocket, Odin rewarded Huginn with a tasty treat. As he did, the ground beneath the citadel began to tremble. Odin's smile grew even wider.

Warriors were returning from Midgard and with a wave of his hand across his ring he travelled instantly to the Chamber of the Valkyries. He prayed that all of them had returned safe and sound.

Kat didn't care if she travelled between the wells as trillions of flashes of light, a graviton wave, or as a cartload of rotten tomatoes.

All she cared for now was that she arrived back in Asgard in one piece, and as free from nausea and sickness as possible.

Blinking violently, she allowed her eyes to adjust to the dim light in the circular Chamber.

"Sangrid!"

It was the excited voice of Ruby as she, and Jameela hurried around the ring and helped the staggering Kat away from her pillar. She pushed them away urgently and doubled up, vomiting as she did so. *By Thor's beard, she hated motion sickness!*

Feeling better, she slowly stood up and pulled them close. The three girls hugged each other ecstatically as Vili and Ve looked on. The brothers had arrived with Jameela at least ten minutes before Kat and they now looked like a pair of coy schoolboys shuffling with embarrassment as they tried not to stare too enviously at the passion of the girls' embrace.

"Greetings, greetings, dear Sangrid and Herja!" Odin trotted down the last few steps and flung his arms around the returning girls. He was enthralled. He could see the artifacts in their hands and it hadn't yet registered that one of their number was missing.

Kat couldn't reciprocate his warmth. Holding her arms rigidly by her sides, she turned her head away in disgust. Too many issues now lay between them. His refusal to send help, the vile way she had parted from Jess, and the many ominous questions Henry had posed. Odin might not be evil, but she certainly couldn't trust him anymore. Violated and angry, her shattered trust was impossible to hide.

Fortunately, her coldness was missed by her sisters. Breathless with anticipation, Jameela battered Odin and Ruby with a salvo of questions.

Had Thor won his duel?

Was Asgard safe?

Had any warriors or maids been hurt?

"Slowly, slowly, Herja—please," Odin replied, throwing his hands up in despair. "Prudr will tell you everything but only when you're on your way to the watchtower. A great battle is about to begin and I'm sure you wouldn't want to miss it."

Ruby stared hard at Odin. He could see the flames of desire raging inside her.

"Yes, of course that means you, too, my dearest Prudr. Go now, take your sisters and honour your mighty name. Kill more giants than there are heroes in Valhalla." He hugged her warmly once again.

"But my lord, who will look after Asgard?" Ruby had to ask—she couldn't just desert her post.

"Vili and Ve. Let's see if we can keep them out of mischief here for a day or so. I'm sure even they can't create too much mayhem," he chuckled merrily. He could feel a happiness inside and there was a twinkle in his eye which had been absent for many weeks.

With a great shriek of joy, Ruby hugged Odin and then dragged the girls up the steps toward the wooden doors.

"Where's Brynhildr?" Odin's gentle enquiry stopped the warriors dead in their tracks. One more step and they would have left the Chamber.

"She's not coming home, my lord." Kat turned slowly, her eyes falling to stare silently at the floor.

"Why not? Has she been hurt? Is she dead?" Odin asked in a voice filled with urgency and dread.

"No, my lord, she's changed, she's...she's different." Kat paused, not really knowing what to say. She wanted to scream 'MURDERER!' at the top of her voice and batter him to a bleeding pulp but now was neither the time nor the place.

"What do you mean?" Odin's voice echoed chillingly around the chamber. An awkward pause developed and it expanded slowly into a deafening silence. The chamber begged for an answer and to everybody's relief, Kat provided one.

"She didn't drink the mead my lord, not for—for five days...," her voice trailed off.

Odin slumped down on the floor and put his head in his hands. He didn't need to hear more. He knew only too well the consequences of such misfortune. There was nothing he could do.

Brynhildr was gone, a much-loved daughter lost. He knew one day she would return—the mead was irresistible—but for now Brynhildr would suffer all the pains of Niflheim as she struggled to fight its toxic allure.

"Are you all right?' Jameela hesitated, before stepping forward to place a reassuring hand on his shoulder.

Odin nodded and clasped her hand in his. "I'll be fine, just give me a few minutes. Please, I beg of you, go, all of you. Fight like tigresses and do so not for me, but to honour your sister Brynhildr. Please, go, now." He turned his head away, not wanting the warriors to see the glistening tears forming in his eye.

Jameela and Ruby needed no further invitation. Whooping with anticipation, they bounded up the stairs from the sacred Chamber.

Kat followed silently in their wake. She felt numb. An empty chasm inside her soul was slowly filling with pain and hate. Perhaps a fight was what she needed, something to blot out the bitterness of her wrongful existence in this place. She tried weakly to force a smile, to feel the joy of the bloodlust which now gripped her sisters.

She would go with them and do as Odin bid. She would fight, but not for him and not for Brynhildr, either. She would fight for herself, drowning her misery in the bloody frenzy of war.

Reaching their rooms, the girls changed quickly and put on their cloaks of swans' feathers. Their excitement for war was finally beginning to deaden Kat's pain. Her bloodlust was rising, too, and she began to crave the swing of a sword in her hands and the roar of battle once more.

With a chorus of loud whoops and trumpets, three elegant swans sped swiftly away from the castle walls. They headed fast and low across the plain of Ida. Their path led west and they flew straight as arrows toward the watchtower.

The battle was about to begin and they didn't want to miss a single blow.

47

The Battle of the Bridge

One of the many joys Kat loved about being a warrior was the ability to transform into a swan. The thrill of the air rushing around her, the fabulous vision, and the wondrous smells that wafted up from the ground below—these showered her in riches that left her senses helplessly reeling.

Add to this the exquisite bloodlust and she could almost forget about Jess. Almost.

Ruby held a tight formation as the three warriors powered their way through the air. There was much honking and whooping among the beautiful birds as they swapped stories and updated each other on events. The journey to the watchtower sped by and the girls were spurred on with the news that Thor and Carmel were racing east from Utgard. The battle would be over if Thor got to the Bifrost Bridge before them. Mjollnir would leave sloppy seconds for a warrior to have fun with.

After what seemed like only minutes, Heimdall's watchtower came into view. They smelt it almost as soon as they saw it—thick, acrid clouds of black smoke billowed up into the sky which alarmed the warriors at first. *Surely the giants couldn't have overrun the mighty fortress so soon?*

In a panic, they flew lower and circled the tower. It was scarcely visible through a choking veil of smoke. To their relief, they could see that the fire was coming from a ditch that barred the exit from the giants' massive causeway. Whooping loudly, the excited girls climbed higher once more and wheeled away to the west. They had changed their plan and would now attack their foe from behind, in a pincer move.

If they hadn't known that Thor was on his way, the idea would have been a disaster. They would be cut off with no line of retreat. However, with Thor and Carmel less than an hour's swift ride away, they knew their diversion was secure. It would help distract the giants' forces that were now heading toward the watchtower.

"Buckle up, ladies!"

It was Ruby who drew her sword first when they landed. "If we don't feast victorious in Asgard tonight then we will dine with honour in Valhalla."

"HAIL, ODIN!"

With a wild, exalted cheer, the three warriors raised their swords high above their heads and charged headlong toward the massive army that lay barely fifty metres ahead of them. They had deliberately chosen to land perilously close to the giants, giving them little time to react to their assault. Their tactic worked beautifully. Caught unawares, the men from Jotunheim watched in amazement as the three graceful swans transformed into their worst nightmares.

They were still watching when, spellbound with fear, the three equally graceful Valkyries crashed into their ranks, hair flowing wildly and swords flashing brightly in the autumn sun as they rained down blow after blow upon the giants' bewildered heads.

The battle had begun, and the Valkyries had struck first.

Heimdall, as always, spotted the beautiful swans before anyone else.

He called to Silk and the other warriors to hurry and join him on the rooftop. They waved and hollered at their sisters as they swooped down low over the castle before circling around them in the billowing clouds of smoke. Reinforcements had arrived from Asgard and not a moment too soon.

Elation quickly turned to despair. *What in Odin's name were their sisters thinking of, banking away and heading across the glacier to Jotunheim?* The smoke must have addled their brains.

When Heimdall eventually confirmed that the warriors had indeed landed behind enemy lines, Silk realised immediately that it must be a diversion. It seemed a suicidal tactic, one that filled her with dread. No one at the watchtower was yet aware that Thor had recovered his hammer and was heading toward them. Without this knowledge, the actions of the three arriving warriors seemed like madness, and left Silk, Zara, Mika, Eve, and Juliet with little choice.

The ditch of tar had been lit and the tower braced for defence, but now the warriors and maids needed to go on the offensive. Their foolish sisters would be slaughtered by the massive giant army and to abandon them to their doom would be intolerable.

The warriors put their thoughts to the maids and were relieved by their unanimous agreement to attack. It was a decision their protégées took with the carefree ease of a summer breeze. Quickly gathering their weapons, the Valkyries congregated behind the massive, barred doors to the watchtower. It was attack or nothing—death or glory.

After drinking deep draughts of mead, they formed a large circle with their swords pointed toward the floor, tips meeting in the centre of the ring.

"HAIL, VALOUR!" Freyja led the salutation.

"HAIL, ODIN!" everybody cheered as they raised their swords straight before them to chest height.

"HAIL, WAR!" The metres-thick walls of the watchtower reverberated as the warriors and maids raised their swords high above their heads and let out a final, wild, bloodcurdling chorus of war cries.

Singing with joy and with chests heaving with passion, the Valkyries burst through the doors and raced like hares toward the flaming ditch. Without breaking stride, they leapt across the blazing mass of tar and wood, only scrambling to a halt when they were standing on the giants' bridge. In a single, graceful movement the Valkyries lined up in three rows, the first crouched low with the others rising in tiers behind them. Raising their shields, they formed a solid and impenetrable barricade.

Behind the Valkyries stood Freyja. The dwarf metal of her armoured breastplate, shield, and falcon helmet shone brilliantly in the watery, midday sun. She looked magnificent.

Caught by surprise by this outrageous manoeuvre, the vanguard of the giant army was stunned into silence. Cowering behind the first of their three massive war mammoths, they stood barely metres away from the Valkyries. Their army outnumbered the Valkyries by over twenty to one and yet they had fear in their hearts. The sight of the ferocious Valkyrie queen standing proud with sword in hand and her chest held high was absolutely terrifying.

"Warriors!" Freyja roared as she pointed her sword at the fractious mammoth. "Let's get this poor beast out of the way. There are giants to kill and I hunger FOR THEIR BLOOD!"

Breaching the first and second rows of giants, Ruby, Jameela, and Kat quickly formed a triangle, standing shoulder to shoulder and back to back. They wheeled gently left and right in a graceful ballet as they danced their way deeper into the enemy ranks.

Unlike Kat's first encounter with the giants when she was a maid in Asgard, she now felt completely at ease. Any dwindling thoughts of Jess were submerged instantly in their fight for survival. Her mighty sword, Talwaar, with its edges now ground to a razor sharpness, swished effortlessly through the air, slicing deeply into the giants' shields, breastplates, and flesh. The motion of her blade felt almost magical in her hands as she darted and weaved with the power and grace of a panther. She felt no fear, no hate, and no pain, only the ecstasy of war. The giants appeared to move like tree sloths: dodging their massive swords and double-headed axes felt like a child's game, and one she had mastered years ago.

It seemed almost a crime to kill them, like taking candy from a baby—an action barely worthy of effort.

Jameela stood to Kat's left and she hummed the gentlest and sweetest of lullabies as her sword sang in a blur of motion before her. She was in a trance, her eyes rolling as the bloodlust boiled over. 'Herja the Berserker' had taken Valkyrie form.

Flecks of saliva began to foam from the corners of her mouth and her sword and chakram shared equally in the bloodbath that grew ever deeper around her. Giants were disembowelled, decapitated, and their limbs hacked from torsos even after they had been killed and crushed beneath her feet. She was untouchable—an unstoppable, swirling fortress beyond the reach of even the most powerful of their foes.

Ruby stood to Kat's right, chanting continuously with a fixed, sardonic grin upon her lips. She was the mightiest of the Valkyrie sisterhood and she left their opponents in no doubt of this. She had no need for ducking and diving and no need to swing her sword as swiftly as an arrow. Ruby stood her ground and traded blow for blow with any giant foolish enough to chance his luck. Her sword was twice the size of Kat's, being made from dwarves' gold laced with iron. This gave it added weight such that she could match or even better the force of the giants' blows.

Time and time again she demonstrated her might by cleaving a shield or helmet in two. Razor sharp and thrust with all her strength, Ruby's sword could easily penetrate a giant's breastplate, skewering him as effortlessly as a seamstress sewing hemp.

Such was the power of the three Valkyries that the giant host around them became angry and confused. The girls were a tiny, savage island in their ocean of muscle, hair, and armour, but like a wasp they couldn't swat, the giants became increasingly frustrated and distracted.

They had to stamp out this irritation, but in doing so, the army stalled in its attack on Asgard.

It was Silk who leapt over the barricade of shields first, jumping up onto the trunk of the mammoth that reared and thrashed in front of them. The poor animal was terrified. Silk felt nothing but pity for the wretched beast weighed down by its massive armour, blindfolded, and pressed forward by the giants' relentless, prodding spears. He was being driven toward a fire he could smell but couldn't see, and from which he had no hope of retreat. Clinging to the stiff hairs of his trunk, Silk hacked the blindfold from his eyes. That was all she needed to do.

Driven beyond madness by the sight of the flames in front of him, the crazed mammoth reared up, bellowing wildly as he twisted sideways in a last desperate attempt to break free.

Although the giants' bridge was strong and wide, even their great skills couldn't build a causeway broad enough for a mammoth to turn on. Still wet from a heavy dew, the logs were slippery and the creature lost his footing. With a desperate trumpeting of despair, the huge beast collapsed onto the surface of the bridge, his hind legs dangling wildly over the gaping chasm below. His body began to slip, and the inexorable force of gravity pulled the behemoth toward his doom. Panicking as his forelegs failed to grip, the mammoth flailed his trunk from side to side, hurling Silk through the air like a feather tossed on a gust of wind. She bounced and spun dizzily across the bridge before finally sliding headfirst off the other side. She vanished from view.

"ATTACK!" Freyja raised the call to arms, but the warriors and maids were already on their feet and charging headlong toward the exposed giant host. With a final anguished wail from his trunk, the mammoth lost its battle with gravity and plunged into the abyss below. He was swiftly swallowed up by the darkness.

The giants had been shocked and cowed by the statuesque figure of Freyja, but they were brave and wouldn't retreat without a fight. Raising their shields and brandishing their spears, they made ready for the fury of a Valkyrie onslaught.

Pausing briefly to allow the maids to unleash a deadly volley of arrows, the warriors slammed into their towering foes. The air was filled with bellowed grunts and shrill battle cries which rose high above the metallic clamour of swords and axes as they locked together in deadly combat. Inch by inch the giants gave ground, allowing the warriors at last to reach the point where Silk had hurtled over the side of the bridge.

"Gunnr!" With a sickening ache in her chest, Zara called out her name. There was no reply.

"Gunnr!" she called again, only louder and more fearfully.

"Hey, are you girls just going to leave me hanging around down here or what?"

After what had seemed an age, Silk's calm voice echoed up from somewhere underneath the bridge. Zara dropped to the floor and held her arm out. To her immense relief she felt the powerful grip of a woman grabbing hold of her wrist. It was Silk. Somehow she had managed to catch hold of the end of one of the ropes that lashed the logs together. Vicki now joined Zara and, safely held by two strong arms, Silk climbed swiftly up their bodies and back onto the bridge.

"Take cover!"

A warrior's voice called out above the roar of battle as rocks hurled by the giants began to crash crazily around them. Vicki raised her shield in front of Silk and held it there until her sword and shield could be brought. Taking a large gulp of mead from her flask and gesturing that she was unhurt, Silk crouched low with her rescuers before snaking forward to join the mêlée ahead.

Capturing the bridge was slow and bloody work.

The giants were packed tightly together and fought like angry bears. Each one had to be prised individually from the timbers, the dead falling swiftly to their doom and the injured clinging to the logs like limpets. All had to be cleared from the path if the warriors were to reach their sisters trapped behind the giants' lines. No mercy was expected and none was given. The giants didn't understand captivity. In a battle they either won or died. There was no middle ground.

The Valkyries fought their foe at close quarters, the safest tactic to avoid being hit by the endless barrage of stones that were being hurled at them from Jotunheim. Each wave of warriors and maids fought until they were exhausted, then they crouched down low and let another wave press forward with the attack. Rising once more, they would take quick gulps of mead from their flasks before firing volleys of arrows at point blank range into the seething mass of flesh ahead.

Their tactics worked and as the minutes crawled by, first one section of the bridge and then another, and another, fell to their ferocity. Freyja herself led the final wave, roaring in triumph when at last her feet landed on the soil of Jotunheim.

The bridge had been secured, but an army numbering many hundreds still lay between them and their beleaguered sisters.

Kat froze, her sword suspended in midair and shield clasped firmly before her. *The mead changes you...*

From somewhere deep inside her mind Jess's words called out, and for the briefest of moments time seemed to stand still. Kat stared intently at her sword and then turned to study her sisters beside her. *What on EARTH was she doing here?*

The battered remnant of Dr. Katarina Neal's soul screamed out in one final, desperate plea. She was begging herself to see the insanity of what she had become. Her anguished voice pleaded from somewhere deep inside Kat's soul, cutting through the rage of battle like a ray of sunlight into a shuttered room. Its light was blinding.

Dr Neal was a saver of lives, not a barbaric, slaughtering warrior.

Dr Neal should be listening to music, going to bars, taking Sunday walks, and relaxing in a hot bath brimming with bubbles and fragrant perfume.

Dr Neal was a compassionate, intelligent, healing woman.

Dr Neal was a—

"Sangrid, are you all right?"

Kat wasn't sure if it was the sound of Jameela's voice or the pain from a giant's spear as it pierced her loin, but suddenly she was back in the battlefield and fighting for her life. Sheltered briefly by Jameela's shield, Kat took a hasty gulp of her refreshing mead. This did its work, plugging a drug-crazed finger over the hole in her fractured mind. The tortured farewell cries from another woman in another world fell silent, dying swiftly in war's raging inferno.

Dodging to the left, Kat's sword sang musically as it sliced through the air. The arrogant giant who had so nearly run her through crumpled and fell at her feet, her blow practically severing his shoulder from his chest. Blood gushed from a gaping cleft which ran from his collarbone to his nipple. He was dead before he hit the ground.

Kat knew she was beginning to tire, as were Ruby and Jameela beside her. Sweat ran in rivulets down their bodies, tracing twisted trails through the blood and grime that covered them.

If help didn't arrive soon, the vast army would overwhelm them.

Thor bellowed loudly as he and Carmel burst from the cover of the forest and galloped onto the battlefield. His roar was so loud that every giant's head turned as the ground shook beneath their feet. Leaping from Gold Mane before Carmel could bring the stallion to a halt, Thor charged forward with Mjollnir whistling malevolently as he spun the hammer high above his head.

This was the final straw.

Under attack on three fronts, the brave hearts of the giants finally gave way. Screaming and tossing their weapons to the ground, the giants lumbered crazily away in all directions. Mjollnir scarcely had time to crack a single head. As Thor charged toward them, the giants scattered like autumn leaves whipped by a storm.

The warriors cheered loudly and redoubled their efforts. The wall of giants which had held so stoically now lay shattered and broken.

Within minutes of Thor's arrival, the battle was over. Exhausted by their efforts, the Valkyries were too tired to give chase and press home their victory. Instead, as the last giants disappeared into the forest slopes around them, the girls stumbled gratefully toward the reassuring figure of Thor. Holding his arms open wide, he hugged and kissed each and every one of them.

Finally, when they had all received his heartfelt appreciation, the party formed a circle in the middle of the blood-soaked battlefield. Raising their swords high above their heads they made ready for one last triumphant cheer.

"HAIL, VICTORY!"

From across the glacier came the ringing sound of Gjall. The horn had been blown by Heimdall and it heralded their mighty victory. Its powerful blast was for all the realms of Asgard to hear—and for all the realms of Asgard to quake with fear.

The gods and Valkyries had been victorious.

48

Feelings

The battle had exhausted the Valkyries so much that it was unanimously agreed to stay the night at the watchtower and return to Asgard the following day.

The elation of victory was tinged with a bitter sadness. Two maids had been killed during the fight, with Vicki being the first to perish. She was lost shortly after offering her arm to help Silk claw her way to safety. A well-aimed boulder had knocked her unconscious and she had fallen sideways, toppling from the slippery bridge.

Freyja had put on her falcons' cloak and hovered for what seemed an eternity over the crevasse into which she had fallen. She could see nothing in the bottomless blackness and the calls from the girls brought no reply from below. It would be impossible to climb down and find her—the crevasse could be hundreds of metres deep with jagged outcrops and fragile overhangs. These would cost more lives.

Beth died later, once they had set foot on the soil of Jotunheim. She was injured and fell as a wave of giants surged forward. Her skull was crushed beneath their trampling feet and her head was now an unrecognisable mess. Scraping together what they could find of her, the warriors built a funeral pyre on the battlefield and said their good-byes as they watched her body burn. No one wanted her to join the endless procession of carts that were taking the giants' bodies to the gates of Niflheim. Her soul deserved to rest in peace, and for that her journey had to be by a different route.

Despite their losses, the party was otherwise in excellent spirits. It had been a tremendous victory over an army many times their size.

Their foe had been crushed and scattered. At least a hundred giants lay slain and there was a widespread belief amongst the girls that this battle was Ragnarok, the war they had all feared. The Valkyries had saved Asgard and its fate could be rewritten.

There was more good news as they chattered noisily at suppertime. Thor had made Carmel a warrior and this delighted everyone, even though it hadn't been formally approved as yet by Odin. With the sad news that Brynhildr was gone, Freyja gave her consent to this accolade. The power of nine wouldn't be violated and no one deserved the honour of being a warrior more than Carmel.

With the use of the word 'violated' Kat's curiosity was aroused, so she enquired as to why there were only nine Valkyries. Freyja's answer was both intriguing and inconclusive.

The number nine was considered lucky in Asgard because it was last number before the cycle of numerals returned to one. It represented both an end and a beginning, the largest single number you could possible have before being reborn as 'One' again. It was also no coincidence that there were nine realms, nine planets around their sun, and that it had taken Odin and his brothers nine attempts to create their universe.

Many other things also came in nines or multiples thereof, but Freyja quickly grew bored of Kat's question and the conversation ended before Kat would have liked it to. Still, she could tick this question off the list that Henry had posed for her.

The party rose early the next day and after bidding Heimdall farewell, they galloped swiftly back to Asgard. During the night messengers and fresh horses had arrived at the watchtower, and they learned that Odin had decreed two days of feasting and rapturous celebrations. All the gods and goddesses from Valhalla were invited, and the main feast would be held in the hall of Gladsheim that evening.

Everybody was thrilled. It promised to be an occasion the like of which hadn't been seen in Asgard for many generations.

When the warriors eventually arrived at the castle they found their excitement was more than justified. The entire town had been transformed into an enormous street party. Bunting was hanging up and down the streets, drums and horns were blowing, and fires were raging fiercely in every kitchen as huge quantities of food were prepared for the festivities ahead. An enormous crowd lined the road from Gladsheim to the castle and the girls were greeted in a frenzy of clapping, cheering, and singing. Flowers were strewn before them and they rode up the gentle rise to the castle on a carpet of fragrant petals.

It felt like a dream, and better was yet to come. Where yesterday had raged the battle from hell, a day when the warriors proved their feminine might, today was going to be a girly day, a day for pampering their feminine right.

Odin spared no expense: a hairdresser, seamstress, and masseuse had been arranged for each warrior and maid and extra slaves had been drafted in to help the girls bathe and cleanse. The communal bathing seemed to last for hours, with endless gossip and speculation as to who might turn up for the evening and what everybody was going to wear. It was a wonderful luxury to unwind, and when bathing was followed by a relaxing, head-to-toe massage, Kat felt like a woman once more.

Indeed, Kat could almost have said she was happy, if it weren't for that final, fateful conversation with Jess. It gnawed away relentlessly like toothache, a pain buried deep inside her head that belligerently refused to fade. What Kat had said to Jess was right, she knew it was right, and yet, in her heart, she bitterly regretted calling her a murderer.

Try as she might, she couldn't hate Jess although she so desperately wanted to. She needed to lash out and destroy everything and everybody around her. She shouldn't be there, here, now in Asgard. This wasn't her destiny.

Her life had been callously stolen from her; a respectable career, family, and her future children—all taken away. Her anger grew every time she thought about her needless death, and Kat was grateful that Hod wasn't around. It wasn't his fault, but she would have used him as a punch bag, beating him senseless until her fists bled. Somebody had to pay for what had happened, and somehow she had to flush the terrible ache of regret from her head.

Jess had brought about her death so she should hate Jess; she must hate Jess; she HAD to hate Jess. That was what she needed to do. *But why did it hurt so much?*

"Are you ready for your fitting, my lady?"

Bobbing a deep and respectful curtsey, a wary seamstress interrupted Kat's morbid thoughts. Kat was grateful for her polite enquiry; the prospect of dressing up in the finest clothes that Asgard could offer might just be the distraction she needed.

With a weary smile, Kat turned her attention to what she would wear tonight. She wanted to look special, to look breathtaking, and the women of Asgard didn't let her down.

For the next two hours they fussed and pampered her, curling her hair into tight ringlets before piling it up into a cascade on top of her head, holding their design in place with a myriad of diamond pins that sparkled like stars as she turned her head from side to side. They fitted her dress, too, and it looked amazing, its colour shimmering somewhere between a deepest pink and a vibrant scarlet. Sleeveless and strapless, it was made from a heavy and luxuriant silk, with a plunging neckline at the front and the rear dipping almost to her behind. The back of the dress was intricately laced, accentuating her already tiny waist.

Odin had given each warrior and maid a gift of jewellery. For Kat, this was a heavy, diamond-encrusted necklace with matching earrings. The jewellery must have been made long ago by dwarves, because the attention to detail and craftsmanship was breathtaking. A curling, snake-like golden armband completed her outfit and she had to admit she'd surpassed herself.

Watch out any handsome, lonely, single gods, because tonight the Valkyrie Sangrid was going to party hard.

Unlike Kat's life, Carmel's couldn't have been rosier.

For once, Odin was pleased with Thor and his decision to make her a warrior couldn't have come at a better time. Dispensing with the usual formalities, she had gone straight to his citadel and been named by Mimir. Carmel had been around long enough to know about the head-in-a-box trick, so meeting Mimir wasn't as big a shock as it had been for Kat.

Carmel's Valkyrie name, however, was.

The woman formerly known as the fair Carmel had become the Valkyrie Astrid. It was a name that had never been given to a warrior before and the reason for this quickly became apparent.

Carmel's new name literally meant 'powerful queen' and she was delighted with this title, as was Thor. He was the first to offer her his congratulations and respect, as she knew he would. Thor was powerful, reliable, loving, kind, trustworthy—Sif was such a lucky woman to have him as her husband.

Carmel felt envious, very envious indeed.

"Hello, gorgeous!"

Loki slapped Carmel's bottom soundly as she entered her room. He had been hiding behind the door and wanted to surprise her, which he most certainly did.

"Would you like to congratulate me?" Carmel enquired, turning around and smiling warmly at her handsome lover. She held out her hand expectantly for him to kiss it, as was the custom when first greeting the new Valkyrie. It was a mark of respect and loyalty, and an important and expected tribute from him.

"Congratulations indeed, my fairest and sweetest Carmel." Loki swaggered forward, trying to take her in his arms.

She pushed him angrily away. "Come on, Loki, don't greet me like that. Stop messing around, please. Offer your respects first. Go on, kiss my hand." Carmel offered this to him again.

"Hey, come on, it's me!" Loki jested as he stepped forward once more. He had absolutely no intention of kissing her hand now or at any other time. They'd been apart for over a week and all he could only think about was her large, comfy bed and her large, comfy behind. Now *that* he would be only too happy to kiss and demonstrate his manly respects to.

SMACK!

Carmel slapped him hard across the face, catching him by surprise. *Surely she was joking?*

"Come on Loki. Stop messing around. I want you to offer your respects properly." Carmel glared angrily at him. *Why was he being so pig-headed?*

All he had to do was kiss her hand, call her 'my lady' and that would be that, respects paid. She could feel his hungry eyes devouring her body and she desired his, too.

Loki met and held her gaze, smiling as he ruefully rubbed his face. *Sweet Odin!* She was a stubborn and hot-headed woman. If she wanted to make a big deal of this, then he was up for it. Two could play that silly game. Loki gave way to no one.

Stepping forward, he hesitated as Carmel raised her hand again. This was it, decision time. He either kissed her left, or felt her right.

Loki stood still, glancing cautiously at the palm of Carmel's hand. Would she back down or would she slap him again? He didn't know. *Dare he risk her wrath?*

Suddenly and with a loud guffaw, Loki dropped to his knee and took her hand in his. She'd called his bluff and won, although his eyes were firmly set on the bigger game—her taut, sensuous body and heaving breasts looking so inviting.

"Congratulations my lady, my lady—"

"AAARGH!" Carmel screamed loudly and tugged at her hair. *How could she have been so stupid?*

The arrogant oaf hadn't even bothered to learn her Valkyrie name! She stomped crossly over to the door and held it open for him. Her message was clear. Until he could behave respectfully, he had to go.

"Oh, come on Carmel, please. Just tell me your Valkyrie name and I'll give you my respects, honest I will." Smirking and giggling nervously like some naughty schoolboy, Loki sidled slowly over to the door and made to leave her chamber. His face was getting redder by the minute, embarrassment and Carmel's finger marks burning furiously upon his cheeks.

"You can be such an idiot sometimes, Loki," Carmel fumed as he passed by. "You're going to have to change your attitude if you want to enjoy my favour, and my bed."

Loki left the room with his metaphorical tail firmly wedged between his legs. Carmel watched his departure with a conceit that surprised even her. She still loved his swaggering charm but why, oh why, couldn't he take her seriously for once? She was a warrior now and she demanded respect.

Her desperate struggle to retrieve Thor's hammer still filled her mind and she hadn't forgiven Loki yet for all the silly pranks he had played. His mischief as regards Geirrod and his daughters could have brought about Thor's death and destroyed them all.

Carmel turned and closed the door slowly behind her. The sudden thought of Thor had brought a warmth to her chest. Their journey, despite its pain and hardships, had been a wonderful time and she'd enjoyed his company far more than she would ever have dared admit. She was still in love with Loki, but Thor had lit a light inside her soul that refused to wane and die.

Thor was happily married with children, and his heart belonged to Sif. He was short, squat, unattractive and built like...what was it Thrym had called him? *Oh yes,* an overgrown dwarf. It was madness to even think about him and yet, and yet...

Carmel stopped dead in her tracks. The very thought of his name had sent another powerful tingle down her spine.

She cursed him lovingly under her breath.

49

Vengeance

Cole's introduction to the Berserker army was almost as short-lived and painful as his introduction to sodomy.

Cole was a big man and a strong man, a man who in Midgard had taken pride in his physique. He had spent hours in the gym pumping iron, honing his six-pack, and building pecs of steel. Unfortunately, in Niflheim, all this counted for nothing. A long period of inactivity, pain, and the sweltering heat and humidity had made him weak and easy pickings.

Lucifer stepped forward into the area cleared by his men. He was in no mood to take prisoners and he attacked Cole as soon as he was up and able to hold his sword and shield. For a brief moment Cole attempted to launch a defence, but this soon crumbled under a welter of well-aimed and powerful blows.

Louis was not a particularly big man, but the time he had spent in Niflheim had been put to good use: working in the mines until his hands bled, sweating rivers in the crippling heat, and fighting with a sword until he dropped from exhaustion.

The duel between him and Cole was one-way traffic.

Round and round he circled Cole, like a wolf that had cornered an abandoned lamb. Blow after blow erupted from Louis's sword until Cole crumpled to his knees, cowering behind his shield.

Now Louis was going to have some fun.

"Sweet," he spat sarcastically as he unleashed a massive blow against Cole's shield. "Who's a fucking worthless piece of shit now, hey?"

Another mighty blow sang through the air and tore the Cole's sword from his hand. It clattered and skidded as it spun helplessly away across the gravel floor.

"You ain't worthy to kiss my feet," Louis continued goadingly, swinging his sword again and again as he shattered Cole's defences.

By now the fight had been reduced to a pathetic spectacle, with Cole clutching his shield with both arms as he crammed his mighty frame behind it.

This humiliating sham didn't bother the spectators. Far from it—the ragtag Berserker army revelled in Cole's misery and they roared their approval. It was magnificent sport to see one of Hel's little girls, her 'pussy boys' as they liked to call them, getting his arse well and truly kicked. Shouting louder still, they urged their leader to finish him off.

By now, Louis was growing bored and fed up with battering such a weak and feeble opponent. Cole was useless, just as he'd guessed he would be. With a final torrent of blows—left and right, left and right—he dislodged Cole's precious shield and sent him sprawling face down across the floor. Breathing hard, he stood over Cole's prostrate form and placed his sword at his neck.

"Did you recognise those words?" he hissed angrily, brown eyes glaring through the narrow slit in the scarf that covered his face.

Cole looked up. His expression said no.

"Do you not know who I am?" Louis bent closer, hoping that the vicious glint in his eyes would spark some recognition in Cole's face. It didn't.

"Do you mean to say that taking my life had so little meaning for you and your evil bitch girlfriend that even now you still can't remember me?" he raged, lashing out a kick to Cole's kidneys that left him screaming in pain.

Louis had had enough. His patience was at an end. Raising his sword high above his head, he decided to hack the evil bastard to pieces.

"You?" Cole's faltering voice was barely audible, but it was just loud enough to stop Louis's sword in mid swing. 'Evil bitch girlfriend' had brought recognition at last to his bewildered eyes.

Louis threw his sword to the ground in disgust before turning his back on him. He walked away slowly, pondering what to do next. Hel had asked him not to harm Colleen—Odin's rotten apple—but he hadn't realised Cole's true identity until they had stood together face to face. It was only then that Louis knew his prayers were answered and he could finally rain down vengeance upon his murderer.

His deal with Hel was off. Cole must die, but he must do so very slowly. He had to feel the terrible agony of despair, the horror of a future being torn from him, just as Louis had once done. As for his evil bitch girlfriend—Louis smiled grimly—her time would come. It must surely come.

"Take him outside, and stake him out on a nice, hot rock," Lucifer commanded and with a loud roar of approval eight Berserkers stepped forward, raising Cole to their shoulders.

"Oh, and one more thing." The men paused, awaiting their leader's orders. "Make sure only one foot gets buried in the filthy, rotting slime. I want the maggots of Hel to eat this worthless piece of shit very, very slowly, one toe at a time."

The men cheered once more and then headed toward a heavy steel door that was being slowly cranked open. A blast of red hot air ripped through the cavern, scorching their upturned faces. The door that was being opened led to the surface of Niflheim.

Cole was going outside.

Cole was finally going to experience the true, unadulterated, fiery horror that was Hel.

50

Astrid's Song

Thor's preparation for the night's festivities was very different to the Valkyries. Next to giant-bashing, his favourite pastime was working at his anvil in the castle's stable blocks. Horses needed shoeing, swords needed mending, and all manner of odd jobs begged for his attention after being away for so long.

He set about his work with gusto, singing (badly) as he hammered and smelted his way through the day. Whereas Odin would hold court in his citadel, Thor preferred informal chats in his forge. Anybody could turn up and ask his advice, or simply talk about the weather, and they frequently did just that. It was a relaxed and informal affair, without any of the pretensions and trappings that would usually go with talking to a deity. Thor loved it this way and the people of Asgard loved him for that. He was approachable and easy to talk to, provided they didn't catch him at the wrong moment. On those occasions things would get thrown, and the only safe tactic was to run for your life.

Thor's morning passed agreeably with a string of well-wishers and requests for minor repairs to farming tools and the like. He paused for about an hour to discuss the evening's entertainment with a group of travelling actors and he spent a very pleasant time greeting and congratulating Carmel on her Valkyrie name.

Her name came as a quite a surprise and a refreshing one at that. Astrid was a pretty name and he was pleased that Freyja liked it, too. The implication that some day Carmel might become a 'powerful queen' hadn't seemed to bother her in the slightest. The name was a good omen, and coming so swiftly after Kat being cursed as Sangrid, that was all she cared about.

Thor fantasised for the briefest of moments that if Carmel were a queen then he might be her king—before slapping himself quickly and telling himself to snap out of it. He was married and her boyfriend Loki was a most handsome devil who just also happened to be his favourite drinking buddy.

Going back to his hammering, he scolded himself gruffly under his breath, the foolishness of the notion slowly fading from his thoughts as he buried himself in his work. Eventually, when the afternoon faded toward dusk, he tipped several buckets of cold water over his head, shook himself dry, and then quickly combed his fingers through his tangled beard. *Perfect.*

He was ready for a night of serious eating, drinking, and merry-making.

During the afternoon, the short spell of autumn sunshine and warmer weather came to an abrupt end. Black, oppressive clouds rolled in from the Great Sea. They were laden with rain and threatened the first major storm of winter. The strengthening, gusting wind and a darkening afternoon sky did little to dampen the carnival atmosphere in Asgard. Everybody was joining in the celebrations, and the main square in front of Gladsheim was full of jugglers, acrobats, fire-eaters, and even a dancing bear. This caused mayhem when he escaped briefly and ransacked a street seller's stall. He was looking for a particularly sweet-smelling jar of honey which the owner kindly let him keep.

Children were laughing and singing, fathers were coming back early from the fields, and mothers were putting on their Sunday best ready for the night ahead. All in all, the victory celebrations of the Battle of the Bridge couldn't have got off to a better start.

As dusk began to fall and to another rousing chorus of drums and horns, the Valkyries made their way by torchlight down the wide, cobbled road from the castle to Gladsheim.

The first big splashes of rain had already begun to fall, and slaves frantically tried to stretch linen sheets above the girl's heads, sidestepping and skipping alongside the women in a desperate attempt to keep them dry. All the people of Asgard seemed to be out to congratulate them, showering them once more with flowers and tokens of appreciation. Led by their queen, the Valkyries looked amazing.

The seamstresses and hairdressers had done a fabulous job, with no two gowns or hairdos looking the same. Every colour of the rainbow was on display and their jewellery sparkled with a grandeur that rivalled the brightest stars in the sky. Silk wore black with two strings of beautiful, white pearls; Ruby wore a sequined white dress which shimmered as she walked; and Jameela looked fabulous in a sky blue strapless creation with sides slit all the way to the top of her thighs. It was a dazzling display of beauty and power and the crowd loved it. The women stopped so frequently to shake hands, accept gifts, and kiss small starstruck children that it took them at least half an hour to cover the short distance to the hall.

Knowing the persistence of the crowds outside, the gods and goddesses had arrived much earlier in Gladsheim to little or no announcements. Kat was shocked when she entered the building to see so many of them present. Nearly everybody was there with only one notable absence: Frigg. No doubt the self-appointed 'queen of shopping' was still in Midgard, living it up.

Thanks to her afternoon in Fensalir, Kat already knew most of the goddesses, but there were several new faces amongst the gods whom she didn't recognise. Forseti, Bragi, and Ull were amongst these, as well as a god called Vali who particularly caught her eye. He was sitting at a crowded table yet looked alone, staring absently at his horn of mead whilst those around him chattered gaily away. He had the shadow of three days' stubble on his chin, and loose, shoulder-length, curly black hair which would have been much smarter if it had been washed and then tied back in a ponytail. His face looked familiar and yet was instantly forgettable, like your typical boy next door. He seemed an oddball, different from the gregarious mob that made merry all around him.

"HAIL, VICTORY! HAIL, VALOUR! HAIL, ODIN!"

Thor led the traditional salutations before they all sat down. Odin stood up and prepared to make his speech. As he opened his mouth, the gathered audience cried "Shush!" and then leaned forward in an exaggerated gesture of listening intently. Everybody fell about laughing, even Odin. He sat back down and smiled, gesturing to Thor to get on with the evening's entertainments.

Thor was lavish in his praise for the Valkyries and the reason for his meeting with the actors earlier in the day soon became apparent. He had arranged a tribute, the *Song of Astrid,* to celebrate Carmel's bravery and the terrible journey they had endured.

Musicians struck up and Bragi, the god of poetry and eloquence, spoke the prose as their epic struggle unfolded. The enactment was heavily laced with humour, courage, sadness, and surprises.

The story began with buckets of flour being thrown over two clowns to represent the blizzard on the plateau. They stumbled about the floor shivering and blindly waving their arms about as they asked guests if they knew the way. Everybody hooted with laughter.

Next, the actor who played Geirrod entered. He wore the mask of a pig and was loudly booed. His daughters were played by two midgets who had crudely smeared bright red lipstick across their mouths. One of their deaths was caused by a hearty belch from Thor that made everybody laugh until they cried. There was loud cheering when the other midget died, run through by the actor playing Carmel.

Geirrod's death, too, caused merriment: a large chicken leg was stuffed into his mouth and he flopped theatrically this way and that before finally falling to the floor in an exaggerated and drawn-out end. Showers of meat spat from his mouth as he choked, lay still, and then choked some more. The audience and actor loved this scene and his comedic death throes continued for ages.

Carmel squeezed Thor's hand and mouthed 'Thank you' to him for the next part of the poem. He had kindly ignored her brutal whipping. For this section, the actor playing Thor merely ran around the stage carrying a squawking chicken whilst Carmel's likeness chased after him, plucking feathers from its back.

Thor reciprocated her squeeze and smiled at her. She looked magnificent in a sleeveless silver dress that plunged steeply into the shapely cleft of her bosom. He didn't know how she had got it, but somehow Carmel had persuaded Freyja to let her wear the Necklace of the Brisings again. This was without doubt the finest necklace in all creation. Without thinking, Carmel and Thor let their hands linger one on top of each other, a gesture which didn't go unnoticed by Sif. She nudged Thor under the table and threw Carmel a filthy scowl. Carmel withdrew her hand.

It was unwise to upset a god, and madness to upset a goddess.

The play moved on to Utgard, with the actor portraying Thrym wearing the mask of an ass. He kept stumbling around and bumping into things, dropping an imaginary hammer on his foot, which made him hop with pain. The presence of Thrym brought forth loud catcalls and jeers. Food was thrown, too, until Odin begged them all to stop. He didn't want the show to get completely out of hand.

Carmel's duel with the giant was next and was the undoubted highlight of the story. A burly serf and a slender Asgard maid had been tied impossibly close together, forcing the maid to perform a breathtaking balletic display as she circled lithely around the man as they traded blows with their arms. Her dance was so gracious and elegant that the gathering begged her to repeat it twice more before they eventually allowed the poem to reach its humorous climax.

With the cockerel released, the actor playing Thor bent over proudly and wiggled his bottom high in the air. This was the finale and everybody howled with laughter knowing what was about to come. On the count of three, and with a single loud and raucous raspberry which everybody helped in blowing, the entire cast crashed to the ground, felled by a blow from Thor's flatulent hammer.

With the performance over, everybody got to their feet and gave the show a standing ovation. It was a masterpiece, and one that would be performed over and over again as the events gradually blurred and faded into the stuff of legends. Thor and Carmel were immediately engulfed by well-wishers and there was a prolonged interlude as the tables and chairs were rearranged for the feast ahead.

The break came as a welcome opportunity for Kat. She had spied the one person she really needed to see that evening. She had a hunger, but it wasn't for food. A different form of nourishment was needed to ease the terrible ache of Jess that had surfaced once more inside her head.

Sashaying seductively over to Freyr, Kat joined him in conversation. He congratulated her on her part in the battle and as he leant forward to kiss her cheek, she whispered in his ear.

For Kat, Freyr was like a blue cross pair of shoes in a half-price sale—completely irresistible and a must-have. If anybody could banish her feelings for Jess, it was he. Smiling broadly, Freyr put his hands behind his back and delicately waved one of them across his ring. They were off to Odin's garden.

Within the same blink of an eye they returned, but the ashen look on Kat's face suggested that something other than love-making had taken place. Whilst everyone else remained preoccupied with the play, Kat took Freyr's hand and dragged him swiftly from the hall. They would have to go to the castle instead.

"I can't believe it," Kat muttered over and over again as heavy gusts of rain lashed around them. The terrible spectacle that had greeted them in the garden was hard to comprehend. Odin's garden stood outside of space and time and reflected the wellbeing of Asgard.

Any premature belief that the Battle of the Bridge was the final, triumphant battle of Ragnarok had been instantly shattered.

The garden was a shadow of its former glory. Its sun now lay hidden behind clouds, and the ground beneath the ash tree Yggdrasill was covered in a thick, rotting carpet of decay. Yellow and brown leaves lay everywhere. Patches of sky were visible through the tree's thinning canopy, and the spring which had once bubbled so musically around its roots had been reduced to barely a trickle. The Norn were still there, but they had stopped their singing and their ash blond hair looked uncombed and uncared for. Their crisp, clean, linen frocks were crumpled and stained, too.

The picture became worse the longer they stayed. The air was still and their ears rang with the emptiness of silence. No birds were singing and the insects had ceased to hum. The garden was dying, and where it led, Asgard was sure to follow. The mighty battle with the giants had been nothing, a mere pinprick compared with the conflict that must surely lie ahead.

Ragnarok was coming like some almighty storm and Odin's garden lay dying in the horror of its expectation. The vision was an unthinkable horror, and Kat gulped hard, fighting to hold back her tears. Their trip to the garden had only accentuated her pain. She needed Freyr more than ever and she attacked him as soon as they entered her room. If ever a god of love could cry rape, this was it.

Shredding his clothes, she threw him onto the bed, straddling his hips as she did. Kat didn't undress, such was her hunger she didn't have time. Hitching her dress up high around her waist she took his thickness immediately, forcing herself down upon his enormous strength, inch by painful inch. The pain of his size was intense, but was exactly what she wanted, exactly what she needed: mind-blowing waves of ecstasy and agony to purge Jess from her soul. Their final words together pierced her conscience like a knife—foul, evil words, cursed words that should never have been their last.

MURDERER!

With lust fuelled by pain, Kat rode upon Freyr's belly in a frenzied crescendo, digging her nails deeply into his flesh and grinding her hips hard against his, begging him to match her fervour. Freyr's manhood was immense and she wanted every last magnificent, manly inch buried to its hilt deep inside her womb.

Gasping loudly, they sprinted toward their climax.

"Jess, Jess, JESS!" Kat's anguished, words tumbled in a frenzy from her lips as her mind screamed *why, Why, WHY?*

Freyr's warmth exploded inside Kat as she burst in all the colours of the rainbow. Red followed orange followed yellow in an endless procession of steep and wonderful waves. For the briefest of moments Jess was forgotten, drowned by an ocean storm seething with emotion. Finally, when the last climactic waves had crashed and then faded from her shores, Kat collapsed into a sobbing heap on Freyr's chest.

He held her gently in his arms. This wasn't the Kat he knew. This wasn't the Kat he loved.

"So, my dearest Sangrid, what was all that furious passion really about?" Freyr had waited a few moments before posing his question. He had guessed long before Kat's collapse that it wasn't his love she craved tonight. With a practised art, he dried her eyes and tidied her hair, all the while gently coaxing her to speak.

Kat's words at first were a garbled mess, punctuated by long periods of sobbing and apologising, but finally her story was told. When Kat eventually finished, she immediately felt better. Freyr was a good listener. A problem shared was truly a problem halved.

"Well," he said when she finished at last. "You know what you have to do?'

"What?"

"You need closure. You can't leave your dearest friend like that, no matter what she has done. We both know that."

Kat nodded and smiled. She knew he was right and she also knew what she had to do. The torment inside was still there, but at least now it was a bearable pain.

"I'm so sorry for abusing you," Kat murmured apologetically as she ran her fingers tenderly through his hair.

"Please, think nothing of it. I'm just glad to be of help," Freyr smiled and then added, "It's not every day I get to share such a passionate tryst. You must truly love her. She's very lucky." He winked knowingly.

"Thank you, thank you so much," Kat kissed his lips. "Will you come back with me to the hall?"

"No, I'm sorry. Much as I'd love to, I can't," Freyr shuffled a little awkwardly. "Duty calls, I'm afraid. Public holidays are always a busy time."

Kat nodded. Frigg had warned her—as a fertility god it was his job, after all. They kissed affectionately once more and with a wave of his hand he was gone.

Taking one last look in the mirror and pinching her cheeks with her fingers to add some colour, Kat walked slowly back toward the hall. The rain had become heavier still, but she didn't care. Her head felt better because she had come to a decision.

As soon as the night was done, she would ask Odin if she could go back to Midgard and visit Jess. She had to talk to her, to let Jess know that she was forgiven and how much she still loved her. The mere thought of this thrilled her and her step lightened as she walked. Now at last she could relax and enjoy the party.

As Kat crossed the square, the sound of the festivities in the hall grew louder. The party was still in full swing. Breaking into a trot, she skipped merrily up the wooden steps and pushed open a heavy door. She hoped she hadn't missed all the fun. Unfortunately for Kat, she had.

The mood inside the hall was very different to the one when she had left.

Events were unfolding that would change their lives forever.

51

Vacation

The journey to Dulles airport was one of the saddest and most depressing Marcus had ever taken.

It had taken Jess a long time to emerge from the café toilets and when she did, he saw that she clearly had been crying. Her eyes were red and swollen and her cheeks were heavily stained with both old and new tears. Marcus had a pretty good idea as to what the problem was, but there was little he could offer in the way of comfort. He knew Jess hadn't killed Kat—that was Mickey's doing—but in allowing it to happen she was guilty by association. It was a tricky issue and he could see both sides of the argument, but he didn't want to take either position. Luckily, Marcus didn't have to.

Jess was in no mood for talking as he drove her to the airport. She sat beside him, staring silently out of the window. She wasn't looking at anything in particular; her mind was miles away. Fresh, large tears fell in spasms as they drove. Marcus had offered to look after her for a while in New York, but she turned this option down. She needed to go, and get as far away as possible from the memories of Kat and her life as a Valkyrie. Being with her mother and starting a new life with her estranged family would be the best thing for her. It would help her forget Kat, Asgard, and hopefully her intense craving for the mead.

The addiction haunted the depths of her consciousness like a spectre, wracking her body and head with spasms of pain and violent shakes when she least expected them. She hoped they would fade and go, but she feared the worst. In truth, her desire for the mead was growing stronger rather than weaker.

Marcus would have liked to talk to Jess about things besides her argument with Kat, because there were other questions burning holes inside him. *Was he still about to die?*

Jess had said that she could no longer feel him, and that held a promise of salvation. It could, of course, just be the absence of the mead that made her feel this way, Marcus couldn't say. But he hoped that his escape from the assassination attempt meant his destiny had changed, his future purged of the spectre of an early death. Perhaps now he had many, many, years of blissful living ahead of him? He wanted children, lots of them, and as soon as he went back to New York, he and Anna would make a start on that.

With the thought of Anna came another, depressing and miserable question. *Would she take him back?*

This question went unanswered for many hours as Marcus helped organise Jess's ticket, sort out some money, and bid her a very tearful and heartfelt farewell. Kat had departed with Jess's mead and Valkyrie knife, but she had kindly left Jess's purse and coin behind. The Dragza Corporation credit continued to hold good and this came as a relief for Marcus. The only thing worse than Jess arriving in Ireland forty years after her death would be if she returned as a penniless vagrant. He shuddered at that prospect.

Reluctantly, Jess had given in to his insistence that she travel first class. She needed the room to rest and the copious amounts of free alcohol might just numb her broken heart.

As he finally waved goodbye, Marcus wondered if he would ever see Jess again. He still felt a deep love for her and he prayed that someday he would.

Heading slowly back toward the car park and a rental car, Marcus faced one of the toughest decisions of his life. He still had his mobile with him, but it had been unused and switched off for the last two days. It was one of the many precautions he and Kat had taken to avoid detection. Sitting in the car, he pulled the silent phone from the glove compartment and turned it over thoughtfully in his hands.

If he switched it back on, what messages lay in wait?

It took some time for Marcus to pluck up the courage to do this. His hands were sweating when eventually he pressed the on button. He could stay on the run if he wanted to, but he knew that a fugitive's lifestyle didn't suit him. He liked his creature comforts way too much and the stigma of being a petty criminal didn't sit comfortably on his honest shoulders. If trouble was waiting then it was best to face the music now.

To Marcus's great relief and happiness, when his phone finally picked up a signal and sprung into life there was a torrent of messages and missed calls, all from Anna.

With a huge smile on his face and a joy that threatened to split his chest in two, he started the car and sped back to New York and home. The journey passed effortlessly, as if it were a dream. In no time at all he was back in Anna's arms and their joyful reunion was vigorously consummated in bed. The furious passion of their lovemaking confirmed the words that didn't need to be spoken.

Anna had forgiven him.

"Is that a promise, then?" Anna asked solemnly when they eventually finished making love.

"Yes, yes, of course," Marcus replied, equally soberly. She wasn't joking and neither was he.

"There will be no more messing about with the Valkyries, their knives, mead, or any other such hocus-pocus ever again, so help you God?" Anna crossed her heart and insisted he do likewise as he spoke. She was a religious woman, unlike him.

"Absolutely not. I won't even think of them, I promise."

Anna tapped Marcus's face playfully and then sank back into bed. She rested her head upon his chest once more. His indiscretion was forgiven, but it could never be forgotten. For now, she was grateful that he was back in her arms and their shattered lives could return to normal. She hated the drama of the last few days and prayed that Marcus really meant to keep his promise. He had an obsessive streak a mile long and she knew she would have to keep a close eye on him.

"Mmmm, what we need now is a good holiday," she murmured as she ran her hand up and down his manly chest.

"Mmmm, sounds like a good idea."

Marcus dwelt on this thought for a while and as he did so, a smile began to grow upon his face. Without her knowing it, Anna had just given him a perfect opportunity, one that was just too good to miss.

"Do you know what," Marcus sat up a little and lifted Anna's head from his chest. "I think I know just the place." Marcus had honestly meant to keep his promise to Anna, but for the moment that would have to go on hold.

Curiosity and obsession always got the better of him.

Agent Woods smiled broadly as he looked out of his office window. He knew he should be furious, but his smile said otherwise. In truth, he was more than a little relieved.

Special Agents Smith and Smith had actually done him a favour by taking the two Valkyries off his hands and also in removing their artifacts. It gave a nice, neat, stitched-up end to their paperwork. No loose ends—just a cold, clinical, surgical cut.

Woods still wasn't sure how they'd executed their escape, but if he had to hazard a guess he would have hung his hat on meta-materials. This was his favourite Valkyrie toy: their cloak of invisibility. It was a pity that he hadn't got his hands on one of those but, hey, never mind. He had what he wanted and that was all that mattered.

Woods was a meticulous and experienced FBI agent, seldom taking chances, and keeping records and backups of everything he did. The Valkyries were no exception to this rule.

Having captured Herja and her prized flask of mead, Woods had carefully decanted half the contents into a cheap, plastic drinks bottle. This was sitting safe and sound in his fridge at home. He was certain that there was more than enough there for the Contessa's scientists to work out what it was made of. So far he had managed to keep his hands off the soothing and refreshing liquid, but it was hard work. Every time he opened his fridge his eyes went lovingly to the shabby bottle. He yearned for another sip, just one, that was all. That would satisfy him—for now.

The rich and aromatic liquid was incredibly addictive, but Woods didn't care. With any luck, he would soon have enough to wallow in the stuff. *So what if he had to drink it for the rest of his life?* The mead was going to make him live forever. Compared to eternal youth, addiction was a trivial inconvenience, nothing more.

Woods absent-mindedly played with the mobile phone in his hands. He had already informed the Contessa of what had happened and she didn't seem too distressed, either. As he had said, it was the mead that mattered and he had managed to keep hold of enough for both of them. He was waiting now for a call from her pilot. The Contessa was sending her private jet to pick him up and take him to her Caribbean retreat. He had never been there before and the thought of all that sea, sun, and fabulous wealth gave him serious goosebumps.

He looked slowly around his bare and shabby office, memorising every last detail in his tidy mind. *Would he miss it?*

Would he really miss all those hours of paperwork, phone calls, and nights of working late? Woods chuckled to himself and returned the phone to his pocket. Hell no—of course he fucking wouldn't! Who in his right mind would miss this shithole?

Woods returned his gaze to the window. He had a good feeling about his upcoming journey, a very good feeling indeed. Somehow he felt certain that he would be leaving his office and FBI headquarters for the last time.

He touched wood quickly to ensure his luck held.

52
The Cruellest Blow

"**I**'m a god, I am immortal! Look! Nothing can harm me, see? See!"

These extraordinary words were being spoken by an extremely drunk Balder. He was standing and swaying at his table while stabbing himself repeatedly in the stomach with a knife.

Of all the gods and goddesses gathered at Gladsheim for the evening's entertainment, Balder would have been the last one you would expect to get wasted and cause such a ruckus. He was without doubt the kindest, the most charming, and the most handsome god in all of Asgard but, unfortunately, tonight he was also the most drunk. He had been sulking since the Valkyries returned from their triumphant victory, being mad at himself and even more so at Silk.

How could he let her send him back to Asgard before the battle?
How could she have deprived him of his share of the glory?

These feelings of frustration had finally erupted tonight. The beautiful play, the lavish praise for the warriors, and far too much mead, ale, and wine had gone to everybody's heads. This had sparked a row between Silk and Balder which had simmered on and off until now. Now it was boiling over and the gods around them were having a field day.

"Go on, Balder, you show her!"

It was Loki, of course, who had led the stirring, taunting each of them in turn with a string of witty, but barbed, comments. First Silk, then Balder, and then Silk again, and so on. What had started out as a petty, lover's squabble had quickly escalated into an all-out row with food being thrown and sides being taken. Predictably, the gods and goddesses backed Balder while the Valkyries backed Silk.

At first, the ensuing conflict was a hoot. There had been a great deal of humour as tables were upturned, makeshift barricades erected, and plates of cabbage, horns of ale, and mutton stew were thrown from one side of the room to the other. There had been tussles and raids, with gods snatching maids, and warriors kidnapping goddesses, all of which had been done with much laughter.

Now, unfortunately, the situation was getting a lot more serious and it was at this point that Kat entered the hall.

Everybody was still having fun, but the alcohol was leading the merrymaking down a dangerous avenue. Balder was daring the warriors and gods alike to harm him, to prove his point that he alone couldn't be killed. This wasn't a sensible game but, then again, when you are all completely rat-arsed, common sense goes out the window.

The cocky maid Lara was the first to have a go, stabbing him in the chest with her knife. Balder felt nothing, and smiled.

Skogul, who really should have known better, was the next to have a go, running him through with a sword. Balder laughed loudly, pulled it out and then thrust it back in again, just to prove his point. The gods roared with laughter, begging him for more.

To everybody's surprise, Ull decided to take a turn. He attacked Balder from behind and buried an axe deep in his back. Balder belched loudly, twisted his arm behind his back and heaved the weapon out. Wiping his blood from the head, he hurled the axe across the hall with such force that it buried itself in the wooden door.

"See? I'm indestructible!" Balder roared loudly as he staggered sideways. He was bleeding heavily, but no one seemed to mind, not even Silk. She was too angry, even encouraging the other Valkyries to have a go. She was furious with him and was about to let rip again when an unexpected voice took up the challenge.

"Can I have a go? Let me see if I can kill my mighty brother."

It was Hod. He had decided to use this moment to show off his reborn skill of archery, his ability to hunt and shoot despite being blind.

"Don't be so daft, Hod." It was Thor who tried to pull him back into his chair. "You can't see."

"I don't need to," Hod replied crossly, shaking Thor's arm from his shoulder. "Loki has taught me how to shoot again. I can put an arrow in his heart if you'll just give me half a chance."

"Go on, give him a chance, Thor. Come on everybody: Hod, Hod, Hod, HOD, HOD—"

It was Loki of course, taking the lead, waving his arms above his head and whipping them all into a frenzied chant of Hod, Hod, Hod. Everybody joined in, stamping their feet and thumping their fists on tables as they shouted his name. This would be great sport, even if Hod messed it up. A blind god flailing around the room hosing arrows at the guests—what a riot!

To Kat's surprise and horror, Thor gave in to their demands and a servant was sent to fetch Hod's crossbow and some of his stumpy green darts. Balder obliging stood against a wall while everybody else took cover behind tables and chairs. You couldn't be too careful—Hod's aim might be truly disastrous.

"Okay, what I want you to do, Balder, is to hold your arms out wide and then clap your hands when I nod my head." Hod held the loaded crossbow in his hands as he stood in the middle of the hall. "That will tell me where you are. Before you can clap your hands a second time, I will have shot you with my dart."

"Hang on a minute." Although Hod's words made perfect sense, Thor was having none of it. "That's too easy," he quipped, chuckling away to himself.

Thor had decided to up the stakes, and the fun. Standing behind Hod, he spun him around three times before letting go. Now Hod would be dizzy, confused, and even more likely to nail any one of the guests with his dart. Everybody roared with laughter and crouched still lower. Who knew where Hod would shoot? The poor, blind fool.

Balder clapped his hands and then stretched his arms out wide to get ready for his second clap. Hod spun around, took aim, and pulled the trigger. The stubby green dart whistled through the air and landed with a dull thud. It was bang on target and Balder fell to the ground like a sack of potatoes. Hod's dart had pierced his heart.

There was a mighty roar of approval from the party. No one believed that Hod could do it and he had proved them all wrong. It was the icing on the cake that Balder had thrown himself on the floor pretending to die.

"Well done, bro!" Thor slapped Hod heartedly on the back as he offered him a horn brimming with mead. "Come on, Balder, get up and join us in giving three cheers to our little brother here."

Balder didn't move. He lay on the ground, still and silent.

"Oh, come on, Balder, do get up!" It was Sif who spoke, eager to get on with the rest of the night's entertainment. She had been enjoying the food fight and was keen to get down to some arm wrestling with Ruby.

Still Balder didn't move, not even a muscle.

"Silk, go and give that silly lover of yours a kick up the arse. I'm getting bored now. A joke's a joke, but don't overdo it." Thor was still chuckling loudly, but he wanted to make his toast and carry on. Balder was wasting serious drinking time.

Scowling fiercely, Silk stomped over to Balder and gave him a none-too-loving kick in the ribs. She would forgive him eventually for starting the argument, but for now she was still too mad to be gentle. Balder continued to lie there, still and silent as a stone.

Silk crouched down and slapped his face. "Come on, enough's enough. Get up you silly, handsome devil you." A hint of anxiety had begun to creep into her voice. She was angry with him, but his continuing silence was becoming unnerving.

"Balder. Balder!" Silk shook him and then placed her head against his chest. "Sweet Odin, will somebody help me? BALDER'S NOT BREATHING!"

Silk leapt up, screaming loudly and hysterically to the bewildered crowd. Only one person in the room could comprehend what was going on and that was Kat. She had already grabbed Hod's hand and pulled him toward the door. She had sensed something wasn't right the instant Balder fell to the floor.

Balder had quite literally fallen like a sack of potatoes, with no regard for his safety. To her trained and still sober medical eye, this was not the way someone pretending to fall actually fell. They would always make sure they protected themselves from harm. Something was wrong, very wrong.

"Hod, what have you done?" Silk hissed furiously through clenched teeth as her eyes roamed around the room in an attempt to find him.

"N-n-nothing! I just fired my dart. Balder's my brother. It wouldn't kill him, it couldn't kill him. It was just a dart! He's messing around—he must be!" Hod's voice sounded nervous. He could sense an air of hostility growing all around him. The gods and Valkyries were beginning to inch toward him and their mood was turning ugly. Very ugly.

"Hang on a minute," Kat raised her voice as she pushed Hod behind her next to the entrance and stood defiantly in front of him. "There has to be an explanation for this. Just let me go and have a look at Balder before you all jump to any hasty conclusions."

"You've killed him, Hod. You've killed the finest god in all of Asgard!" Silk was coiled up like a tiger ready to pounce and she did so as she spoke. Luckily, Thor and Tyr were able to grab her before she could sink her sword into Hod. She had made her mind up already. Hod had killed the love of her life and she was going to skewer the sick bastard like a stuck pig.

"HEY!" Kat waved her arms above her head, shouting loudly to grab everyone's attention. "What's Loki doing?" She pointed an arm toward him, emphasising her point.

All eyes turned in his direction.

"Loki! What in Odin's name…," Thor's voice trailed off as Loki looked up like a rabbit startled by a fox, his eyes flashing green and yellow. He had been caught red-handed. Hel's cursed black dagger was in his hands and plunged through Balder's heart. It was beginning to glow, but in the shock of discovery Loki had let go of its handle for a split second.

"GRAB HIM!" To everybody's amazement, Odin had raised his voice.

Turning as one, they lunged toward Loki. They could see with their own eyes what was going on. Loki had taken advantage of the situation and was taking Balder's soul to Hel.

Loki quickly seized the knife once more and prayed that it would hurry up and do its job.

A hand reached out to grab Loki's shirt, but in that instant a brilliant flash of red light burst from the blade. Loki snatched the knife from Balder's chest and, waving his hand over his ring, he was gone. The hand clutched at thin air.

"Come on, Hod," Kat whispered coarsely as she manhandled him through the door. "We've got to get out of here."

For the moment, her distraction had worked. All eyes had been on Loki and she made good her opportunity to escape with Hod. Balder was dead—of that she had no doubt.

Loki, who she suspected was behind this whole dastardly plan, had fled to the safety of Niflheim and his wicked daughter, leaving just Hod—the poor, innocent fool who had pulled the trigger—to face the wrath of the gods.

Kat gulped hard, trembling as she barred and bolted the heavy doors behind her. Hod was a dead man walking—and so was she.

The stunned and drunken guests in the hall behind them would quickly come to their senses and their anger would be beyond compare. With a sickening jolt, Kat realised that she was now on the wrong side of the law. Her bravery—or stupidity—in saving Hod from a lynching could only lead to one thing: the terrible vengeance of the gods and Valkyries raining down upon her as well.

Kat shuddered violently and then charged off into the howling rain. Hod stumbled and shouted wildly as she dragged him along behind her.

They had to get away—far, far, away—and fast.

53

A Rock and a Hard Place

Nothing could have prepared Cole for the shock of the surface of Niflheim. All his experiences so far—his finger amputation, his battering by Lucifer, his forced sodomy—were mere pinpricks compared to the inferno of Hel.

Lifted high above their heads, Cole was carried outside to a chorus of jeers and raspberries. Not that he heard them or even cared. The shockwave of the atmosphere hit him like napalm, a searing blast that clung to his flesh and raised instant blisters on his face and lips. He would have liked to scream, but he didn't dare open his mouth. The air was dense and foul beyond imagination. Every breath made him cough and gag. The intense heat burned his throat as each forced gasp tasted as though he were inhaling sewage.

If someone had given him a knife, he would have cut his own heart out rather than live another second in Hel's fiery hole.

Beneath him he could hear the squelch of the Berserkers' iron-clad, hobnailed boots as they slithered through the rotting mire. Their boots had been given an additional protective coating of Hellinium and they certainly needed it. There was a continuous clanging and scraping noise which sounded like a cat running its claws down a blackboard.

Huge, hideous, armoured worms and deadly scorpions lurked in the rotting detritus that the men were wading through. Giant leeches were leaping at the Berserkers' legs; their suckers lined with hundreds of razor-sharp teeth scratched and scraped as they fought to find a purchase on their heavy boots. These sounds blended into a cacophony of noise, as did the buzzing of a myriad of beetle wings. Swarms of insects darted like shadows in the twilight surrounding them. Occasionally the men would stop, and Cole would hear the heavy swish and thud of a sword being used on creatures far bigger than beetles, maggots, or leeches that were blocking their way. Cole shuddered to imagine what these could be.

It felt like hours, but it was probably only five minutes before the men found what they were looking for. They had travelled slowly and carefully, gingerly picking their way around deep potholes of sludge that would have swallowed them whole. They were travelling steadily uphill and as they did, the squelching of their boots seemed to lessen somewhat. Perhaps the putrid slime was thinning, Cole couldn't tell.

He tried to look around him, but the dark sky was partially smothered in a thick blanket of steam that made visibility difficult. He could just make out vast swathes of poppies spreading in all directions. Their luminous scarlet stamens swung lazily in the air, while ragged clusters of worn, ochre rocks punched their way skyward between their swaying bloody fields.

KABOOM! The ground shuddered and shook as a plume of molten rock and lava exploded violently in an eruption barely two hundred metres from where they were. Cole wished it had been closer. It would have killed them instantly and put an end to his suffering.

Rocks showered down around them, bursting into a hail of sizzling shrapnel as they landed. The slimy ground beneath them erupted too, now hissing and fizzing as the mixture of rotting flesh and feeding bugs became pockmarked by the incinerating, white-hot shards.

After travelling a few metres farther, the men stopped and laid Cole down on a coarse, angular slab of rock. His arms were locked into crude, iron manacles but his legs were left free. Cole quickly discovered why. The rock was barely long enough to accommodate his head and torso. Just as Louis had requested, his legs would be left to dangle in the air.

In a final, spiteful twist of cruelty, Cole was safe from being devoured by the ravenous slime for as long as he could keep his feet suspended. It was a test of endurance, both physical and mental. *How long could he stay awake?* How long could he keep his feet from sinking into the filthy, seething mess around him?

The Berserkers didn't care. With a final farewell chorus of kicks, curses, and spits, they left him to his fate. Louis would have his wish. When eventually Cole lost his strength the bugs would eat their fill, digesting him inch by screaming inch as they crawled their way hungrily up his legs. They would gnaw, suck, and dribble acidic bile as they digested Cole alive.

Cole looked up to the dying remnant of the sun above him. It filled almost a third of the sky. Brilliant yellow and white flashes of nuclear explosions rippled across its blackened surface, spewing huge plumes of plasma that eventually slammed into the atmosphere high above the surface of Niflheim. This firestorm created a continuous aurora of garish, dancing lights, a dazzling display that cast brilliant reflections from a slender ring of tiny rocks and dust that orbited the planet's equator.

The spectacular aerial display would have made for a beautiful sight, but Cole wasn't admiring it. His eyes were now tightly shut and he was muttering something under his breath, something he had never done before.

He was praying for a miracle.

CLINK—CLINK—CLINK

Ganglati had managed to find a Zimmer (walker) frame somewhere in the depths of Niflheim and was grateful for its discovery. It was now easing his slow and painful progress as he neared the door to Hel's royal chambers. He had come from the hall of the Berserkers where, some time ago, the message he was supposed to deliver would have been considered urgent.

Hel had left strict instructions with him. Cole mustn't be killed. Harmed definitely, maimed possibly, but killed—no.

Unfortunately, as Ganglati neared her door, these instructions clashed with another command she had issued. She absolutely, definitely didn't want to be disturbed under any circumstances whatsoever. She was busy relaxing, and for Hel, relaxing was serious business.

Ganglati raised his hand to knock, and then paused. He was caught in a paradox. If he knocked and interrupted Hel, he would get a kicking— of that he was certain. If, however, he didn't knock and Cole were eaten alive, he would still get a kicking—and of that he was equally certain.

Ganglati scratched his head as he tried to focus on these options. Just like his legs, his brain wasn't too sprightly these days. One ironic thought crossed his mind as he mulled over his choices. He was in a lose-lose situation and, in a peculiar sort of way, his plight mimicked Cole's.

He, too, was caught between a rock and a hard place.

54

Vali

"It's all my fault. I'm responsible," Odin muttered quietly as he knelt beside the still body of Balder. He was carefully examining the end of the short, green dart which lay embedded in Balder's heart.

"Don't be so silly, Father," Thor encouraged as he stood behind Odin and nudged him reassuringly in the back.

The hubbub in the room was gradually subsiding as gods and warriors alike gradually came to their senses. The full horror of the tragedy was slowly sinking in.

"No. It is my fault." Odin hung his head and fell silent. He was too consumed by grief to continue talking for the moment.

"It can't be," Thor offered once more. "You didn't whittle the dart and you certainly didn't ask Hod to shoot it, so how can it possibly be your fault? If you ask me, it's that wretched Loki who's to blame. Look how quickly he scarpered with Balder's soul, hey?"

"No, Thor. I agree that all you have said is true, but the dart was made from mistletoe." Odin's voice, barely louder than a whisper, was choked with grief.

"So?" Thor didn't understand what Odin was getting at and neither did any of the other guests who were close enough to hear his utterings.

"Balder was invulnerable to injury from any plant or object native to Asgard," he began, rising slowly to his feet. "But I'm afraid mistletoe isn't a native plant. I brought it back from Midgard many years

317

ago. It seemed so decorative and people had such fun with it at Christmas time. It seemed so pretty, so harmless—until now."

Odin buried his head on Thor's shoulder and Thor hugged him warmly. For once the two were united in a common cause: grief at the loss of a son and a brother.

"You stupid fool!" Sif was the first to break the eerie silence that had descended on the hall. Odin's revelation was shocking and she was the only goddess brave enough to express what was on everybody's mind.

"Frigg will go absolutely mental. You can count on that, you idiot. She'll skin you alive—or worse—I promise. However, instead of crying over spilt milk, what we need to do right now is to focus, and focus hard, on catching the evil culprits. As Thor said, you didn't fire the dart and neither did you make it."

There was a loud murmur of approval at this point as they all looked around, trying to find Hod. He was nowhere in sight.

"Where's Hod?" Silk snarled through clenched teeth. He had surely killed her lover, not Odin.

"He must have left," offered Carmel who strode over to the door and tried to open it. The door wouldn't budge.

"Come on, Thor, get your hammer and open that door for us," Odin was beginning to recover his composure. "Hod couldn't have locked it by himself so someone must have helped him."

The gods and Valkyries looked at each other as they tried to work out who was missing. The veil of confusion cast by such an excess of alcohol was slowly clearing.

"Where's Sangrid?" Ruby exclaimed loudly and suddenly.

THUD!

"Damn her!" Odin cried as he slammed his fist down hard upon the table, making everybody jump. "She has to be in on this plot as well. There can be no other explanation for her actions. Why else would Mimir choose such a name for her? 'Sangrid'—great treachery and cruelty. I'm such a fool! I trusted Kat and now look how she's repaid me. How could she do this to me?"

"Calm down, dear," Freyja stepped forward, putting her arm around his shoulders. Being the Valkyrie queen she couldn't stand by and listen as one of her warriors was insulted. "We need to hear her side of the story before we jump to any hasty conclusions. Come on, Thor, hurry up. Get this door open already."

"Where's my hammer?" Thor enquired as he scratched his head. Somewhere in the confusion of the play fighting he'd misplaced it.

"I can't have hurt him…I can't have killed him…that's impossible!" Hod babbled deliriously as he half ran, half stumbled toward the castle.

"Just shut up, Hod!" Kat hissed angrily as she dragged him up the hill by the scruff of his neck. She slapped him hard, making him yelp, and then slapped him again. She didn't mean to take it out on him, but she was furious, not only with Hod but also with herself. They had precious minutes to escape and she didn't have time to hear a sorry tirade of excuses. Balder was dead and they would be, too, if they didn't get away.

The wind was howling all around and rain lashed against their bodies in icy, horizontal squalls. She was shivering violently with cold and fright and they were both already soaked to the bone.

"Get a slave to give you the fastest horse he can find and then wait for me here," Kat yelled, throwing him roughly in the direction of the stables. Racing inside the castle, she flew up to her room. Grabbing her sword and a bottle of mead, she slit the leg of her dress with her blade. She would have loved to change into her warrior tunic, but there wasn't time. Hastily she ripped the bottom of the dress off. The ragged tear left her hem far too high on her thigh for her usual liking, but modesty wasn't a priority tonight. Leaving Asgard alive was all that mattered.

Bounding down the stone staircase two steps at a time, she raced back across the courtyard. To her great relief, Hod was standing there with a large stallion by his side. It wasn't Sleipnir, but the horse looked strong enough.

"It's Gold Mane, Thrym's horse," Hod offered helpfully as Kat leapt on its back and then hauled him up behind her.

"Giddyup, Gold Mane!" Kat dug her heels in hard and yelled at the stallion without acknowledging Hod. "Hold on tight!"

Gold Mane whinnied expectantly, and then reared up on his hind legs before bolting across the yard and out of the gates. Kat gasped with amazement and excitement. He was a fabulous steed, the fastest horse she had ever ridden. Within seconds and with a thunderous clattering of hooves, Gold Mane had galloped down the hill and across the square in front of the hall. Kat could barely see where they were going. The rain lashed about her face, blinding her with its howling ferocity.

As they clattered over the bridge across the River Ida, Kat heard the loud explosion of the door to Gladsheim. It had been shattered into a million pieces. Thor's hammer must have done its work and the gods would soon be after them. They had escaped—but not a moment too soon.

"Where should we go?" Kat yelled over her shoulder as she spurred Gold Mane to gallop faster still. "Fensalir?" she suggested, hoping that they would be safe in Frigg's secret hall.

"No. We can't go there. I've killed my brother. Mum will never forgive me." Hod slid his arms farther around Kat's waist, clutching her tightly. He was drunk and terrified.

"Then where, Hod, WHERE? Where in Asgard will we be safe, hey?" If Kat had had a hand free, she would have slapped his silly head off. It was pitch black, pouring with rain, and the whole of Asgard was about to rise up against them. Their plight was hopeless. For what it was worth, they might as well stop running now and give themselves up.

"Take the road south to Middle Sea!" Hod yelled in her ear.

"Why?" Kat asked before adding, "Are we going to the elf kingdoms?'

"No!" Hod shouted resolutely in her ear. The storm around them was gaining in intensity and fingers of lightning now danced across the horizon. The roar from the wind and thunder was deafening. "We're going to bear west and head toward the cleft in the mountains."

"Ah, hah!" Kat nodded. She knew the deep gash in the mountain range, although she had never travelled in that direction before. The valley lay about a day's ride to the south of Heimdall's watchtower and about half a day's hard ride from where they were now. With any luck, they could be there by noon tomorrow.

"Why go there, Hod?" Kat hollered once more as a gust of wind lashed her face with a cocktail of sleet and hailstones. "Will we be safe?"

"Yes!" Hod bellowed. "We're heading to the Valley of Sighs and the bridge over the River Gjoll."

"Why?" Kat asked again. She hadn't heard of either of these places before and she was curious.

To her surprise, Hod said nothing. He just held her tightly, pressing his head against her back.

The night was still young and it was going to be a nightmare of a journey.

It took the party in Gladsheim at least five minutes to find Thor's hammer and then the merest fraction of a second for him to blast the door to smithereens. With a satisfied grin on his face, he led the party outside and into the howling winter's storm. The gods and Valkyries followed, with Odin being the last to leave. They looked around. Neither Hod nor Kat were anywhere in sight.

"Where's Vali?" Odin enquired as the guests parted apologetically, allowing him through to the front.

"Here I am, Father." Vali stepped forward and bowed deeply on bended knee. His long, black, curly hair was already soaked and dangling around his heavily-stubbled face.

"I want you to find them for me," Odin asked and Vali nodded.

Crouching down on all fours, Vali began sniffing the cobblestones around him. He then placed an ear to the water-soaked ground. Odin waved at everybody to stand still and be silent. They did so.

Within a few moments Vali looked up. To Carmel's surprise, he had twisted his neck almost full circle, like an owl or a bird of prey. Indeed, his eyes seemed to have enlarged, becoming more yellow and slit-like than they had seemed just moments before.

"I have them, Father," Vali spoke softly. "They are on a single horse heading south. The horse is strong and fleet of foot, but it isn't Sleipnir. I know his gait."

"It must be Gold Mane," Thor offered, and the gathering murmured in agreement. That would be a fine horse to make good an escape.

"My lord, I will take my leave of you now." Vali stood up once more, bowing stiffly. "What would you like me to do with them when I catch them?" he added.

Odin paused for a while as he stroked his beard thoughtfully. He stared long and hard at the floor before looking up. When eventually he did so, his eyes were cold and hard as stone.

"What shall I do with Hod, sire?" Vali ventured once more.

"Kill him." The gods and Valkyries gasped in amazement. "He is dead to me, the treacherous cur!" Odin spat vehemently.

"And the Valkyrie Sangrid, my lord. What about her?"

Odin paused once more. "Kill her, too. Kill both of them," he replied resolutely. She had betrayed him and her fate was sealed.

"But my lord—" Freyja began, pleading with an angst-filled voice.

"Enough!" Odin raised his hand to silence her. He had no time for mercy. "I have made my decision and my order stands. Be gone, Vali, and make good speed."

"As you wish, my lord." Vali turned and with a single, almost silent flap of his wings he was gone, vanished into the howling gale.

Vali, half-god and stepson of Odin, was a shape-shifter. In the blink of an eye he had transformed into a magnificent eagle owl and in two near-silent beats of his mighty wings, had passed stealthily into the night.

55

Taller

To Ganglati's great surprise, when Hel eventually emerged from her chambers she gave him a great, big, slobbering kiss right in the middle of his forehead—before clipping him hard around the ear and sending him sprawling across the corridor.

The leopard hadn't changed her spots.

Hel was, in fact, delighted for an excuse to end her marathon pop-corn-eating, horror flick-watching, and video game-bashing session with Henry—hence the kiss. It wasn't that she hadn't enjoyed her time with her new toy, far from it. It was just such horribly hard work being 'nice' for so long. She had to get out and stretch her legs, in a manner of speaking.

She honestly didn't know how angels could hack being, well…so damned angelic.

Ganglati's slap was therefore a welcome release for Hel, a return to more familiar territory. It was also his punishment for allowing Cole to be put in harm's way.

Quickly changing into her more customary black bodice, studded belt, and tight leather trousers, Hel made her way toward the Ber-serker hall. Slaves were sent scurrying on ahead to make sure Cole was retrieved from the planet's surface, and she picked up a couple of hounds, just in case.

The sight that greeted Hel when she arrived at Cole's side wasn't pretty.

He was deeply unconscious and barely breathing. His body, cov-ered in blisters, stank like a flame-grilled steak. Slaves were anxiously waving large bundles of poppies under his nose in a desperate attempt to revive him. To Hel's relief, she felt confident that he would survive his ordeal, but he would definitely need a new pair of feet. His had been digested down to the bones, which now gleamed a ghostly, ivory white against the rotting background goo of partially dissolved flesh and muscle.

Cole really wasn't a pretty sight.

"Who's responsible for this outrage?" Hel shouted angrily at the men gathered around her. Her eyes blazed red and orange as she slowly cast her gaze amongst them. The dogs at her side began to bark and bare their teeth; sensing their mistress's anger had aroused them. Someone was going to pay for disobeying her orders and they would be having a very literal piece of him.

"Begging your pardon, ma'am. It was me, your majesty." Lucifer stepped forward, knelt on one knee and kissed her hand. It was his fault and he would take the rap.

"Louis, sweetheart, why?" Hel cooed in a sickly-sweet voice which was laced with a malicious undertone.

"Because he's the one, my queen. He's the one who sent me to this place. Cole is the reason why I agreed to serve you and why I have stayed with you until I could take revenge upon the man who stole my life."

Hel withdrew her hand slowly and stood back. As far as she was concerned, Cole was Odin's starter of Ragnarok and nothing more. This revelation came as a complete surprise, but she knew she mustn't say so. She had convinced Louis that she knew who his killer was when, in reality, she neither knew nor cared. Louis was the sexually repressed but oh-so-brilliant leader of her army, and this inspired quality was all she wanted of him—except perhaps for a little teasing and flirtation now and then.

"Why of course he is, stupid," Hel replied as she tapped Louis's masked face lightly with her hand. "That's why I sent him here, for you to punish him, not to kill him, don't you see? Remember that nasty, cheap, trashy little girlfriend of his?"

Louis nodded.

"Well, we need to keep Cole alive by using him as bait to lure her down here. That's why you mustn't kill him just yet, you silly sausage!" Hel frowned, pouting petulantly as she spoke. Louis hung his head. She was right. What she said made sense in her uniquely warped and twisted sort of way. "Good. Well, I'm glad we've got that sorted out."

Hel offered Louis her hand once more and he kissed it again. She didn't have a clue as to who Cole's girlfriend was, but yet again she didn't care. The idiot child would tip up sometime or another, bobbing up and down on the Nastrond along with the other rotting garbage. It was just a matter of being patient, that was all. Anyway, she had other more important matters on her mind right now. Cole's injuries screamed for punishment and her bloodlust was rising fast.

"Will someone get me a sword?" she enquired politely. Hel was in dire need of entertainment, relief from being nice for so long. After a short pause, a suitable blade was found and cautiously presented for her approval. She took it.

"Now, Louis, would you be a treasure and select five of your best men for me to play with?" Hel had a sword in her hand and she yearned to slake her thirst.

Louis had to think fast. He could see the fire in Hel's eyes; the brightly flashing colours betrayed her need. Blood would have to be spilt, but he could ill afford to lose five of his best men. For that matter, he really couldn't risk his own life either. In her current mood, if he offered his life instead of theirs, she would take it without a moment's hesitation. Act first, regret later: that was the way Hel operated. Her life was driven by impulse and what she wanted she always got.

Somehow, there had to be a middle ground, a way out of this mess that didn't involve killing. Luckily for Louis, he had a flash of inspiration.

"Your majesty. Would you accept my hand in place of five men, five of my fingers as punishment for my disobedience?"

Louis rolled up his sleeve, clenched his fist, and held out his arm. Hel smiled mischievously and nodded. That just might do for now, and besides, it would be great sport to see how well he took the pain of amputation.

Louis waved to one of his men and a chopping block was quickly brought. He knelt and placed his outstretched arm upon it.

"Your majesty, I await your justice. Please accept my hand for displeasing you." Bowing his head, he looked away.

Hel strutted arrogantly around him and after taking the heavy sword in both her hands, she raised it high above her head. This was going to be fun.

"Oh, my lady! Oh, my lady!"

Hel's arms froze in midair. A disturbance had come from the corridor and she could hear the agitated voice of Ganglot. She sounded breathless and Hel could see her now, shuffling her bloated and mis-shapen body toward them across the blood-soaked floor of the cavern.

"Oh, my lady!" Ganglot paused, fighting for breath. She hadn't shuffled this fast in as long as she could remember. "Great news, my lady. The best news ever, my lady," she garbled as she arrived, panting hard, beside her mistress.

Hel slapped her across the head. She'd got the 'great news' bit already. Now what exactly was so important as to interrupt her fun?

Gasping frantically, Ganglot filled her in. "My lady, your father has arrived and he has brought with him a great god of Asgard, the big-gest god of Asgard ever."

"What do you mean? He's brought Odin?" Kat's eyes blazed green with excitement. *How could this be possible?*

"Oh no, my lady, that's not his name. No, he hasn't brought Odin. He's brought Taller, that's who he is. Your father has brought the great god Taller with him."

Hel thought for a moment and then squealed loudly with excite-ment, jumping up and down with joy. "You stupid imbecile!" Grab-bing Ganglot by her ears, Hel pressed her face to her chest, kissing her forehead firmly with her lips. "The god's name is Balder, not Taller, you idiot!"

Hel threw the sword to the floor, all thoughts of taking Louis's arm forgotten. She had to return immediately to her chambers and see the best present she had ever received. She made to go—and then stopped abruptly. She had one last piece of business to attend to.

"Ganglot, do you think you could dig out a nice pair of feet and stitch them onto Colleen for me?" she waved disparagingly in Cole's direction. Even he didn't matter anymore. Nothing did, now that she had Balder.

"Oh, of course, my lady. You can trust me," Ganglot replied, bob-bing an almost unrecognisable curtsey as she spoke.

Hel gave Ganglot one of her stares. *Trust her? I should coco!*

56

Divisions

The storm engulfing the whole of Asgard continued to rage throughout the night. Torrential rain driven by swirling winds lashed mercilessly at everything and everyone that dared to stand in its way. The heavens opened as lightning crackled and thunder growled relentlessly from horizon to horizon. So violent was the storm that countless trees became uprooted, torn asunder by the howling gale's incessant brutality.

After galloping swiftly away from Asgard, Gold Mane gradually slowed his pace to a canter and then to a more leisurely trot. He had no choice. Kat could barely see where they were going and the path beneath his hooves had become hidden in a quagmire of rain and mud. Luckily, Gold Mane was as sure of foot as he was fleet. He remained completely fearless of the terrible storm as it raged all around them, never losing his footing, not once.

To her great surprise, Kat gradually realised that they weren't being pursued. She listened intently as the minutes ticked by, expecting at any moment to feel the thunder of galloping hooves and hear the excited cries of warriors as they picked up their trail. Fortunately, all that greeted her ears was the reassuring 'clip-clop, clip-clop, splish-splash, splish-splash' as Gold Mane's tireless pace pounded out the waterlogged miles beneath his hooves.

Kat couldn't sleep. She didn't even feel tired. Fear and frequent, deep, draughts of mead spurred her forward, holding at bay a bitter chill from the freezing rain. Hod sat behind her and required the occasional prod as he drifted in and out of sleep. He was still the worse for

327

wear from the night's heavy drinking and she didn't need him falling from their trusty steed. Besides, the warmth of his body pressed close to hers was a comfort and a reminder that she wasn't completely alone in this ferocious storm.

Was Hod guilty?

The question often crossed her mind as the hours trotted by. Hod had shot the dart, but he clearly hadn't intended to kill Balder. He was his brother and Hod was simply too naïve to scheme such a thing. She remembered seeing Loki moving toward the stricken Balder as they left the hall. He must be behind the killing—that would be right up his street.

Why hadn't the gods given chase?

The mood in the hall when they had left was ugly. Very, very ugly. They would have killed Hod there and then if given the chance. Perhaps the gods already knew where they were heading? If this was the case, then the gods could easily afford to stay at the castle and wait until the storm eased. Certainly the Valkyries would be able to overtake them in a matter of hours once transformed into swans. In some ways, Kat's suffering now seemed pointless, her desperate attempt to rescue Hod a futile gesture that flew in the face of overwhelming odds.

Kat's mind also turned to Jess. Her pain was almost gone, replaced by the warmth of love. Kat had sworn that should she get through this mess, she would return to Midgard and seek Jess out. This clarity of thought comforted her and gave her the resolve to carry on. Wherever Hod was taking them, they had to survive and prove his innocence. Odin and the rest of the gods would have to listen to him. She would make sure of that. For Jess's sake, they had to stay alive.

After a few hours' ride, Kat found the junction that headed west toward the cleft in the mountains. It was marked clearly with deep, flooded potholes and muddy ruts. The route had to be well travelled and Kat was curious as to why she had never heard of it before.

Between his naps, Kat tried to press Hod for more details. Unfortunately, all he would repeat was that they would find sanctuary in the Valley of Sighs. They would be safe there from Odin, the gods, and the Valkyries alike. Kat should have taken comfort in his words, but she didn't. The Valley of Sighs didn't sound like the sort of place where you would find food, warmth, and shelter.

As dawn broke, the storm gradually abated, having blown itself out in a one night stand of madness and mayhem. The winds slowly subsided and the torrential rain turned first into a chilly drizzle then stopped altogether. Everything around them was sodden, such that throughout the morning they had to endure frequent and unpleasant soakings from trees anxious to relieve themselves of their burden of rain.

As the morning progressed, the landscape around them rose steadily steeper. Their path picked its way at a leisurely pace; winding slowly this way and that as it meadered through the foothills toward the mountains beyond. Dwellings were becoming fewer and farther between and the early patchwork of cultivated fields and meadows gave way to a much more coarse and haphazard scrubland. Heather, gorse, and briar patches now surrounded weathered rocky outcrops, each richly festooned in lichens and mosses. As they continued, they passed only occasional, isolated shepherds tending straggling flocks of sheep and goats. The shepherds tipped their hats and nodded polite 'Good days' as they passed. It would be some time before the news of Balder's death would reach these lonely souls.

With almost imperceptible slowness, the deep cleft in the lofty mountain range was drawing steadily nearer, forming a threatening and distinctive blackened gash, one that split the snowy mountain range in two. Immediately before this haunting and forbidding chasm, the Valley of Sighs awaited.

"Sorry," Hod muttered. Kat didn't reply.

"I'm sorry for getting you into this mess," Hod tried again after they had journeyed in silence for several more minutes. He had been steadily sobering up throughout the morning and was keen now to apologise to Kat and thank her for saving his life.

"Huh!" Kat huffed grumpily, digging an elbow sharply into his ribs. "I should be flogging you, not rescuing you, you—you idiot!" she fumed. "What were you thinking of, Hod, getting all drunk and fooling about with a crossbow like that? It was always going to end in trouble, you should have known that, you buffoon!"

"I know. I'm so sorry for being so stupid. Thank you, thank you for saving me. I'm really, really grateful."

"Why did you do it then, Hod, why, hey? Why did you go and kill your brother of all people? What crazy spark of lunacy inspired you to do such a thing?" Kat enquired angrily.

"I don't know. I didn't mean to kill him. I just wanted to show everybody that I wasn't completely useless as a god anymore. I wanted to impress them, all of them. I, I wanted to impress you," he ended, lamely.

"You're crazy," Kat muttered irritably. She felt tired and sore, and the fact that Hod's act of insanity was turning out to be some daft, crackpot scheme to win her affection didn't help matters one jot.

"I know and I'm sorry," Hod sighed. "I guess I'm just a stupid, blind, idiotic fool—who happens to be madly in love with you," he continued, finishing his sentence in a whisper just loud and obvious enough for her to hear. He desperately needed to know how she felt.

Kat didn't respond, allowing Gold Mane to continue walking for some minutes, splashing and squelching his way through the puddles as they rode together in silence.

"Well?" Hod enquired eventually, with a nervous gulp.

"Well, what?" Kat huffed.

"Do you love me, too?"

"Oh, do shut up!" Kat scolded, trying to stifle a grin. "How can you ask me such a ridiculous question when your father, the gods, and all the Valkyries are about to tear us apart limb from limb, hey? Honestly! I despair of you, I really do."

Digging Hod in the ribs once more, she spurred Gold Mane into trot for a while before letting him return to a more leisurely pace. She really didn't want to answer his question. Not now. Not in this situation, of all places. *The besotted halfwit!*

"Well, do you?" Hod enquired again, determined to get an answer to the question that was tearing his heart in two.

Kat wanted to stay mad and punish him with a cruel and stinging rebuttal but, in truth, she knew she couldn't. He was a kind and loving friend, and in reality just as much of an innocent victim as she now was. Kat knew he wasn't guilty; he didn't have such wickedness in him. That evil finger of blame pointed unequivocally at Loki, Loki, Loki.

Turning around with a sigh, Kat smiled and stroked his worried cheeks before planting a tender kiss lightly upon his lips. Hod's face lit up like a beacon.

"Despite the fact that you always somehow manage to get me into trouble," Kat paused, deliberating on how best to put her feelings for him, "let's say that you're growing on me."

"Then you do love me, don't you!" Hod exclaimed ecstatically, hugging her tightly as he cuddled still closer behind her.

"Shush! I never said that, so don't push your luck," Kat teased, slapping his thigh soundly with her hand as she spurred Gold Mane into a canter. She hadn't said yes and she hadn't said no, but for now she'd had enough of this silly talk.

After about another hour of much more cheery travelling, their journey neared its goal. Rounding a final small rise of scrubland, their destination came into view. From a distance it appeared to be a richly wooded valley, densely forested with mature oak, elm, beech, and chestnut trees, their leaves now painted in all the colours of an autumnal palette. Kat could see the road pass into this woodland through a narrow break in the dense foliage. The pathway was, however, blocked. A simple wooden gate barred their way and it seemed to be unlocked.

If this was the sanctuary and the gate its only defence, then Kat really didn't fancy their chances. The end of their quest must surely lie somewhere farther ahead, deeper inside the secluded vale.

Kat nervously studied the skies above them. A few buzzards circled lazily overhead, their leisurely, spiralling flights mobbed by angry crows. To her relief, there was no sign of Freyja's falcon nor the telltale V of a flight of Valkyries.

Suddenly, a large owl slipped silently from a tree and glided effortlessly down to the ground in front of them. Kat craned her head forward, eager to glimpse what the impressive bird had caught for his meal.

Scarcely had she moved her head than her eyes were blinded by a brilliant flash of light. Kat blinked before rubbing her eyes in surprise. The owl was gone, replaced by the figure of a heavily-armed man who looked vaguely familiar.

He was blocking their way and clearly meant business.

Frigg received the news of her son's death while she was engaged in her favourite pastime. Dressed in a bikini top and jodhpurs and with a warm sun beating down upon her back, she was trotting her horse through the breaking surf of a beach on their private Caribbean island. It was a passion that easily eclipsed the glamour and bling of shopping and socialising, a joy she could relish for every single day of the eternity she knew she would be living.

It was during these leisurely rides that she could relax and let her mind wander, allowing her thoughts to meander through events both past and yet to come.

Frigg hated her husband with the passion of a woman scorned. She had loved him once, enduring his countless mistresses and bastard children who seemed to crawl from under every rock and stone in Asgard. She had known that he was a womaniser long before she married him. She tolerated his affair with Rind and even the one with the grotesquely voluptuous giantess, Grid. Odin was welcome to those vile and wanton women if that was what took his fancy. So long as his affairs remained discreet and of no consequence, she would hold her tongue. Besides, Frigg herself had never been short of suitors. She evened the score by taking a lover for each and every one of his. She had an army of handsome boy toys begging to share her bed, with Ottar being just the latest in a long line of dashing admirers.

No—what had turned Frigg's love to hate and crossed her line in the sand was his flagrant affair with Freyja. She was a fellow goddess and had once been her best friend.

Their liaison was unforgivable, a damning humiliation she had had to endure both in Valhalla and in Asgard. She could never forgive him, never. That was why she strove to frustrate his plans and to undermine his dreams for a mighty army. Anything that caused him pain and suffering brought contentment to her heart. That was why she now worked for Hel. Their bold and secretive alliance being her finest triumph, her greatest victory over her pompous, selfish husband.

Frigg knew all about Ragnarok, the prophecy, and even the trouble with 'Λ' (Lambda) which had so vexed Mimir when he was whole. She could even forgive Odin for that horrendous blunder, but not for his affair with Freyja. Not the loss of her best friend. Ragnarok was coming and she would be on the winning side, unlike her husband. She would make sure of that.

This dream was one she shared with Hel, a dream that someday Odin would end up trapped in Niflheim, imprisoned and forced to endure its cursed fate, the one that he'd created. Together they would see him stripped of his powers, chained up naked and crying like a little, whipped pup. Now that was a doom worth savouring.

Frigg's blissful daydreams came to an abrupt end with the sound of a galloping horse drawing close behind her. She turned hastily and caught sight of her maid Gna riding hard to catch her up. This was an unexpected intrusion, and one which suggested unwelcome news.

Frigg had three maids: Lin, Fulla, and Gna. She always took one with her to Midgard and left one of the others in Valhalla and one in Asgard. That way, she could be updated quickly with any news or gossip from the realms. The maids changed places frequently, although Gna should, by rights, be now in Asgard. Her presence here heralded trouble. Frigg leant sideways and listened with deepening gloom to her distressing news.

When at last Gna had finished, Frigg dismounted and gestured for her to take the mare back to the mansion stables. In normal circumstances, Frigg would have been guarded about what she did next. But this wasn't a normal day. Her face was ashen with shock and anguish. After flexing her riding crop angrily between her hands, she waved one hand across the other and departed in a flash of brilliant light.

For once, she didn't care who might have seen her departure. All she could think of was Asgard, and her fallen son.

"Step aside, Valkyrie, I have no quarrel with you."

The man standing before them had drawn his sword and his intention was clear. He had come for Hod, dead or alive.

"Do you know this man?" Kat whispered quietly as she prepared to dismount. To her dismay, Hod replied loudly and in a voice that their adversary could easily hear.

"Yes, that's Vali, my stepbrother. He's the son of Rind and he was at the celebrations last night. He's one of Odin's trackers." Hod had recognised his voice instantly.

Kat vaguely remembered him now. He was the quiet man with long, curly hair and an unshaven chin. It was strange how easily she could forget his face.

"You're absolutely correct, Hod." The man spat on the floor as he spoke his name. "But you've missed one crucial detail."

"Oh, yeah, that's right," Hod sneered as he spoke. "Vali hates my guts. But don't worry, the feeling's mutual."

Kat glanced up at Hod and then looked at Vali again. Their history of bad blood must go back a long way. She'd never heard Hod speak so contemptuously before.

"What do you want with your brother?" Kat enquired, raising her sword as she spoke. The two of them began to square off.

"To do Odin's bidding," he replied sarcastically.

"And what might that be?"

"To kill him, and you, too, if needs be. But that would be a pity." Vali waved his sword in the air as he practiced a few gentle strokes.

He looked skilled and at ease with a blade in his hands. He would make for a dangerous opponent.

"Why would killing me be such a pity?" Kat was a little taken aback by this statement. They hadn't really met, so why would her death cause him even the merest hint of sorrow?

"Because I owe you, my lady Sangrid. You saved my life once and a favour begets a favour."

"What in Odin's name are you talking about? I would surely remember if we'd fought or if I'd rescued you. I'm sorry, but I don't remember any such occasion." Kat was becoming increasingly perplexed; he clearly knew a lot more about her than she did about him. This was troubling.

Vali stopped circling and stood still. He put his sword down. "You really don't remember me, my lady, do you?"

"No, I'm so sorry." Kat kept her sword held high, ready for any trickery he might be contemplating. She wouldn't be lulled into a false sense of security, not just yet.

"Perhaps if I reminded you of your real name, fair Kat? That might spark your memory—the memory, perhaps, of one Dr. Katarina Neal from St Luke's-Roosevelt Hospital Emergency Department?"

"What?" Kat gasped in amazement. This time it was her turn to lower her sword. *Wow…!*

57

Poolside

"*A*aah…this is the life."

Woods sighed deeply and settled back in his recliner. He closed his eyes and let his face soak up the powerful rays of sunshine that streamed down from a cloudless Caribbean sky. He could hear the rustle of a gentle breeze as it stirred the fronds of the coconut trees that stood all around the magnificent marble pool.

He had arrived at the Dragza Corporation's fabulous private island only a matter of moments after the Contessa had hurriedly left. At first, he'd been annoyed that he'd missed her, but now, this didn't matter anymore. Her secluded haven was a paradise which not only exceeded his wildest imagination, but one which he intended to enjoy for a very, very long time. Reaching his arm down to his side, he gave his knapsack a reassuring pat. The cheap plastic bottle half-filled with priceless mead lay inside and he wasn't going to let it out of his sight, not for anyone.

"Hello. Would you like some suntan cream, sir?"

Woods opened his eyes and looked up. The voice came from a beautiful blond girl who had crept up on him unawares. *Wow!* She looked absolutely gorgeous in her tiny bikini. His heart skipped a beat.

"Uh, yeh, that would be great." Woods wished he could have said something a little wittier but, like most men faced with overwhelming beauty; his brain had turned to mush. "By the way, what's your name?" Woods enquired, hoping that this would be a better way of striking up a conversation.

The girl squatted down beside him and began to rub oil onto his chest. "Christina. And those girls playing in the pool are Olga and Vika. Lia is sitting over there."

Woods followed the waves of her hand and decided to spend a moment studying the eclectic group of individuals who had become his new poolside companions.

The four women, including Christina, were all young and incredibly beautiful. He guessed by their accents and faltering English that they were Eastern European. The two girls in the pool had been playing a riotous game of water polo with two well-muscled gentlemen who were now sitting on its edge, smoking cigarettes. The men were clean-shaven, with crew-cut hair styles typical of the armed forces.

In fact, Woods could infer further. He had recognised the tattoo on the arm of one of the gentlemen as being that of an American submariner. He also suspected by the English accent of his friend that he, too, was probably a naval officer. Interestingly, they both had a large, curious V-shaped scar on the left side of their chests. Woods intended to ask them about these if and when he got the chance.

The third girl, Lia, was sitting under the shade of an umbrella next to a distinguished-looking and portly gentleman in his sixties. He was also American and spoke with a loud and commanding Southern drawl when he occasionally opened his mouth. He was engrossed in a newspaper and it looked as though he intended to read it cover to cover before paying attention to his beautiful companion. This seemed a pity, because she was the best-looking of the four girls.

Her blond hair was tied up in a tight ponytail and her eyes were hidden behind large, reflective sunglasses. She had a beautiful upturned nose and lush, pouting lips, ones that could pour scorn or platitudes with equally seductive allure. Not that Woods was complaining about his new companion, Christina, who had now finished applying suntan cream to his chest and legs. She was fabulous—and way out of his league.

"By the way, my name is Woods. I mean—Tom. Do you know who these other gentlemen are?" Woods could have kicked himself. He must get out of the agency habit of calling himself by his surname.

Christina paused for a moment. "It's probably wise not to ask too many questions about the other guests. They tend to like their privacy, if you get what I mean."

Woods nodded knowingly. "Aren't you and the other girls guests here, too?"

"Goodness me, no! We're your hostesses," Christina laughed comfortably as she pulled a recliner up alongside his. "Would you like some company? You can choose another girl if you prefer."

It took a few moments for Christina's words to sink in, and when they did, Woods glanced lustfully over to the girl sitting at the table. Christina followed his gaze and, giggling sweetly, pulled his face back toward her.

"I'm sorry, she's off limits. The 'Senator' (she mouthed this word silently as she spoke) always books her for the duration of his stay."

"Oh, oh, I see!" Woods smiled apologetically, before allowing his gaze to return and roam greedily up and down her body. *Christ!* He didn't really give two shits about the other girl—his hostess was a goddess and his for the asking. Silently, he gave thanks to the Contessa. She really did know how to wine and dine her guests in style, and that now included him.

"Look, why don't you go and have a dip in the pool and I'll sort out some drinks for us. Would you like a Piña Colada?" Christina offered obligingly.

"Any chance of a cold beer?" Woods suggested as he started to walk over to the pool.

Christina nodded and then strutted elegantly over to a small bar which was staffed by a West Indian waiter. He was immaculately dressed in white, from the top of his colonial-style hat to the bottom of his shiny leather shoes. He was even wearing a pair of white cotton gloves. Whilst Christina organised their drinks, Woods seized the opportunity to strike up a conversation with the two men by the pool.

"Hi, I'm Tom, nice to meet you." Woods shook both their hands warmly and was impressed by the equally firm and confident grip of their hands. They didn't volunteer their names.

"Those scars on your chests, they look very unusual. Do they mean anything?" he enquired hopefully.

The two men looked at each other and then burst out laughing.

"Yeah, pal." It was the American who spoke first. "We went to the same fraternity." They both chuckled once more, obviously enjoying an inside joke.

"Oh, and where was that?" Woods continued, desperately trying to reignite their fragile conversation.

Both men got up from where they had been sitting and one of them slapped Woods playfully but deliberately on the back. It was a firm, slightly menacing slap, one which nearly toppled Woods into the crystal water.

"Hey, I could tell you, mate, but then I'd have to shoot you—know what I mean?"

The American made a pretend shooting gesture with his fingers, winked, and then pushed his friend into the pool. Jumping in behind him, the pair swam lazily away to rejoin their companions. Their message for Woods couldn't have been more abrupt, clear, or embarrassing: no questions.

Feeling his cheeks beginning to smart, Woods beat a hasty retreat to his sun lounger. Luckily, Christina was already there with the drinks and she smiled reassuringly at him as she patted his recliner. She beckoned for him to sit down beside her.

"I did warn you, you silly man," Christina scolded in a teasing manner which was immediately disarming and made him forget the rather unpleasant snub. "Come on, why don't you rub some lotion on me now?"

Christina rolled over and helpfully untied the back of her bikini. Trying to control his trembling hands, Woods tentatively began to massage some oil into her back. Her figure was amazing.

"That's an interesting tattoo," he murmured as he reached her firm, peach-shaped behind. It was just visible on her left buttock above her bikini. It looked vaguely like a small, black poppy with a bright red centre.

"I'm glad you like it," Christina replied cheerily as she took a sip from her Piña Colada which filled a decorative, hollowed-out coconut shell.

"Does it mean anything?" Woods enquired as he began to work more lotion into her shapely legs.

"You naughty boy, you just can't stop asking questions, can you!" Christina rolled over and playfully took a swipe at him with her large, floppy sun hat. She hoped he'd get her message soon, for all their sakes. *No questions!*

Woods gulped hard. Her tattoo was well and truly forgotten, replaced by a vision of her incredible breasts. Firm, tanned, and perfectly proportioned, with nipples enticingly erect, too. He was certainly living the dream.

"Well, are you going to rub some lotion into these puppies or aren't you?" Christina enquired playfully as she poked her tongue out. Taking hold of one of his hands, she pressed it tightly against her bosom.

"Don't worry," she teased. "They don't bite."

58

The Gateway to Oblivion

Kat listened in astonishment as Vali's story unfolded before her. Once again she reeled with the knowledge of how little she truly knew about Odin, Asgard, and the ways of the Valkyries.

Vali was a tracker and one of Odin's best. His job was simple: to find people who Odin and his warriors couldn't. Mimir's well and the Valkyrie sixth sense didn't always glean enough information to locate a hero, an evildoer, or a future maid, and that was where he came in.

With features designed to blend in with those around him, he stalked the earth visible to all, yet with a face that was instantly forgettable. That was why Kat had had such difficulty in remembering him.

Kat had been one of those people whom Odin couldn't pin down. Vali had found her, and he was in the process of leaving New York when he had been knocked off his motorbike. In a bizarre quirk of fate, he was the very last patient Kat tended to before she left the hospital on that fateful Friday evening. He was the injured biker with a collapsed lung and she had indeed saved his life. In doing so she had stayed on late, bumped into Jess, and then walked alone to her doom.

In a very real sense, he was just as responsible for her death as Jess was.

Vali's revelation was incredible. It was yet another piece of the puzzle that surrounded her death. However, interesting though this information was, it didn't really help them in their current situation. Vali would let her pass unharmed, but that was all. Hod was his for the taking and Kat had sworn to protect him. It was a classic Mexican stand-off.

She would have to dig deep if she was going to break their dead-lock.

"Okay, Vali, you win," Kat sighed and turned when he finished his tale, handing her sword and shield to Hod. "I'm sorry, Hod, I tried, but I'm not going to risk my life to save yours. You're on your own now, I'm afraid." Turning back to Vali, Kat held her hand out. "He's all yours, but just to be sure you really will spare my life, let's shake on the deal."

"A wise decision, my lady. I swear no harm will come to you," Vali smiled and then stepped forward with his hand outstretched. He was equally eager to seal their deal. He really didn't want to kill such a beautiful Valkyrie.

Unfortunately for Vali, he had missed one small detail in their agreement. Kat hadn't sworn not to harm him.

Withdrawing her hand abruptly, she jabbed him hard in the face with her fist. He reeled backward, stunned by her blow. Stepping quickly forward, Kat unleashed an uppercut with her left, which landed squarely under his chin. Vali's head jerked violently upwards and he staggered back again. His nose was already gushing blood and his senses were dazed and confused, but he didn't go down. Kat stepped forward once more and swung a powerful right hook that connected perfectly with the side of his chin.

This time, she noted with a smirk of satisfaction, he did go down, collapsing into a sprawling heap at her feet. Vali was down—and he wasn't going to get up.

"What's going on?" Hod shouted, twisting his head this way and that in a desperate attempt to work out what was happening. He had heard the thuds of blows. *Who had struck whom?*

Kat turned and with two steps she leapt up behind him on the horse.

"Hold on tight!" she yelled, gripping him hard between her arms as she took one last, lingering look at the god lying prostrate in the mud. She was now a powerful woman with toned and muscular arms. Few men could take more than one or two blows from her steely fists and it had taken three to put Vali on the ground. He had indeed been a strong and formidable opponent.

"GEE-HAAH!"

Kat dug her heels into Gold Mane, and with a startled whinny he reared once more before galloping toward the wooden gate. In one giant leap he cleared the puny obstacle and was hurtling down the leaf-strewn valley which lay beyond. Hod and Kat had entered the Valley of Sighs.

"Whoa! Slow down, Kat, you lunatic!" Hod screamed frantically at her. "By Thor's beard, tell me when you next intend to make a jump like that! You nearly scared me half to death."

Kat giggled wildly, and tickled Hod's ribs as she reined Gold Mane back to a more leisurely trot.

"Go on, Hod, admit it—you enjoyed that bit of excitement." Kat tickled him some more, laughing heartily as he squirmed in front of her. It was an incredible relief to have reached their destination unharmed. However, looking around her now, it really did seem a most peculiar place for someone seeking sanctuary.

Kat and Hod tussled for a while before she finally relented and stopped her cheeky assault. As her high spirits began to settle, Kat slowly took stock of the valley surrounding them.

The path they were now following was sloping gently downward and appeared to be following the course of a stream that was gaining in width and strength. Hod informed her that this was the River Gjoll and many other streams would join it before it reached its final destination. He mentioned numerous tributaries but Kat could remember only Svol, Vid, and Leipt. There was a path on the other side of the river and a cave which opened onto this at one point as they continued with their journey.

She mentioned these details to Hod, but he just grunted and said nothing.

The rich carpet of autumnal leaves that lay strewn beneath their feet muffled the sound of Gold Mane's hooves as he walked. Indeed, other than then muted gentle lapping of the river, the whole valley echoed with an eerie stillness. Even when Kat strained her ears, she couldn't hear the sound of a single bird or the gentle hum of a bee or dragonfly. It was deathly quiet, and the canopy of trees thickening above them shaded their path with an increasingly menacing gloom. As a child, Kat had been afraid of the dark and this was now rapidly becoming one of the spookiest and creepiest places she could ever remember being in. The deafening silence and the stifling, breathless air added to its sense of sinister foreboding.

It therefore came as a welcome relief when Kat first heard, and then caught sight of, an oxcart creaking slowly toward them. A young family was on board and to Kat's surprise they didn't look up nor acknowledge their presence as they passed solemnly by. The faces of the parents and children were tear-stained, and heartfelt sobs rose in stifled bursts from the cart.

Alarm bells clamoured loudly in Kat's head. This didn't look good.

"Hod, where in Asgard are we?" Kat commanded tersely, pulling Gold Mane to an abrupt halt. She had had enough. If Hod didn't tell her exactly where they were or where they were going, she was going to give him a damn good beating. Leaning forward, she slapped him hard on the side of his arm to ensure he got her message. The time for cloak-and-dagger secrecy was over.

"This is where the dead are brought," Hod began hastily, which neatly explained the tearful occupants of the cart.

"So how exactly does that help us?" Kat enquired menacingly, slapping his arm again. She wanted more and Hod had no choice but to oblige. Kat's harsh blows had left him under no illusion. He couldn't bluff or ignore his way out of her questions this time and he certainly didn't want to end up being thrashed like Vali—Odin only knew what state she'd left him in.

"It's not just the dead of Asgard, but the dead from all the realms," he blurted. "The path on the other side of the stream is for giants' corpses and the cave you noticed back there leads to the dwarf realms. There is an ancient agreement that no weapons be drawn in this valley as a mark of respect to the dead and grieving."

"Thank you, Hod," Kat replied sarcastically. "But I still don't understand why you had to be so secretive about all of this and how that really helps us."

They were cornered, and she felt certain Odin could find some excuse to break this agreement and force them out of the valley if he chose to. There had to be more to Hod's plan than this, surely?

Thankfully, there was.

"Because we're not staying here, that's why."

"What do you mean, not staying here? What's at the end of this valley—a graveyard or something?"

Kat still wasn't satisfied but she was slowly getting to the bottom of their mysterious journey, bullying the truth from Hod. His fear felt good, provoking her bloodlust, which was exactly what she needed right now: a burst of anger to stave off her exhaustion.

"Yes, it's more the 'or something' bit, Kat. Look, we must be nearly at the end of the valley by now. Can you see a bridge?" he enquired hopefully.

"No, not yet. Should we ride on?" Kat suggested. Encouraged now that something important lay ahead, she urged Gold Mane into a gentle canter. She wanted to see this bridge and her wish was soon granted.

Within a short while, the valley around them became abruptly steeper, coinciding with their entry into the deep cleft that split the mountain range. These peaks now towered majestically on either side of them, giving rise to vaulted, precipitous cliffs that hemmed them in as the valley narrowed dramatically. The River Gjoll, too, had changed its demeanour, frothing and foaming excitedly beside them, joyful now as it rushed toward its journey's end.

Rounding a final tight corner, they were hit by the loud roar and spray from a waterfall. Its icy mist covered their faces and partially shrouded the view of the wooden bridge which now loomed large in front of them. This was it: journey's end for them as well.

Kat screwed her eyes up tightly and tried to study the ghostly vision before her.

Just as Hod had suggested, there was indeed a slender, arched bridge over the seething river. It was made from thick, rough-hewn wooden logs thatched together with a golden thread that shimmered in the occasional shafts of sunlight falling upon it. A simple rope pulley was suspended across the bridge with a winding handle at either end. Its purpose was clear. Anything intending to cross the bridge had to be winched across, not carried. Beyond the bridge lay the mouth of a craggy cave and it was into here that the roaring river cascaded and fell to become lost from view.

Almost completely hidden by the spray that billowed in clouds from the falling waters, Kat could just make out the shadowy figure of a woman. She was dressed in black and her face and head was covered by a thick scarf from which only her dark eyes were visible. They twinkled ominously in the gathering gloom.

"Hod, we're here, and there's a woman standing on the far side of the bridge." Kat leant forward, whispering hoarsely in his ear. Kat didn't know why she whispered—the roar of the waterfall was almost deafening.

"That's Modgud. She's the keeper of the bridge and beyond her lies Eljudnir, our final destination."

"Hod, what do you mean? There's only a cave on the other side of the bridge and we're completely surrounded by cliffs. I can't see any sign of a hall or castle, or any other building for that matter."

Kat stared hard at Hod's back. She could have sworn his voice sounded strained and uneasy at the mention of Eljudnir. Whatever that place was, she sensed he really didn't want to go there.

"Eljudnir's at the bottom of the waterfall. Come on, spur Gold Mane on and let's get over the bridge." Hod didn't want any more questions. It was time to end their quest.

Kat dug her heels into Gold Mane once more and he trotted forward obligingly. The woman on the far side of the bridge spotted them and she held her hand up, signalling for them to stop.

"Greetings, weary travellers," the woman cried in a voice which rose high above the clamour of the falls. "I see no dead amongst you?" she enquired, sounding a little perturbed.

"Greetings, Modgud. I am Hod and I intend to pass. We mean you no harm." To Kat's surprise, Hod had taken charge for a change.

"I know who you are, son of Odin and god of Asgard. And you, I know you, too, noble Valkyrie. My lady Sangrid, you are free to pass, but Hod—you know the price you will pay if you attempt to come with her. Do so at your peril. I will not stop you nor will my hound."

The woman stepped back, revealing a huge beast with jet black fur, pointed ears, and bright yellow teeth and eyes. He looked ferocious.

"What does she mean by 'price,' Hod, and 'at your peril'?" Kat yelled, but she could see that Hod wasn't listening. His mind was firmly focused on the cave beyond.

"Is there a dog with her, Kat?" Hod enquired calmly and Kat obediently turned her head to stare at the beast once more.

"Giddyup, Gold Mane!"

Seizing the brief opportunity afforded by Kat's distraction, Hod grabbed hold of Gold Mane's neck tightly and spurred him to gallop forward. Oblivious of the danger that lay ahead, the horse sprung into action. Before Kat could stop him, the stallion had galloped the few paces across the bridge to the far side.

Kat knew instinctively something was wrong the moment Gold Mane's hooves touched the ground on the other side of the bridge. She felt his body go limp and his legs crumpling beneath him. Hod, too, had slumped forward like a ragdoll in her arms. They had both collapsed instantly and without making a sound.

Gold Mane's powerful body ploughed slowly into the gravel; the momentum of his gallop continued to propel the three of them forward. Skidding wildly and out of control, they travelled the last few metres to the edge of the cavern as a sprawling mass of limbs and fur. Teetering momentarily on the bank of the river, they toppled slowly over its edge before plunging into Gjoll's freezing waters. In an instant they were lost from view, cascading helplessly over the waterfall's lip and falling, falling, falling, into the darkness below.

Modgud watched them as they slipped from view. Her eyes were unblinking and her face expressionless. Hod had been warned. He would now have to face the consequences of his actions.

Only the dead and undead could safely cross the bridge. All living souls who attempted this journey died the instant they set foot on her side.

The cave was indeed the end of their journey. It was the gateway to Niflheim and it spelt the end of life itself. The powerful waterfall that cascaded through its mouth fell a very long way. When next their bodies came to rest, Hod's would be as a corpse floating on the Nastrond.

Hod had found his sanctuary, but at a price that was truly terrible.

It had cost him his life.

59

What's Wrong?

addy, what's wrong?"

For the first time, Hel's voice had a sense of panic about it. She had been pushing and prodding and shaking and rattling Balder for about five minutes and he still hadn't responded to anything. He just sat there, slumped and breathing sonorously at her sumptuous oak dining table.

He didn't look at all well. His face was a nasty, pale, mottled-blue colour and his eyes were rolled up into his head. You could have pinched or kicked him as hard as you wanted but he would never have stirred, not in a million years.

"Um, darling, there was a bit of a problem when I took his soul," Loki began cautiously, wringing his hands nervously as he spoke. He had a hunch he knew what the problem was, but if he was right, there was absolutely nothing they could do about it.

"What?" Hel shouted angrily as she bent over in front of Balder and wobbled his head from side to side. It moved like a rag doll's, flopping worryingly whichever way she pushed it. Things really didn't look good.

"I was interrupted when I plunged my knife into him. I, I, I sort of…let go of the handle," Loki ended quietly and apologetically. Hel was going to lose it; he was certain of that.

"What do you mean, you let go? You know you have to wait until the light flashes!" Hel looked up in astonishment. She was too surprised to be angry. This was elementary 'soul taking' they were talking about, not rocket science.

"I was flustered, okay? They tried to jump me and I just panicked. I'm really, really sorry, my angel." Loki held out his arms out in a gesture that suggested he needed a cuddle. Unfortunately, his reward was a well-aimed goblet of wine. This ricocheted off his right shoulder before bouncing from the wall behind.

"You bloody idiot! Honestly, Father, I don't know what gets into you. I swear I don't."

Hel hardly ever swore and for her to do so suggested she was seriously ticked off. She began to pace up and down, pinching her lower lip nervously between her fingers while chewing at it with her teeth. This was a mess and for once she was stumped.

Balder was her ultimate prize, her dream god, but to have him here in this state made her feel as though her heart had been shredded. What made it worse was that there was absolutely nothing she could do. When Loki removed his hand from the knife, he had interrupted the stream of data coming from Balder's body. Balder's brain pattern must have become jumbled such that he was now in essence, a brain-dead zombie. His genetic blueprint had been transferred safely, but his mind hadn't.

The only hope of rectifying this situation would be to go back to his body in Asgard and start all over again. She just prayed that Odin wouldn't be in too much of a hurry to hold his funeral just yet. If he was, and Balder's body were cremated, then that was it—game over. The soul of the most handsome god in all of Asgard would be reduced to the state of a dribbling jelly baby for all eternity. That would be just her luck.

"We'd better get him to his room," Hel sighed at last, snapping her fingers for slaves to come and take his body away.

"Oh, which room is that?" Loki asked with feigned interest. He seemed to have escaped one of Hel's screaming fits, at least for the time being.

"The one opposite mine," Hel replied absentmindedly. She would go with Balder, of course, making sure he was handled with the same tenderness she would give to a newborn litter of puppies.

"But I thought that room belonged to Rhett?" Loki enquired innocently. For as long as he could remember, this name had been scribbled on the door in handwriting that he assumed must be his daughter's.

"Oh, Daddy, you're so silly. Balder is Rhett!" Hel shook her head and smiled. Sometimes dads could be so behind the times.

"Oh, yes. Oh, of course he is—how stupid of me." Loki pretended he understood what she was talking about, although of course he didn't. "And, well, I suppose that explains why the name on your room is Scarlett, then, doesn't it?" he suggested in a voice filled with hope rather than surety.

"Absolutely, Daddy. You're learning," Hel smiled sweetly, and in a gesture of love which caught Loki completely by surprise, she playfully kissed him on the cheek before following Balder out of the room. He had made a lucky guess that was all.

As she walked slowly toward the royal chambers, Hel felt a child-like thrill rising once more inside her heart. Despite his dire condition, Balder was here at last. Her childhood crush had come to Niflheim. This alone was cause for riotous celebration. The fact that he was a complete vegetable was neither here nor there. Odin's favourite son was by her side and that was all that mattered. Odin would have to listen to her demands now.

One way or another, this time Hel would definitely be getting the hell out of Hel.

Frigg arrived in Asgard like a shockwave blasted from the gates of Niflheim. She was so completely consumed by grief and rage that she scarcely noticed the sense of despair which smothered the town like a blanket forged from lead.

The square in front of Gladsheim was deserted and a single sodden, black flag hung limply above it. The streets were silent and empty, with children kept indoors and serfs taking the day off work. The surrounding fields lay deserted and still, save for the baleful sound of cows mooing, impatient to be milked. The whole realm was in a state of shock, unable to come to terms with the loss of its favourite son. It would be many days before the full horror of the tragedy would sink in, and many joyless weeks longer still before some sort of normality could return to their daily lives.

Asgard couldn't have been more grief-stricken if Odin or Thor had perished, such was the love the Aesir held in their hearts for Balder.

Finding Gladsheim empty, Frigg stormed up to the castle, crop in hand. Odin was seated in the feasting hall and as soon as she set her eyes on him she saw red, attacking him with a vengeance and screaming in a garbled tirade as she lashed out with her riding crop. She didn't care that his beloved Valkyries were all around—he was her adulterous husband and she, his broken-hearted wife. She had every right to beat him black and blue and that was exactly what she intended to do.

All the pain of his endless mistresses, Freyja, and now her cherished Balder poured from her soul as she rained down blow after blow upon his face and body. It was a frenzied attack, one fuelled more by grief than hatred. How could he have brought mistletoe to Asgard? How could he have undone all the months of enchantments she had cast to protect her dearest son?

These thoughts spurred her on to ever greater ferocity. *How could he have been so bloody stupid?*

Hod was there in her anguish, too, his name being etched on many of her pulverising blows. How could he send that cursed, half-caste, bastard Vali to kill him, to murder their only other child?

The thought was too vile to comprehend, and she prayed that Kat would save Hod from that monster. Of all the Valkyries, Kat was the only one who gave her heart any warmth. Perhaps she could find a way of keeping Hod from harm and spare Frigg the nightmare of a double funeral. Kat was now his sole protector.

To Frigg's surprise and to Odin's credit, he didn't try to defend himself from her beating; neither did the warriors try to stop her. Thrashing Odin was her right, although her ferocious attack was in reality a waste of time. Her husband was dead inside.

His looks betrayed this fact. The sparkle had gone from his eye, opening an empty window into a barren, shattered soul. Grey-faced and with cheeks hanging limp and sallow, he barely made a sound as her crop sang its vicious, biting tune, swishing mercilessly back and forth as it hurtled through the air. Frigg lashed out with all her might, stroke after stroke after stroke, but her blows held little menace. Odin was a broken man and nothing she could do could make him feel any worse. She could have run him through with a sword and he would have barely felt it.

Finally, when her arm ached with a tired satisfaction, Frigg spat her final, anguished curses before retiring to Fensalir. She now needed time alone, time to cry the endless tears that she so desperately needed to shed. However, she wasn't going to leave the castle empty-handed. Bullying Odin mercilessly, he reluctantly agreed for Balder's body to go with her. This she laid in state, surrounding his body with the same mixture of embalming leaves and herbs that cradled Mimir's severed head. For now, there would be no talk of funeral pyres.

Balder's body may be dead, but his soul had gone to Niflheim and with that came a glimmer of hope. Hel was Frigg's friend and there was a slender chance she might allow him to return to mortality. It would be tricky. Frigg knew only too well of Hel's feelings for her son, the overwhelming crush she had had on him since before she could remember. Hel alone had the power to grant a pardon, to release him from his eternal slumber. The question now was: could she, would she, do this for Frigg's son?

Could Hel find it in her heart to release the only man she'd ever loved?

Marcus let his hand trail lovingly in the crystal clear waters that lapped lazily around the gunnels of the boat. He was tired and exhausted, but curiosity spurred him on. His destination was finally looming before him, growing larger with every passing minute.

After agreeing to organise a vacation for himself and Anna, Marcus had struck lucky. A last-minute cancellation had given them the opportunity of a bargain of a lifetime in a hotel at the southern tip of Cat Island. Frantically packing their suitcases the very same day, they arrived at JFK airport with minutes to spare. Their flight took them to Exuma International Airport in the Bahamas, which wasn't ideal. The airports of Nassau or Rock Sound International would have been closer, but at least they'd got a flight. A fast ferry ride to Devil's Point had followed and they eventually arrived at their hotel just in time to enjoy cocktails on the veranda of their exquisite, thatched-roofed suite of rooms. They sipped these lovingly as the sun set through all the colours of the rainbow before slipping lazily into a tranquil Caribbean sea.

Anna couldn't have been more pleased, and her energetic lovemaking the night before had reflected her gratitude for this welcome break. Unfortunately, this pleasurable memory left Marcus feeling more than a little guilty about what he was doing today.

They had both been tired and, after making up some feeble excuse about wanting to go fishing, he set off alone from their hotel leaving Anna swinging sleepily in a shady hammock on their idyllic beach. Common sense screamed at him to stay there with her, immersing himself in their slice of paradise, but obsession drove him on.

Grabbing a taxi, he set out for the harbour at Arthur's Town, the northernmost point of Cat Island. Here he spent some time trying to find, and then persuade, a fisherman to take him on the thirty-kilometre boat trip to Crescent Cay. This was the three and a half thousand-acre private island owned exclusively by the Dragza Corporation. Marcus paid many times over a normal rate for this journey. Nobody wanted to take him there and he sensed a widespread reluctance to approach this place. In the end, he cajoled an elderly fisherman into agreeing to take him. His trip, however, came with one proviso: they didn't land.

This was where Marcus was now, watching with growing awe and admiration as the coconut-shrouded beaches of Crescent Cay rose majestically out of the sea before them.

Cutting the engine abruptly, the skipper indicated that this was as near as they were going to get. With the deafening, rhythmic throb of the engine now silenced and the sickly, aromatic smell of petrol fumes beginning to fade, Marcus picked up a pair of binoculars and began to study the shore in front of him.

The island was large and very impressive. A long, white, sandy beach seemed to stretch from one end of his view to the other. Beyond the breaking surf and honey-coloured shore, he could make out clusters of buildings dotted amongst the copious palm trees. There were, however, no signs of the orchards he and Jess had spotted from Google Earth. They must be there, farther inland, buried somewhere deeper beyond his field of view.

Marcus drifted like this a mere three hundred metres or so from the shore for what seemed an age, before eventually the skipper coaxed the sleeping engine back to life. He had done his duty and pocketed a very easy hundred dollars as his reward.

As they began to turn away once more, Marcus spotted a boat approaching at high speed from around the western tip of the island. The boat was grey in colour and camouflaged in the manner of a military patrol. To his surprise and immediate consternation, he noted a large calibre machine gun mounted on its prow.

Now he could understand the reticence of the fisherman to bring him to the island. Voyeurs were unwelcome.

ACK-ACK-ACK-ACK!

The urgent, chattered burst of a submachine gun sent Marcus's heart into a paroxysm of palpitations. Brilliant spurts of flames and puffs of smoke burst from its muzzle as plumes of water erupted in front of them. A ripple of speeding bullets had slammed into the sea around them. Marcus cowered down and then peered over the gunnels. The motor boat was still heading their way at full speed and its canon was aimed directly at them.

Marcus's gamble was black and white: stay in the boat and chance that the crew would be content with the single warning salvo, or jump overboard in advance of a second, more deadly burst.

A sixth sense cut in, the primitive instinct of self-preservation seizing control of his body. Almost as an unconscious reflex, Marcus dived overboard and began to swim deeply down.

ZIP- ZIP- ZIP- ZIP!

The sound of bullets fizzing past him in the water told him that his instincts had been correct. He swam deeper into the crushing ocean depths.

KABOOM!

The sudden, violent shockwave of an explosion rendered him dazed and semi-conscious; confirming that for a third time he had cheated fate.

The boat above him had been destroyed, its laden fuel tank erupting in a blazing fireball which left nothing but a smoking remnant behind, bobbing peacefully up and down on the surface of the languid waters.

The Dragza Corporation definitely didn't welcome uninvited guests.

60

Lord of the Gallows

din couldn't live with himself.

"It's all your fault. You have to do something. You have to get our son back."

Frigg's parting words cut through his skin far deeper than any of the lashes from her crop. She was right—he held himself responsible for Balder's death even if those around him didn't.

This sense of guilt now made his life unbearable. He hated himself and yet, being the most powerful god in all of Asgard, there was no one to punish him for his crime. Frigg's whipping had felt like pinpricks, the mere bites of ants upon the soles of his feet. They did nothing to scourge the bitter pain of despair from his heart. For that, he needed something far more brutal.

Vali returned from his hunt empty-handed and with a broken nose to boot. Secretly, Odin gave thanks to Yggdrasill for the safe deliverance of Hod and Sangrid. He realised now that his foolish command had been driven by a blind and drunken rage. Hod hadn't intended to take his brother's life and fair Kat had played no part in his death. Even the wicked trickster Loki wasn't to blame. In truth, he was just the messenger.

The real culprit lay in a realm buried beyond his reach. Her evil fingers burrowing deep beneath the soil of Asgard to seize its finest prize.

What vexed him now in equal measure to his guilt was his feeling of utter helplessness. He was the supreme god of Asgard, ruler and creator of this realm, and yet he lacked the power or knowledge to bring his son back to life. In an act that now seemed like insanity, he had bequeathed this priceless gift into the hands of a wicked and teen-aged temptress—Hel, his nemesis. *How could he have let this happen?*

Grieving now with the double burden of guilt and impotence, Odin sat in the castle hall staring blankly at the wall in front of him. He needed a plan. He needed to do something, anything, which could ease the throbbing pain of self-hatred. All his plans for Ragnarok, his brilliant scheming to mask Lambda's curse, would be meaningless without his cherished son by his side.

As he sat and thought, an idea began to germinate inside his mind. It started as a tiny spark which quickly grew into a seed. This laid down roots and sent forth leaves such that a healthy sapling emerged. Growing stronger with each passing minute, this first tiny flash of inspiration finally burst forth into a mighty tree. Odin had a solution.

He would punish himself, sacrifice himself in such a manner that he might discover all there was to know about the magic of his realm. Surely then, his guilt would be assuaged and he would discover how to return Balder to his empty bosom?

Summoning Freyja and his Valkyries to his citadel, he laid out his plans before them. His mind was made up. His agonising journey would begin immediately, and so it did.

For nine days and nights without cessation, Freyja and a warrior would drag Odin to Yggdrasill in his beloved garden. There he would be stripped, bound, and suspended by the neck such that his toes could barely touch the ground. The warrior would pierce his side with Gungnir and then she would depart along with Freyja. At first he would be left alone, writhing in agony, choking and hallucinating as he teetered on the narrow ledge that seperated life from death.

As he hung there gasping in a state of near delirium, the gods and goddesses would bring the finest minds to stand before him: seers and old women, witches and druids, people all blessed with the wisdom of ages. They would teach him their secrets, recite ancient incantations, and read the runes which they scattered on the ground before him. He would pluck each strand of knowledge they possessed and weave these into a tapestry, a patchworked masterpiece that would slowly take shape, growing day by day in both clarity and texture. Here he hoped to cure his impotence. Somewhere hidden deep within its intricate weave, Odin hoped to find his answer, the key that would unlock the gates of Niflheim—secret, ancient words that would compel Hel to release his beloved son.

Freyja would take her rest during the day; her gruesome role in Odin's torture taking place in the night ahead. As dusk fell across the realm, she would return with one of his Valkyries. Their role was as simple as it was brutal: to assuage his guilt. Whip in hand, the chosen warrior would thrash Odin until his back bled and he howled in anguish.

This was a duty his devoted Valkyries found especially hard to stomach. They loved their lord with all their hearts and didn't hold him responsible for Balder's death. Many wept as they whipped, with Silk bluntly refusing to take part. She locked herself away in her room, too proud to show her tearstained face in public. Only Herja managed to punish their lord with any conviction. She was furious at his refusal to allow her to cross over to Valhalla. Because of his troubles, Odin had broken his promise to let her join Ben. She alone could take pleasure in his suffering.

By night, Odin's ordeal continued. Beaten and bleeding, he was then chained to the foot of his lover's bed. Here, Freyja would bring suitors and taunt Odin with displays of hedonistic lovemaking. This was the part of Odin's anguish that Freyja loathed the most. It brought back memories of a time long past, a shameful secret she had kept buried deep within her soul.

Freyja's disgrace had taken place during the time in her life when she acquired the fabulous Necklace of the Brisings, the source of all her power.

In her youth, the motives which ruled her life had been very different from now. Vain and selfish by nature, her life was consumed by arrogance and greed. She took pride in winning wagers and she made one with the four dwarf rulers who had created the exquisite masterpiece. Freyja's lust spurred her to acquire the beautiful necklace for her own, but to succeed in the endeavour she had to sleep with the realm's foul rulers. Giving herself to each in turn, she was forced to endure a night of passionless lust, submitting herself to their depraved and ugly cravings.

Freyja won her bet, but in doing so she lost her virtue. Even now her reputation was tarnished by speculation about those shameful deeds.

This time, fortunately, her intentions were far nobler. Her nightly trysts were driven by love and compassion. Freyja truly adored Odin and if through his pain and suffering he could find redemption, she would submit to his need for cruelty. If that was what it took to cleanse his soul, she would gladly make the sacrifice. Such was Freyja's devotion to the god she loved.

Hours turned into days as Odin's relentless torture continued, and while he suffered the nightmares of his sins, all those around him suffocated under a heavy shroud of wintry clouds and tearful mourning. Joy had left their realm as surely as the warmth of summer sunshine.

Until Odin could forgive himself and return from purgatory, all their lives remained on hold.

61
Surprises

Somehow Marcus managed to survive being torn to shreds on the razor-sharp coral reef that lay barely metres from where his boat had been destroyed.

Gasping for air, he half swam, half drifted the short distance to the sandy shores of Crescent Cay, his mind wrestling to fight back waves of darkness that threatened to drown his consciousness and drag him down to the ocean floor. His ears whistled noisily—both eardrums being left torn and bleeding from the concussive blast of the boat that had exploded so close above his head.

The anonymous crew of the launch which destroyed the vessel didn't hang around long. They hadn't seen him slip overboard, so they didn't expect to find any survivors. Without waiting to search, the crew took off and headed back around the tip of the isle, confident that their mission had been accomplished. None of them spotted his desperate struggle to reach the shore alive.

Exhausted and on the verge of collapse, Marcus eventually reached his goal. Crawling through the surf, he finally came to rest lying face down in the sand, a warm sun beating down gleefully upon his back. Soothing waves lapped invitingly around his legs, each trying to entice him back into their carefree embrace as they slunk once more into the ocean's gentle swell.

The silken sand felt divine and he could have lain there for many hours if it wasn't for another unpleasant interruption. Marcus listened in a whistling daze as the deadened sound of galloping hooves drew rapidly nearer to where he lay. The horse whinnied loudly as it pulled up to an abrupt halt and the heavy thud of dismounting boots was swiftly followed by the shuffling sound of approaching footsteps. Someone was coming to his rescue. He looked up through a hazy blur of sand and salt. It was the figure of a woman, and she was stooping now to tend to his battered body.

It was the roughness of the kick that rolled him over that gave the first clue that this woman was no angel of mercy.

Grabbing hold of his short, curly locks, she pulled him roughly into a sitting position before kneeling in the soft sand behind him. Taking a firm hold of his head in the crook of her arm, a knife flashed briefly into view.

"What the fuck?" Marcus croaked despairingly as the tip of her blade bit deeply into the sensitive skin beneath his left jaw.

"Sorry, nothing personal," the woman volunteered briefly as she made ready to slit his throat.

"Wait, wait, I—" Marcus struggled, desperate to find some words that might just save his life.

"Is that it? Are those your final words?" the woman scoffed as a sneer spread across her lips. He could feel the warmth of blood as it began to trickle down his neck.

So this was it. His moment of death had arrived.

"Frigg," he croaked as the woman pressed his head forward and began to carve her fatal, slender groove. "I need to speak to Frigg."

The movement of her blade stopped instantly. His words had worked their magic. No mortal soul in Midgard should know this name and Fulla froze in her tracks.

Perhaps she shouldn't take his life?

Flipping the knife in her hand around, Fulla cracked the heavy black handle against Marcus's head and he slumped gratefully into the dark embrace of unconsciousness. He was past caring about what would happen next.

Fulla stood up slowly and let him sink backward into the sand. Taking her mobile from her pocket, she called for assistance. She would have Marcus bound and brought back to the mansion with her. It was best that the Contessa knew of his extraordinary words before a decision about his fate was sealed.

For a fourth time in as many days, Marcus had cheated death out of the pleasure of his company.

"GANG—GA—LOTTTT!"

Hel yelled angrily at her servant as she shuffled away in a desperate attempt to avoid the kick she knew was coming. Ganglot failed, and collapsed in a howling heap onto the floor.

"I'm so sorry, my lady, I think I got it wrong," she whimpered, knowing that Hel had spied the shambling, limping shadow of Cole's former self as he stumbled pathetically away from them down the corridor.

"Got it wrong! Have you seen him? Look, Ganglot, look." Hel grabbed her by the ear, thrusting her neck forward.

"I think I may have put them on the wrong way round my lady. Oh, please, please forgive your foolish servant," Ganglot whined in a voice that always irritated her demanding mistress.

"You didn't put them on the wrong way round, you dummy," Hel raged, "You gave him two left feet!"

"I'll try again, if it pleases you, my lady." Ganglot was on her knees and clutched at Hel's legs now. She needed to stay close to avoid another vicious kick.

"I think you've done quite enough damage as it is, you, you—ohhhhh, I don't know what to call you, you blithering idiot!"

Hel wrenched herself free and headed briskly back toward her chambers. She was angry, but not completely furious. She had received some excellent news from Henry and, to be truthful, she could see the funny side of Colleen's predicament. She knew she shouldn't have entrusted Ganglot with the task of sewing on new feet, but it would be great sport to see how Cole now coped with her servant's bumbling ineptitude.

Besides, Ganglot's mistake was of no consequence compared to Henry's astounding breakthrough. He had finally cracked the mechanism to the well and Hel at last held the key to its control. This was a monumental achievement and she fully intended to reward Henry with a lengthy session of popcorn, games, alcohol, and quite probably copious amounts of sex.

It was such fun teasing her darling, innocent little genius, the idiotic fool who still believed he was in heaven with his guardian angel.

"Oh, my lady!"

What now? Hel had just arrived outside the door to her chambers when she heard the frail voice of Ganglati echoing down the corridor. It was coming from the direction of the Nastrond. Tapping her foot impatiently, she tutted in annoyance as her geriatric manservant hobbled toward her.

"Great news, my lady!" his voice wavered excitedly as he stumbled ever nearer.

"Well, what is it?" Hel enquired angrily, raising her arm to cuff him should he dare to keep her waiting a moment longer. Something interesting must have surfaced in the pool ahead.

Fighting to catch his breath, Ganglati knew he had to speak immediately if he didn't want to feel the full force of her hand upon his face. "A horse, my lady—a horse! There's a horse in the Nastrond," he gasped at last.

"Don't be so stupid, you silly old fool." Hel lowered her arm as she contemplated what to do next. His eyesight must be playing tricks on him again and he most probably had seen another large rat. They had a habit of toppling into the cascade from Asgard.

Hel stared hard at him before grabbing hold of the scruff of his neck. "Come on," she hissed angrily, dragging him along behind her. "You'd better not be having another one of your hallucinations or you'll be for it."

Hel was an inquisitive child and she couldn't resist taking a peek. If what Ganglati said was actually true, then a horse would be the sweetest of icings on her birthday cake.

First there was Balder, then the key, and now this: the possibility of a fine steed for her to ride on when she marched her army out of Hel.

62

Friend or Foe?

at really, really wanted to hate Hel, but try as she might, she simply couldn't find it in her heart to do so.

Kat's arrival in Niflheim couldn't be described as her finest hour, but then again, Hel wasn't exactly her first choice in destinations. Her recollection of the fall over the edge of the waterfall was blissfully limited. Having hit her head on a rock almost as soon as she entered the water, she missed all the tossing and tumbling with the freezing cascade as it hurtled through the wormhole. This spared her the trauma of the long, long, fall to oblivion.

Kat's first impressions on coming to were the thunderous sound of the waterfall crashing around her and the icy bitterness of its chilly waters. She found herself swirling slowly around in a pool along with dozens of corpses with more arriving by the second. On the bank of the pool she could make out a group of bare-chested slaves. They were busy heaving Gold Mane out of the water and waving peculiar-looking garlands of flowers under his nostrils. Whatever these were, they seemed to work. Almost immediately he reared up and careered around the cavern whinnying loudly and kicking his legs out behind him, the whites of his eyes rolling wide in terror. Gold Mane could sense the evil around them, as indeed could Kat. The unpleasant stench of burnt, rotten eggs filled her nostrils despite being mixed with a heavier and more insipid fragrance. She guessed this came from the flowers—or the rotting bodies.

Kat's first sight of Hel herself was a bit of an anti-climax. Dressed in her usual attire of figure-hugging black trousers and bodice, she appeared so much younger, prettier, and happier than Kat could ever have imagined her to be. From the terrible stories she had heard back in Asgard, Kat had built up an image of a grotesque and disfigured ogre, spitting hate like a cobra spits venom.

The beautiful woman dancing about excitedly before her was anything but.

Hel quickly spotted Kat and Hod amongst the floating corpses and with squeals of obvious delight she waded into the chilly waters and carefully pulled them to the bank. Her excitement and enthusiasm was infectious, as was her wide and disarming smile. She looked every inch an excited child, one who had received so many Christmas presents she simply didn't know which to open first.

Jumping up and down, Hel clapped her hands, shrieked for joy, and generally made a huge fuss of the three of them, flitting from Hod to Kat to Gold Mane and back again in a bewildering blur of confusion. More slaves were quickly summoned and they brought thick towels for Kat and Hod to snuggle into as they were courteously guided away. Hel then devoted her attentions to Gold Mane.

This became a vision which endeared her immediately to Kat's heart.

Gold Mane was terrified, his nostrils flaring wide with fear as he backed himself into a corner, rearing up onto his hind legs the moment anyone tried to approach. Sidling cautiously up to him, Hel cooed softly as she dodged between his prancing legs. Grabbing hold of his mane, she whispered something soothing in his ear which seemed to calm him instantly. Gently stroking and massaging his powerful chest, she ran one hand along his flank and onto his back. Then, wrapping her arms tenderly around his neck, she slid her lithe body up on top of his. She lay there for a while, motionless, stretched out along his back and neck while continuing to whisper sweet words into his ear.

Finally, he was calm enough for her to control.

As Kat left the chamber, her last memory of Hel was seeing her cantering round and round the pool, waving a hand in the air and shrieking with joy. Her happiness with her newfound stallion was overwhelming and Kat struggled to comprehend how anyone who possessed so much love could possibly be so evil.

Kat was taken to her chambers; which were sumptuous by any standards. Her room was huge with a large, imposing, oak four-poster bed and a carpet on the floor which was the deepest shade of burgundy red. This felt infinitely soft and luxurious beneath her feet. The walls were whitewashed and subdued lighting came from dozens of red candles in gilded candelabra. There was no window to the room but this came as no surprise. The palace of Eljudnir lay buried deep underground.

A large and powerful shower was run for Kat and as she closed her eyes and let the warm water caress her face, she felt the softness of a woman's hand upon her shoulder. It was Hel. She had slipped into the shower beside her and was offering to help her relax and get cleaned up. Kat accepted her kind invitation. She was used to bathing with her Valkyrie sisters and the prolonged and firm massage which Hel so generously provided was more than welcome.

After the shower, which lasted an age yet seemed to finish all too soon, they dried themselves and got dressed together.

Although Hel was several years her junior, they were surprisingly similar in size and shape. They talked about everything as they busied themselves getting ready. A blizzard of questions poured from Hel's lips as she asked about Asgard, Midgard, Odin, the Valkyrie warriors, and their maids. Her questions cascaded in a tangled jumble which made Kat laugh. It was an intensely girly time and Hel begged Kat to dress up like twins. Carefully trimming Kat's hair the same length as hers, Hel dug out clothes identical to her own.

Once dressed, Kat decided to educate Hel in the art of applying makeup. She had already stifled a giggle watching Hel's crude and disastrous attempts. This closeness brought tears to Hel's eyes, a point not lost on Kat. It had been so long since Hel had enjoyed the company of a woman she could call her equal, and the warmth which blossomed so rapidly between them was both genuine and heart-warming.

Hel's greatest sorrows with her exile had been the loss of her bonds with animals and her Valkyrie sisters. In a single stroke, Kat and Gold Mane had redressed these. She couldn't have been happier.

Finally, when they were ready, the two Sangrids stood side by side in front of the mirror. They definitely looked like sisters, twins almost, the blond Sangrid standing shoulder to shoulder with the brunette variety. They laughed as they twisted from side to side, admiring and comparing each other.

"I do love your tattoo," Kat purred as she caught sight of a flower with a bright red centre on Hel's left shoulder. It looked identical to the garlands of flowers she had seen earlier and those scattered around her chamber, too.

"Oh, thank you," Hel squealed as she hugged her tightly for the umpteenth time. She was in paradise with her new best friend. "You must get one, too. It won't take a minute and it doesn't hurt—honest."

"Hmmm. I'm not sure," Kat wrinkled her nose as she considered her offer.

"Oh, go on, do—please! It really would be lovely. Then we could be proper sisters."

"I don't know…" Kat was wavering.

"Please, please. Oh, do say yes. For me, for your sister Sangrid," Hel pouted as she ran her fingers seductively through Kat's hair.

"Oh, go on then. It would be fun and it's such an unusual and pretty flower." Kat's mind was made up and she gave Hel a big hug. After all, what harm could a little tattoo do?

"Oh, goody!" Hel squealed once more, clapping her hands for a slave to make the necessary preparations. "It'll look fabulous on you."

Kat nodded enthusiastically as she allowed Hel to sit her down in a chair. She had never had a tattoo before and she prayed it wouldn't hurt.

When the tools were brought, Hel set about creating an identical flower with the greatest of care. The significance of this moment wasn't lost on her, even though it passed unnoticed by Kat. Hel was branding Kat with her mark, the mark reserved only for her most loyal subjects. These were the elite of Niflheim. These were the angels, her angels—

Hel's Angels.

Frigg wasn't sure for how long she'd been watching Marcus. He seemed deeply asleep and was snoring peacefully as he lay in the soft bed in her island mansion. A tiny smile curled around her lips as she smoked and studied his face. He was an extremely handsome man and such a lucky one, too. She had had so many opportunities to take his life and somehow he had dodged them all. Her hired assassin in New York, the attack by her guards in the boat, and now Fulla's knife—somehow he had scraped through all of these by the skin of his teeth. He must have a charmed life and that could mean only one thing.

He was alive for a reason, a greater purpose which lay beyond the horizon of her view.

It was perhaps this sense of destiny which had saved him from death at her hands, too. She was across the street when Brynhildr greeted him and Sangrid on the steps of the FBI headquarters. It was her familiar face that Brynhildr spotted, but couldn't quite make out. Frigg knew instantly that the aged woman was Jess; she could read her mind even from that range. Despite her half recognition, Frigg could have pressed home her attack if she had wanted to. However, something had stopped her even then, just as it was stopping her now. A strange sixth sense was preventing Frigg from smothering him as he lay on the bed.

Marcus must be alive for a reason and she was curious to know what that was.

"Have you been there long?" Marcus's sudden question startled Frigg. She thought he was still asleep.

"No, not long. How are you?" Frigg asked as she got up and strolled around the bed to sit down beside him. She stroked his hair away from the egg-shaped bruise on his forehead and he winced as she did so.

"Do you remember much about your accident?" she enquired casually as a courtesy. She didn't really need to pose the question, since his thoughts were already pouring into her head. His reason for coming to their island, for instance, had already been discovered. It was the apples, of course, the countless acres of well-groomed trees, each laden with a thousand golden promises of immortality.

"Yeah, pretty much everything I think. You must be, are you, I mean, you're Frigg, aren't you, right?" It was a bit of a garbled jumble, but Marcus got there in the end.

"Yes, and you must be Marcus Finch, I presume." Frigg held out her hand and to Marcus's great surprise, he kissed it rather than shook it. It must have been something in the elegance of her dress or the extreme sophistication in the way she moved and spoke. Frigg was class personified.

"Why, thank you. That was most polite." Frigg got up from the bed and walked toward the French doors, which were open. It was after dark and the untiring refrain of noisy cicadas was audible through a mosquito net that rippled in the slightest of evening breezes.

"Do you feel up to joining my other guests for dinner?" Frigg enquired.

To Marcus's surprise, he suddenly realised that she had made no attempt to apologise for nearly having him killed—twice. That was odd, but he decided he would wait and see if she brought it up of her own accord.

"I think so." He sat up, feeling the world spinning wildly around him. "Just let me take a minute."

"We always dress for dinner," Frigg continued casually as she pressed a button that called silently for a servant to come. "I can organise a dinner jacket if you like."

"Thank you. That would be most kind." With great care, Marcus swung his legs slowly over the side of the bed. The dizziness was beginning to subside.

"Are you travelling alone?" Frigg enquired.

"No. My wife Anna—she's at our hotel." *Christ! He'd almost forgotten about her!* She'd be worried sick.

"Would you like me to call her, let her know that you're alright?"

"That would be great." Marcus was grateful for her consideration. She seemed the perfect hostess—*so why had her staff tried so hard to kill him?* The question was beginning to bug him. Marcus decided to bite the bullet. "I don't mean to be rude, but why did your servants shoot at me?"

"Oh, do forgive my manners. I should have apologised sooner. Their actions were quite unforgivable. Please accept my sincere apologies."

"That's all very well, but it doesn't explain why." Frigg sounded genuinely apologetic, but Marcus wasn't letting her off the hook that easily. "Last time I checked, murder was illegal—even here in the Bahamas."

"Point taken, Marcus, point taken." Frigg paused briefly. "Look, to be honest, we entertain a lot of high profile guests on our island. Politicians, movie stars, pop stars, and such like. They value their privacy and we get so many paparazzi poking around—my staff do have a habit of over-reacting. I am sorry, genuinely sorry. Will you please forgive me?"

"I guess so," Marcus mumbled lamely. Her explanation sounded totally plausible, and coming from those beautiful lips, the apology was impossible to decline.

"Look, please let me make it up to you." Frigg's face suddenly lit up in a smile. "Why don't I arrange for a boat to pick up your wife and the pair of you can stay here for free? I'll even take you home on my jet and refund the cost of your holiday if you like. Would that help?"

"Sure, that's great." Marcus suddenly stopped. He had just had a very nasty thought. "Um, my wife doesn't know I'm here and she really won't be happy if she finds out this place has anything to do with the Valkyries and all that stuff."

"Oh, Marcus, you silly boy," Frigg laughed gaily as she stroked his face affectionately. He really was a desperately handsome devil. "Why don't we say that you had a little fishing accident and were washed up on my shore? After all, that's not so very far from the truth is it?"

Marcus nodded. That would definitely do.

"Oh, and while we're on the subject of Valkyries, would you mind awfully promising me one thing?" Frigg asked. "Would you please address me as either the Contessa or Fran? I really don't like people knowing about my…," she hesitated, "my Valkyrie connections."

"I'll do my best," Marcus replied politely.

"Oh no, Marcus, I'm sure you'll do better than that." A slight iciness had crept into Frigg's voice. "I know you wouldn't want to disappoint me, would you?"

Marcus didn't reply. The question was rhetorical and the tone of her voice left him with a sudden and unexpectedly bitter chill.

Frigg, the Contessa Francesca Dragza, definitely wasn't a woman to be messed with.

63

The Mouths of Fools

"**S**o why did you do it? Why did you kill Balder? Why?"

Kat launched her verbal assault on Loki as soon as the main course of dishes had been cleared from the table. In contrast to Kat's friendly chat with Hel, her conversation with Loki couldn't have been frostier. They sat together—Hel, Loki, Kat, and Hod—through a very congenial meal in Hel's reception room, gossiping politely about hunting and clothes and other meaningless tittle-tattle. Now it was time to talk turkey—to find out what was really going on.

Taking Kat by the arm, Loki strolled with her over to the window and pretended to show off the breathtaking view of the surface of Niflheim.

"I think you should be asking Hod that question," he began with a customary mischievous twinkle to his eyes. "After all, he fired the dart."

"Don't be so silly, Loki. How could Hod get hold of mistletoe up a tree and know that it would harm Balder? Do you think I'm stupid or something?"

"No, of course not. I never said you were stupid, my dearest Sangrid. And, might I say, you look absolutely ravishing tonight." Loki tried to kiss her hand, but Kat pushed him away. He was flirting and she wasn't going to be fobbed off by childish flattery. The stakes were too high.

"Are you going to answer my question or aren't you?" Kat was growing impatient. He was a handsome devil of a rogue and on some other occasion she might have enjoyed his advances, but now was neither the time nor the place. Besides, she didn't want to upset Hod, who could so easily overhear his silly overtures.

"Leverage, dear Sangrid, leverage," Loki eventually replied with a sigh. "By the way, what do you think of my daughter? Do you really think she's evil and vile, capable of doing all the terrible things you've heard?"

"I can't really say. I've only just met her. She's being very nice but it could all be a show, a pretence put on especially for me," Kat replied cautiously.

"Well, you'll just have to wait and see, I guess. I believe she's misunderstood and has been unfairly punished by Odin, deliberately blackened by exaggerated tales of her cruelty. It's time for her to return to Asgard as the great Valkyrie warrior she once was. That's what this is all about. We'll release Balder when Odin allows Hel to return."

In an unusual turn of events, Loki had chosen to be frank with Kat. "By the way," Loki continued as his eyes flashed a blaze of glorious green. "Did you know that Odin keeps her here for reasons other than just punishment?"

"Oh, yes. And pray, what might that be?" Kat scoffed, sensing a lie on its way.

"You know how your sword is made from dwarf gold, as are all the weapons and armour of the Valkyries. Where do you suppose all that metal comes from—the dwarves?" he enquired mockingly.

"You're not trying to tell me…?" Kat shook her head with disbelief. Her eyes were beginning to open wide.

"That's right. It all comes from right here." Loki pointed to the ground beneath them. "Odin keeps her here to ensure his supply of dwarf gold. That's why he won't stop me visiting her—because he can't, not if he wants his precious metal. It's his greed and not her evil that keeps her locked up here."

"You're lying!" Kat blurted out explosively. *Loki had to be, surely?*

"Well, next time you see him why don't you ask him where it all comes from?" Loki was beginning to enjoy getting on his soapbox. Alcohol and impressing pretty women had a habit of loosening his tongue. "Oh, and while you're grilling him, why don't you ask about his agreement with my daughter, too? The one where she inherits his beloved Asgard."

"Come on, Loki. You surely can't expect me to believe that. That's just plain nonsense," Kat shrugged. She'd almost believed the rubbish about the dwarf gold but this talk of some crazy agreement was far too outlandish, even for Loki's fanciful imagination.

"It's true," Hel chimed in eagerly. She'd overheard their rising voices. "When he's finished with the realm and it's all been blown apart by Ragnarok, guess who's going to be Asgard's new ruler?"

Kat couldn't answer. She was dumbstruck.

"That's right," Hel continued sarcastically, "Moi! I will have the pleasure of inheriting a burnt-out useless husk of a planet—my reward for all the hard work in digging up that priceless metal. Now tell me, Kat, do you really think that's fair?"

"But what about Odin? Where will he be?"

Hel shrugged and shook her head. "I don't really know and frankly I don't really care—that's his business. But that's why I want to get back, get there before it all happens. If anyone is going to save Asgard from Ragnarok then it's me, not Odin. He knows he's going to lose the final battle and all he cares about is saving his and his other precious gods' scrawny necks, that's all. It's a shame really, because I thought he loved the place."

"So did I, so did I," Kat murmured as the three of them slowly returned to the table. Dessert had arrived and she suddenly felt the urge to sit down.

What Loki and Hel had just said sounded preposterous—a lie to make her feel sympathetic to their cause. *But what if it were true?*

It would be easy enough to find out about the dwarf gold, but the truth behind Odin's other plans would be much trickier to uncover. Besides, if Odin really were going to lose Ragnarok and abandon Asgard, a far bigger problem reared its ugly head.

Where would he and the other gods go?

Kat didn't have to search too deeply to find the answer. The promise to unblock the forbidden realm on Hod's ring, the fabulous wealth of the Dragza Corporation, and the acres of orchards on Odin's Caribbean island: all the pieces fitted nicely together and pointed ominously in Midgard's direction.

As she played with these thoughts, Loki's and Hel's words suddenly had a particularly bitter taste to them.

Suitably dressed in a very fetching and immaculately cut white dinner jacket, Marcus linked Frigg's arm through his as he escorted her out onto the veranda. Frigg, of course, looked absolutely stunning and Marcus felt fit to burst with pride as they stepped outside. Taken aback, Marcus struggled hard not to look too awestruck by the splendour that greeted him, but it was difficult, very difficult.

A huge black marble table lay on what seemed like acres of terracotta patio in front of the biggest swimming pool he had ever set eyes upon. Ribbons of lights festooned the trees and citronella candles burned brightly to discourage any mosquitoes tempted by the bare flesh of all the exquisitely-dressed ladies. A string quartet played melodically in the background whilst numerous servants scurried efficiently back and forth from the table. They were busy delivering a continuous procession of magnificent food and drinks in a complicated but extremely well-oiled routine.

Frigg graciously introduced each guest in turn and Marcus politely shook hands with all of them. Introductions were strictly first names only and Marcus hadn't expected to recognise anyone at the table. Fulla, the woman who so very nearly taken his life, was there of course and she shook his hand warmly as though the event had never happened. Marcus also recognised a senator whose grip was firm and reassured. Marcus had seen him many times on television, but he seemed so much less grand and pompous in real life than the rumbustious character he portrayed on chat shows and the evening news. Interestingly, he had a small, tattooed 'v' on the inside of his right wrist. Marcus might have dwelt on this peculiarity longer had it not been for the very last guest he was introduced to.

"Hello, Finch." It was agent Woods, and he seemed equally as surprised by their meeting as Marcus was.

Introductions over, a beer was hastily brought for Marcus as the other guests drifted back to their rounds of small talk amongst themselves. Marcus was 'a nobody' and as such they would afford him the zero conversation time his currency was worth. Marcus didn't mind. He had been sat next to Woods and quite clearly they needed to have a chat.

"I didn't know you knew the Contessa," Woods began with a hint of jealousy in his voice. How could a common detective like Finch know his stellar, celebrity connection?

"Actually, it's the first time we've met. She's sort of a friend of a friend, if you know what I mean." Marcus could sense Woods' hostility and he didn't want to get embroiled in an argument, not tonight. He wanted to enjoy the evening's opulence.

"When you say 'friend of a friend,' would I be right in assuming that these might also be my friends?" Woods asked pointedly, highlighting 'friend of a friend' with air quotation marks.

Marcus nodded without saying a word. They were speaking the same language. Valkyries.

"Hmmm," Woods paused before lowering his voice to almost a whisper. "Did you know all of our little friends managed to escape?"

Marcus nodded. *Frigg had helped them, too.*

"And they took their artifacts with them," Woods continued. "The Contessa wasn't at all pleased, I can tell you." Woods shook his head knowingly. He certainly wasn't going to tell Marcus that he'd managed to save some of their precious mead; that was his and the Contessa's little secret.

"Displeased? Are you sure?" Marcus replied quizzically, looking more than a little surprised. Perhaps he'd misheard Woods.

"Yes, she was furious. If you had anything to do with their escape," he stared hard at Marcus, "then you'd best not mention it to the Contessa. She has friends in high places, if you get my drift."

A smile began to grow on Marcus's face; a curious fact had dawned on him and he hoped his face wouldn't give it away. *Woods didn't know the Contessa's true identity!*

Woods didn't know the Contessa was one of them, a being from another world. *Wow!* This really was a turn up for the books.

"I don't see what's so funny," Woods exclaimed indignantly, misreading Marcus's smile. He and the Contessa went back a long way and he knew stories about disappearances that would soon wipe the sneer from Finch's face. You didn't mess with the Contessa, not if you wanted to live.

"Oh, it's nothing. Please excuse me—it's just a little joke someone told me earlier, that's all," Marcus apologised profusely while praying that a servant would come and interrupt them soon. He really couldn't tell Woods the truth; he'd given his word to the Contessa not to reveal her identity.

"I'm glad to see you two getting on so well." It wasn't a servant's voice but Frigg's that thankfully interrupted them. "But I'm afraid I'm going to have to split you two gentlemen up," she laughed gaily, lifting Marcus out of his seat by the arm. "If I don't, you won't mingle and that would be so unfair to all my other guests, don't you think?"

With a cheery flourish of her hand, Frigg marched Marcus along the table and sat him down next to her. He was opposite the senator once more and sitting beside his extremely attractive daughter, if that was who she really was.

Marcus continued to smile gratefully for his rescue, before prattling off some small talk and then tucking into his hors d'oeuvres. He guessed the reason the Contessa had come to separate him from Woods was the same as the reason behind his own smile. She obviously didn't trust him to keep her secret.

Talking of secrets, Marcus decided to reflect on another loaded question. *If Woods didn't know the truth about the Contessa, how much of an expert on the Valkyries was he, anyway?*

Frigg smiled and nodded politely to the senator as they resumed the conversation they'd been having a few moments before. Chatting away amiably together, Marcus's thoughts were coming over to her loud and clear.

Whilst Marcus deliberated on how much Woods knew about the Valkyries, Frigg was delving deep into his mind and deliberating on precisely the same subject.

Exactly how much Marcus knew about their mutual 'friends' would seal his doom.

64

Issues

While Odin suffered his torment and searched for the darkest and most elusive secrets of the realm, life around the castle struggled to return to some sort of normality. Fields needed tilling, crops needed harvesting, and animals needed to be tended. The Valkyries, too, had duties to attend to. Despite their mighty victory, the borders of Asgard still needed to be patrolled and prisoners needed disciplining and punishing.

It was against this backdrop that Carmel, the latest Valkyrie warrior, set to work.

Whereas Kat had inherited Hlokk's arena with its meagre number of aging and docile prisoners, Carmel had inherited Brynhildr's. This had an altogether motlier band of Midgard scum and lowlifes. Carmel was keen to stamp her authority upon them with a vengeance. Her name Astrid described her as a powerful queen, and that was what she intended to be.

For wrongdoers, however, she intended to add a third dimension: ruthlessness.

Over the course of several days Carmel executed four of her prisoners and flogged the rest. Two she beheaded herself and two more she gave to the Aesir to stone to death. This was a popular punishment in the realm and one that always attracted large crowds, particularly women. Carmel loved the limelight and she was determined that her arena would become the most popular. Discipline, fear, and entertainment were her watchwords, and news of her unique brand of justice quickly spread. Even in times of mourning, the Aesir weren't above a bit of titillation.

It was on one of these days that Thor turned up unexpected at her arena, catching Carmel unawares. Like the rest of the gods and warriors, Thor had been subdued for many days, confining his activities to labouring in his forge by day and drinking heavily in the taverns by night. He looked tired and drawn, but Carmel didn't mind. They had hardly spoken since that fateful evening's feasting and she hugged him enthusiastically. She had certainly missed his company and the wryness of his wit.

"Would you like to go hunting this afternoon?" Carmel enquired hopefully, plucking up the courage to ask a question she prayed he would say yes to. It would certainly brighten up what had been a succession of same-old days.

Thor rubbed his beard and deliberated for quite some time before answering. "Well, you know I'm not too partial to riding, but if you can stand travelling in my chariot, then it's a deal."

Laughing loudly, he held out his massive hand for her to shake. Carmel did so in a heartbeat. She couldn't care less about the goats that pulled the chariot. Thor would be her companion for the day and that was all that mattered.

Dancing merrily back to the castle, Carmel picked up her cloak and bow, and then raced off toward the stable block. Thor was already there and waiting with his gilded chariot and trusty goats Tanngnost (tooth gnasher) and Tanngrisni (tooth grinder).

The waiting trio were impatient to be off and as soon as Carmel climbed on board, the goats sprang into action; clip-clopping merrily down the cobbled road, over the bridge, and then into the woods beyond. The ride was surprisingly smooth and rapid, and soon Carmel and Thor were deep inside a heavily wooded valley several kilometres from the castle. It was an ideal spot for hunting boar—and for being alone together.

"Have you missed me?" Carmel enquired cheekily as she took Thor's hand in hers and squeezed it tightly. They set off from the chariot with Carmel skipping lightly by Thor's side, kicking up clouds of crisp, golden leaves that carpeted the forest floor beneath them. Despite a sky sagging with the burden of rain, none had actually fallen in Asgard since the storm.

Thor gave her a peculiar stare and then smiled. "Of course I have, my lady. It's been such a depressing time, that's for sure."

Carmel slid her arm around his waist and he did likewise. They carried on walking together like this in silence for several minutes more. Neither wanted to speak, and neither wanted to break their warm embrace. It was Carmel who eventually broke their silence.

"Why doesn't Sif spend more time in Asgard?" she asked quizzically.

"She prefers the company she keeps in Valhalla," Thor replied with a resigned chuckle. "The heroes, the other goddesses, and the pointless chitchat—pah!" Thor finished with a resounding spit. Clearly, Valhalla wasn't to his liking.

"And you—which is your favourite place?" Carmel decided to press him further, tickling his ribs as she spoke.

"You already know that answer, my lady," Thor replied, returning her playful gesture. It felt good to be close again, but perhaps just a little too good for his comfort. Feelings he shouldn't have were beginning to stir uncomfortably inside him.

"Are we just going to talk, or are we going to get down to some serious hunting?" he enquired, wrestling his mind away from carnal fantasies about her lithe and shapely body.

"I don't know…which would you prefer?" Carmel teased, letting go of his waist and prancing away to stand with her back pressed against the trunk of a tall beech tree. She was flirting outrageously, like some adolescent schoolgirl, but she didn't care. Thor's bear-like strength and enchanted power was an irresistible allure, and she yearned to ensnare his spirit, harnessing his will to do as she desired.

Thor paused before walking slowly over. Placing one hand against the tree trunk above her shoulder, he leant forward, studying her face intently.

She was so beautiful, so fragrant, and so sensuous—a perfectly-formed flower he could barely resist plucking. *Why in Odin's name was she taunting him like this? Couldn't she see the flames that she was fanning?*

Pouncing like a cat, Carmel grabbed Thor's head and pulled his face roughly toward hers. She could feel the warmth of his breath as she held his face close to her cheek. An unbearable desire held her in a vise-like grip and open-mouthed she let her eyes roam longingly around his face; her soft and inviting lips teasing fragrantly a whisker from his weathered skin.

"I love Loki," she gasped passionately, breasts heaving against Thor's mighty chest. She was fighting to control her bloodlust.

"And I'm married to Sif," Thor replied in a whisper as he wrapped a mighty arm around her waist and pulled her exquisite body close to him. He couldn't stop this fever.

"We absolutely mustn't—" Carmel moaned, biting Thor's lower lip such that a bead of blood glistened upon it. Emboldened by desire, she allowed her lips to caress his cheeks while her tongue darted furtively, longingly, thrilling to the taste of his manly sweat.

"I know, we mustn't—" Thor muttered, taking her ample bottom firmly in his grasp. Her body was perfection, a temple he begged to worship in.

"Would another whipping, help—help, stop—?" Carmel panted, sinking her teeth passionately into an earlobe. Sliding her hand down his stomach, she forced her way deep inside his trousers, purring appreciatively as she released his manhood. It was already proudly swollen, throbbing with the intensity of his desire.

Thor groaned loudly before raising a flag of surrender. He had succumbed to passion's desire. His coarse hand was between her silken legs and the heady musk of her sweetness had crossed his point of no return. Pressing Carmel back against the tree, he hoisted her legs from the ground.

Carmel responded. Flinging her thighs around his waist, she held him tightly in her grasp. Guiding him with her fingers, she took his thickness prisoner in a single powerful thrust of her hips, screaming in ecstasy as their bodies united as one.

Thor and Carmel made love in an urgent frenzy, their coupling seething with the intensity of their desire. The strength of its denial making this final, lustful surrender so very much the sweeter.

Having made love so passionately, neither Carmel nor Thor wanted to return immediately to the castle. Walking deeper into the forest, they came across an abandoned cottage and agreed to take shelter there for the night. Such overnight stays weren't uncommon amongst the gods and Valkyries and certainly wouldn't arouse suspicion. Neither of them wanted others to know about their tryst. It was a private affair and one they believed was already over.

Their lust had been by fuelled by the intimacy of their ordeal, nothing more. Now that it was sated, they were certain it would fade as rapidly as it had begun.

Thor quickly organised a fire and a tempting pile of bracken and leaves on which they could lie. To Carmel's great surprise, he slaughtered one of his two goats, skinned it, and then roasted it upon a makeshift spit above the crackling logs. They were both famished and the meat was so sweet and tender that between them they consumed the whole beast.

As they picked the last of the meat off the bones, Thor made sure that Carmel threw each one back onto the skin of his slain goat. This seemed important, but he wouldn't explain why. To her later chagrin, Carmel enjoyed the meal so much that she sucked the marrow out of one of the thigh bones before she threw this too upon the pelt. She felt sure it wouldn't matter.

Licking their hands clean and downing some mead, they settled into each other's arms and gently dozed as the dying embers of the fire faded and crackled their last farewell to the sky above.

Despite their declarations of love for others, Carmel and Thor enjoyed several heated trysts that night. Each occasion was more tender than the one before and, like a horn filled with mead before being left to stand, the sweetest draught was always the last.

Silent and deadly, the chains of love stalked each fervent embrace, winding themselves invisibly around their unsuspecting hearts.

The pair rose early the following morning, a sunless sky greeting them as a solitary distant cockerel heralded the start of yet another cheerless day.

To Carmel's great surprise, she was greeted by the bleating of not one but two goats outside the cottage. Thor's enchanted creatures had revealed their greatest magic, though her careless treatment of a thigh bone hadn't passed unnoticed: one of the goats was slightly lame and Thor wasn't impressed. Normally he would have bellowed loudly and thrown a terrible rage, but because he was smitten by the fairest Valkyrie in all of Asgard, he merely chuckled wryly into his beard.

Skipping breakfast, they headed swiftly back to town. To their surprise, the sound of horns could be heard and an orange flag had replaced the black flag of mourning above the hall of Gladsheim. Something important was about to take place and Thor urged the goats to quicken their pace. They did so, breaking obligingly into a swifter trot.

Crowds of people were beginning to gather in front of the hall, and as Carmel and Thor drew near, familiar names materialised from fragments of gossip snatched from those assembled.

Loki, Kat, and Hod had returned from Hel.

65

An Olive Branch

The frozen orb that hung suspended in the sky above Niflheim fascinated Kat as she struggled to make sense of a world without time. Like Cole before her, she began by counting her periods of being awake as days, but she soon became muddled with these. Besides, if she were destined to spend the rest of eternity here in Hel, then there was precious little point in keeping track anyway. She might as well kick back and enjoy herself—Hel made for an entertaining and unusual hostess.

The friendship which had sprung up so quickly between them continued to grow and blossom. Hel was rapturous about it, telling everyone how much 'in love' she was with her wonderful new friend. Kat, however, was a little more reserved. Hel's reputation was fearsome and yet Kat found her childlike charm and rampant enthusiasm wonderfully infectious. Little by little, Kat found herself succumbing to the sweetness of Hel's seduction.

Of Hel's three new guests, Kat, Hod, and Gold Mane, the latter proved to be the most difficult to accommodate in her realm.

Try as they might, they couldn't squeeze the mighty stallion into any one of the rooms in her royal chambers. In the end, he was forced to wander forlornly up and down the corridor outside the reception hall, munching away at oats, apples, and hay which Hel had quickly appropriated from one of her indebted deities.

Not for Gold Mane was a diet made from the disgusting, reconstituted goop from her kitchens. He was a horse fit for a queen and was treated as such, with Kat and Hel taking turns riding him, often hopping on his back and sitting astride him together. Whooping with joy, they would canter around the edges of the Nastrond or gallop across the massive hall of her Berserker army.

No one else was allowed to ride Gold Mane, and Hel never let him stray far from her sight. The risk of so magnificent a beast 'accidentally' finding his way into her cooks' stewing pots was one too great to take.

In spite of her outward display of enthusiasm, Hel was both cautious and economical in the way she introduced Kat to her realm. Her vicious brutality and sadistic whims were prudently hidden from view. Kat would come to know Hel at the pace which Hel dictated. She wasn't going to risk a premature end to their budding sistership.

At first, Hel and Kat dressed in the same black clothes which Hel was most accustomed to wearing. However, after Kat's introduction to the vast wardrobes in Hel's chambers, the pair quickly became addicted to rummaging through these and choosing different themes for their numerous tours around the palace. To hoots of laughter, they dressed up in garish, 1960s-style mini-skirts and on another occasion in bell-bottomed trousers, afro wigs and platform boots reminiscent of the glam rock era. *Dynasty*-style suits and shoulder pads weren't overlooked either, with their constricting pencil skirts, sky-high stilettos and wide, glossy belts. The best time of all was when Kat found clothes from the Victorian era. The pair paraded proudly up and down in hats, parasols, and heavy pleated dresses which had the most enormous bustles Kat had ever seen.

For the brief duration of Kat's stay, it was as though a shaft of sunshine had arrived in Niflheim. There was a happy, almost carnival atmosphere which rippled through the countless tunnels and caverns, embracing all it touched with its festive mood. It was as though a lead weight had been lifted from Hel's shoulders and she could finally breathe again.

After a solemn and respectful tour of the frozen souls in Old Niflheim, Hel took Kat to her kennels and introduced her to her hounds. To Hel's great surprise and relief, the hounds greeted Kat enthusiastically. They seemed to sense she was a kindred spirit and they behaved like puppies in her presence, wagging their tails ecstatically until they practically fell off. Together, the two Sangrids would collar up a brace of dogs and walk arm in arm along the torchlit corridors, chatting and laughing merrily as their footsteps echoed cheerily around them in the gloom.

Next on Hel's agenda was the moment when Kat set eyes on Balder. It was both a joyous and a sad occasion to see him lying so peaceful yet unmoving on his sumptuous bed. Kat wept and laid a bouquet of poppies on his chest whilst Hel explained about the accident during the transfer of his soul. She hadn't intended to reveal this, but Kat took the news in her stride. As an undead soul herself, Kat understood the vagaries and risks of Loki's hasty actions. She agreed with Hel, too, that the only way to restore him to consciousness was by reuniting him with his body once more.

This acknowledgement was extremely convenient to Hel, because it would aid her in the next stage of her plan.

The Berserker army was introduced shortly afterwards and Kat felt sure its leader was Cole. She had never met him during his short stay in Asgard but the polite, heavily-disguised black man with his head swathed in a scarf certainly fitted his description. Quite why he chose to call himself Lucifer was anybody's guess.

With a heavy, sinking feeling inside, Kat quickly realised that Mimir's prophesy might soon be fulfilled. If Ragnarok was to be a war waged against the Berserker army, then the rotten apple from Midgard would certainly be bringing a fire with him to Asgard.

To the delight of the assembled troops, Hel and Kat often took up arms and sparred together. Kat found the strength of their black armour and weapons impressive but far too heavy for her liking. In their fights Hel was the superior warrior, but after each bout Kat felt she had grown in stature. Hel was an excellent teacher and only too willing to pass on tips honed by aeons of practice. The soldiers around them acknowledged the skill of 'Sangrid's sister,' and it was widely agreed that between them they gave the finest display of sparring they could ever remember.

As Kat relaxed and became ever more at ease with Hel and the workings of her realm, further, more exotic, introductions were made. Hel showed Kat her harem and introduced her to the playroom—although most of the toys were judiciously kept locked away. Kat was impressed with her selection of lovers and fully understood her womanly needs. After all, back in Asgard she herself had enjoyed the seductive lure of Freyr. Indeed, to her mortification, she gave in to temptation and joined Hel in her playroom on more than one occasion. Kat, too, was an explorer, and her bloodlust craved to examine the many facets of her sexuality. In spite of her deepening feelings for Hod, the temptation of a handsome hunk was far too great.

While Hod slept peacefully, Kat's fickle virtue slipped ever further from his hopeful grasp.

Kat's willingness to accept her realm led Hel to draw back even more veils of secrecy. Among the last of these were her VIP chambers, the area where customised tortures took place. Despite the horror of the countless cells echoing with screams of agony, once again Kat understood and accepted their place in the realm. The brutality inflicted wasn't Hel's doing—she was merely undertaking the wishes of disaffected kings, sorcerers, and outraged gods. It was a job like any other and not dissimilar to the one she witnessed over and over again in the prisons beneath their own Valkyrie arenas.

In a strange way, the weird and freakish tortures decreed by the prisoners' curses held a macabre fascination for Kat. Sadism held a distinct allure, and she fought to control the desire to join in the endless rounds of whippings, brandings, and other fiendish torments.

Although time had no meaning in Hel's realm, it seemed to pass all too swiftly. Shortly before Kat's departure, two surprising shocks materialised before her. These came in the shapes of Henry and Hod.

Henry's presence was supposed to be a secret, but with typical forgetfulness, he wandered into view yawning and wearing nothing but a towel and a boyish grin. Kat was as amazed as he was by their meeting. They hugged and embraced and then spent a long time discussing the wonderful toys that festooned Hel's chambers.

Unfortunately, Henry's mind was something of a blank as regards the circumstances of his death. He remembered going out on a date with some 'amazing blond,' but couldn't remember her name. He attributed his untimely death to passing out and inhaling his own vomit. He didn't seem too disturbed about his premature demise, either—he was in heaven and delighted that Kat had found her way back there, too.

To Hel's great relief, Kat didn't shatter his delusion. After all, Henry was happy and was clearly being well cared for. For him, the absence of green fields, fresh air, and exercise were more than offset by a limitless supply of video games, junk food, and the companionship of a beautiful angel. He was in 'La-La Land,' and it wasn't Kat's place to tell him otherwise.

Kat's second surprise was even more astonishing and came after a prolonged and unexpected break from Hod. Although the two of them had adjacent rooms, there had been little time to nurture their growing friendship or share a deeper intimacy. Hel was besotted with her new best friend and demanded all of Kat's attention.

Knowing Hel of old, Hod decided to step back, confident that history would run its usual course. Hel was bound to trip herself up sooner or later, either by growing bored of Kat's company or by revealing her inner ugliness. To his surprise, this didn't happen.

Hel had other ideas and she begged Hod to help her organise a special gift, one that would have far-reaching consequences for the three of them. Far from being horrified by her proposal, Hod was elated.

If she could pull it off, he'd be the happiest man alive—or dead, as the case may be.

"Hello, my lady Sangrid. You look fabulous," Hod commented casually when he finally bumped into Kat again. He held out his hands to greet her.

"By Odin's grace—you can SEE!" Kat shrieked with joy as she leapt into his arms and smothered his face with kisses. *This was amazing!*

"Thank you, thank you so much, Hel," Kat gushed, turning to her as tears of gratitude streamed down her face. "I don't know how you managed to do this, but I will be forever in your debt."

"Oh, it was nothing, just my way of thanking you both for your company," Hel blushed.

Genuine praise for her surgical skills was unheard of and, to be truthful, she could have done a much better job. Hod's new eyes didn't exactly match (one was green and the other hazel brown), and she was sure one of his eyelids was drooping. Still, at least he could see again and that had been her goal. Kat was in her debt and the time was right to hold this forfeit.

Her unwitting sister was ready to do her bidding.

"My dearest Kat, it's time for my father to take you and Hod back to Asgard," Hel began as a lump grew steadily inside her throat. This was her plan, with Kat being the last piece of a jigsaw puzzle that had kept her going through centuries of incarceration—*so why did using her hurt so much?*

"I'm going to miss you," she continued shakily with a gulp. She'd fallen big time for her Valkyrie twin.

Kat pulled her close and hugged her tightly. "I swear I'll do everything in my power to persuade Odin to release you. I swear that with my life."

"Thank you, thank you, my darling sister," Hel whispered as she wiped a tear from her eye. "That's what I want, my release along with Balder's. And as gesture of good will and proof that I'm a reformed character, I'm letting Hod go free with his sight restored. Now please, my dearest Kat, I must also entrust you with a special gift for Odin: final, compelling proof of my honourable intentions. It's for his eyes only and must only be opened in his citadel, nowhere else. Will you promise me this, please, my dearest friend?"

Kat nodded and hugged her once more. It was the least she could do.

"I will go and get it if you like," Hel offered, and then added, "but I will say my goodbyes now, just in case I'm too upset to return. I'm hopeless with farewells."

Hugging each of them in turn, Hel left swiftly. True to her word— she didn't return.

After what seemed an age and most probably was, Ganglot eventually shuffled her bloated carcass back into the reception room and handed an elongated box to Kat. It was wrapped in an identical manner to the present Hel had given Cole, complete with a bright and flamboyant scarlet bow.

To Kat's surprise, the gift felt heavier than she would have imagined for a box of its size. She wondered briefly what could weigh so much, but it never crossed her mind to take a peek inside. She had given Hel her word and she intended to keep it. Odin would receive her present exactly as Hel had requested: unopened and strictly for his eyes only.

With growing nervousness, she took her position alongside Loki. To further sweeten their return, he would be taking another heavily-laden chest of dwarf gold with them. It was yet another gift for the arrogant and ungrateful god who continued to hold his darling daughter captive.

After indicating that they were ready, Loki waved his hand slowly over his ring.

Loki, Hod, Kat, the chest of dwarf gold, and Hel's present left the realm of Niflheim. Very soon, Hel's master plan would be complete.

If she could have laughed with joy, Hel most certainly would have done so.

66

A Rage in Gladsheim

*I*t was on the ninth hour of the ninth day of Odin's ordeal that the answer he had been searching for was finally unveiled. A volva (learned sorceress) from a far-flung corner of the realm spoke the words he had yearned to hear: his son could be saved.

Despite his terrible suffering, the tears he wept when Freyja cut him down from Yggdrasill were tears of joy. He was exhausted, unshaven, and stank of stale sweat and excreta, and yet Freyja still held him tightly as she caressed his aching head. His punishment was over and they rejoiced at his redemption.

Pausing only for the briefest of cleanups and refreshments, Odin mounted Sleipnir and rode triumphantly from the castle to the hall of Gladsheim. Horns blew, drums were beaten, and people quite literally wept for joy. Their lord was back and life could at last return to Asgard. Even the heavens seemed to hear their happiness. A single shaft of sunlight pierced the clouds and a songbird could be heard singing high above the hubbub of the crowds. Hope sprung anew and a warmth spread across the realm from the shores of the Great Sea to Heimdall's distant watchtower.

The jubilation that welcomed Odin was in stark contrast to the wall of silence that greeted Kat, Loki, and Hod when they had arrived in Asgard only hours before. Until Odin deemed otherwise, the trio were branded as villains, conspirators in Balder's foul abduction.

Dressed in Hel's tight black outfit and carrying her sword and shield, Kat looked every inch the treacherous messenger they believed her to be. Hostility was muted, but it hung in the air like the scent of rotting corpses. Everyone feared the warrior Sangrid, and their love affair with the maid formerly known as Kat was over, her beautiful, kindly soul now lying buried beneath that cursed and evil name.

Kat felt nervous and her legs wobbled like jelly, but she refused to show her fear to the disgruntled mob. With head held high and an unswerving gaze, she entered the mighty hall with Loki and Hod at her side and made her way toward the empty thrones. Standing silently and nervously, the trio waited impatiently for Odin to arrive.

Within a matter of minutes, the Valkyries swept down to the hall to greet the returning travellers. There role was simple: to keep the three of them there until Odin had determined their fates. Secretly, the warriors were delighted that Kat had returned, but before the gathered townsfolk they had to appear stern and forbidding. The most support they could dare to offer their sister was the briefest of waves or a shy, silently-mouthed 'Hello.'

Silk was absent from the gathered Valkyries. She remained stubbornly locked in mourning and confined to her room.

While everyone awaited Odin's arrival, speculation mounted as to what might become of Kat. Expulsion seemed the most likely outcome, and seeing Kat's bold attire and Hel's tattooed poppy proudly emblazoned upon her shoulder, they feared the worst. Mimir had foretold a treacherous fate and this now seemed inevitable.

Hod was treated much more kindly by the crowd and Kat was grateful that he remained by her side throughout their ordeal. She squeezed his hand appreciatively as they exchanged frequent and reassuring glances.

By now no one blamed Hod for Balder's death. The poisonous dart made from mistletoe was to blame and this had been fashioned by Loki's hand. The crowd rejoiced in his restored eyesight and prayed that Odin would quickly forgive his estranged son.

The people of Asgard feared Kat, forgave Hod—and hated Loki. He had stolen Balder from them and his presence was repugnant. Everybody booed and jeered him, with some throwing rotten fruit and eggs. Without the Valkyries present, he might well have been lynched.

The atmosphere was tense, laden with emotion, and promising violence if Odin didn't arrive and settle matters soon.

"HAIL, WAR!"

"HAIL, VALOUR!"

"HAIL, ODIN!"

The hall erupted in a stampede of foot-stamping, raucous cheering, and sword-beating when Odin and Freyja finally arrived and took their places in front of their thrones. The crowd wouldn't be silenced and it was a long time before a hush could fall and Odin was allowed to speak.

"Greetings to you all," he began, waving his arms in the direction of the Valkyries and townsfolk, deliberately avoiding the gaze of the three miscreants before him.

"I have great news. I have learnt many things as I hung from Yggdrasill and I am enriched now with the greatest wisdom of our realm. I have learnt all there is to know and all that can be known about our fair land, and I bring you great joy. Balder can be saved. Balder will be returned to us."

The crowd erupted once more and Odin waved his hand in delight as he took the cheers and adoration of the Aesir. Flowers were thrown and soon they formed a fragrant carpet at his feet. This was the moment he had been looking forward to, the moment when he stumbled from torment's darkness into salvation's glorious light.

Eventually, when the crowd finally settled down once more, he turned his attention to the three conspirators.

Hod was the first—and easiest—to deal with. His son was greeted warmly and immediately forgiven. After giving thanks for the miracle of sight, Thor embraced his brother before dragging him away to stand beside him and the warriors next to Odin's throne.

Pausing for a moment's contemplation while he studied her appearance, Odin turned his attention to Kat. "Greetings, my lady Sangrid," he began softly and politely, without smiling and without a cheery twinkle in his eye. He had seen the mark of Hel upon her shoulder and his heart was gripped with an icy chill. He had loved Kat more than most, and felt betrayed.

"Greetings, my noble lord."

Kat bowed low as she kissed his hand. She wanted to show her respect but, like Odin, she too felt wary and distrustful. Too many questions lay unanswered and until she heard the truth there could be no love in her heart.

It was a stalemate. Old friends now separated by a chasm of suspicion.

"I bring you a gift from the great Queen of Niflheim," Kat continued as she pulled the glossy present from a sack. "It is her tribute to the mighty Odin and is for his eye alone to see!" she exclaimed loudly, holding it above her head for all to see.

Odin raised his eyebrows and studied the box intently. He had heard rumours of Hel's presents and felt uneasy. The heavy chest at his feet, laden with dwarf gold, was more than welcome but this…this gift baffled him. *Why would Hel offer him a tribute?*

"Will you unwrap it for me now?" he enquired hopefully.

"I cannot, my lord. Hel has given me strict instructions. Whatever lies inside this box must be opened by you and by you only. She has asked that this be done in the privacy of your citadel."

Odin stroked his stubbled chin, and after some consideration he gave in to Hel's demand. He was curious. *What gift could Hel give him that required such secrecy?* It was a mystery and one he was intrigued to unravel.

Choosing to leave Kat's fate undecided for the moment, Odin turned his attention to Loki. Their friendship was over, destroyed by his kidnapping of Cole, Idun, and now his son. No platitudes, gifts, or pledges of allegiance could spare the wicked trickster. His deeds were beyond forgiveness.

Frowning and with a face that threatened a thunderous earthquake, Odin prepared to pass judgement.

CRASH!

With the sudden violence of a volcanic eruption, the doors to Gladsheim burst open. Standing silhouetted in the harsh and watery rays of sunlight was the figure of a woman. It was a warrior, a heavily-armed Valkyrie who charged quickly down the aisle and smashed Loki to the floor with a single blow of her outstretched shield.

Placing her foot upon his chest, her sword glinted menacingly as she pressed its tip deep into his throat.

"Any last requests, you filthy, scheming cockroach?" Silk hissed in a voice that seethed with fury. She was here to avenge her true love and nothing was going to stop her.

Loki gulped hard and looked anxiously around him. Holding his arms out wide, he began to beg for mercy, desperately playing for time in the hope that Odin or one of the Valkyries might come to his rescue. Silk wouldn't spare him and the vengeance in her eyes confirmed that fact.

She wanted blood—his blood.

"I can't let you kill him." Carmel had drawn her sword and held it pointed at Silk's throat. It wasn't Silk's place to take his life; that was Odin's prerogative.

"Nor I," Kat added as she drew Talwaar, placing this, too, at Silk's throat. Until Odin revealed the truth, Loki remained innocent.

Silk looked slowly from one girl to the other, smiling scornfully as she did so. "Do you think you can stop me, Kitty Kat? Or you, my dearest little Carmelita, do you really think you can stop me, too?" she sneered. She was ready to die if it meant Loki would join her at the gates of Niflheim.

"Put your sword down, Gunnr." Freyja's calm voice echoed chillingly around the silent hall. She had slipped stealthily behind Silk's back and her sword now lay flat on her shoulder, the blade's razor sharpness pressed firmly against the tender flesh of Silk's neck.

"You touch one hair of his head and, though I love you as my sister, I swear I will take your head and deny your place in Valhalla." Freyja's words sent a palpable shudder around the room.

No one could remember such a confrontation: Valkyrie against Valkyrie and their queen ready to decapitate one of her own. It was unprecedented, and the hall fell silent as a tomb. Nobody breathed nor moved a muscle as Silk's eyes darted from Kat to Carmel to Loki and back again. She pressed her sword still deeper into Loki's throat and felt a trickle of blood as Freyja's blade responded, digging deeper into her neck.

"If Loki dies, we all die," Freyja whispered quietly. "That is the truth behind Mimir's prophesies. His destiny is to live and his fate cannot be undone."

Unmoving, Silk continued to hold her sword at Loki's throat. Her soul cried for justice, but Freyja's words screamed louder still. *She couldn't bring about their doom.*

"Brokk should have taken your head years ago," she muttered furiously, dropping her sword such that the harsh, metallic clatter of its fall reverberated eerily around Gladsheim. Stepping forward, she hawked before spitting vehemently in Loki's face. Without saying a word, she turned on her heel and left as swiftly as she'd arrived.

Freyja sighed deeply as she lowered her sword to the ground. It had been a close call. Extending his arm, Thor helped an extremely shaken Loki to his feet. "You'd better stay in my room tonight," he offered gruffly before looking expectantly at Odin.

Odin nodded. Loki was off the hook.

Freyja was right. He couldn't kill Loki; Loki's life was guaranteed—Ragnarok forbade any harm should come to him, much as he would have wished otherwise. Besides, if he did allow Loki to walk free, he might yet be able to turn Balder's kidnapping to his advantage, playing a father against his daughter.

Turning to Kat, Odin took her hand in his. "Come, I think it's time you and I had a little chat," he informed her bleakly, waving his hand across his ring.

Hel lay on the bed next to Balder, just as she'd requested.

She looked at peace, a warrior resting serenely with arms folded across her chest and fingers wrapped tightly around the hilt of her long, black sword. This lay atop the length of her body.

Hel's eyes were closed with lids unfluttering, and her porcelain skin felt as cold as ice. Her beautiful, pouting lips were stained the deepest shade of purple-blue, and no fragrant breath would ever leave her chest while her heart lay as still and silent as her childhood sweetheart's.

Hel was dead.

This was as she had wished.

This was as she had commanded.

Hel had taken her own life in a final, desperate, gamble—the chance to break free from her frigid, lonely tomb.

67
Truth or Dare

Kat exploded like a firework the moment they arrived in the citadel. She didn't even give Odin a chance to sit on his throne. Sword in hand and gift tightly clasped behind her back, she began her assault.

"Why did you abandon us in Midgard?" she snarled angrily.

"What? Don't be so silly, Sangrid, I did no such thing," Odin tried to stay calm. The venom in her attack had caught him unawares. "I sent Vili and Ve. You saw them in the chamber and Herja can confirm that my brothers rescued both her and Brynhildr."

"Frigg said you refused to send anybody," Kat retorted crossly.

"She's lying. She was the one who refused to help, not I. She hates us all, you included. She hates all my Valkyries because of my love for your queen. She'll do anything to hurt me, and now it appears so will you. Is that why you're showing off Hel's mark, hey, Sangrid? Are you one of Hel's Angels?"

"No," Kat answered crossly, not really understanding quite what he was referring to. "It's just a pretty tattoo, that's all."

"Oh, and you expect me to believe that, do you? Honestly, Sangrid, I would have thought better of you." Odin sat down upon his throne. It could just be the truth. He didn't consider Kat to be a liar but she'd been with Hel a long time and anything was possible. *Could he take the risk?*

"Why did you have me killed, Odin, why? Why did you send Vali to track me down and then have Jess stall me so that I would get caught up in a fight and shot?" This question cut Kat to the bone.

"Because, my dear Sangrid, you were destined to die a hero. Yesterday, today, tomorrow—it was always going to happen sooner or later. It was better to speed up your death and make sure that Brynhildr was there to save you, rather than otherwise. You should be thanking me, not hating me. I have given you another life and more— you can now live forever." Odin felt indignant at her ingratitude.

"What if I didn't want to die? Why, why…why couldn't you give me the choice?" Kat stammered. Odin's answers were too smug and well thought out for her liking.

"Oh, come on, Sangrid. Get real!" Odin chuckled. "Does the guy who steps out under a bus get a choice? Trust me: your death was imminent and if Brynhildr hadn't been there, you would be feeding the worms right now."

"Okay, okay," Kat flustered. She couldn't fault his logic and that was annoying. She decided to try another line of attack. "Why can't we go to Valhalla and see the heroes?"

"Because you won't come back," Odin replied condescendingly. "When I first started my army, the Valkyries used to join them but they loved it so much there they wouldn't come back. Trust me, Sangrid, when—or should I now say, if—you go there, you'll understand."

Odin finished his answer with a thinly-disguised threat. He needed Kat to understand that she wasn't arguing from a position of strength. To anger him was unwise.

"Why are you still recruiting heroes, then? Taking modern soldiers from modern wars? What good are they with a sword in their hands?" Kat felt confident that the question would make him pause.

It didn't.

"Because like you and my other dear Valkyries, the heroes from Midgard are strong, brave, and—most importantly—clever. I can't help it if your technology has moved on. Besides, just because you carry a gun doesn't mean you can't learn how to fight with a sword," Odin scoffed. He was winning their war of words hands down.

"Talking of technology, what is your Dragza Corporation doing back in Midgard and why are you growing millions of apples on your island? Enough to feed all the gods, I shouldn't wonder." Kat's eyes gleamed as she posed this question. *Gotcha!*

"Firstly, the Dragza Corporation is trying to haul your civilisation into becoming one like mine. How do you think you got to the moon and have personal computers now? You've got my brothers and I to thank for that."

Odin paused, allowing his mood to soften just a little for his explanation to the second part of her question.

"The apple trees are, sadly, a series of mistakes. I've tried over and over again to grow a second source for Idun's apples, but they just aren't the same. The orchards you see are the proof of this failure. Do you honestly believe that if they were a success I wouldn't have snapped my fingers and got a load brought back to Asgard when Loki kidnapped Idun? Do you really think I'm that stupid?"

"No," Kat replied tersely. "But you could be lying."

"Be careful what you say, Sangrid," Odin's face darkened as he stubbed a finger angrily at her. "I've taken a lot from you, and remember—I'm still your lord and master. Don't make me angry."

Kat gulped hard. She had been pretty rude so far.

"I'm sorry, my lord," she apologised contritely. "But what about your mead? Why do you make it so addictive? You should have seen what it did to Brynhildr—it nearly killed her."

"That's an unfortunate side effect of its powers. I haven't been able to change this. I've tried. Believe me, I've tried." Odin hung his head and shook it slowly at this point. He seemed genuinely upset—*or was he just being an extremely good actor?*

Kat began to mellow. *Damn him!* She needed to stay angry.

"What about the third part of the prophecy?" Kat's words leapt from her mouth before she realised she'd even asked the question.

"There's no third part," Odin replied bluntly.

"Frigg said there is, but she didn't say what it was," Kat conceded.

"There—" Odin paused and then looked up, staring long and hard at Kat as he toyed with the disk in his pocket. Suddenly, the enigma of Kat's role in Asgard's fate had fallen into place. Perhaps she was like Loki: a messenger, a go-between, a conduit by which he could manipulate Hel, needling her to deliver what he wanted. Through Kat he might be able control Hel, and through Hel he would get the solution to his problems: the war to end all wars—Ragnarok.

Odin stood up and paced slowly up and down. A silence fell upon the room and it lasted for several minutes as he deliberated on what to say next.

Truth or dare?

"There is a third part to the prophecy, and when I tell you what it is you will understand why I have kept it secret. Perhaps then you will trust me, my dear Sangrid?" he enquired hopefully.

Kat nodded and waited impatiently for his reply.

"The third part of Mimir's prophecy speaks of my death at Ragnarok. It states that Fenrir will kill me. That is why I had him bound and that is why I have been so passionate in recruiting my army of heroes. I want to live as much as anybody else." Odin paused before looking Kat in the eyes once more. "Now, dear Sangrid, have I earned your trust? Have I earned the right to open Hel's gift?"

Kat said nothing as she handed him the heavy box. Everything sounded so believable, so plausible, especially this last bit. It all fitted together so perfectly and yet...and yet...?

Perhaps that was the problem: it all fitted just a little too perfectly. Particularly the sob story at the end to get her sympathy. Suddenly her head hurt. *Was Odin really telling the truth?*

She desperately wanted to believe him, to trust the kind, compassionate god who she had once so adored.

"Sangrid, is this some kind of a joke?" Odin exclaimed loudly, interrupting her thoughts. He had unwrapped the box and was now holding the present in his hands for Kat to see.

The gift was a black Valkyrie knife, identical to the one that Kat had seen in Frigg's handbag. Odin grasped the knife by the handle and stared thoughtfully at its shiny black metallic blade.

"Perhaps it's meant for you—" Odin began, when a brilliant flash of red light exploded from the knife's handle, filling the room with its brilliance.

Temporarily blinded, Kat heard Hel's cackle rather than saw her as she materialised naked in the room. By the time Kat had rubbed her eyes and could see once more, Hel was already behind Odin and pushing him to his knees. The knife was in her hands and she had it pressed against his throat.

"Pleased to see me, you filthy, rotten maggot?" she hissed in his ear.

Odin looked up at Kat, but he didn't need to ask the obvious question. Kat's face said it all.

"I didn't know anything about this, I swear!" Kat exclaimed in amazement. "Hel! What in Asgard's name are you doing here?"

"I want my ring and my cloak—or else," Hel threatened, ignoring Kat as she pressed her blade deeper into Odin's flesh.

"Or else what, Hel?" Odin enquired in a remarkably calmly manner for a god with an assassin's knife at his throat. "You'll kill me, will you? Is that what you'll do?" he sneered arrogantly.

"No, Hel, please. You mustn't," Kat blurted. "He's supposed to die at Ragnarok, the third part of the prophecy. Fenrir's going to kill him, not you."

"Why, Kat, what a good idea. I'd never have thought of that one. That would be 'poetic justice,' wouldn't you say, Odin?" Yanking his head back abruptly, Hel pulled her knife away. "Still lying, I see," she added sarcastically.

"What do you mean?" Kat asked, still shocked by Hel's dramatic appearance, and the fact that she'd been used.

"Well, I thought Frigg said the third part of the prophecy went something like this: 'When Asgard is consumed by fire the gods will inherit paradise,'" Hel chanted, mimicking Frigg's voice to perfection.

"Is that true?"

Odin averted his eyes. He'd lied. The expression of guilt was written all over his sheepish face.

"I want my ring and my cloak," Hel demanded furiously once more.

"You're not getting them. I know you won't kill me, and you certainly won't be killing your new best friend. The only way you're getting out of my citadel is when I send you back to Niflheim," Odin growled defiantly. He was still the most powerful god in the room and holding all the cards.

"Oh, yes, that's right," Hel began to smirk as she strutted confidently away, holding her finger to her bottom lip as she spoke. She was toying with Odin. "Now let me see. I can't kill you and I won't kill my sister, so just what does a girl have to do—to GET HER THINGS BACK?" she yelled angrily.

Hel was by the cask now. "Gracious me!" she exclaimed, raising her hands theatrically in mock surprise. "By Thor's raggedy beard, what do you suppose could possibly be hiding inside a quaint, little old toy box like this one?"

Before Odin could open his mouth, Hel raised the lid and dragged Mimir out by the roots of his hair. Tossing him high in the air, she caught his head in her outstretched hands.

"Tongue feeling a little looser now, hey, Odin?" she cackled harshly.

"Oh, Hel—please, please put him down," Kat tried to plead, but she wasn't listening.

"Hey, Odin," Hel tapped Mimir firmly on the cheek then rubbed his face salaciously between her naked breasts. "You really aren't taking very good care of your friend, are you? Look at the state he's in."

A wicked grin was growing from one ear to the other. "He's lost a lot of weight."

"Hel, please stop," Odin's voice sounded horrified.

"Tell me what I want to know and then I'll let your friend go—oh," Hel chanted, trying to make the words rhyme. She was having such wicked fun.

"I can't," Odin pleaded.

"Or won't! Hmmm, now let me see." Hel paused before placing Mimir's head very deliberately on the floor between her legs. "You know, all that travelling from Niflheim and not a toilet to be had any-where." Bending her knees, she squatted suggestively.

"Oh, Hel, that's revolting. For Odin's sake, please!" Kat felt dis-gusted.

Suddenly, and to everyone's surprise, Mimir opened his eyes. They roamed wildly around the room before focusing on Kat. "Lamb-da," he rasped slowly, fixing his stare upon her.

"What did he say?" Hel enquired.

"Lambda!" he croaked louder, widening his eyes in terror such that they seemed to pop right out of his head.

"It's in the cask," Odin surrendered quietly. Mimir had already said too much and Odin was determined to silence him before he could say more.

"What was that?"

"Your ring, Hel. It's in the cask," Odin repeated his words of capit-ulation.

"And my cloak—where's that?" Hel almost sounded disappointed. She'd been looking forward to pissing on Uncle 'Mimi'.

"In the Chamber of the Valkyries," Odin sighed as he rose slowly from his knees. Defeat didn't suit him. He looked exhausted.

Hel stood up and quickly rummaged amongst the leaves in the bot-tom of the cask. With a triumphant squeal, she held her ring aloft for them to see and then slipped it on a finger. Jerking Mimir up into the air once more, she kissed him cheekily on the lips before replacing him in the cask.

"Hel, you wouldn't have really peed on him, would you?" Kat asked breathlessly as Hel walked over and put her arm around her. This was the evil side to Hel she hadn't seen before, and it scared her.

"Maybe yes, maybe no—now we'll never know…" She paused reflectively. "Certainly would have brightened up his day though, don't you think?" she cackled coarsely.

Neither Odin nor Kat joined her laughter. They couldn't see the funny side to her crude and vulgar display.

"So Kat, are you coming with me?" Hel enquired, posing the six million dollar question as easily as if she was offering her a slice of cake.

Kat hesitated. Odin was a liar and a cheat, and he had proved that now conclusively. He hadn't stopped Hel from humiliating Mimir out of compassion, either. He had surrendered her ring because he wanted to shut Mimir up, that was all. Whatever 'Lambda' meant, it must be important, so Kat decided to make a mental note of the word.

Hel's question was really quite a good one. *Why in Asgard should she stay with a god she didn't trust?*

Unfortunately, Kat already knew her answer. She did have one good reason to stay, and it happened to be the most important reason in her life right now.

"I'm so sorry, Hel, I can't come with you. There's someone— Jess—I need to see. I hope you can understand…," Kat's voice trailed off as she hung her head apologetically.

"Do you love her?"

Stepping closer, Hel lifted Kat's chin up cautiously with her finger. For the first time her words sounded soft and full of kindness. Kat nodded.

"As much as I love you?" she added, softer still. Again Kat nodded. "Then you have to stay."

Pulling Kat's hips to hers, Hel kissed her tenderly on the lips. For the briefest of moments, Kat was back in Jess's arms and she parted her lips hungrily, pulling Hel's head firmly toward her. Hel returned her fire before drawing slowly away and sneering once more at Odin.

She had wanted her cursed enemy to see the strength of her bond with Kat, and Kat had just delivered that in spades. Hel couldn't have been happier.

"Look after yourself, Sangrid, and remember—*I'll be back!*" Finishing her sentence in her best *Terminator*-style voice, Hel waved her hand over her ring, and was gone. Hel's greatest gamble had paid off.

Back in Niflheim she had taken her own life by drinking a powerful poison, an extract made from the roots of the magical poppies. Ganglot had then stabbed her through the heart before Kat innocently carried Hel's soul back to Asgard as a gift—hidden inside the black Valkyrie dagger.

In a reckless oversight, Odin's enchantments had only bound Hel's body to Niflheim, not her soul. Freed from her physical form, Odin's grasp upon the handle had activated Mimir's well, re-uniting Hel's soul with a burst of energy that condensed into corporeal form; thus completing the cycle of her resurrection.

Between the two of them, Odin and Kat, they'd not only brought Hel back to life…

…they'd set her free.

68

Crescent Cay

I t must have taken Marcus all of ten minutes to work out that the Senator's daughter sitting next to him wasn't, in fact, his daughter. She was a high-class call girl, as almost certainly were all the other beautiful women seated at the dinner table, Frigg and Fulla excepted.

This fairly simple observation quite probably saved Marcus's life, again. Frigg's probing of his mind had become increasingly disrupted by frequent storms of erotic thoughts emanating from his amygdala. Marcus was quietly enjoying carnal fantasies about the guest next to him and this was interfering with her investigation. Growing bored with the constant interruptions, Frigg decided to end her eavesdropping. Marcus clearly knew too much about the Valkyries to leave the island, but the question as to whether he knew enough to secure a death warrant was a matter that could be put on hold—for the time being.

Later that evening, Frigg contacted the hotel where Anna was staying and early the next day a launch was dispatched to collect her and their luggage. Anna eventually arrived on the island close to dusk, and even closer to tears. Once again Marcus was in the doghouse; going AWOL and dodging death were becoming something of a habit with him. Anna was both furious and relieved in equal measures.

Fortunately, her need to beat her husband to a sticky pulp evaporated quickly as she took in the splendour of their new surroundings. As Marcus tactfully pointed out, if he had to get shipwrecked anywhere, he couldn't really have chosen a more idyllic location. Their hotel back on Cat Cay had been five stars, but Frigg's mansion blew

that away by a considerable margin. Anna was truly spellbound and
overwhelmed by Frigg's generosity, and to Marcus's great amusement
she bobbed an awkward curtsey every time she saw the Contessa.

There was more good news for Marcus, too. To his surprise, Anna
produced his mobile phone. It wasn't resting in a watery grave somewhere among the coral reef; in his exhausted stupor he had forgotten
to take it when he left their hotel. Anna slapped him playfully for this
oversight. Not only had he been shipwrecked, but he couldn't have
called for help! Between them, they agreed amicably that Marcus was
indeed an idiot, and on that happy note they decided to start their
vacation anew.

Crescent Cay was the ultimate Caribbean dream and Anna didn't
want to waste a second more of it through arguing and fighting.

Frigg was kept fairly busy most days, but she was so appalled by
Anna's dowdy and meagre wardrobe that she took the whole of the
next day off and insisted on taking her to Nassau for a day of leisurely
shopping, all at her expense. Anna had to virtually tape her jaw in
place when they took off in her private jet and headed for the most
exclusive boutiques they could find. While Anna enjoyed endless
glasses of chilled champagne and couture dresses, Frigg enjoyed wading through her mind, and it didn't take her long to find what she was
looking for.

Anna knew nothing.

Her only knowledge of the Valkyries seemed to be restricted to the
name and her hatred for 'Jessica.' Frigg was both shocked and fascinated by the discovery of her affair with Marcus. Brynhildr, well, she
could expect that of her...*but Marcus?* Perhaps he wasn't such a blue-
eyed, holier-than-thou detective boy she had considered him to be.

His handsome standing suddenly rose considerably in her esteem.

Returning home late that same evening, Anna's verdict on the day
could best be measured in the countless beautiful dresses and shoes
that Frigg had bought her. Frigg's verdict was less effusive: Anna was
harmless and could leave the island whenever she pleased. She knew
nothing of consequence.

While the women shopped, Marcus seized the opportunity to
explore the island around him. There were no obvious restrictions, no
barbed wire fences nor padlocked gates, but if he strayed where he
wasn't welcome a helpful servant or security guard would pop conveniently into view. He would then be politely but firmly redirected
elsewhere, usually with a cover-all excuse that where he had intended
to go was undergoing routine maintenance or that it was a 'Health and

Safety' issue. He didn't mind too much, being able to glean almost all he needed to know from one of the two craggy knolls that lay at either end of the isle. These rose to approximately fifty metres in height and provided excellent vantage points from which to study the island's layout.

He had intended to climb to the top of one of these but, to his surprise, he practically fell over a well-concealed missile battery near the top of the eastern one. Muttering profuse apologies to its guards, he retraced his steps back down the slope and eventually settled upon on a weathered rock some distance below. From there, he could take his time and study the island's topography.

Marcus already knew from his and Kat's Google search that the island was over 3,000 square acres in size (twelve to thirteen square kilometres), but what the numbers couldn't convey was just how large the Dragza's slice of paradise actually was.

As the name suggested, the Cay had an elongated, roughly crescent shape which lay on a southeast to northwesterly axis. At both ends of the island were the two craggy knolls; the beach where he had come ashore was on the western side of the isle not far from where the sprawling mansion complex opened onto it. This beach ran the whole length of the island, unlike those on the eastern shore which formed a series of shallow, sandy coves. On the eastern side, too, a large artificial harbour had been created, and moored there was what Marcus could only describe as the most fabulous yacht he had ever seen.

It had to be at least fifty or sixty metres in length, a figure which put it firmly in the league of billionaire super-yachts. It was a gorgeous, three-decked affair and he hoped that during their stay they might get a chance to board it. Beyond the harbour, a deep channel had been dredged which cut a dark, navy-blue gash in an otherwise turquoise sea.

Surrounding much of the island lay a shallow coral reef beyond which two grey launches endlessly circled the island. Add these to the missile defences on the knolls and a large satellite dish hidden discretely within the mansion complex, and the island was armed to the teeth. It was like a fortress, which begged the obvious question: *Were its defences intended to keep fishermen and tourists out—or to keep the Dragza's secrets in?*

The centre of the island was wide and flat and had been mostly taken over by the swathes of manicured orchards so clearly visible on Google Earth. A mile-long paved runway stretched from roughly the centre of the isle and ended in a complex of large buildings and hangers which lay close to the western tip of the isle and farthest from his view. There was a constant hive of activity around this area with at least one or two large transporter planes landing every day. Equipment and personnel scurried between the planes and the hangers, but they were much too far away for Marcus to make out any detail, even with the aid of a pair of binoculars he borrowed from an obliging servant.

A final oddity struck Marcus as he began his descent back to the beach. Frequent minor tremors shook the island. They were reminiscent of the subway back home and he couldn't really call them earthquakes because the disturbances were too small. They didn't seem to correspond with the movements of landing aircraft or any other obvious phenomenon.

They were a mystery, but one he decided to make a mental note of, rather than obsess about.

Springtime had to be the best time of year for a holiday in the Caribbean. Each day dawned with a cloudless sky of the deepest blue, and each day seemed more pleasantly warm than the previous one.

Marcus and Anna quickly settled down into a luxurious and leisurely routine. Breakfast was served late on the veranda and their mornings centred around the pool. This was the time when Marcus would try to strike up conversations with Woods and the other guests.

To Marcus's disappointment, Woods (or 'Tom,' as he preferred to be called on holiday) was becoming increasingly irritable. Each day he became more agitated and withdrawn, constantly asking to speak to the Contessa and trying to steal her precious time for private conversations. What they discussed, Marcus didn't know, but Woods' agitation was accompanied by sweating and an episodic and violent tremor. He didn't look well, and this troubled Marcus.

The only times when he seemed at ease were when he was with his hostess, Christina. She had the same interesting tattoo on her bottom as Frigg had discretely hidden on her derrière. Marcus had noticed it peeping over her bikini as she got out of the pool one morning. Not that he was intentionally looking at Frigg's behind—it just happened in one of those peculiar, typically 'bloke moments' (or that would be how he'd justify his furtive glances).

Along with Woods, the other guests at the mansion gradually became a source of curiosity for Marcus. He found he could conveniently divide them into the 'Haves' and the 'Have nots.'

Apart from the obvious divide—guests and servants—there were other, more subtle and intriguing ways the sorting could be done. Take, for example, the 'Have an apple' and the 'Not have an apple' groups.

Despite the island being carpeted in an orchard, the apples that were plucked from the trees were not freely available. Only some of the guests were given them and these were only on demand. To qualify, you had to have either a large V-shaped scar on your chest or a smaller v-shaped tattoo on the inside of your right wrist. If Marcus asked for an apple, he would be given one, but not one of the distinctive variety produced on the island. When he pushed for an answer, he was informed that they were a 'genetically modified crop' and that the other guests were guinea pigs. Reluctantly, Marcus decided to refrain from offering to become one, too.

Guests continued to arrive and leave throughout Marcus and Anna's stay, most staying for two or three days at a time. These people were pleasant and conversational up to a point—happy to chat about the weather, items of news, and the hotness of the girls around the pool. They were considerably less happy, however, to talk about themselves or their jobs, restricting their answers to "Yes, we serve in the forces" or "I'm afraid that's classified."

Marcus was careful not to pry too hard. Woods had told him of the veiled threat he had received when he first brought up the subject of the scars and Marcus heeded that warning well. If the scars did come from a fraternity, then it must be one with global aspirations. At least half the guests were from overseas. One detail Marcus managed to glean did seem to be of interest: most of the men with big V-scars served in the navy.

As the days rolled by, a pattern began to emerge for the 'Have apples' guests. They would arrive, unwind, spend time with the hostesses by the pool, and before they left they would have a private consultation with Frigg in a special room in the mansion. Marcus peeped in there on one occasion and was taken aback by its appearance.

The area was a large conference room with a central round table with nine seats around it. One wall was completely taken over by a well-organised library and another by large maps and detailed charts, particularly those of the oceans. There were multiple computer terminals and plasma screens throughout the room and blackout blinds for the single, wide, floor-to-ceiling window. The door appeared reinforced and blast-proofed.

If he hadn't known better, Marcus would have said the room looked like the Situation Room of the White House

After the visitors had their private meeting with Frigg, they would leave the island. The guests were a disparate group of individuals who seemed to talk even less to each other than they did with Marcus. Occasionally some were old friends, like the pair Woods had met, but by and large the guests kept to themselves, ate an apple a day, and relaxed with one of the many beautiful hostesses.

Interestingly, the hostesses could also be divided into 'Haves' and 'Have nots.' The Contessa, Fulla, and Christina all had poppy tattoos, whereas the others didn't. From what he could make out, those with the tattoo also ate an apple a day.

Marcus pondered on these findings for some time before he eventually arrived at a startling conclusion. The guests had to be members of a secret society; there could be no other sensible explanation. Inwardly, he speculated wildly as to what this might be. His most likely bet, and the one which satisfied Frigg the most when she plundered his mind, was that they were a kind of 'Valkyrie support group'—people working behind the scenes, smoothing the path for the warriors when they came to the Earth.

It was not until the eighth day of their stay on the island that Marcus had his ultimate dream fulfilled. All the guests were invited by Frigg to spend a day on the super-yatch, fishing.

The day dawned with a clear blue sky as usual, and the party set off early for the boat. Loaded with crates of beer, champagne, and wine, the vessel set sail and headed out to explore more distant and uninhabited isles. They snorkelled, swam, rode jet skis, tried their hand at Marlin fishing, and lounged around in the giant Jacuzzi on the sun deck. The yacht was fabulous and with two huge engines it could travel as swiftly as the finest upmarket speedboats, having a top speed in excess of thirty knots. Every facility was available on board, including a gymnasium and a magnificent home cinema room complete with pre-release samples from all the major Hollywood studios. It was a veritable Aladdin's cave of boys' toys, and made Marcus's stay almost complete. Only one thing now was missing, and by a strange coincidence Frigg offered it that very same evening: a guided tour of the island with her as their hostess.

Saddling up horses from the stables the next morning, Frigg led Marcus, Woods, and Anna away from the beach and into the endless groves of apple trees. This was what Marcus had been waiting for, an opportunity to get up close and personal with the fruit that had been of so much interest to Kat.

The apples were indeed peculiar and Frigg went to some lengths to explain how and why they'd been created. This was best demonstrated when she cut one in half.

The apples were seedless and had an unusually thick and waxy skin which she explained was where the goodness lay. The apples had been cultivated by a program of cross breeding and selected to have minimum waste and maximum nutrition, hence the lack of a core and the thickened skin. Each tree had to be grown from a graft, and the apples hadn't as yet been formally named. Marcus suggested 'Golden Francesca' had a nice ring to it and his suggestion was greeted with some merriment. Their skin did indeed have a rich and golden hue, changing colour and shimmering according to the way sunlight fell upon it.

Frigg offered slices to each of the trio in turn, but they all politely declined. This pleased Frigg enormously although her face didn't show it. She had read each of their minds as she offered them the fruit and none seemed to know the true nature of the apples. This came as a huge relief and one that all but guaranteed Marcus and Anna's safe passage from the island.

This lack of knowledge would have guaranteed Woods safe passage, too, were it not for his knowledge of the mead and his tortured addiction to it. In true Woods style, he hadn't given all the mead he had brought with him to the Contessa; he was keeping a secret stash hidden away as another insurance policy. Unfortunately, his craving for the liquid had caused him to sip thimblefuls each day such that by now his covert supply had run dry. That was why he was getting increasingly crotchety and irritable.

He was becoming delusional. *Surely the Contessa must have synthesised the mead by now?*

His craving and her failure to inform him of progress was giving rise to ever-deepening suspicions. Little by little, a rational perspective was being distorted by delusions. He was convinced that the Contessa had already started its production and was deliberately hiding it from him.

Unfortunately for Woods, the Contessa was aware of this fact, and of his deteriorating mental health. The time was fast approaching for her to deal with him. Woods had served his purpose and had been amply rewarded. It was time for him to go—permanently.

"Your tattoo looks a little faded," Frigg commented to Christina when they returned poolside from their tour. "It could do with a little touch-up, don't you think, Tom?"

"Looks all right to me," Woods nodded as he peered suspiciously at it.

"No, it's definitely fading and needs…refreshing, Christina," Frigg continued pointedly.

"If you say so, my lady," she replied obediently. "Would you like me to do this sometime soon?"

"Hmmm, perhaps in the next couple of days, whenever it's convenient," Frigg finished nonchalantly as she made to walk away.

For the briefest of moments, Marcus caught an exchange of glances between the two women. Instinct told him that their conversation had nothing to do with tattoos. It was a code, but one he didn't understand. Frigg and Christina did, however, and the message was clear and unambiguous. Wood's fate had been sealed, with Christina his chosen executioner.

"Come on you," Marcus sighed as he nudged a tired and contented Anna beside him. "It's time to get changed for dinner."

With some reluctance, Anna followed Marcus away from the pool and back inside the mansion. Frigg wasn't far ahead of them, but they didn't quicken their pace to catch her up. She had spent the best part of the day with them and they didn't want to strain her friendship any further. Besides, she was overdue some quality relaxation time with her 'man hunk,' Ottar. He had joined the party a couple of days previously and was clearly her love interest.

Reaching their bedroom, Marcus was surprised to hear his mobile phone ringing. Racing over to it, he pressed the answer button the moment before it switched to voice mail. With hindsight, Marcus might well have wished he'd waited for just one more fateful ring.

"Hi, Marcus, is that you?" a familiar voice began falteringly from the other end of the line. "It's me—Jess," the faint but beautiful Irish voice continued. "I, I…," she paused, and Marcus could hear her quietly sobbing.

"I want to go home. Please help me—you're my only hope."

69

Berserkers—

The first the Valkyries knew about Hel's escape from Nifl-heim was when the alarm was sounded in the castle. Zara was the warrior who raised it. She had found Ruby collapsed and bleeding heavily on the steps leading down to the Chamber of the Valkyries. She'd been run through by Hel with her own sword.

Despite the severity of her injuries, Ruby refused to succumb to unconsciousness. Taking huge gulps of mead, she explained how she had met Hel coming up the steps from the Chamber wearing her cloak of black swans' feathers. They had fought, but despite Ruby's great strength and vast experience, Hel was simply too fast and strong for her. Ruby wasn't sure what she had been doing in the Chamber, but she was adamant about what Hel did next. Chanting the ancient words, she had transformed into a swan and taken flight.

This news came as a terrible shock to Odin, almost as bad as the appearance of Hel in his citadel. He desperately needed to find Vali, and the warriors wasted precious time looking for his son. He was around somewhere, but not within the castle grounds.

Growing impatient with the delay and sensing exactly what was at the back of Odin's mind, Freyja put on her cloak of falcons' feathers and sped off at great haste. She headed due south toward Middle Sea, the same direction she was confident Hel had taken. Minutes ground relentlessly into hours as Odin sat nervously in the feasting hall. He was alternately biting his fingernails and pacing irritably up and down. When at last Freyja returned, the news was as grim as he'd anticipated. The guards to the prison on the Isle of Lyngvi had been

411

killed and the fortress sacked. The cell that had held its only captive lay open and the door hung creaking ominously from its rusted iron hinges. Loki's wolf had been released.

Hel had taken Fenrir back to Niflheim.

Almost as soon as Freyja arrived back with the news, the ground beneath the castle began to shake and groan. The well had been activated and the warriors dashed frantically down into the Chamber.

Hel had been a busy girl. Armed with knowledge gleaned by Henry, she had put it to good use. Another gateway to Niflheim had been opened and its flow modified. What had once been one-way traffic was now two: the dead could return to the living.

Odin struggled desperately with the controls but to no avail. He'd been so confident that Hel couldn't escape from Niflheim, they'd never bothered to reset the access codes. They were voice activated and Hel had put her mastery of mimicry to good use. Imitating the voice of Freyja, she'd entered the Chamber and then used her talent once more to open the well and fiddle with its controls. She'd also registered a new voice command locking Odin out.

All the well's energy and power was now diverted to only one thing: creating a portal from Niflheim to Asgard. Odin was impotent and helpless, reduced to being a bystander as the forces of evil began their march.

As a tepid sun slowly set behind the mountains of Jotunheim, the direction of Hel's attack soon became apparent. A large, dark, swirling cloud started to envelope the towering volcanic cone in the realm of Muspellheim. The cloud grew blacker by the minute. Here was where the worm hole had opened its doorway; here was where Hel's army would gain their foothold in Asgard.

Events unfolded quickly once darkness crept across the land. An endless procession of torches could be seen filing their way out of the volcano's crater and winding their way slowly down its sides. From the castle the appearance was surreal, like the dance of a thousand fireflies on a moonless night. Hour after hour, the numbers steadily increased until the whole hillside was bathed in an eerie glow.

No one slept that night.

At first, while the evening was still young, there was considerable debate amongst the warriors as to what to do with Kat. She had brought Hel's soul to Asgard concealed in a modified Valkyrie knife. There were cries to have her imprisoned, or even stoned to death, but Odin quickly silenced these calls.

In truth, his options were far more limited than his loyal Valkyries had grasped. Their situation was perilous and he would need every available warrior to stand tomorrow in the battle for Asgard. Kat had stayed with him and for that reason and that alone he would give her one last chance to prove her loyalty.

The gravity of the situation worsened when word reached the castle that Heimdall was on his way from the watchtower. Nothing could usually make him stir from his vigilant watch, so the situation had to be deadly serious for him to take such a drastic step. Travelling by chariot, he blew the ringing horn of Gjall all the way. His horses galloped hard across the plains of Ida and were drenched in sweat when they ultimately arrived at the castle.

Gjall's call was a call to arms—the alarm for Ragnarok—and its piercing blast could be heard in every corner of the land. Every able-bodied farmer, serf, peasant, and soldier got out of bed and made ready for war.

Weapons and farm implements were taken out, dusted down, and then nervously sharpened. Meals were cooked and hastily eaten, and with tender farewells spoken to families who they might never see again, the menfolk marched to the town of Asgard. Delicate rivulets of torches could be seen threading their way around hills and woods as, little by little, Odin's army took shape.

By the first grey light of dawn, a reassuring mass of cold and weary men was assembled on the banks of the River Iving. They must have numbered at least two thousand strong, but as the cold, grey light of day grew in strength, the magnitude of their foe became all too apparent.

Through an early morning mist which hung like a veil of finest lace, row upon row of Hel's soldiers could be seen marching across the fields and through the woods which stood between the castle and the foothills of Muspellheim. As they marched, they beat their swords upon their shields and chanted a dark and evil incantation. It echoed harshly in the pallid light of dawn, chilling the blood of all who heard it.

The beating and chanting was relentless, as were the tireless, heavy, trampling footfalls that covered the many kilometres between them and Asgard.

By mid-morning Hel's army came to an abrupt halt. They had reached the strip of land chosen for the battle. This was wide, well-drained, and on a slight slope which offered them the advantage of higher ground. Had Freyja had the choice, she could not have found a better place to prosecute a war.

At the head of Hel's imposing army stood their leader, dressed in black but with the chocolate-brown of his forearms exposed for all to see. He led his host with confidence, though his face was covered in a scarf that concealed all features other than his eyes. Among the warriors there was little doubt as to his identity. It was Cole, Odin's rotten apple, the starter of Ragnarok, who was at the helm.

Breakfast at the castle was a hasty and muted affair. The normal excitement of the warriors for war had been replaced by a sense of fear and foreboding. Their enemy was dressed in distinctive animal skins that covered their heads and faces as well. This was a Berserker army, the most dangerous and ferocious fighting foes they could ever dare to face. What made the girls' apprehension all the greater was that this battle would be a leap into the unknown: no Valkyrie force had ever engaged an army of the dead before.

Their nerves were stretched to breaking point.

Kat's arrival at the breakfast table sent a further shockwave around the room. She came dressed not in the leather fighting tunic of a Valkyrie warrior, but in the tight black trousers, belt, and bodice of Hel. Her shoulders were bare, and she proudly paraded the mark of the Black Valkyrie before all those present. For a moment, Odin feared the worst—Mimir's twisted prophesy would be fulfilled. Kat would cross the line and take up arms with his mortal foe.

Sensing her sisters' fear and hostility, Kat raised her hand and indicated that she would like to speak. She felt relaxed and confident, so very different from the nervous maid who had once feared a tiny band of masons.

"Fellow warriors," she began loudly and defiantly. "Please do not fear my attire. Although I no longer trust your lord and master, I pledge my life to fight with you. I will join you today in battle, though it will not be to defend the honour of your lord. I join you to defend our queen, to defend my beloved sisters, and to defend the realm of Asgard. HAIL, VICTORY!"

To Kat's surprise, the room erupted into a wild chorus of cheering and stamping of feet. For the moment her differences with Odin were forgotten and both Silk and Carmel urged her to come and sit down beside them. It was like old times once more, and Kat hugged and kissed them all warmly. They returned her embrace with gladness in their hearts. After all, who knew if their hugs and kisses would be their last?

Breakfast over, Odin, Freyja, the warriors, and all the gods Odin had been able to muster made their way across the narrow stone bridge. Their thin, silver line of hope now trailed up through dew-soaked meadows and fields of golden stubble to join the Aesir soldiers who had already confronted the enemy host.

It was clear to Odin that his army was inferior but to his relief, his ring and those of the other gods were still functioning. He had sent for his brothers Vili and Ve, and they were now hard at work in the Chamber of the Valkyries desperately trying to override the well. If they succeeded, then Odin could call upon his mighty army of heroes should they be needed.

As the tiny host of gods and warriors trotted toward the front line, a single, icy blast of air descended from the mountains of Jotunheim. With it came a brief flurry of snow. Odin traced the path of a single, delicate snowflake as it curled and pirouetted down like a ballerina upon his outstretched hand. This was it, the final, stark omen that Ragnarok had begun.

This battle was surely the beginning of the end, and Odin prayed silently that Mimir's prophesies would be fulfilled according to his wishes. It wasn't quite how he'd planned it, but like the prophecies, much of the final conflict remained a mystery, hidden from view. Only its outcome was important, not the hows, whys, and whens of getting there.

"All hail the cockroach Odin!" Hel yelled caustically as she whipped her army into a loud chorus of jeers and sarcastic laughter. The miniscule size of the Valkyrie forces and the inexperienced youth of the Aesir were all too apparent to her and her soldiers. The confidence of her host was at boiling point and under Lucifer's brilliant leadership, defeat seemed impossible.

Whilst the soldiers around him hurled their taunts, Louis himself remained deathly silent. His eyes were fixed on the shapely figure of his nemesis. The woman who had condemned him to Hel's brutal realm was clearly visible. Revenge would be his. Anger burned like fires in his eyes.

Ruby, too, stood impassive. The Valkyries were immune to the insults of inferior warriors. Her bloodlust was rising fast and her eyes were fixed unblinkingly on the leader of Hel's army. Justice would be done and she alone would hack Cole down, destroying Odin's rotten apple.

"Hel," Odin began calmly as the jeering of the Berserkers slowly subsided, "I will give you one last chance to return Balder to me and retreat to your realm. If you do not, you will face the mother of all defeats."

"Odin, lay down your weapons and I swear I will spare your life."

Unfazed by Odin's threats, Hel raised her sword triumphantly above her head, looking every inch the proud, conquering warrior queen. She sat astride Gold Mane dressed in scarlet leather trousers and a tightly-laced matching bodice. The brilliant colours of her clothes cut a dash against the muted brown, blacks, and greys of the furs that cloaked her soldiers. She was their figurehead and this was her victory dress. Her garish ensemble was designed to inspire her army and strike fear into the hearts of her enemies.

Odin shook his head and turned to his warriors. "We have no choice, the die is cast. Today we fight not just for our lives but for life itself!"

"HAIL, VALOUR!"

Thor led the battle cheer with a loud bellow.

"HAIL, ODIN!"

The Aesir joined in the cheering.

"HAIL, VICTORY!"

With a tremendous rallying chorus of battle cries, the Valkyries leapt from their horses and spread out before the enemy lines. The ranks of bear-skinned soldiers seemed to stretch from horizon to horizon, standing in rows which in places lay ten deep. The Berserker army was well armed and well trained—and they had another, terrible surprise in store for the Valkyries.

"Prepare to attack!" Hel shouted shrilly as she waved her sword once more above her head before galloping back between their ranks.

With a massive roar that echoed like thunder around the battlefield, the Berserker army threw off their animal skins to reveal their true colours.

This was no ordinary army of flailing, demented berserks driven to madness by a cocktail of Amanita mushrooms and bog myrtle. Beneath their animal skins they were heavily protected by armour coated in Hellinium, the secret weapon of Niflheim. On each soldier's back was a black metal cylinder and fine plastic nasal prongs curled from this to their nostrils.

This was one of Henry's brilliant ideas. Hel's soldiers would inhale the fragrance of their poppies as they fought, its powerful healing properties making them nigh but invincible.

"CHARGE!"

Ruby's voice rang out, and the Valkyries hurled themselves at the enemy host with the greatest ferocity. The bloodlust was at fever pitch and it screamed to be sated.

Lucifer raised and then lowered his sword, unleashing a terrible force.

Each Berserker held a log-sized clay canister in his hands which he hurled at the approaching warriors and soldiers. As the canisters landed and exploded, the deadly effects and horror of this hideous weapon spread chaos amongst the brave men of Asgard.

Each missile contained a sticky mixture of white phosphorus and carbon disulfide (Fenian fire), igniting everything it touched. In an instant, the battlefield was transformed into an apocalyptic nightmare, a fiery furnace that burnt as fiercely as the surface of Niflheim itself. Its devastation was indescribable. The screams of the Aesir soldiers as they slowly burned to death could be heard across the realm.

Truly the horrors of Mimir's prophesy had come to pass. A rotten black apple had indeed sparked a fire that would consume them all.

Odin smiled grimly. So far, so good. *But where was Fenrir—and where were the Guardians?*

As the smoke began to clear and the warriors tried to calm the terrified men around them, it became apparent that one of the Valkyries had been killed in this first assault. Prima had taken a direct hit and was amongst the dead. This loss spurred the warriors into an even greater fury and they renewed their assault upon the waiting Berserkers with a venomous rage in their bosoms.

The armies engaged with a thunderous roar and the superior weaponry of the Berserkers quickly became apparent. Arrows and spears struggled to penetrate the shields and armour of the enemy soldiers, and the Valkyries' swords fractured and broke in the violence of their exchanges.

Dwarf metal was strong, but Hellinium was stronger still.

The Berserker army began to move forward, crushing the lines of Aesir soldiers rapidly as they crumpled beneath their overwhelming might. Only the silver line of the Valkyries held firm. Their strength and fighting skills could keep the Berserkers at bay, but couldn't force them into a retreat.

Even Thor was struggling, the mighty power of his hammer being limited by its restricted access to the well. He could kill individual Berserkers with ease and was by far the mightiest warrior on the battlefield, but that was all—enemy tactics had been devised to hold his vengeful rage at bay.

Louis had considered every angle. Instead of rushing blindly at Thor, the Berserkers surrounded him in a defensive ring, shields raised high and retreating as he lunged toward them with his hammer. He killed one or two on each advance, but it was exhausting work and he was becoming isolated. 'Containment' had been Louis's watchword, and this tactic was clearly working. Thor was fighting in an insulated bubble and had little impact on the greater battle raging all around.

The only area where the Berserker army ceded ground was where Kat was waging war. To her dismay, they retreated with each and every one of her attacks. She hurled herself against their shields but they wouldn't strike a single blow in their defence. Within minutes, she had passed clean through the enemy lines and was standing at the feet of Hel.

"Why won't they fight me?" Kat screamed furiously. Her bloodlust was raging and her body consumed by its need to fight and kill.

"My soldiers will not harm a queen of Niflheim," Hel laughed as she lowered an arm to lift Kat up beside her on the back of Gold Mane.

Infuriated, Kat leapt up beside her sister. She must have misheard Hel.

"You're my sister," Hel continued as she shouted in Kat's ear. The clamour of war around them was deafening. "And as such you're their queen as well."

Kat looked at Hel in astonishment. For a moment the mad absurdity of her situation flashed briefly into her mind. In less than a year she had gone from doctor to warrior and now this: co-ruler of the damned. *Surely there could never have been a more meteoric rise to infamy?*

Kat craned forward and yelled passionately in Hel's ear, "Please, I beg of you, if I am your sister then so are the other Valkyries. Please don't kill them."

Hel nodded and sent messengers swiftly forward to the front line. Like Kat, she had seen first Prima fall, then Mist, and now the maid Yuko. One by one, the Valkyries were being destroyed.

"You cannot fight any more," Hel begged Kat. "And I have instructed my soldiers to do your bidding. Your sisters won't be harmed. Now, please, why don't you sit with me and watch the battle unfold?"

Kat thanked Hel and squeezed her tightly against her. To Odin and Freyja she must have looked a traitor sitting there beside their bitter enemy. But in a bizarre and perverse twist of irony, it would be thanks to her that so many Valkyries would survive this terrible day.

Hel was true to her word.

As each warrior grew weary and ran out of arrows, swords, and spears to break upon the enemy, the Berserkers would slyly force them back toward the River Iving, nothing more.

Hel's army was winning the battle and Odin knew it. Worse, this wasn't how it was supposed to be. Ragnarok was his creation and Lambda's curse couldn't be consumed by this pitiful rag-tag bunch of Berserker nobodies. He needed Fenrir and the Guardians—*but where were they?*

Something was wrong, and he cursed the evil Sangrid. They'd made their agreement and Hel knew her fate, yet still she'd chosen to defy him, daring to challenge Ragnarok and change their destiny.

Hel had brought the wrong army to Asgard.

Toying nervously with the Doomsday talisman in his pocket, Odin looked pleadingly toward the castle for hope, a sign that Vili and Ve had done their job: wrestling the well's control from Hel's evil grasp.

Whilst news of clemency toward the Valkyries rippled up and down their lines, one soldier chose to ignore the command. Slowly but surely Louis was fighting his way toward the beleaguered Ruby, and behind him limped an embittered Cole. He, too, had spotted Ruby amongst the warriors and his heart was set on revenge. Reaching her position first, Louis quickly joined her in combat.

He was enraged as was she; and they fell upon each other like a pair of rabid wolves.

"Your head is mine!" Louis yelled at the top of his voice, raining down hefty blows upon Ruby's shield, which groaned and cracked alarmingly.

"I should have killed you long ago," Ruby snarled, trading blow for blow with her masked attacker. Cole was slightly behind him, and the lingering smoke of the incendiary bombs still hid his face from view.

"You will soon join your vile lover as my guest in Hel," Louis taunted as he struggled to gain the advantage. His sword was stronger, but she was a ferocious warrior and more than an equal in skill and power.

"My lover?" Ruby's attack began to falter as the limping soldier behind her assailant came slowly into view. His features were as unmistakeable as the truth that hit her like an axe. The man she was fighting wasn't Cole.

"Who are you?" she screamed, lunging forward once more with her sword.

"Death's worst nightmare, you evil whore!" Louis growled as he took a pace backward. The beautiful woman was almost too strong for him.

"Unmask yourself!" Ruby yelled as she pressed forward her advantage. She was gaining the upper hand, and soon the leader of Hel's army would be lying slaughtered at her feet.

Parrying a blow, Louis stepped sideways and lost his footing on the muddy ground. He slipped backward and Ruby's sword was swiftly at his throat. With a triumphant yell she placed her foot on his chest and pressed down upon her blade. He was pinned beneath her feet.

"I say again," Ruby hissed as she leant forward, staring coldly into his eyes, "unmask yourself so I can see the vile dog I'm about to kill."

Indicating that he would do as she asked, Louis began to unwrap his scarf. Starting at his neck, he unwound it slowly, coil by coil. Finally, the last coil of his disguise was ready to be undone. Holding it carefully in his hands, he revealed his cheeks, mouth, and nose.

"YOU!" Ruby gasped, swaying violently as she fought not to collapse with astonishment. "It's not possible," she muttered in complete bewilderment.

There, before her eyes, was the unmistakeable face of Elijah.

"The black apple rotten to the core" as foretold by Mimir wasn't Cole after all. They'd got it wrong.

The man who had stirred her passion was the Berserkers' mighty leader, and his rage had been all Ruby's fault. She was the cause of the passionate fire that had burned in Elijah in Midgard, and her failure to save his life had triggered a rotten hatred in his soul.

Elijah was the true starter of Ragnarok and Ruby was overcome by despair.

"Come on," hissed Elijah as he lay before her. "Kill me yourself this time, you heartless, evil, cold-blooded bitch!" He spat the words disgustedly, as vehemently as though he'd been stung in the mouth by a hornet.

"Oh, Elijah. My dearest, sweetest, Elijah," Ruby dropped her sword and held out her hand to lift him up. She could understand his rage and it broke her heart completely.

"You let me die at his filthy hands," Elijah fumed as he rose to his feet, stabbing a finger angrily in Cole's direction. Cole's sword was also raised and he was having trouble containing the urge to kill Ruby.

"I'm so sorry, my angel." Tears welled uncontrollably in Ruby's eyes. "Please forgive me," she blurted.

"Fight on, bitch!" Louis picked up his sword once more and held it out in front of him. He was having none of these fake tears. "This time it will be your turn to burn in Hel."

Ruby dropped to her knees and lowered her head. *How could she fight the man she loved and had abandoned to a gruesome fate?*

Overwhelmed by remorse, she lowered her hands to her sides.

"I love you, Elijah, and I have wronged you terribly." She spoke softly as sobs threatened to drown her words. "If taking my life will ease your pain and bring you peace, then I give it to you gladly."

Bowing her head, Ruby parted the hair from the back of her neck. She was ready to die.

Elijah raised his sword high above his head and as he did so, Cole seized the opportunity to strike. He lunged forward. It would be his sword that killed the despised and murderous bitch.

Elijah swung his sword with all his might. Ruby heard its cruel swish as it hurtled through the air. She didn't flinch. Her death was nigh and she embraced it with open arms. This was her destiny. A terrible wrong would at last be put to rights.

Elijah's sword flashed through the air and landed with a dull thud, but it wasn't Ruby's head that fell to the ground. It was Cole's. Elijah had seen his movement in the corner of his eye and had heard Ruby's final impassioned words. The vehemence of his rage concealed a much darker, deeper, more terrible truth, a truth he had denied even to himself since the moment of his death.

He was, and always had been, madly in love with her.

Slowly Ruby raised her chin and the roar of battle overwhelmed her senses once more. She was still alive and Elijah's hand was now helping her to her feet.

"Am I forgiven?" she sobbed as she struggled to look him in the eyes.

"Do you even have to ask?" Elijah smiled as he pulled her close.

There, surrounded by a seething mass of blood and hatred, they kissed with a passion that eclipsed the battle's fury.

Shortly after their embrace, and while the fighting was still boiling at its peak, Odin ordered Heimdall to blow Gjall once more. He was ordering a retreat, but it wasn't one born of defeat. Word had arrived from the castle that Vili and Ve had been successful—they had regained control over the well. They couldn't deny Hel her access, but at least its power was now available to Odin.

With the slyest of twinkles in his beady eye, Odin thumped Gungnir on the ground. It was time to destroy Hel's motley crew.

It was time to bring on his heroes.

70

The Gilded Cage

"**V**alkyries!" Anna hissed furiously. "She's one of them, isn't she? Isn't she?"

Anna erupted as the reality slowly dawned upon her that everything about their vacation was a lie. Far from promising to keep away from his Valkyrie obsession, Marcus had organised their wonderful holiday of a lifetime around them. If she had held a Valkyrie knife in her hands, Anna might just have used it on him now. As it was, Marcus stood in their bedroom grinning and staring sheepishly at the floor. He had been caught red-handed and all he could do was let her storm break over his head, and hope that that was the only thing that got broken.

Marcus had received the extraordinary phone call from Jess just minutes before. He had then hurried down the hallway and handed the phone to Frigg who would, naturally, be in the best position to help Jess with her urgent plea. Marcus had hoped that they were out of earshot, but Frigg's rather loud and unhelpful "Brynhildr, how are you?" had spilled the beans. Hence the ruckus now.

He couldn't blame Anna—he thoroughly deserved her wrath. He had made a promise and had broken it. The only blessing was the fact that today had been the planned end to their holiday. They would be leaving tomorrow, so they could pick up the pieces of their shattered marriage on the way home.

Unfortunately for Marcus, the telephone call did more than just upset Anna. It upset the Contessa as well. She had already made her decision about Woods, and this phone call now sealed Marcus's fate, too. Anna could leave, but he couldn't.

It was just a question of putting a suitable plan in motion, and after instructing Fulla to attend to this, she retired to her suite with Ottar.

Tomorrow promised to be a day full of surprises.

"Is this the bag in question?" asked the detective who had arrived on the island at approximately nine in the morning. He was accompanied by two uniformed police officers.

"Yes, I'm afraid so, officer." Frigg hung her head and spoke with all the sincerity and solemnity she could muster.

A brief dab into the bag with a wetted finger and a quick taste on the tip of his tongue confirmed the identity of the mysterious white powder inside it. It was cocaine, and of a surprisingly high quality. After a brief discussion with the detective, Frigg asked one of her servants to round up the suspects. Within ten minutes or so, a rather groggy and befuddled Marcus accompanied by Anna was standing in her office. Marcus could offer no explanation for the presence of a sizeable quantity of cocaine in his luggage other than the obvious one: he'd been framed.

Unfortunately, the fact that he was a police detective from the NYPD didn't help matters, neither did the production of his badge. If anything, it made things worse. The police in Nassau had a fairly jaded and colourful view of corruption amongst mainland American cops. The fact that he worked in a crime-infested city like New York only compounded his guilt.

Much to Anna's horror, they decided to take Marcus into custody. The officers would complete their enquiries back at police headquarters in Nassau. Before they cuffed him, Marcus begged for a few brief moments alone with his wife. As a special favour to the Contessa, they agreed to his request and stepped outside.

"You know I've been set up, don't you?" Marcus whispered as he tried to stem the floods of tears which were streaming from Anna's eyes. She nodded yes although he felt sure she wasn't listening.

"Please, listen—this is very important, do you understand?" Marcus tried to console her. He just hoped she wasn't so distraught that she wouldn't remember what he was about to say.

"Look, I'm sure I can clear this mess up quickly, but if you haven't heard from me within two days then you must contact Agent Woods, all right? He'll know what to do."

Anna nodded. She was listening—sort of. It was this wretched Valkyrie nonsense all over again and she was sick of it.

"Oh, and if he doesn't answer, then you must call Jess and explain the situation to her. She might be able to help, too," Marcus added.

Up until this moment he had considered Frigg to be his friend and ally, but now he wasn't so sure. He found it hard to believe that she would have had someone plant drugs in his room, but who else could have done it? He was a friend and supporter of the Valkyries as was she, so there didn't seem to be a motive.

The situation was confusing and until he'd got things sorted out, he decided to hedge his bets about her friendship and give Anna Jess's mobile number.

"I know you hate the Valkyries, but please—Jess may be our only hope if things go pear-shaped, all right? Will you promise me you'll call her, please?" Marcus pulled Anna close to him and cuddled her hard. To his relief, she folded the piece of paper with Jess's number on it and put it in her purse. Despite her distress, she seemed to have got the importance of his message. *Thank goodness.*

A few moments later, the detective and police officers returned to the room. After putting Marcus in handcuffs, they took him to their shiny white police launch and set off heading west, in the direction of Nassau.

With a certain amount of frosty politeness, Frigg organised some servants to help Anna pack their belongings and she arranged a first-class ticket on the next available flight from Nassau. Frigg kindly agreed to allow Anna to keep the beautiful dresses and shoes they'd bought together, but Anna didn't have the heart to pack them. Her dream holiday with Marcus was in ruins; the combination of a Valky-rie-infested island and his arrest had turned their vacation into a nightmare. All she wanted to do now was leave and as quickly as possible. Frigg understood, and got the jet fuelled and in the air within the hour.

Marcus was a few kilometres away from the island when he heard the roar of engines as the plane took off from Crescent Cay. He knew it had to have Anna on board and as he shielded his eyes to watch its departure, the butt of a gun landed heavily on the back of his head. Marcus collapsed unconscious onto the floor of the boat.

As soon as he was down, the detective ordered the captain of the launch to turn the vessel about. Had Marcus been more observant and aware of police uniforms in the Bahamas, he might have noticed that his captors were frauds—and the intensity of the smell of fresh paint that pervaded their vessel.

The shiny white 'police launch' was now returning home—to Crescent Cay.

Christina's execution of Woods was as efficient as it was clinical.

After a leisurely breakfast, she suggested that they go water skiing. Taking a powerful motorboat from the harbour, the two of them headed a few kilometres out to sea. They both took it in turns to ride the exhilarating wake behind the launch, and after an hour or so Christina could sense that Woods was tiring. An overly zealous turn and sharp acceleration was all that was needed to capsize the inexperienced agent and leave him bobbing helpless and stranded in the water. Gathering up the tow rope and turning around, it was simplicity itself to run him over. To her satisfaction, Christina felt the dull thud of his head as it struck the bottom of the vessel. She felt certain that one of the powerful outboard motors must have also struck him because when she powered the boat down, he was nowhere in sight.

At first, the lack of a body bothered her. With the engines on idle, Christina slowly circled the spot of her kill for at least fifteen minutes. Woods's body didn't surface but a fine slick of fresh, bright red blood did. He had to be dead, and even if he wasn't, they were far enough from shore to make a swim to safety out of the question.

His blood in the water was the coup de grace. The sea around Crescent Cay was heavily shark infested and these would already be homing in on the scent of their next meal.

With one final leisurely circuit, Christina fired up the engines and set off back to the isle at full throttle. Woods was dead and she wanted to break the news immediately to Frigg. Competition to become one of 'Hel's Angels'—signified by the poppy tattoo on her bottom—was intense and she was under pressure from Lia (the Senator's 'daughter'), who was desperate to join their elite. A prompt and clinical kill would earn her merit points and keep her rivals at bay.

Eternal youth was the Contessa's gift for her chosen Angels and this was a prize more than worth killing for.

Marcus drifted slowly back into consciousness with a splitting headache and intense nausea. He threw up almost immediately and then waited patiently for his blurred vision to focus on his new surroundings.

The sight which eventually greeted him was far from heartening.

A few hours before he had been sitting at a marble table sipping coffee from fine bone china and enjoying the warm sunshine of the Caribbean on his back. Now he was lying behind iron bars on a coarse, straw mattress. The only warmth to his two by three-metre concrete cell was being provided by a single naked electric bulb which dangled from the ceiling of the narrow corridor beyond. There was no window in sight and instinct told him that he must be underground.

A gentle rumble and rattle to his room aroused his curiosity immediately. It sounded and felt exactly like the ones he had experienced back on Frigg's island. It struck him as odd that these tiny tremors—for want of a better word—could travel all the way to Nassau, unless, of course, *he'd never left the isle?*

"Hello, Marcus."

Frigg's aristocratic voice cut through the air like a knife. The clanking of a lock at the end of the corridor had already interrupted Marcus's thoughts and alerted him to the prospect of visitors.

For some reason, he wasn't altogether surprised to find that Frigg, accompanied by one of her servants, happened to be the first. After placing a cheap moulded plastic chair in the corridor opposite the cell, the servant departed and closed the heavy door behind him with a heavy, ominous thud.

Alone at last, Frigg took her time to sit down comfortably on the chair, light a cigarette, and then study Marcus's face intently. All the speculating and connections Marcus had been making over the last few days had caused her increasing concern. Now, with the telephone call from Jess, Frigg needed to seriously reconsider what she was going to do with him.

Killing him would be all too easy. With Anna out of the frame, Marcus could easily suffer a tragic accident, although she hoped this wouldn't be necessary. He had such a lovely face.

Keeping him alive was the thought that really bothered her. He had cheated death so many times that there really must be a higher purpose to his continuing existence. However, not knowing what that purpose might be gave cause for concern. Keeping him alive for the wrong reasons could lead to her and Hel's undoing. Her dilemma was, therefore, complicated.

Dead Marcus or alive Marcus—it was a tough call.

"I think, Detective Finch, we need to talk," the Contessa began at last.

71

—and Heroes

Silk was furious as she slowly retreated from the battlefield. It was unheard of for the Valkyries to be defeated and their withdrawal added insult to an already deep and crushing humiliation. It had been obvious for some time that the Berserkers were denying the warriors a noble death. Once the Valkyries' swords were broken and their arrows exhausted, the Berserkers had toyed with them, adopting a defensive wall of shields to ease the warriors gently backward.

This was an unbearable slight and one that made Silk feel physically sick.

Even when she had hurled herself at the Berserkers and tried to tear down their shields with her bare hands, they still hadn't killed her. She had earned her place in Valhalla and that right had been denied. If her sword hadn't been broken, she might well have fallen upon it that very instant rather than tread this ignominious path.

Glancing around her, she could see that the other warriors and maids felt the same way, too. The short journey back to the River Iving was the longest walk any of them would ever have to make. There was only one tiny ray of consolation to greet them as they regrouped along its bank: a small, golden disk was glowing with increasing brightness from beyond the castle. It was a sight they hadn't seen before and she hoped, like all the rest of them, that it meant what they believed it did.

The heroes were coming to save Asgard.

Odin sat on Sleipnir and surveyed the carnage of the battlefield before him. There were more bodies of the brave but inexperienced

Aesir soldiers than he cared to count, yet perhaps fewer than one hundred dead Berserkers. Hel's army had been victorious and if it weren't for the imminent arrival of his heroes, Ragnarok would have been undone and Asgard would have lain at her mercy.

It had been a close call.

Smiling wryly under a banner of truce, he urged Sleipnir to trot forward across the bridge and carry him to the centre of the battlefield. He could see the two Sangrids sitting proudly astride Gold Mane.

Their parley was certainly going to be interesting.

"So, Sangrid, you've finally revealed your true colours, just as Mimir predicted," Odin sneered, taking a snide swipe at Kat.

"Odin, it's not what you think," Kat began, but she wondered if it was really worth the effort of trying. "If it weren't for me, all your Valkyries would be dead by now."

Hel nodded in agreement. "Yeah, that's right, you filthy pig. You should honour her, not taunt her."

Kat prodded Hel in the back. "Please, show Odin some respect. I know you hate him, but he's still a god," she hissed quietly.

"Well said, Sangrid, well said indeed." Odin had overheard her comment. "I am a god, the very greatest of all gods, and for that reason I will give you one last chance to return Balder. Lay down your arms, and return to Niflheim."

"What?" Hel nearly fell off Gold Mane in surprise. "Excuse me! Your army is slaughtered, your Valkyries humiliated, and you expect ME to surrender?"

"Um, in case you haven't noticed," Odin smiled smugly as he waved his hand in the direction of the castle. "I have control of the well again and my heroes are coming. Trust me, Hel, when I say this: you do not want to fight them."

"Oh, boo-hoo-hoo!" Hel rubbed her eyes in fake, sarcastic crying. "I'm so scared. Come on, Sangrid, let's turn Gold Mane around right now and flee for our lives." Throwing her head back, she howled with laughter.

"You may laugh now, but trust me, you'll regret it if you choose to stand and fight. You are condemning your brave soldiers to a terrible fate." Odin paused, staring intently at Hel's face. She was in an exuberant mood and he could see that she wouldn't be persuaded. Hel had absolutely no idea what he was about to unleash, and that was going to make his destruction of her rabble so very much the sweeter.

"Hel, please, I think we should consider Odin's offer," Kat began cautiously. There was something about Odin's serenity that unsettled her. Hel's Berserkers were strong, brave, incredibly well-armed, and had been led by a tactical genius. This was obvious to all who had fought or witnessed the battle. However, if—in the face of this overwhelming superiority—Odin was still confident of success, then he must have a truly amazing card up his sleeve.

"Oh, come on, Kat, you can't be serious!" Hel twisted around, kissing her lightly on the cheek. "The idiot's bluffing!"

"I don't know. I just don't trust him. I've got a bad feeling about this," Kat sighed. She knew Hel wouldn't listen to her and as she considered what to say next, the golden glow in the sky behind the castle suddenly quadrupled in size and intensity. Hel had obviously seen this too, because she let out a triumphant roar.

"ODIN!" she yelled such that her troops could hear her reply. "Bring on your heroes if you think they're hard enough!"

With her arrogant challenge left ringing in Odin's ears, Hel dug her heels into Gold Mane and galloped back toward her vantage point. As Gold Mane's hooves pounded beneath them, Kat could hear the wild cheering of her Berserker army. They had crushed Odin's Valkyries and were in no mood to stop now. Fresh faces for slaughter were exactly what they wanted. Battle fever held them tightly in its grip and its thirst raged like a fire inside them.

"You will regret this, Hel, I promise you," Odin warned as he thumped Gungnir on the ground once more. The golden rift grew brighter still until it rivalled the brilliance of a summer sun. The bridge between Valhalla and Asgard was open.

"The power that you will see is the mere flexing of my little finger!" Odin called after them, raising a hand in the air and reinforcing his words by gesturing as such. Turning quickly, he headed back across the bridge.

It was time for the heroes to take to the battlefield.

Pregnant with expectation, the hubbub of jeering, taunts, shieldbanging, and foot-stamping gradually subsided from both opposing lines. Before long, an eerie silence descended across the entire battlefield as all eyes focused on the blazing gateway.

For a long time, no sound could be heard coming from the portal. Then slowly, when the warriors had almost given up hope, a distant rumbling began. The sound grew steadily louder, and as it did the warriors started to cheer. The noise seemed like the pounding of a thousand galloping horses as they thundered their way toward Asgard.

The Valkyries'excitement mounted as the deafening roar grew steadily louder.

COUGH—SPLUTTER—GRRRRHHH!

The cheering died instantly.

The thunder they had heard wasn't from the hooves of horses, nor was there a mighty army of warriors with long, flowing, golden locks sitting astride their backs. Instead, rolling into view from the direction of the beach came two huge khaki-coloured metal monsters that vaguely resembled a pair of giant beetles. The strange noises the armies had heard were accompanied by the belching of black fumes as the heavy beasts gathered pace and rumbled toward them down the cobbled road and across the square in front of Gladsheim.

Where were the heroes?

These strange monsters had to be a joke. Both were squat and ugly, with a flattened head, invisible eyes, and a long, pointed snout that wheeled slowly from side the side.

With an almighty crash, the first giant machine smashed onto the bridge and ground its way swiftly across it. The enormous weight of the beast could be appreciated for the first time as the stone walls on either side of the bridge shattered, splintering like matchwood beneath the blur of two spinning, belts of wheels. The bridge creaked, groaned, and cracked under its heavy load, but it held firm. The second behemoth followed the first and the two giant monsters fanned out noisily before taking up their positions at the front of the remnants of Asgard's shattered army.

The Valkyries looked on in amazement. Most had never seen such strange monstrosities before, but the frantic whispering of a few suggested that some knew exactly what they were.

WHUMPH—WHUMPH—WHUMPH!

A different, mighty noise now came from Valhalla, and all eyes turned once more and tried to peer inside the fiery, golden gateway. The silhouettes of two giant, black dragonflies sped quickly into view. The roar of their spinning wings and their massive downdraft engulfed the Valkyries as they passed low over their heads before coming to rest hovering malignantly above their two sinister-looking compatriots.

Finally, and with a thunderous roar that sounded louder than all the devastation of the previous battle put together, a strange metal bird streaked low across the parapets of the castle and then turned its nose skyward, climbing vertically as two sheets of flames erupted from its tail. Eventually, when the creature was little more than a speck in the sky above them, the monstrous metal bird turned and began to slowly circle round and round.

Odin's army was complete, and he raised Gungnir high above him.

"Quick, Hel, we must take shelter now!" Spurring Gold Mane into a canter, Kat headed in the direction of a small patch of rocky scrubland. She knew exactly what these strange creatures were and the mysteries of Valhalla were now laid bare, spewed like vomit before her.

"ATTACK!" Odin hollered as he thumped Gungnir down hard on the floor in a triumphant flourish.

The command was issued. The strangest army ever to set foot in Asgard began its assault.

Sheets of flames leapt from the 120mm cannons of the two M1A1 Abrams tanks, as round after round of anti-personnel shells exploded into the ranks of the Berserkers. Multiple machine guns erupted simultaneously from their turrets and their deadly chatter spat death and destruction into the terrified army as they fell in waves before them.

The two AH-64 Apache helicopters hovering above the tanks now began their own leisurely dance of death. Gliding like hawks, their bodies turned slowly left and right as a flurry of Hydra missiles spat from their bellies. The 'saw' of M230 chain guns could be heard as bursts of 30mm tracer shells flashed like hail through the air. Shields and armour were shredded as easily as though they were made from eiderdown.

The total devastation of twenty-first century warfare bore down on Hel's defenceless army, ripping them to pieces in a matter of minutes. By the time the F-22 Raptor swooped low and delivered two massive five-hundred-pound bombs into their ranks, the fight had long been over. Not even the fragrant power of Hel's poppies could put their mangled, dismembered corpses back together again.

The spattered, blood-soaked battlefield looked like a slaughterhouse, and Odin's face bore the demented mask of a madman. He was cheering his army on to even greater fury, willing them to blast apart each and every last Berserker.

From the vantage of their shelter, Kat peered out and felt sick. The carnage could have ended long before it eventually did. Odin's victory had been assured even before the first gun was fired. Hel's army never had a chance and Odin's maniacal jubilation chilled Kat to the bone. Turning around, she went to cuddle Hel who she felt sure would be totally devastated.

To her intense surprise, she wasn't. Hel was smiling quietly and chuckling to herself. *She must have lost her mind.*

Eventually, the roar of gunfire subsided and the tanks and helicopters turned around and headed back once more across the river. As they did, the body of a man fell from one of the helicopters, plummeting swiftly toward the ground. The soldier must have been aiming for the water but he missed and landed heavily amongst a thicket of briars and gorse.

The helicopter didn't stop. Blinded by their overwhelming victory, its nameless, faceless crew hadn't noticed the suicidal leap of one of their men.

No one cheered as the heroes departed. The terrifying shock was too profound to even raise a smile. Asgard had been saved, but not through a heroic victory. The Valkyries wouldn't kill vermin the way Odin had exterminated the brave and fearless Berserkers. It wasn't a proud and honourable host that had won the day, and the Valkyries shed tears for their butchered enemy.

Odin's obvious rapture at his terrible massacre didn't help their mood. His jubilation left them feeling dirty and uneasy inside.

Asgard had been raped, and the heroes who the Valkyries held so dearly in their hearts were responsible for this sacrilege. It was impossible to believe that these men they adored had controlled such terrifying and omnipotent machines, and far worse to believe that their hands had been behind so cowardly a slaughter.

This horrific thought raised an ugly spectre in all their minds. *Was Odin a kind and compassionate god after all?* Suddenly, the lord they had worshipped and trusted had blood on his hands and it wasn't easily going to wash away.

Before the battle could at last be declared at an end, Odin had one final, chilling horror left in store.

As the F-22 Raptor twirled and blasted its way back through the portal to Valhalla, a solitary flying machine whooshed leisurely from the golden void and sped out across the battlefield, heading in the direction of the volcano.

"Look away, Hel!" Kat yelled as she turned Gold Mane's head around. It had taken a long time to register that the speeding object was a cruise missile and that it wasn't about to drop a cargo of lollipops onto the gateway to Niflheim.

The brilliance of a nuclear explosion lit up the sky as an apocalyptic mushroom cloud formed where once had stood the volcano's majestic cone. Moments later, the ground shook violently and a scalding blast of red hot air ripped angrily through them. Luckily, the weapon's yield was low and the distance between them and the volcano was sufficient to spare their lives.

Odin's final, grandiose gesture had been designed to shock and dazzle but, unfortunately, its vengeful blast had already been surpassed. A much more urgent and impassioned plea had grabbed the attention of his Valkyries.

"Herja, come quickly!" a lonely voice cried frantically from the river bank. A maid was calling as she crouched beside the injured body of the soldier who had tumbled from the sky.

"It's Ben!"

72
Aftershocks

"Odin!" Hel yelled defiantly as she and Kat cantered swiftly across the battlefield. "This war isn't over!"

Odin turned and smiled. Good—that was exactly what he wanted to hear: a declaration that she'd return to complete the job she'd botched.

"You may have won this battle but you know you can't win the war," Hel continued menacingly as she started to consider her options.

She had taken a gamble, a very big gamble, in bringing her Berserker army to Asgard—and she'd lost. The appearance of Odin's heroes and their ferocious firepower had been a surprise and one she hadn't anticipated. Some annoyingly brilliant geniuses (she guessed, correctly, that it was his brothers) had snatched control of the well and this had given him the upper hand, which was a pity. She'd come so close to victory, to rewriting destiny. Now she'd have to start all over again, and rethink her tactics.

Ragnarok, she mused, was becoming like a game of cards. She'd played her queen and Odin had trumped that with his king. However, the ace—as they both knew only too well—was in her hands, and this begged the obvious question.

Dare she play it?

Odin certainly wanted her to and Mimir's prophecies for Ragnarok demanded that it be played, that she release the Guardians to do his bidding. This would assure her victory, *but was the price too great?*

Destroying the realm she loved purely for the sake of winning would be no recompense for a land reduced to a scorched and barren wilderness. Where would be the joy in that hollow triumph?

No, this wasn't what she wanted and luckily, with the queen and king now played, she held the jack in her hand, too: Balder.

While he remained securely locked within her realm, Odin was at her mercy, leaving everything to play for. This promised hope. Hope that she would have her victory and not the one that Odin desired. For now, her ace—her terrifying quartet of Guardians—would stay put. Time was on her side, not Odin's.

Seeing her nemesis swaggering proudly from the battlefield, Hel decided to taunt him one last time. "You'll never get Balder back— that I swear!" she hollered belligerently.

Odin didn't turn and he didn't look back. He had already discovered the dark magic to secure his son's release, and he knew Hel couldn't stop him. As to her other insults, he couldn't care less. Ragnarok had begun and he was banking on her returning to the battlefield. She wouldn't be able to resist the temptation and even if she did, there were many, many ways to needle the vicious, psychotic teenager into making a mistake. Immaturity and lack of control were her weaknesses and ones he intended to exploit to the full. The countdown to oblivion was underway and he itched to clash swords with that evil minx again.

Ragnarok couldn't end until Fenrir and the Guardians of Niflheim took to the field.

Then, and only then, would Asgard's destiny and all their fates be decided.

"Louis! Will you return with me?" Hel called out to the figures of two warriors who loomed in front of them. It was Ruby and Elijah, who by some miracle could be counted amongst the tiny band of survivors.

Elijah turned at the mention of his pseudonym and Ruby pulled him close. They had taken shelter in the crater of one of the earliest exploding missiles and by covering themselves with layers of shattered shields they'd survived the terrible carnage.

Ruby was now with her one true love and there was no way she was letting him go. Elijah obviously felt the same and he shook his head. He wasn't going back.

"Too bad," Hel sighed, plucking a spear from the ground and hurling it furiously at him. Her glorious commander was now a foul deserter and execution would be his reward.

Seeing the deadly missile in flight, Ruby didn't hesitate.

Pushing Elijah aside, she spread her arms open wide and took its full impact upon her chest. It tore clean through her body and she staggered back impaled upon its shaft. Finally, she'd repaid the terrible debt she owed him.

Ruby didn't care if Hel's spear took her life—the knowledge of her love's survival filled her soul with joy.

Kat closed her eyes and shuddered before pulling Hel tightly toward her. That had been a monstrous thing to do. She was about to chastise her sister when the sound of hooves approaching distracted her.

"Wait, Kat, wait!" Hod yelled, pulling his horse up abruptly beside them. "I want to come with you."

"What, Hod—are you mad?" Kat cried, stunned by his ludicrous request. "I can't go back to Asgard because Odin thinks I've betrayed him. But you, you can go back—he still loves you. Please don't do this, I beg of you. You mustn't come with me to Niflheim—the Berserkers will have your head!"

"I'm sorry, Kat, I'm coming and that's that. You need me," he announced resolutely.

"No, she doesn't!" Hel interrupted. "You're only coming because you're sad and madly in love with her," she fumed, sticking her tongue out at him. Turning around, she grabbing hold of Kat's head and kissed her passionately on the lips. Her message was clear and bristling with hostility: Kat was hers.

"You're mad, Hod," Kat spluttered. "You know you won't be able to help me and I, I, I don't…" she paused, blushing violently.

"Oh, yes, you do, Kat. You DO love me, so don't you dare try and deny it. I know that in my heart. Why else did you save me, hey?"

"Because, because…," Kat was struggling for words. She felt furious inside, furious at Hod and furious at herself, too. Part of her really did love him but she so desperately wished it didn't. Every time they got together, trouble just seemed to follow—and Niflheim was filled with a hate that would surely spell disaster for a son of Odin.

She had to stop him from coming. She had to be tough for both their sakes.

"If you come with us, I won't look after you and I won't vouch for your safety. You will also have to serve me, do you understand? I'm a queen of Niflheim now and you'll have to honour and obey me and you won't enjoy that, I promise."

Hod nodded. "I trust you Kat. You have a good heart and you're going to need my help in stopping that Black Valkyrie from corrupting you."

"Hey, Hod! That's my sister you're talking about—apologise to her at once!" Kat shouted angrily.

"Sorry," he murmured insincerely. No matter what she said or what she did, he'd die for her if that was what it took to win her heart.

"Nice one, sis. That'll teach the lovesick dolt," Hel laughed haughtily before deliberately kissing Kat once more.

Kat was hers—and the secret power of her poppy tattoo would ensure that she remained so.

To Hel's great relief, Odin's terrible missile hadn't succeeded in destroying the gateway to her realm. It had blasted the top of the volcano to smithereens, but the unworldly, black portal remained intact. Unfortunately, Odin's nuclear blast had inflicted other much more unpleasant damage, causing harm that would have serious repercussions for both their realms.

Deep gashes were already beginning to form around the volcano's rim as seething cauldrons of molten lava bubbled swiftly toward its surface. The violence of the explosion had stirred the mighty volcano into activity, and this had stirred other sleeping giants as well.

Surt, the ruler of Muspellheim, had been awakened.

He and his ancient army of giant dragons had been peacefully sleeping away the eons in cosy nests buried deep within the volcano's bowels. These nests now lay shattered and the disturbed beasts were waking one by one from their enchanted slumbers—and they weren't pleased.

Repercussions didn't end there, either.

The violent shockwave of the nuclear explosion had travelled through the wormhole to Niflheim and erupted into the palace of Eljudnir, shaking it to its foundations. Ceilings had collapsed and heavy iron doors had been flung from their frames, two of which were now hanging ominously from their hinges.

These had been the locked doors of the two incarcerated Guardians. Freed at last from their imprisonment, they greeted Ganglot and Ganglati with wild jubilation. United once more, the four Guardians of Niflheim could taste the incredible power that had once made their hideous forms so unstoppable. With a portal now open before them, they hungered for its freedom. The worlds above them had been sheltered from their ghostly dance for too long and they cast their eyes lovingly in that direction.

The gateway called with a song that was irresistible.

As Hel and Kat wound their way slowly back through the foothills to the volcano, Kat had plenty of time to think. Her heart still bled with love for Jess and now that a gateway was open to Niflheim, Hel had promised she could return to Asgard whenever she wished. This would be her priority once she discovered the truth behind Ragnarok. This was the problem that vexed her to the core.

Everything was so confused.

Was Odin really going to die? Could he have possibly been telling the truth? What about his incredible, twenty-first century army—what was all that about? And why was Hel not devastated by her ignominious defeat?

What really was going on between her and Odin?

Kat desperately wanted to quiz her sister, but she knew that it would be a waste of time. She couldn't trust her answers any more than she could Odin's. She loved Hel dearly, but she wasn't fooled by her childlike façade. Hel had secrets every bit as deep and sinister as Odin's and she'd already abused Kat's trust with the gift she'd been duped into giving.

Hel couldn't be trusted, and neither could Odin.

Wow! What a choice. Two rulers, and each as devious as the other.

Was Odin really going to abandon Asgard?

Hel's retelling of the third part of Mimir's prophecies was very different to Odin's and suggested a chilling alternative. If Asgard were going to be destroyed, then the paradise the gods would inherit had to be Midgard, home to so many dear and distant friends.

Hel's interpretation created a paradox and one that caused Kat the most confusion. Asgard already WAS a paradise, so why surrender it?

Odin had access to a mighty army of heroes, the wizardry of twenty-first century technology, and the incredible knowledge of an advanced civilisation that made the human race look like something from *The Planet of the Apes.*

Surely Odin could prevent whatever disaster Mimir had foretold?
This question really had Kat stumped and made her head hurt. Something truly terrible—something really, really horrific—must be lurk-
ing beneath the prophecies if Odin had no choice but to abandon
Asgard to its fate.

The truth was out there, of that she was certain, and it lay hidden
somewhere between Hel and Odin's lies. Kat desperately wanted to
find out what it was, but this posed the ultimate question: *Could she
unearth the truth before Ragnarok consumed them all?*

Kat continued to wrestle with these thoughts as the shadows
around them lengthened and the day slowly drew to its close. Leaden
clouds filled the sky once more, and fresh snow began to fall across
the realm. The bitter winter of Ragnarok had arrived, exactly as the
prophecies foretold.

Ragnarok wasn't over.

It had barely just begun.

Unbeknown to Kat, her shrewd reasoning was correct. Asgard's
deepest and darkest secret, the curse that stalked the realm, lay yet to
be uncovered.

If she could only understand it, the answer to all her questions was
really rather simple:

$$\Lambda$$

(Lambda)

TO BE CONTINUED…